The storm has passed, but the
true reckoning has only begun.

The
INDOMITABLE
SENTRY

ANACOSTIA MILLER

HOT TREE PUBLISHING

FARLIGHT
VIOLETTA SILVER'S HAVEN
THE WILDS
THE FAE OCCUPIED GULLIES
FISHERMAN GULLY
BLISS THATCHER'S COLONY

The Ivory Keys
rbor
Farlight Keep
Pike Estate
The Isles of Farlight
West Algar Sea
Shipwreck Bay
Lucky Bartram's Outpost
Anchorage Cove

THE INDOMITABLE SENTRY

THE GUARDIANS OF FARLIGHT ISLES
BOOK THREE

ANACOSTIA MILLER

HOT TREE PUBLISHING

For information, contact the publisher, Hot Tree Publishing.

WWW.HOTTREEPUBLISHING.COM

EDITING: HOT TREE EDITING

COVER DESIGNER: BOOKSMITH DESIGN

E-BOOK ISBN: 978-1-923252-50-9

PAPERBACK ISBN: 978-1-923252-51-6

CONTENT WARNING

The Indomitable Sentry is the third book in the GUARDIANS OF FARLIGHT ISLES series. To understand this story, you need to start with book one, *The Last Leviathan*, and continue with book two, *The Monarchs*.

This book is darker than the other two. At its core, it's about how far your spirit can stretch and bend before it snaps. It's about rising from the ashes. It's about howling at the moon because they could never break you. As dark as the story gets, find comfort knowing that it has a happy ending before the finale in book four.

These content warnings do contain spoilers, but I care about your mental health and want you to be prepared.

This book contains heavy themes of war, death, and misogyny.

There are instances of implied sexual assault and domestic abuse (not Maeve), and threats of sexual assault that never happens. There are references to what happened to Ronin when he was trapped as Nathaniel Pike's prisoner.

There are plenty of examples of torture, blood, violence, and gore. This includes disembowelment involving the villains, experimentation on one of the main characters, and body horror elements.

Scenes include side character deaths, funerals, and major injuries.

Mental health is a smaller theme in this book, but it revolves around rage and exacting vengeance over those who have harmed you. There are quite a few examples of female rage.

There is less sexual content than the previous books, but you can still expect graphic sexual content including oral sex, manual stimulation, bodily fluids, and penetrative sex. This is accompanied with a whole lot of *I love you*.

This book molds Ronin and Maeve into the people they need to be to save the world in book four. Hang in there.

PROLOGUE

"This body weakens," Varric said, eyes fixed on the foggy mirror before him.

It had been in his possession as long as he could remember. Though, it was once a looking glass before he used the shards to craft a more worthy vessel to commune with the beyond. Now it stood, grand in size, framed in black and detailed with gold flake.

She deserved no less.

With spindly fingers, he twisted the amulet around his neck, its black crystal cracked and on the verge of shattering. Like with his mask, he struggled to keep the pieces together.

In the reflection of the mirror, a glowing figure brushed Varric's shoulders in a gesture that seemed too fond to be a mistake. Like an echo of who she once was, she flitted in and out of focus. Fabric flowed around her like blood in the water, and her eyes shone like polished amethyst. Her skin had grayed, dark veins winding like rivers all over her face.

Varric didn't notice her yellow teeth or the patches of dark hair that had fallen out in clumps. What was left of her was hardly human, but he saw the same woman he married a lifetime ago.

"I'm running out of time," he mused. "I feel the power draining more every single day."

"Then give her to me," the figure demanded. "She's strong enough—"

Varric shook his head. "You don't know Maeve. She's far more resilient than you think. I will not risk you."

"Sounds like you'd rather not risk your adoptive daughter. She doesn't care for you as much as you care for her." She twisted her neck, canting it at an unnatural angle. "You always wanted a daughter. But I *need a vessel.*"

"In time, my queen." Varric bowed his head.

"*Sentimental,*" she chided. But even with disapproval in her tone, her voice echoed through his ears, the sound of it like a caress to Varric's soul.

"You used to find it charming." He sighed, drinking in her presence. "But it is not my sentimentality this time. Maeve is more useful as an ally."

She waved her hand dismissively. "Fine. Do things your way if you must. Take her gift, use the heir, and slay the dragon. May ash rain above you."

"In your name," he responded with a hint of sadness. Then he sighed, placing his hand over hers in the reflection.

As always, she disappeared too soon. Her presence ebbed away, and Varric remained, staring into the dark reflection of himself. He stroked the glass, relishing the chill. "I will free you soon, my queen. But not by using Maeve. Not yet."

A knock came at the door, too soft to be a guard. It was Katherine. His wife, but not his queen. She always knocked on his study too lightly, as if she didn't want to be heard. Didn't want to be seen. Katherine was exactly what he needed at his side: a forgettable woman.

Mousy.

Subservient.

"Enter," he answered, and the door cracked open. "What is it?"

Katherine kept her head down, her eyes fixed on the floor. "The Heads of the Houses are awaiting you in the Great Hall."

Right on time.

The Heads of the Houses were many things, but late was not one of them.

As Varric passed Katherine, he snatched her chin, drawing her gaze up. "At least pretend like you love me."

Her eyes were glazed over, pupils blown to oblivion. The product of too many opioids combined with too much to drink. It was a miracle she hadn't succumbed to the poison over the years, but her misery wasn't Varric's concern. He would keep up appearances, and Katherine would be the invisible wife.

She didn't respond, a mere pawn in Varric's grasp. Perhaps it was better that she was incoherent. She was less of a bother that way.

After releasing her, he didn't spare Katherine another glance, but he did hear her stumble across the hall. She was a shadow of the woman she used to be before Varric awoke within his new vessel. Too many memories clashed together. It was difficult to keep them straight.

Who he was then and who he was now.

Once upon a time, a piece of him loved Katherine. She was brilliant and made him laugh. But that was when they were young and he was useless. Before he found his looking glass and restored his memories.

He'd leave her in the ash like he had everyone else. Once she served her purpose.

The servants pulled open the grandiose doors to the Great Hall, revealing six nobles seated around a long oval table. They stood when they saw him and waited for him to take his seat before joining him. Varric's armchair was positioned at the head of the table, separated at a far distance from the nobles.

"Good evening," Varric greeted.

One of the nobles—none other than Samuel Pike, an older man who took as much pleasure in vexing Varric as his son, Nathaniel, did—swirled a chalice of wine, disrespecting Varric by putting his feet up on the table.

"I hear you have your daughter back in your custody," he commented before taking a deep drink. He held the wine in his mouth, swishing it before swallowing.

Varric nodded. "She is being brought to Nathaniel as we speak." He looked around the table. "I have gathered you all today to discuss the coming months. I have—"

"Are you sure you want her back?" Samuel asked. "Last time that *girl* was under your roof, she released the Royal Leviathan and committed high treason. Destroyed half the port on the way out. As far as I'm concerned, she's a pirate."

Varric narrowed his eyes. "Her name is *Maeve*. And while our treaty with your son fell through, you must remember that my daughter is a victim. Unfortunately, she suffers the same ailment as most women. She is ruled by her emotions, which makes her the perfect pawn for leviathan charm."

Samuel didn't reply, only repressed that snakelike smile that lingered on his lips.

He knew the truth. Only a very few nobles did. Knowledge wasn't a gift Varric awarded easily.

Varric knew leviathans couldn't control minds, but most nobles didn't think that far ahead. All he had to do was give them a special gift, say the right words, and their loyalty was his.

Fickle creatures. But they answered to power and greed.

Offer them the world, and they'd burn it to fight over the smoldering ashes left behind. They were easy.

The commoners required more thought. Careful lies and organized attacks on rebellious villages. No witnesses. Point the finger at the ever-elusive leviathans, and any uprisings fell apart. They never knew better. Once that lie had been planted all those years ago, it flourished. Soon enough, neighbors were dragging leviathans out of their homes in broad daylight under the misapprehension that lifelong friends had manipulated them.

Of course, Varric had to tend the garden on occasion. Conscript new blood as needed. Cull whatever invasive pest that threatened to disrupt what he'd spent decades cultivating. He maintained the order.

One well-placed lie set Varric's reign in motion. Twenty-five years later, he had hundreds of thousands of blindly loyal subjects. What was the alternative? To *admit* what they had done?

Never.

Varric intended to keep it that way.

He tapped his fingers together and gestured for the court scribe to start taking notes. "Now, we are one step closer to uniting Farlight Isles with Algar again. An entire continent for the taking. Let's discuss what you can offer me in exchange for your own piece of the treasure."

PART I
THE FIRST BATTLE

1

MAEVE CROSS

WHO CAN YOU TRUST?

As Death's realm vanished into the ether, I felt renewed with a sense of purpose.

I knew who I was.

I knew what I needed to do.

Whatever came next, whatever pain I had to endure, I knew I'd survive.

I floated above the darkness and stroked the veil between the realms. With a gentle press, the veil parted at my touch, springing back like a bowstring.

The light above me drew closer, and the warmth encompassed me again. All my mortal tethers weighed on me at once. My belly rumbled, and the summer wind whistled above me. Heavy boots clapped against the wooden deck nearby.

Gentle waves struck the shallow hull.

I'm close to the water. I have to be on a sloop. Minimal crew.

There was something on my face.

I blinked, slowly coming back to myself. Light permeated a bloodied sheet that was draped over me. My heart squeezed hard as I remembered the devastation of Shipwreck Bay, the pirate hunters, and the siege.

Violetta's crushed ribs.

The beams of the tavern falling on top of Wesley and Enya.

Gunny flying into the dirt as a cannonball blew a door off the hinges.

Luther bleeding to death on the cobblestone.

I didn't see what happened to anyone else.

My throat grew thick, but the longer I lay there, the farther away I'd be from my family in Shipwreck Bay. I didn't know where I was, but I knew I wasn't with Ronin anymore.

I felt for a cutlass at my waist but found nothing.

No sash.

No gear.

No weapon. No idea where I am. Fantastic.

I listened closely for another pair of boots but only heard one. The ship turned suddenly, but I stayed still, waiting to glean more information.

"To the Gods, I wish you were here. Give me a sign, *skelmis*. Tell me I'm not fucking everything up."

That voice.

That bastard kidnapped me!

I jolted, quelling the fury churning in my belly, taking a deep breath to steady myself. It was not the time to react out of anger. I had to be smart about this.

"*Draugr*," he huffed, and I heard those boots approach me. The shadow of his lean form blocked out the light above me.

Godsdamnit! Now or never.

I flung the sheet off me, coming face-to-face with none other than the Skadian heir. He was bent at the waist over me, his hand fastened on the hilt of his blade.

Those unique yellow eyes blew wide open. "What the fuck!"

In response, I flung my leg forward and kicked him in the face. I had no intention of dying on his sword twice.

He recoiled, shouting a gruff noise of pain and cupping his nose. I rolled back, scrambling to my feet and taking a defensive stance. My fists came up as Ronin and Luella had taught me.

He might have a sword, but I wasn't going down without a fight.

My blouse stuck crustily to my abdomen where his sword had speared me. The blood had long dried, but I could still taste it on my lips and feel it on my skin. Judging by the storm clouds rolling away, it had to have been an hour or two ago at least.

"You were dead! *Dead!*" the elf shouted, removing his hand from his face to reveal a stream of blue blood where I'd hit his nose.

"What can I say? I'm full of surprises," I retorted. "Where am I?"

"I'm returning you to your father," he claimed.

"Like the Hells you are!" I yelled.

"Not all of us get to run from our problems, *Princess*," he hissed. "Now, you can sit down for the ride, or I can bind you to my fucking mast. You're going—whether you want to or not."

If he had met me six months ago, on the night when I first met Ronin, I would've been too afraid to fight back. That princess would've bent and bowed. All words and no action.

But I wasn't a princess anymore. I was a *pirate*.

And I was going to commandeer his ship.

I glanced out the side of the ship into the big blue. Silver smoke bloomed around the clouds. "You have one chance to get out of my way."

The elf's entire demeanor changed. He straightened up, wiping the blood from his nose with the back of his hand.

"You think you can beat a blue-blooded Skadian warrior, *kona*?"

I squared my shoulders, putting both my fists up. "Only if you stop talking so much."

The corner of his mouth twitched as he unbuckled the sheath from his waist and let it clatter onto the deck. He mirrored my pose, watching me intently as a flare of something I couldn't place came into his eyes.

While he watched my hands, I swung my foot out to clip him in the knee, but he moved, anticipating me. I countered, slipping my knee between his legs to get him in the groin.

But my leg came into contact with something hard like plate mail, and I winced, losing my focus briefly.

Both his hands came around my biceps, gripping them tight. "That was a low blow, Princess. Did they teach you dirty fighting at the castle?"

I threw my weight backward, freeing myself from his grasp. "Depends. How often have you been kneed in the groin that you need to wear a cup?"

Before he could reply, I struck him again in the face. My knuckles ached, splitting against his cheekbone. But as my hands bloodied, they knit back up, taking the pain with them.

Faster than before....

I didn't have the time to ponder what it meant or how I had changed since speaking with Death. I could speculate all I wanted once I got off this sloop and made it back to my family.

This heir might have the skill, but I had the endurance.

What was it Luella used to say?

"If all else fails, strike them in the groin or the throat."

I dodged another punch, fisting my hands so tight that my nails cut into my palms. I swung forward, catching him right in his throat. The elf gagged, choking on his breath. He doubled over and grasped at his neck.

The glimmer of his broadsword caught my gaze, and I dropped down to grab it. When I rose up, he glared at me and hissed something under his breath. The smell of a winter hearth enveloped me, chilling my muscles.

It disoriented me until a wide arm grasped me from behind my thighs and flung me backward over his shoulder onto the deck. The air was knocked out of me instantly as the elf retrieved rope from netted storage.

He kicked me onto my stomach before straddling me to tie my hands behind my back. I tried to rock him off me, but he was too strong.

"Get your blasted ass off me!" I screamed, rage heating my face.

"Gladly," he croaked, rising to walk back over to the helm.

"You can't handle a fair fight?" I twisted violently, rubbing rope burns into my wrists.

The elf rotated the helm, getting us back on course. "Failure is not an option for me. I'm delivering you back to your father, and he is going to send me home."

I glared at him from where I lay prone on the deck. "What about *my* home? The one you destroyed!"

Locking his jaw, he pinned me with a withering stare. The scent of smoke filled my nose again, the chilly blaze of his fury coloring his face a darker shade of purple. "*Your* leviathan should've thought about that before he sent assassins to murder my wife."

"What in the blazing Hells are you talking about?"

"Don't play coy. I'm not a fool."

I scoffed. "Agree to disagree, then. Did Varric tell you that? He's a liar."

"He wasn't lying," he replied, wiping another stream of blue blood from his nose. "I'd be able to tell."

"Eels hide their teeth. How would you anticipate a bite before it was too late?" I wriggled, my wrists rubbed raw as I fought the knots, my blood tinging the yellow fibers red. It was fine. I'd heal. "Where is *my* leviathan?"

"Gone. I barely escaped a surge of electricity," he replied.

"Electricity?" I inquired, ceasing my struggles.

"I'd been taught that dragons breathe fire. Not him."

Ronin shifted? My heart thudded, elation pulling the sides of my mouth into a grin. "Oh, you're *fucked.*"

He shook his head, a grim expression on his face, and I didn't miss the way his narrow pupils contracted in fear.

Good. He should be afraid.

"I'm going home. I deliver you, and then I leave for Skadi."

"Is that what they told you?" I asked, rolling over onto my back to sit up straight. "Ronin is going to kill you. Assuming Varric doesn't kill you first."

The Skadian heir shook his head. "They need me."

"Sure they do," I crooned. "They'll use you and kill you. But if they fail, *my* leviathan will have that honor. You destroyed our home. You led a siege against my people. You'll pay for it." I rolled my shoulders, wriggling my wrists, but the knot was too tight. No matter how much I twisted, I couldn't get out of the ropes.

"I didn't—" He stopped himself, turning his head completely away from me. "I didn't have a choice."

"There is always a choice." I narrowed my eyes. "And ignorance is yours."

"Once you're home and that leviathan's influence isn't swaying you, you'll be thankful for your father," the heir said, sounding more like he was convincing himself than he was trying to sway me.

"Did my *father* tell you that too?" I asked. "Another lie."

A tic formed in his jaw, and he squeezed his eyes shut before he focused on the current in front of us. I ground my teeth together as the ropes bit into my wrists. Unnatural healing ability or not, it still hurt like the Nine Hells.

"Stop doing that," he said. "You're going to hurt yourself."

My eyes shot over to him, and another mocking laugh spilled from my lips. "Says the man who killed me. That hurt too."

"You didn't have to dive onto my sword," he retorted. "I wasn't trying to kill you."

I tilted my head to the side and stated, "No, you were trying to kill my best friend." I paused, noticing how the line in his lips turned farther down. "Answer this. If you had the choice between yourself and your wife, would you take her place?"

"Without hesitation," he replied, reaching into his shirt to caress his marital pendant. He stared at the wintery magic, shoulders sloping downward.

"So loyalty is *not* a foreign concept to you."

"You turned your back on your kingdom, so I don't expect you to understand this. My home is on the verge of war with Edessa. Your leviathan ordered the assassination of my wife, *Edessa nobility*. My disappearance will line up with her murder, and the peace agreement will fall apart. I would've lost my wife and my country," he explained through clenched teeth, an urgency rising in his tone.

I leaned back against the wall of the sloop. "Where did you end up?"

"What?"

"When you came to Farlight Isles, where did you end up?"

His eyebrows came together. "I followed the assassin into the—" He stopped himself. "That's not relevant."

"Let me guess. You ended up right in front of Varric."

"That was a coincidence. He didn't stop me from killing the assassin. He must have wanted them dead," the heir insisted, even though his face was pinched with doubt.

"Or he had a better opportunity," I pointed out. Varric was opportunistic to a fault. He burned bridges. Cut ties. Flipped sides on a whim. He didn't have an ounce of loyalty in his blood.

The heir shook his head, fine white hair escaping from his braid. "You're trying to get in my head."

I pressed my tongue into my cheek. "Is it working?"

His nostrils flared as he glared at me, that familiar smell of smoke wafting over to me, melding with the scent of the sea. It reminded me of the ovens in Butcher's galley and how the scent would stick to my clothes after my rounds. "Keep speaking and I will get something to put over your mouth," he threatened.

Yes, it's working.

"Tell me something first. Who has more to lose? Me, a princess who fled her marriage and joined the pirates, or a usurper? Who can you trust?"

He didn't answer me, but he did tie a bandanna around my mouth.

That was answer enough.

2

RONIN MURDOCH

I WANT BLOOD

Acrid smoke flooded my nose from burning buildings. Ash rained above us, blotting out the sun that cut through black storm clouds. Screaming filled the air.

It was a living nightmare.

My leviathan had sapped the energy from me. Luella and Andra had to drag me through the mud as exhaustion weighted my bones.

I did this. I put these people into this position. I failed.

The beast writhed within me like a wild animal railing against the bars of my flesh. It refused to fall into another slumber. It was angry, enraged by Mae's capture, by the devastation of our home.

My mind circled back to Mae again, her body crumpled in the dirt. She was there, and then she was gone. She was either dead or being taken into Pike's care. Death would be more merciful.

But deep in my bones, I *knew* she was alive.

She was going to the place I'd been trying to protect her from. After everything Pike told me when I was his prisoner, I knew what was waiting for her.

There isn't anything I can fucking do about it. She can handle this. She has to.

I would do my part, and she would do hers.

The abyss beneath me licked at my ankles, encouraging me to sink into the tar. Toss and turn until I was so tangled up in despair that I was no use to anyone. I'd never be free of it.

The lump in my throat thickened, but I swallowed it down. I couldn't crumble. Everyone would be looking to me for guidance. Even if I desperately wanted to sink to my knees and break, I couldn't.

Bringing prevalent authority figures here was a bad decision, and anyone who died in the crossfire was *my fault.* There wasn't any way around that. I'd carry their deaths on my shoulders. No matter how much I buckled under the weight, that was my burden. No one else's.

Mine.

And I wanted *vengeance.*

I replayed everything that happened, mulling over every fucking thing I did wrong. The despair twisted in my chest, contorting into something far more dangerous.

Malice infested me, growing in intensity like an uncontrollable tremor.

Scorching the pirate hunters wasn't enough. I wanted blood. I wanted to be fucking saturated in it like a risen *monster.*

I'd watch fear dance in their eyes as I became the last thing they saw.

But I was in no shape to go on a full-scale rampage, so I did something I never did.

I prayed.

What else could I possibly do?

Cliohde, I want blood. Help me make them pay.

I was lost in my head as Luella and Andra held me up on

unsteady legs, completely naked except for Luella's jacket around my muddy shoulders. It had only been a few hours since Mae was taken and Shipwreck Bay was sieged. My leviathan had broken through again, shredding my clothing and releasing the power bottled inside, but it was still too late for me to save her.

Just a few moments earlier and I could have....

No. I couldn't dwell. Because that didn't change the reality of the situation, did it?

I waited a moment with my eyes closed for Cliohde to answer. To give me something—anything—to ease the despair that wrecked my entire being, but my prayer was nothing but a drop of water in the ocean.

Answered only by silence.

I tried to quell the anger twitching in my muscles.

Worth a shot, I guess.

I took a deep breath, steeling myself for the fight ahead, not only with Pike's men but the fight to lead no doubt terrified people into trusting that I was who I said I was. How was I supposed to walk into the tunnels and tell these people that Captain Leviathan was an *actual* leviathan this whole time?

Not only that, but that the dethroned prince, the rightful heir to the throne, had been hiding among them for years. Why should they follow me now after the tyrant had laid waste to their homes?

A tyrant who I had fucking *brought here.*

I'm going to put his head on a fucking stick.

Guilt blew a cold, heavy breath against my naked neck that felt like a piece of ice sliding down my back. It cooled the heat blazing inside.

Luella and Andra each had one of my arms over their shoulders. Was the growl that rumbled out of me mine or my leviathan's? I didn't know.

"Into the river," Andra said, guiding us in the direction of the bank that led to the tunnels under Shipwreck Bay.

"I can walk," I muttered as the water licked at my ankles.

The brackish water gave me strength as I pulled away. My legs buckled briefly, but I quickly found my balance. It felt as if the strength of the ocean salved my wounds and filled my lungs with fresh salty air.

"*Vengeance?*" a feminine voice whispered from below me, speaking directly from the water.

The voice startled me, and when I slowly looked toward my feet, I was met only by murky blue. I wasn't entirely sure that it wasn't exhaustion playing tricks on my mind, but I still replied, "I want them to pay."

Luella paused beside me and asked, "Who're you talking to?"

I waited to hear the voice again, but it never came.

Hearing voices now?

Of course I was.

It was only a matter of time before all that pressure cracked me. And without Mae beside me, I felt like a bridge with no supports. The water pounded at the stone, wearing it away to nothing until all that was left was the molten fire at my core.

A mixture of anxiety and uncertainty welled inside me, but I pushed it all down. I couldn't flounder. If I did, my failure would be even worse.

I shook my head. "No one, Wraith."

She gave me a cautious side-eye but didn't press. She looked me up and down. I was clad in only her jacket. "I think there should be a fisherman's cache around here somewhere. You're intimidating enough without that thing swinging around."

Despite the circle of the Hells we'd been in the past few hours, her crude statement made me laugh. And that fleeting moment of mirth snuffed out the rage and applied a balm to my heart that had been cleaved in two somewhere inside my chest. "Don't make me laugh right now."

My sister patted me on the shoulder and said, "I don't want to see you naked on a good day, and we've just had the worst day."

I took a deep breath. "I don't know how much I can take. The blood. The death. Everything falling apart again and again."

She squeezed my shoulder while Luella waded through waist-deep water that led to a small cache underneath a wooden platform. It wasn't much, but it supplied the retired sailors who would set up chairs and fish off the lip where the stream became a roaring river on its way to the ocean.

"You can do this. If not for yourself, then for Mae. For Howler. For Mama and Lucky. For everyone they've taken from us. This has to matter, Levi." Andra's voice broke. "All of this has to matter."

I softened. *All of this has to matter.*

One more deep breath, and I reached to my shoulder and gave her hand a reassuring squeeze. "It *will* matter."

Her shining brown eyes met mine in kindred under-standing before Luella called out, "Found some waders!"

Fishing waders?

You've got to be fucking kidding me.

Andra helped me over to the shore, and Luella passed me the waders. I shrugged off her jacket and stuck my feet into the wide trousers and all the way into the attached water-proof boots. I felt fucking ridiculous, but I'd rather that than be stark naked.

"Don't distract anyone with that ass, Cap," Luella said as I pulled the straps over my shoulders.

I glanced over at her and rolled my eyes, but her jest

helped calm the pattering in my chest. "Time to move," I said and swiped my hair back.

The water was waist-deep as we approached the tunnel grate, the scent of the sea mixing with the sewer. The dread built. My chest felt unbelievably heavy as the rage came back.

I struggled to hold on to my control, but I felt volatile. Like one wrong word, one wrong move would release it like floodgates opening. This was not the time to lose my temper and frighten these people any more than they were already.

I opened the grate, ignoring the smell as Luella and Andra climbed inside before me.

Familiar voices echoed through the tunnel system. I recognized how the townspeople spoke and that distinct Shipwreck Bay accent that had permeated my own voice. It especially came out whenever I played cards at the tavern.

That felt so long ago now. When all I had to worry about was how much coin I'd be taking and who I'd bring upstairs for the night. If I could see that man again, I wouldn't recognize him.

As we followed the voices through the undercity, we saw parents holding their children. Babies were crying. Adolescents had their arms wrapped around themselves as tears streamed silently down their faces.

There was no order. Just chaos. My mind raced with ideas on how to take control of the situation, each new thought overtaking the last one.

If there was anything more dangerous than the pirate hunters outside, it was a scared mob of people.

Among the faces, I saw Pinky staring at a wall, eyes wide. His hands were shaking as they clasped his shoulders in a tight embrace. Violetta's blood still painted his face, tracks of tears revealing his blue skin. Udine was blotting it off his cheeks with a dirty cloth. Her crescent-pupiled orange eyes bolted upward to gaze at me.

The wounded had been laid out in the darkness lit by oil lamps. More poured in by the moment. Tension was sky-high, and panic thickened the air.

I needed to give these people some direction or they'd start coming to blows. They'd shove and scream, and there'd be no coming back from that. My grip on my temper was wavering, but I had to do this.

I would get my revenge, but I had to take care of these people first.

"You!" a voice roared as a stout figure rushed me.

I barely had time to react as fist after fist collided with my chest. I grunted as the punches landed, their knuckles snapping back to strike me across the face. The skin under my cheek split. Pain erupted as my lip got caught in their gold ring. They hit me hard enough to knock me flat onto the ground.

"Get the fuck off my captain!" Luella demanded, hoisting them off me with Andra's help.

Blue fire spat up into my belly, electrified like lightning in the water, but I grabbed my temper with both hands. My fists curled onto the brick pathway, fingernails scraping the grout between the grimy stone. *Keep it the fuck together. Don't indulge Bliss's rage.*

"You *fucking bastard*!" Bliss screamed, golden skin completely flushed as they surged to their feet. They thrashed, breaking out of Luella's hold to pull a knife from their sash. "Look what you've done! I should've slit your throat back in Fisherman's Gully!"

I got to my feet clumsily in the fucking fishing waders before Andra got in front of me. "Show some fucking respect!" she snarled. "This is the man who took out ten—fifteen of those pirate hunters by the tree line!"

Bliss threw their head back in a rueful laugh. "*This* man?

The one who *ran* when the rest of us were crushed under the tavern?"

I fisted my hands so tightly that my nails bit into my palms. I tasted blood from where my lip had been cut open. "That's not fair, Bliss. My mother and my brother were trapped under that tavern. Did you manage to help them get out?" I snapped.

That gave Bliss pause as they gripped their knife, golden eyes darting back and forth between my mates and me. Their silence was enough.

"You think I didn't lose anyone in this, Captain Bliss?" I pushed past Andra, my temper rising before I could catch it. "My fucking girl, *my Mae*, was taken prisoner on Pike's ship. So get off your fucking high horse."

Bliss's throat bobbed, but they didn't put their knife down. "Fuck your alliance. Two-thirds of your council are buried under the tavern."

"That is enough, Bliss," Udine said suddenly from next to me. She looked at me, placing a clawed, webbed hand over my chest. I flinched at her touch even though it was accompanied by "I'm so sorry, Ronin."

"We will get her back. I'm going to get them all back." The vow slipped from my lips easily. This was a promise I had all intention of upholding. "They will *pay with their blood.*"

Gripped hard in Bliss's white-knuckled fist, the knife glimmered in the dull light. "With what army?"

"Mine," Udine declared. Her gaze never left mine. "You have my warriors."

"Are you fucking serious right now, Udine?" Bliss seethed, betrayal apparent on their face. "*He* damned us. *He* led Pike to us. Leviathan is a threat."

The crowd had quieted down and was listening to us intently.

Udine shook her head. "The war was bound to find us."

"I didn't agree to a war," Bliss shouted.

The merrow matriarch straightened her back, holding her chin high with a regality kings and queens only wished they could emulate. "I did. Hoping and wishing for this war to never touch us doesn't change the reality of poison in the water. I came here to make the Besieger pay for everything he's done."

The crowd hung on to every eloquently spoken word as Bliss's face fell.

"I will do this with or without you. Serving a Royal Leviathan is an honor I've long dreamed of." With that, Udine turned to face me completely and knelt on one knee. "You will have my warriors and my service, Ronin Murdoch."

Whispers erupted through the crowd, questioning my legitimacy. They had all known I was a pirate captain who liked to spread stories of leviathans, but they'd never realized I *was* one.

A complicated feeling welled in my chest, and I held my hand out to her. "Don't kneel before me. We do this together."

Udine took my hand with a flourish, rising to her feet.

"If you expect me to bow at your feet, then you will be disappointed," Bliss spat.

"No, but I do expect you to work with me," I said. "You don't have to like me, but if we're going to stand a chance of getting our home back, we need to do it together. Don't you want revenge?"

Finally, Bliss sheathed their blade. "I can do revenge."

"Good. Then we need to move," I stated.

"Do you have a place in mind?" Udine asked.

I dipped my head. "I do."

3

MAEVE CROSS

THE SHIELD

THE SKADIAN HEIR REFUSED TO LOOK AT ME AS HE SAILED US toward a man-o'-war that sat barely out of sight of Shipwreck Bay. I could only see a sliver of the port town, plumes of smoke in the air. I could smell the fires and hear the distant cries as the pirate hunters raided my home.

Rowboats came and went from around the man-o'-war as the heir brought the sloop right up beside the massive ship. It was not much larger than *The Ollipheist*, but this was a vessel made for war, while the ship I called home was built to carry treasure.

A flag with a barracuda embroidered on it fluttered back and forth with the wind. Nausea settled in my stomach.

Nathaniel.

A thick rope clapped onto the deck next to me, and the heir sighed and grabbed my binds. "Come on, get up. Time to go."

I glared at him, muttering around the gag in my mouth, "You're making a mistake."

He didn't reply, pulling me to my feet and fastening an

arm around my waist. He hauled me right up against him, and I took the opportunity to stomp hard on his foot.

He winced, jerking his foot out from beneath mine. "Cut it out!" he hissed.

"I'll bite next," I hissed, my voice muffled by the fabric.

He narrowed his eyes at me and stepped back to tie the rope in a knot around my waist. He looked up and shouted, "Pull her up first!"

I dangled from the rope as they hauled me up, kicking my foot out to hit the heir in the face, but he dodged me as a second rope thudded against the deck.

Whatever happens next, I'm not going down without a fight. Even if it hurts.

Men grunted as I crested over the half wall and clattered onto the deck, my hands still tied behind my back. I groaned when I hit the planks, glaring up at uniformed soldiers when polished boots entered my field of vision.

"Look at you," Nathaniel chuckled, curling a finger around the scrap of fabric and pulling it out from between my teeth. I nearly gagged as his fingers brushed my face. "I knew it would only be a matter of time before you bowed at my feet."

I reeled back on my knees and met those icy eyes. They were void of any warmth but full of cruel glee. He grasped my jaw, pinching it hard. My eyes settled on his crooked nose, and a taunting laugh crawled from my lips.

Last time I saw Nathaniel, I broke his nose before I rendered him unconscious at Farlight Castle.

He glared at me as he released me. "Why are you laughing?"

"They didn't reset your nose properly."

He struck me across the face with the back of his hand. My head snapped back from the force, my cheek throbbing briefly as I pressed my tongue into it. Like everything else, the pain left nothing but a memory and the taste of metal.

Behind Nathaniel, I watched one of the cabin boys slap a hand over his mouth to stifle the gasp of horror. He darted his eyes from side to side to gauge the reactions of everyone else. "That's the princess," the cabin boy whispered to another equally disturbed sailor, this one older and wearing an officer insignia.

"Quiet," the officer barked, tucking the cabin boy behind him as Nathaniel turned to look at whoever was disrupting.

I knew fear when I saw it, but that small flicker of rebellion gave me hope.

Before Nathaniel could set his sights on the cabin boy, I spat out the blood that had bubbled up in my mouth over his polished shoes to distract him. "You can hit harder than that."

The dissent was forgotten as his gaze snapped back down to me. He curled his fingers, about to backhand me again for my insolence, probably to make an example out of me, when the heir's boots padded on the deck next to me.

"What is this, Admiral Pike?" the heir demanded. "Where I'm from, men don't strike their wives."

With the taste of metal still in my mouth, I hissed, "Oh, he does worse. Don't you?"

Nathaniel grabbed my face, twisting my jaw in an attempt to silence me before he straightened up, eye to eye with the heir. "Prince Fryner, thank you for returning Maeve."

"Freynir," he corrected with a growl. "I said, *where I'm from, men don't strike their wives*," the heir—Freynir—repeated, an added bite to his voice.

"Then I'm lucky she's *not* my wife," Nathaniel replied with a flourish, as if that made his behavior acceptable. "Here, in *Farlight Isles*, wives don't fuck other men." He released me before I could sink my teeth into the fleshy part of his hand.

"We never consummated our marriage, and with your infidelity, it was easy enough to void that contract. And a man like me needs a wife, so I've found another woman for my needs."

What? Panic filled my chest. He took another wife? Whoever she was, her fate would be the same as everyone else's. She'd end up dead, and that would be the only mercy Nathaniel ever gave.

"What is it, Maeve?" Nathaniel toyed with my hair, sending sparks of disgust all through my body. "Don't worry. You'll be in my care until we get you back to your father. I have other needs you can fulfill, Princess."

Freynir grabbed Nathaniel's hand, forcefully removing it from me. "No. I'm going to take her directly to Cross, and then I'm going home." He shoved Nathaniel's hand back and grabbed me by the restraints, pulling me up to my feet.

For a brief moment, relief swelled in my chest. I might not *like* the Skadian heir, but it would be Hells easier to survive on a sloop with him than on a man-o'-war with Nathaniel and dozens of equally cruel pirate hunters.

The Royal Navy was distinguished in name alone; they were no better than the mercenaries who hunted the oceans for a bounty. No better than the kidnappers and death dealers.

Nathaniel tsked. "Oh, you're not going home."

An officer came from behind Freynir and attached a collar around his throat imbued with a black crystal that glittered blue—draconite. He released me, and both his hands came up to pull on the collar. That wintery magic filled the air, but as soon as it did, the fog dissipated, and he screamed.

"We've got plans for *you*, Prince."

I could hear the crystal searing the side of his throat, forcefully halting any magic. Panic fell over his face as he grabbed at the collar. "What? No!"

I scrambled to my feet, taking the opportunity to make a

break for the half wall. Freynir had made his choice despite my warnings. Another guttural scream filled my ears as he tried and failed to cast another spell.

"Get her!" Nathaniel ordered.

A dozen footfalls followed me as soldiers moved into action to grab me. I dodged their hands, using my small stature to my advantage.

I could hear Freynir coughing and sputtering on the ground behind me, the scent of burning flesh in the air. It smelled like the pyres from my childhood.

For a split second, I could hear the distant screams that haunted my nightmares, quieter than before. The pit of despair beneath me crackled but didn't swallow me. If anything, it emboldened me to *fight*.

I flung my leg over the half wall, ready to plummet into the cold water. The sounds of agony from Fisherman's Gully morphed and became Freynir's panicked screams as draconite branded his throat. I tried to shut it out of my mind.

I needed to get back to Ronin. I had to save them.

But Nathaniel broke Ronin. What would he do to another man he imprisoned?

For just a moment, my feet faltered. Then I froze.

I glanced up at the smoke in the distance, and something pulled inside me. I knew what would happen to Freynir if I left. If I stayed, I could spare another person Nathaniel's cruelty.

Death told me I was the shield. Is this what they meant?

Two different sets of hands seized me and sent me lurching from the half wall, twisting my shoulders back until they whined from the angle. I muffled a noise of discomfort as they dragged me back to where Nathaniel and Freynir were posted by the center mast.

Nathaniel grinned, all teeth like his coat of arms. "Take him to the brig with Officer Seymour."

Sailors wearing blue frock coats lifted Freynir up, using the same type of draconite chains to lock his wrists together.

"Don't worry," one of them said, "I'll give you a bucket to piss in. If you're lucky, we'll even hold your prick for you."

Freynir shouted, writhing in pain and indignance as they took him away, while several other sailors surrounded me in case I made another break for it.

Nathaniel approached me and extended one of his fingers to stroke the side of my neck, barely pricking the skin with his one sharpened fingernail and marveling at how it stitched itself back together again.

"How is the leviathan? Hmm? Does he still wear my marks? I was hoping they'd scar," he crooned, cruelty flashing in his eyes as he pressed his thumb against my vein where my heart was hammering. "Men and women aren't too different, Maeve. Snap the right cord and listen to the music."

My hands twitched with the fantasy of closing around Nathaniel's neck and wringing it until he was blue, like when he'd strangled me in the carriage—but I wouldn't let go. Nothing could stop me from squeezing until the capillaries in his eyes burst.

"Do you want to know how his tears tasted?"

I snapped my head forward, but he dodged my attack. Then I reared back and spat in his face. "I'll fucking *kill* you."

The soldiers gasped, but Nathaniel only laughed. "Such a filthy mouth. Perhaps forgoing dinner will teach you some respect." He took out a handkerchief to wipe my spittle away before gesturing to one of the sailors holding me. "Take her to the brig, Ensign Adams. And while you're at it, clip her wings."

"Yes, sir," he replied too eagerly, tightening sun-worn calloused hands around my biceps.

He shoved me down to the ground. I grunted, trying to push myself up, but Adams ripped my arm back, and I screamed as my elbow dislocated.

Nathaniel watched, a cruel smile on his face as his sailor stepped on my back to pull both my shoulders out of their sockets. The sharp pain echoed through my entire body. It blurred my sight as tears bled from my eyes, my muscles and tendons straining to shove the joints back into realignment.

A shriek ripped from my chest that was followed by relief as my unnatural healing popped everything back into place, and I fell slack.

"Whenever she misbehaves, you have my permission to do that again," Nathaniel said, voice smug.

My breath felt as if it had been rattled out of my chest, stealing any possible response I could have made.

"Yes, sir," Adams said, yanking me back up onto my feet.

My head lolled back and forth as I fought to keep my body upright.

The ensign whispered, "Do you hear that, little girl? Anytime you misbehave."

He dragged me down to the bilge, where I noticed three or four cells. I could only imagine how *The Ollipheist* crew had been crammed into them under lock and key. Any remaining sailors were probably chained to the deck on both ships under the blistering sun. The heavy door opened, and I was thrown inside. In the cell next to me, Freynir was coiled on the dirty ground, clearly beaten and barely conscious.

One of Adams's worn leather boots collided with my stomach, making me huff out in a brief moment of pain, but it was gone as soon as it came. Then he chuckled and did it again, making me curl inward on myself. I grunted, but any damage he did ebbed away quickly. He grabbed my hands roughly and attached my cuffs to the cell wall opposite Freynir.

Maybe I could kick the Skadian heir if I *really* tried.

But unfortunately, there was no way for me to touch his collar and shatter the draconite immobilizing him. I glanced at the keys on the pirate hunter's belt. *If only I could—*

Adams spat on me, shattering my thoughts, and slammed the door to my cell, taking the key to my binds with him. He even made a show of sliding it into his pocket, patting it, and grinning at me.

Bastard.

I looked around, taking in my new cage. Not nearly as nice as my tower in Farlight Castle, but it felt the same. A pretty cage was still a cage, nonetheless.

There was an officer seated at a small wooden table with his lunch in front of him. His blond hair was tidy and slicked back, and he wore a blue jacket with an insignia indicating his rank. Several keys hung from hooks beside him. He was probably in his late twenties, while Adams had to be nearing forty.

He was thin, as if he'd been on rations for so long that he'd lost weight, his cheekbones gaunt and his eyes sunken. Even his complexion seemed sallow, teetering on a sickly green when he should have a heathy olive sheen to his skin.

He twisted his fingers, clearly uncomfortable, but he kept his head down.

Adams licked his split lip and said, "Admiral said she doesn't get dinner. You know what happens if we catch you feeding strays again, don't you, Seymour?"

The guard didn't dare to look at him, only nodding, refusing to move as if worried that would set the ensign off.

Adams chuckled and stuck his pointer finger into his mouth before leaning down to swirl it in the younger man's tea. "I want to hear you say *Yes, sir*. I'm your superior," he taunted.

Seymour gulped and murmured, "Yes, sir."

The ensign looked back at me, eyes raking up and down my bloodied blouse like filthy fingertips. "Don't miss me too much, Princess. I'll be back for you in the morning."

"Can't wait," I muttered under my breath as I leaned against the cell wall.

Once he finally left, the petty officer physically relaxed, but his hands were shaking when he grabbed his tea and moved it away from himself.

"They treat you poorly, too, huh?" I asked.

Seymour looked over at me, voice quiet when he said, "I can't talk to you." The unspoken message was clear as day: *It's not safe.*

I narrowed my eyes, but I didn't prod. Instead, I turned my attention to the dark elf next to me. "I hope you're real happy, Freynir. How does that collar feel?"

When he didn't answer, I stretched my foot out as far as I could to kick the bars, earning a dull clank.

"Answer me, fucker! Are you happy?" I shouted, slamming my foot between the bars to hit the white-haired prince in the back of his head. "How does it feel to be caged like an animal?" I punctuated each word with a clang. His lack of response only made me angrier.

Kick.

Kick.

Kick.

After the fourth kick, he rolled away from me, not bound to the bars like I was. He grumbled wordlessly, propping himself against the back of his cell with a noise of pain. "Why did you stay?"

"What?" I asked, caught off guard by the question.

"You were about to jump off the side of the ship. What

stopped you?" he asked, wiping blood and sweat off his brow with the back of his hand.

A lump formed in my throat as I debated answering his question. I looked at him closely, inspecting the way his shoulders drew up and how he picked at his bloody cuticles. "Well, I suppose we're equally fucked at this point, aren't we?"

Freynir lifted his chained wrists to pull on his collar. "You could say that."

Bitterness welled in my chest. "Ronin never liked to talk about what happened to him when Nathaniel captured him. I don't know how badly they hurt him, but I know they almost broke us."

Freynir was quiet, watching me with his stark yellow eyes, a blood vessel broken in one of them appearing like an ink spill in his sclera.

My shoulders slackened. My breath came easier. "Hells. They *did* break us. But we… made it work. We were fine with being broken as long as all those jagged edges fit together. We completed each other that way."

He stared at me for a long moment, his expression indiscernible. "He didn't send an order for my wife's assassination, did he?"

I crooked an eyebrow at him and shook my head.

It was right then that I saw him for what he was—a grief-stricken husband.

"I… I arrived in Farlight Isles when I pursued the assassin right back into the throne room. Cross told me the leviathan sent them and kidnapped you in the process. That he seized the throne, and the Royal Leviathan pirate had stolen your mind as the leviathans had stolen the minds of the citizens."

"That's ridiculous," I said. "Frankly, I don't know when we would've had time for all that."

Freynir sighed. "It sounded really convincing at the time. His heart rate didn't even change—"

"You can hear heart rates?" I inquired.

"Few people lie so easily," he answered, falling slack against the bars. A man accepting defeat.

I stared at him for a long moment, wanting to reassure him despite my better judgment. "Are you one of those elves who can smell pheromones too?"

"...Yes," he said, his voice going up a little at the end. His eyebrow crooked like he wasn't sure if it was a serious question or not.

"That's rather disturbing."

Freynir looked at me for a long moment before bursting into laughter. "It's normal in Skadi!"

My shoulders shook as I laughed too. It felt so preposterous, sitting on Nathaniel's ship right next to the man who'd hunted Ronin and me down and was equally imprisoned.

Once the laughter simmered down, I finally said, "I heard you scream."

"What?"

"How badly did that collar burn?"

Hesitantly, he reached up to his neck and explored the small gap between his skin and the draconite. His nose scrunched up, eyebrows pinching in pain as he brushed the newly formed blisters. His throat bobbed a few times as he swallowed down the discomfort, but he didn't answer.

"I know what happens to Nathaniel's prisoners. I just…. I *couldn't* leave." I leaned my head back, knocking it against the bars so it resonated with a clang. "Ronin can handle this. I know he can."

Freynir slackened and said, "I'm sorry, Maeve."

"*Sorry* doesn't get me out of these chains. *Sorry* doesn't unburn my home. *Sorry* won't protect my family, Freynir."

He reached into his shirt and pulled out the frosty marital

pendant he showed me at the tavern when he approached me the first time. "I did this. I will make it right."

"You should hide that," the guard said quietly. "They'll take it."

Freynir looked over at Seymour, his grip tightening on his pendant. "Over my dead body."

Seymour tilted his head down, eyes darting to the hatch and back to Freynir's yellow ones. "Not your dead body, but your bloody one. Hide it." His fingers tapped against the table nervously. "If it's important, they want it."

What did they take from him?

The Skadian heir gave his pendant one more look, bringing it to his lips before tucking it under the collar of his shirt.

4

RONIN MURDOCH

ALL EYES ON YOU

EACH NEW SURVIVOR WHO TRICKLED INTO THE TUNNELS brought another wave of dread with them. I hadn't seen Mama or Wesley.

No Lucky Bartram.

I watched the ceiling fall on top of them, but I couldn't stay to see if they managed to make it out. The beams would've trapped me underneath the rubble, and then I'd be on my way to Cross.

Like Mae was.

Pain rippled inside my chest. I'd feel better if she were by my side. If I could feel her soft hands, roughened slightly by hard work, soothing my worry. If her wide eyes looked at me like she always did—with wonder and determination.

Like she believed in me. Even when I didn't have any in myself, she had enough faith in me for the both of us. She cleaved my heart right in half and tucked a stolen piece away in her chest to beat alongside hers.

Fuck, I'd give her all of me if it'd bring her back.

But I wouldn't be complete until I burned the Ivory Keys to the ground and took her into my arms again. She looked so lovely with my rings dangling from her neck. Maybe I'd take Pike's eyes and fashion a pendant for her like Cross had done with other leviathans.

Soon, I reminded myself.

I'd bring her home with whatever it took, but we were in no shape for a battle. I glanced around the tunnels, forming a plan. We had to get the injured people out first. If I were going to get my revenge, it wouldn't be at the expense of the other victims.

We'd celebrate Pike's death together. Then I'd tear Farlight Castle apart to give each and every one of them a share of Cross's treasures.

After all, I wasn't interested in the gold. The only treasure I wanted was Mae.

There were plenty of caches and even a community house at Anchorage Cove. We'd never taken care of *this* many people, but I'd make room in my cabana for as many as I could. My privacy wasn't as important as making sure the civilians and children had a roof over their heads.

If we needed supplies, I could send my crew out for them.

I will be worthy of leading. After all, this is just a large ship, as Mae said back at the meeting before it all went to shit. How will I captain it?

The injured were off to the side on pallets, being cared for with the minimal supplies we had. A corked sheepskin of bourbon and volunteered shreds of clothing went a long way. Oil lamps offered the bare minimum for light. Merchants and cornerstones of our community stepped up to take care of them, namely the blacksmith, Ingrid, and the baker, Theo. A few parents came forward to soothe the lone children, while several of the adolescents made themselves useful. They would fetch supplies, sit near lost children, or simply be available like my cabin boys on *The Ollipheist.*

Everyone wanted to help, even if they didn't know how.

Shipwreck Bay was more than a place. We were a people, and we took care of our own, no matter the devastation. This town had taken care of me time and time again, and now it was my turn to return the favor.

But as I stared at the grimy brick walkways and inhaled the stale scent of blood and sewage, hope felt out of reach. Water splashed along the sides of the stonework, and I'd already watched several people slip away into Death's care.

Bleak wasn't enough to describe how I felt. After everything that happened, my grasp on leadership was fragile at best. They were uncertain of me, and after Bliss's speech about me leading Pike to their homes, I felt as if someone was waiting for the chance to stab me in the back.

We were waiting for nightfall to transport all these people under the cover of darkness. It was unlikely that the pirate hunters would go out searching in an unfamiliar place the first night, but the next few nights, we wouldn't be so lucky.

The Ollipheist should still be operational for fishing trips or to suddenly move a large number of people, but it was only one ship. Several others had been destroyed in the harbor.

It was a marvelous galleon, but it wasn't enough.

Not to take on Pike.

I needed more.

More sailors. More ships. More fucking captains.

What the fuck am I going to do?

My foot tapped incessantly against the stone path beneath me. If the pirate hunters found us, the tunnels were too cramped to defend ourselves. It'd be like shooting fish in a barrel. We wouldn't be able to hold the line, although we'd die trying.

Before I could think of anything else, the entrance door slammed open again. Two of the gunnery crew were dragging Gunny through the muck while his head bobbed back and forth.

"Cap?" one of the gunners shouted as soon as they saw me. "Is that you, Cap?"

"What happened?" I asked, moving toward them with purpose. "Follow me."

I forked off toward Ingrid while the gunners followed, panicked.

"We found him in the dirt. He got hit!"

"Ahoy, Cap," Gunny said weakly as they laid him down on the makeshift pallets made up of nothing more than balled-up jackets and scrapped wood, the scent of blood thick in the air.

In the dim yellow light, I saw that his eye was bloodied, caked with mud and fluid. "What the fuck happened?"

"I'm fine," Gunny argued, struggling to get up.

"Like the Hells you are. Ingrid!" I yelled, keeping him down with one hand.

Ingrid scurried over. Despite her age, she was all brawn from her years of wielding the hammer and anvil. "Oh, fuck, Gun! Your eye." She knelt, working frantically to get the debris out of his eye with a waterskin of filtered water to debride the wound.

"It doesn't hurt," Gunny claimed, falling slack against the pallet. "Is Spider here?"

"I haven't seen him," I replied. "He was with you during the attack."

Gunny shook his head, lip trembling. "The cannonball hit the door, and I don't remember much after that." He jolted up suddenly. "I need to find him."

I grunted in disapproval and pushed him back down onto the bedroll. "You're in no shape to do that."

"Someone has to!" he shouted, shoving at both me and

Ingrid with all the strength he could muster—which wasn't much. "He's my best friend! I need to find him!" But then he fell limp, the fight suddenly gone out of him. "He's my best friend, Cap."

I put my hands on his shoulders and looked him directly in the eye. "We will find him, Gunny. One way or another. But you are my gunner, and you *will* stay here. That is an order. Do you understand?"

He gulped hard and averted his gaze. "Yes, Cap. Now leave me, please."

GODS, I WAS SO FUCKING ANGRY THAT I COULD BARELY THINK straight. My pulse still roared, and my jaw ached from how hard I'd been clenching it. It was easy to fall into old habits. I'd fought so hard for control that I pushed Mae and my family away. But I couldn't repeat my mistakes.

I made that promise to Mae, and I would keep it.

But *fuck me*, all I wanted to do was take my vengeance and damn all the consequences. It'd feel good for a moment, but then I'd be left with the aftermath. Perhaps an even bigger mess than I was already dealing with.

Hanging my head, I could still hear the screaming and smell the fire in the distance. It would only get worse if I couldn't get these people out of here. I'd be burying them en masse.

The sun was getting low in the sky. I stood outside the gate to the tunnels, remaining on watch while Udine and Luella prepped the survivors for the trek to Anchorage Cove. Most of the conscious injured could walk, but the rest would have to be carried.

The gate creaked behind me, and Udine stepped out. "We're almost ready."

I crossed my arms and said, "Good. Have you given the orders to your warriors?"

"Captain Bliss and two of mine will remain to help guide any stragglers," Udine replied with a dip of her head. She hid it well, but worry deepened the circles under her eyes.

"Wraith is my best. If anyone can get them back to Anchorage Cove safely, it's her. And we need as much information on the siege as possible."

If anyone could scout the area without being detected, it was Luella. And as much as Bliss hated my fucking guts, our survival counted on their cooperation. They wouldn't sabotage us. Not yet at least.

"I know that, Captain Ronin," she replied. "But I appreciate the reassurance."

"Thank you for having my back in there," I said. "But I want to know why you put your colors behind me so easily."

Udine leaned against the gate, crossing her arms over the sea glass armor that glittered like jewels were peeking through the smeared blood and mud. "Cliohde speaks to me, you know."

"Does she?" I asked, repressing my desire to scoff. "What does she think of our predicament?"

She shrugged. "Your guess is as good as mine. She doesn't so much speak directly to me as she sends me signs. The return of the leviathans and the return of our Blessing might as well have been a foghorn."

"Blessing?" I asked aloud, even though I already knew she meant Mae. A slash of pain crackled through my chest. I saw her in the mud whenever I closed my eyes.

"Maeve. I'm so sorry they took her."

"There's nothing I can do about it until we're ready for that fight." It was a grim reality.

"I'll be with you when that happens."

"You're putting a lot of blind faith in me," I commented.

"Any fool will follow a man who is king in title, but I choose to follow one who is a king in blood and service." Udine glanced back toward the gate as it creaked open. "All eyes on you."

All eyes on me.

5

RONIN MURDOCH

THE LONGEST NIGHT

"IF ANYTHING HAPPENS TO MY KIN, I WILL GUT YOU WHERE YOU stand, Leviathan," Bliss promised before I could take my place at the front of the first cluster of townspeople to make the trip to Anchorage Cove.

Two of my crew would lead each consecutive cluster in groups of twenty. Merrow would help carry the wounded and keep anyone from wandering too far away. After each group arrived at Anchorage Cove, a member of my crew would go back to lead the next group, over and over again until everyone was safely relocated where we could defend them.

"Look after mine, and I'll look after yours," I said, nodding toward Luella, who was giving Andra a kiss good-bye. My sister cupped her face, bringing their foreheads together to share a few hushed words.

A tic formed in Bliss's jaw as they replied, "My word is my bond. I can't say the same for you."

I was getting really fucking tired of Bliss questioning my character.

I parted my lips to say something, but Andra came up to

my side to join me in the first group and then be the one to lead the second group. "We're ready, Cap."

I looked back at Bliss, meeting their authoritative gaze with one of my own. "I don't have time for this. We can talk in my cabin at Anchorage Cove if you still have this bug up your ass."

Bliss narrowed their eyes, running their tongue over their teeth, but they didn't reply, instead turning away to join Luella and the scouting party.

Walking to Anchorage Cove was one of the longest nights of my life.

With no moon in the sky, I led my crew and townspeople by instinct. As little noise as a crying baby could give away our position. If I failed, I'd draw the pirate hunters directly to the tunnels, proving everything that Bliss thought of me was right.

I will not fail. Not again.

Due to the storm, a lot of the path had been flooded out, and our feet sloshed through the thick mud. I recognized some sailors from both Lucky's and Bliss's crews helping where they were needed, but with all the dirt and blood, no one could tell who wore whose colors. Any division between crews blurred into the same creed.

Us versus the corrupt monarchy.

When the dim lanterns surrounding Anchorage Cove swam into my vision, it truly felt like I'd come home. My crew split into their designated jobs, leading people to the community building and a few of the fishing shacks we had available.

It wasn't much, but it was only temporary. We set up tents from supplies the retired sailors would use for fishing. Blankets and tapestries made decent bedrolls. Andra started the trek back to the tunnels alone, and I trusted her to get the job done.

Before the next group made their way up the hills, I went to my cabana for a fresh set of clothes. Anything but fishing waders. I also gathered a few items to take to my cabin on *The Ollipheist*: my lucky red sash that I only wore at sea, a set of Mae's clothes so I'd have clean ones ready for her, and her pillow. It was one of the few things I had that smelled like her. My chest tightened. I wanted to keep a little piece of her for as long as I could.

Most of my things stayed put for Udine and her merrow warriors to use as they needed.

More people trickled in, including Butcher and Conway. *Thank the Gods they survived.*

With one eye and his mobility aids caked in mud, Butcher shook with exhaustion but clearly didn't want to stop moving. As soon as he saw me directing sailors to take the injured into the prepared shelters and tents, he rushed over.

"What can I do, Cap?" Butcher asked. "Give me something to do."

Conway's milky eyes seemed distant as he watched my shadow move across the muddy ground. "We will do what we can. Anything."

"You'll do what you do best, Butcher," I said. "These people are going to be hungry."

Butcher swallowed hard, barely blinking away overwhelmed tears. "Luther's gone. I could've used the extra help."

"I'll help, love," Conway promised.

Luther... that poor fucking kid. But he was just one of the many we lost during the siege.

I wasn't ready to prepare the funeral rites. I didn't want to think about the blood that ran through the cobblestones lining the port. It was hard to lose a sailor on the water, but it was always worse to lose them on land.

When that happened, I couldn't blame the ocean for claiming them.

"The baker, Theo, should be coming in one of the groups. I'm sure he'll want to help," I said, trying to fight back the welling feeling of devastation that I'd been repressing since the moment I saw Mae cold in the dirt.

I clenched my jaw in an attempt to repress my growing temper.

"Yes, Cap," Butcher replied.

I knew my suggestion wasn't the comfort he'd been seeking. Nothing I said would've comforted him at that point.

Conway pulled at his arm. "Take me to the greenhouse. We'll have a lot of bellies to feed."

Butcher gave a resigned nod and set off toward *The Ollipheist* without another word.

IN MY WORN LEATHER BOOTS, I STOOD OUTSIDE WESLEY AND Isa's home. I didn't know if Wesley had survived the beam that fell on top of him when the tavern came down, but I needed to talk to Isa.

What the fuck am I supposed to tell her?

More and more people were flooding into Anchorage Cove, but Andra and Udine had it handled. This news shouldn't fall on anyone else to deliver. I was Wesley's captain, and this was my responsibility.

From my position at the front door, it was hard to believe that Anchorage Cove was bustling. I couldn't see the port town. The cliff face dropped off into the ocean, making me feel as if I was far away from the siege on a little slice of paradise.

Crickets chirped, and the ocean roared as it slapped against the cliffs. It sounded nothing like cannonballs or screams. It was easy to forget about all the terror I'd experienced the past several hours.

I knocked.

It took a few moments for someone to answer, and I assumed that Isa was putting the last of the kids to bed. When she opened the door, I took my hat off, pressing it against my chest.

"Levi? What are you doing here?" Isa asked, the blue-toned umber of her skin flushed nearly purple, as if she had been running around the house all evening. She looked behind me, appearing suspicious that I didn't have any company.

"Can I come in, Isa?"

She recoiled, catching on to my tone. "Where's Wes? Where is my husband?"

"Can I come in?" I requested, not wanting to have this conversation outside.

Her dark eyes widened, and she looked back and forth, upper lip curling in a seething response. "Tell me where my fucking husband is, and then you can come inside."

"He's still at Shipwreck Bay...." I paused, wanting so desperately to put it delicately, but I couldn't. "Pike attacked. The tavern collapsed."

She averted her eyes, curling one hand over her face to quell a soft sob. "Is he alive?"

"I don't know," I answered honestly. "He and Mama were next to each other. They're either trapped under the rubble or the pirate hunters took them hostage."

"Luella and Andra?"

"They're down at Anchorage."

She thinned her lips, bobbing her head in shallow nods. Then she slapped her palm against the doorway. "I told him to stop pirating. Did he ever tell you that?" Her words were tight as her eyes darted over to me, filled with overwhelming *accusations*.

"No. He didn't."

She shook her head, tears leaving tracks down her cheeks. "No, I don't suppose he did. He never wanted to let his brother down." A sudden sob retched from her chest before she could stop it. "Look where it got him."

"Isa—"

"Get the fuck off my doorstep," she said, stepping back into the house to shut the door.

"He could be alive. I'm going to bring him home," I promised before she could.

"I knew if he kept going with you, I would get him back in a box or in pieces. What am I supposed to tell the kids, Levi?" She gulped hard, tears falling faster now. Her voice broke as she repeated, "Get the fuck off my doorstep."

I dipped my head, taking a full step back. "I'm sorry, Isa."

She didn't reply, just slammed the door in my face.

6

MAEVE CROSS

A PAINFUL DEATH

"Come on, Princess." Adams jostled me from a shallow sleep.

Morning already? Godsdamnit.

My wrists ached from the bindings, rubbed raw even as they quickly healed.

Adams and two other hunters stood outside my cell. There was no fighting my way out of this.

I groaned, a brief sensation of pain from sleeping on the hard floor washing through my bones before it was gone and I felt refreshed like every morning. I blinked slowly, glancing over at Freynir, who looked worse for wear.

He was bruised to all Hells, but that didn't stop him from standing on shaky legs and slamming his fists against the bars. "Don't touch her!" he snarled. "Leave her alone!"

"Shut him up." Adams yanked me up to my feet by my irons. The other two opened Freynir's cell to beat him within an inch of his life. "One day you'll learn to keep your mouth shut. Prince or not, you're a prisoner now."

They beat him relentlessly. Kicking his ribs. Smashing his fingers under their boots. Bruising his face even more than it was already. All Freynir could do was curl into himself, his arms locked around his head for protection.

Adams crooked his head to the side, looking Freynir over thoroughly. "Is that real silver?"

It took me several moments to realize he was talking about Freynir's multiple facial piercings. They decorated his ears and dangled from his nose.

I huffed, forcefully jerking my cuffs out of Adams's hands—though not without blistering my wrists again. "Keep your hands off!" I demanded.

Adams grabbed my irons again, slamming my hands into the cell bars with enough force to break several of my fingers. I cried out, my fingers bent at odd angles before they popped back into place one by one. He knocked me down onto the ground, then slammed the door closed to enter the cell next to mine.

"Of course it's real silver. You're a prince, after all," Adams said as the other two officers lifted Freynir for him. A gleeful cruelty danced in his eyes. He didn't look at the jewelry. He watched the blood run from the prince's nose.

He didn't want the silver. He wanted the *power*.

"You have enough to spare. How about one for me..."

Adams hooked his finger into one of the hoops along the cartilage of Freynir's extended ears. He tugged, earning a shout of pain as he tore one out. Blue blood spat from the fresh wound as Adams toyed with a hoop dangling from Freynir's earlobe.

"And one for my friend here."

The Skadian heir muffled another shout as Adams ripped the hoop out.

"I heard body piercings are popular in Skadi. Is that true?" Adams asked.

Freynir sneered but didn't answer.

"Another time, I'll take those too. But there's enough

silver on your face to buy a few rounds at the tavern when we get back to the Keys." He laughed and added, "Oh, and I can't forget one for my other friend."

Freynir couldn't muffle the next shout as Adams took another hoop and then handed them to the officers holding the heir like a trophy.

"Do you want one, Princess?" Adams asked, malice flickering in his light-colored eyes as he looked over at me.

I shook my head, terrified of setting him off and making him hurt Freynir again.

"I don't want to be greedy," he said, one of his hands shooting up to tear Freynir's nose ring out. The shout became a scream as tears tracked down his face. The ensign admired the septum piercing before he threw it into my cell. "You might heal faster than any of us, but he doesn't."

Finally, the men dropped Freynir onto the ground, his face and ears bleeding steadily as they left him alone. But I knew they'd be back for him. They'd hurt him again and again. A hard lump formed in my throat, and despite everything Freynir had done, I couldn't find it in me to hate him.

He didn't deserve this cruelty.

Adams came back into my cell and yanked me up to my feet, holding on to my cuffs.

My vision narrowed in on him, anger clouding all my thoughts. I threw my head back and headbutted the bastard in the face. He recoiled but didn't let go of me, dragging me into a hard headlock. I coughed as his arm tightened around my throat.

"Pike was right. She's feisty." He spat a wad of blood onto the floor of my cell. He raised an eyebrow and gave me a bloody grin. "I like a good fight. I can clip your wings again, little girl."

He twisted my arm, but before he could snap my elbow in two again, Seymour shakily cleared his throat, looking unbearably uncomfortable in the presence of the other two men. "Admiral Pike requested an audience with her immediately."

Adams pouted, blood oozing from his split lip. He brushed my face with his knuckles, making disgust curdle in my belly. "Another time, then. Don't want to keep the admiral waiting. Though he always makes it worth my while."

I glanced over at Freynir, motionless on the floor of his cell except for his labored breathing.

Adams grabbed a fistful of my hair and ripped my head back to force me to look up at him. "You know, women are supposed to be bad luck on board, but having you here makes me feel very lucky."

My upper lip curled into a snarl, but I didn't say anything. I swallowed the bile that thickened in my throat. I maintained eye contact, a million promises of violence bouncing around in my head.

I'll rip your throat out.

Suppress it. Don't give them another reason.

When he released my hair, I ducked my head down. He led me up to the upper deck, where the captain's quarters were located underneath the helm rather than behind it like on *The Ollipheist.*

I felt the eyes. I heard the snickers. But where the laughter was cruel, there were also whispers of another kind. Sailors who didn't want any part of it and were probably conscripted like much of Varric's army. There was a clear difference between those forced to be here and those who *chose* it. The hums of a mutiny waiting for the spark.

But what could be the spark?

Slowly, I raised my eyes to the cabin boys. They weren't scrubbing the deck or learning under different crews. They were treated as less than servants. Sickness churned in my belly when I watched higher-ranking sailors bang the smoking ashes of tobacco over the heads of the younger men.

They remained perfectly still, but their eyes were wild. They were *terrified*.

On *The Ollipheist*, cabin boys were at the bottom of the barrel, but that didn't mean they weren't treated with respect. They did their jobs. Hard work was rewarded. This was *nothing* like that. I'd never seen a cabin boy look at their superior officers like this.

Like they were sure the wrong word or movement would be their last.

I knew without a doubt that this behavior would've been shut down instantly on *The Ollipheist*. If not by Luella, Andra, or Wesley, then Ronin would end it. It was *unacceptable*.

Did Pike even have control over his crew? Or did he encourage their behavior?

A hyperventilating cabin boy, likely only in his late teens, sat upon the lap of one of the older officers, who held him there so he'd squirm. Hot rage swirled within me even as I watched some of the lower-ranking officers stiffen, none of them having the authority to stop it.

A swell of protectiveness came over me. These were *kids*. They should be back home with their parents, living their lives carelessly and happily. They should be making mistakes and learning from them.

But Nathaniel had them on his ship, dying for a cause that killed their friends.

The humiliation didn't stop until a lieutenant stepped in, not much older than Nathaniel but rigid in how he held himself. He ordered the lower-ranking officers to get to work. His obvious concern for the younger men wasn't lost on me as he shooed them to other tasks, much to the relief of the cabin boys.

I needed sailors like him. Enough of them, and Nathaniel didn't stand a chance.

Adams brought me to the captain's quarters, straightening up as he knocked on the door.

I heard Nathaniel's voice inside. "...then *find them*. Next time you report, you better have some good fucking news, or I'm stuffing your head as a trophy." A pause. "Come in."

Adams opened the door, and I got the first glimpse of Nathaniel's cabin. He was speaking into a calling glass the size of a shaving mirror. I imagined that was how Varric kept tabs on Nathaniel's progress and he maintained control over his army wherever they were.

I would've saved a lot of time meeting with the monarchs if we had one. But the journey was worth it.

There was an opulent bed made neatly, like Nathaniel hardly spent any time in his cabin. An ornate desk was placed against a wall of windows. A few stacked papers and a polished dagger rested on the oiled surface. The shelves were not full of personal baubles or books but trophies of various conquests. There were a few trinkets, one of which I recognized from Ronin's cabin: his cracked compass.

I bit my tongue until I tasted blood. I would hold all of my cards close to my chest. I wouldn't tell Nathaniel a godsdamn thing.

Across from his desk, there was a chair, stained with brown blood, leather straps for both the hands and feet.

I gulped thickly. *Whatever happens to me, I'll survive.*

"Ah, Maeve. That's right. I've been waiting for you. She didn't give you any trouble, did she?" Nathaniel asked, rising from his seat. He was dressed in a distinguished coat with fancy embellishments. Golden buttons. An embroidered barracuda.

All teeth.

"No, Admiral. No trouble at all. I'm enjoying this responsibility," the ensign said meekly, bowing his head.

Nathaniel crooked a brow. "Ah. Yes. Well, put her in the chair. We have a lot to catch up on."

He forced me down into the bloodied chair, and I submitted. I needed to save my energy for whatever came next. Adams undid my irons and tied my wrists to the arms of the chair. As he strapped me in, I didn't break eye contact with Nathaniel.

You don't scare me. Let me show you why they say women are bad luck.

After my wrists and ankles were restrained to his liking, Nathaniel looked me over, his eyes catching on the tear in my blouse. "I'm only going to say this once, Adams. You can have your fun, but you are not permitted to fuck her."

The ensign stiffened, all color leaving his face. "I wouldn't—"

Nathaniel's face gave nothing away as he said coldly, "If you value your prick, you'll keep it to yourself. Leave."

"Yes, sir," Adams said, beating a quick retreat out of the room.

I narrowed my eyes, twisting my wrists in the binds.

Nathaniel hummed under his breath before glancing at me. "Those aren't my orders. If it were up to me, I'd let you experience the same treatment as that leviathan, but your father would have my head."

A flare of heat beaded in my chest and spit up past my lips. "What did they do to him?"

He watched me closely, a smile spreading across his face until it showed all of his teeth. "Anything they wanted to."

Tears pricked behind my eyes, all my protective instincts roaring within me. Fantasies of taking his life into my hands overwhelmed me. My fingers twitched. My heart ignited like a wildfire. "When I take your life, Nathaniel, you'll be bowing at my feet."

"You're so precious when you threaten me."

"Go fuck yourself."

He sighed, clicking his tongue in disappointment. "Such a filthy mouth. Unsuitable for a noblewoman. But you threw that away the second you chose the pirates over us." He took the dagger from the desk and slid it over my arm, watching as the skin split, only to knit itself back together. "Marvelous. You would've been an ideal addition to my estate. I don't think I'd ever tire of this."

I winced, groaning deep in my throat as he slid the blade up my skin, ruby-red drops spilling from the incision to puddle on the ground. Again, my body healed.

Nathaniel watched, prodding the freshly healed wound. Then his icy blue eyes shot up to mine, and he watched my reaction as he slit my arm open again. I couldn't hide my hiss of pain. There was no numbness. It was sharp and fresh every time.

He tilted his head, observing the twist of discomfort as I reflexively tried to get away from him.

The corner of his mouth twitched, and he finally put the blade down. "You're going to tell me where that leviathan went, Maeve, and then I will personally restore your status. I'll even give you an officer's cabin to rest in. You'll be treated like a proper lady."

A pained laugh bubbled up my chest. "No."

"No?"

"*No.*"

Then *he* laughed. A chilling eruption of glee as he leaned back and clasped his hands together. "You'll be a challenge, but I'll enjoy it. A thousand cuts. How does that sound? A thousand cuts from my crew. When they're done, it'll be my turn. You'll be groveling before sunup."

I didn't react and kept my head bowed. I gulped down every awful word, every snide retort, because that was what Nathaniel wanted. My nails bit into the armrests, but I resisted.

"I used to love the sound of a woman crying. Pitiful, but beautiful. Even better when the note was snipped before it finished, like the twang of strings as they snap. But that was before," Nathaniel mused.

He wanted a rise out of me. I wouldn't give it to him.

"Before I heard the prettiest cries out of that Royal Leviathan. What was his name? Ronin?"

Hot breath blew out of my nose as my gaze snapped up. My throat bobbed at the thought of Nathaniel's guts being spilled at my feet. "Keep his name out of your fucking mouth."

A cruel grin spread across his face. "He said yours frequently. You know, before he begged me to stop. I don't know how much of it he remembers considering he was incapacitated for most of his stay." He walked his fingertips up my arm. "A shame, really. Watching him break was a euphoria most people only dream of."

The wooden armrest splintered under my fingernails. "I should have killed you."

"Please, Princess. Don't make me laugh. You don't have it in you. When this is over, you'll be using that filthy tongue to shine my boots. You're a pretty sight when you're on your knees." He glanced toward the door. "One more chance to tell me where they are before I watch you bleed until morning."

My lip curled into a sneer. "I'd rather die."

Nathaniel leaned in until he was a breath away. "Then let's find out which death hurts the worst."

7

MAEVE CROSS

A VISIT FROM DEATH

It didn't take long for Nathaniel to rip a scream from me. Agony swallowed my thoughts. Each death took longer to recover from, but the moment I came to again, pain erupted through me until my body was broken.

The force of will inside me swayed, desperate for a reprieve.

Everything inside my head felt blurry, the veil between this world and the next thinner than ever before. I clawed onto my spirit, begging myself not to crack, not to break.

Nathaniel could break my body, but he couldn't break my spirit. The moment he did, I would fail and he would win.

He enjoyed every moment of my anguish. He relished every cry. I swallowed down my urge to beg for mercy. That was what he wanted from me. He wanted to stand above me and push me until I shattered. He wanted to deliver me to Varric in pieces, afraid to raise a hand.

I can't take any more.

Just let me die.

"Come on, darling. Give me another scream," he demanded, my blood painted all over his hands, splattered on his face like the aftermath of a mad artist. "Your voice sounds so pretty when it breaks."

No. I will never scream for you again.

A sob left my lips as I thrashed in that damn chair. Then I swallowed down every yelp, every cry. I wouldn't give him the satisfaction of hearing me scream. I cursed him, I cursed Varric, and I cursed the fucking Gods. Why must I suffer over and over again?

How is this a gift?

"Tell me how badly this hurts," he said with utter glee as he plunged a thin blade into my chest, puncturing a lung.

It felt as if my lungs had filled with fire, drowning me with frothy blood as it sputtered from my lips. My last moments went on for what felt like eternity. My chest burned as everything grew cold.

I couldn't succumb to the dark easily. I fought for every breath, clawing into the armrests until my nails were bloody. Black curled along the edges of my vision as my head finally lolled back.

The pain disappeared, evaporating like morning fog rolling over the ocean. I fell into a peaceful abyss beneath me. All the mortal tethers like the pit in my belly and the fire in my lungs ebbed away into nothing. The veil curled around me, gently lowering me onto the familiar greenery.

Death's realm.

As green as it appeared, I couldn't smell the grass. I couldn't feel the warmth from the sun. It was a void, though a peaceful void. But something about it was different. As if the realm itself was reaching into my chest to grasp my heart.

Relief spread through me as I brought my knees to my chest. I cried. Even if tears didn't stream down my face, every sob was a wave of liberation. I had tried so hard to hold my tears while in Nathaniel's cabin that everything now crested over the surface, and I couldn't stop myself from wailing.

"I'm sorry, Maeve," Death said, appearing from the fog behind me. Moonlight dappled their hands, giving way to spots of tawny skin. Half of their face flickered like a skull in the light.

They were a duality. Life and death. Chaos and peace.

I cried, "I-I can't do this." My chest shuddered as I tried to quell my despair. "I'm not strong enough for this."

"You are," Death replied quietly.

I looked up over my knees, seeing Death standing with their scythe fastened across their chest with a worn leather strap. A skiff floated in the rushing river behind them. Souls took their seats along the boat, waiting politely for the everlasting peace. Death removed the short instrument from their chest, only slightly longer than a sickle, and extended it to its full length, using it in a sweeping motion like a shepherd utilized a cane to guide their flock.

Not meant to cut or clip, but to reap and harvest what life had sown.

Rage broke through my pain, and I shouted, "Why did you do this to me? Why can't I escape this?"

"Is that what you want, Maeve? Do you want to move on?" they asked, propping their scythe straight up so the blade curved high above their head.

I swallowed thickly as the skiff beckoned me. I could give up. I could finally choose peace. But if I did that, then everything I did, all I'd sacrificed, it would all be for nothing. Would I be able to rest knowing that I passed up my opportunity to see Ronin again?

Death already knew my answer.

I won't rest until I see him again.

"No," I answered. "Not yet."

"I warned you that what came next would test you."

"I didn't think it would be this hard," I replied, using my palm to dry my tears. My hands didn't feel wet even though I could see the glistening on my skin. Death's realm would always be a contradiction.

The Reaper stared at me for a long moment before floating closer, kneeling beside me in a way that felt too mortal for Death themself. "You are my champion, Maeve. I wouldn't have chosen you if I didn't think you were strong enough."

"That's not comforting."

"It's not my job to comfort you. It's my job to prepare you." They sat with me for a long moment.

"I feel different," I said. "This place—it feels the same, but different."

They hummed. "Each time you come into my realm, the power passes through you. Each death will make you stronger."

"Stronger?"

They pinned me with a cold, knowing stare. "You will rise where others fall, Maeve. They can't take anything from you."

I let the information wash over me. The strange sensation cascaded through my spirit, making me feel oddly warm in a cold place. I swallowed and asked, "Is Ronin okay?"

"Cliohde is with him. He will have her guidance in the battles to come," Death answered abstractly.

"But is he okay?" I asked again. "Is he whole?"

Death hummed again. "I'm unsure how to answer the question, child. He's in pain, and he cannot be whole because you've taken a piece of him with you." They pressed their pointer finger into my chest. "Just like you can't be whole until you've returned to the leviathan you're sworn to."

My brow furrowed. "Sworn to? Is that something else you did?"

They chuckled, fondly tucking some hair behind my ear like a parent with their child. "No, Maeve. You've done that yourself. Your fates have been tangled together for quite some time, but we never meant for you to fall in love with him."

"Why? I was a guard under his mother—"

"You are *not* her anymore, Maeve. Same soul, but you're a different being with different experiences. That is what makes the person. Not only the soul or body, but everything else as well. Your heart is far stronger than hers was. Duty engulfed her in every aspect of her life, but your compassion rules you. That is not a bad thing."

Their words struck a new chord of hope inside me. It was exactly what I needed to hear. "Thank you."

Death straightened up. "I have souls to tend to, and you must return to the Realm of the Living."

"Can I stay a little longer?" I asked. "Just a little while?"

Death's gaze softened. "You can. Not forever, but you can catch your breath."

I sighed and settled into the peaceful void for as long as Death would let me.

8

RONIN MURDOCH

CLIOHDE'S GIFT

I HADN'T SLEPT IN NEARLY TWO DAYS.

So when I finally stepped foot into my cabin on *The Ollipheist*, it took everything I had not to collapse directly onto my floor in an exhausted stupor. I kicked my boots off and placed my hat on a hook behind my desk. My sash and weapons found their place across the wooden tabletop.

My temper had threatened to swallow me, so I directed all of it into work. It had been a grueling forty-eight hours of finding shelters for displaced townspeople to sleep in, which necessitated cleaning our caches and sheds to make room for everyone. I also pored over our rations to make sure everyone was fed. Not enough, but it was something.

Thank the Gods that Siggi found his way to Anchorage Cove after the attack. I set him up in my cabana with the merrow, and he got to work sewing together scraps of fabric into blankets and clothes. I promised him a drink when we were finally granted a moment of peace, but I didn't think we'd ever get it.

There would be no peace, no paradise—not a fucking

moment of it while the pirate hunters had a foothold in Shipwreck Bay.

There hadn't been enough time for me to process what happened to Mae. She wasn't the only person I lost during the siege. I didn't know where to fucking start with Wesley and Mama. They were buried in the wreckage like Lucky was.

I had to trust that they were still alive, but considering how Violetta was blown away in front of me—

Fuck.

Violetta's dead.

I can't do this anymore.

My legs nearly crumpled under me as I sat down on my bed. I buried my face in my hands, inhaling deeply before running them through my hair. It's not like I ever loved Violetta romantically, but some part of me adored her.

More bite than bark, she said what she meant, even if she enjoyed toying with me while she did it. I respected her. She was my friend.

Violetta was sworn to her family. She was loyal for a price, but once it was paid, she never swayed. I couldn't imagine what Pinky was going through. I still had hope that my loved ones survived, but Pinky had watched his best friend become red mist in front of him.

Violetta had known the cost of what we were doing, but her death wasn't fair. When Andra and the ship crew got the ketch stocked and ready, I'd send correspondence to the Haven. Maybe I could get reinforcements. That would also be the perfect time to get the families and the children out of here.

I didn't know what was going to come next. I didn't know when the pirate hunters would lay siege to Anchorage Cove, so I had to act. If they stabilized their foothold, we'd lose Shipwreck Bay permanently.

Like fuck I'd let that happen.

But all I have are injured sailors, frightened farmers, and retirees.

What the fuck am I supposed to do?

"*Me-row,*" came a familiar chirp from under my bookcase.

I looked up to see two wide green eyes reflecting the oil lamp as Lieutenant Commander Lazlo's fluffy body wormed out from his favorite spot. He didn't wait for permission before wiggling his haunches and pouncing onto my bed.

"I'm happy to see you, Lazlo," I said, so relieved that my cat survived the attack. I didn't think he'd ever traveled far enough to be in Shipwreck Bay, but it was a weight off my shoulders to know he was safe.

I sank my fingers into his black mane, scratching under his chin. He released a monstrous purr, vibrating the whole bed. Lazlo headbutted my hand, demanding more affection.

When he couldn't take any more, he backed away and trotted over to the side of the bed where Mae slept. He bumped her pillow with his nose and meowed loudly.

"They took her."

He blinked owlishly at me and tilted his head to the side.

"I'll get her back, Lazlo." I reached forward and rubbed his ears before he made himself comfortable between Mae's pillow and mine. The massive cat took up as much room as possible, making sure I'd have to hang off the bed if I wanted to sleep.

Knock. Knock. Knock.

What now? I didn't want to talk to anyone else ever again after the past two days, but captains didn't get to take a day off. Not while their crew was in danger. I grunted and pushed myself up.

When I opened the door, I was mildly surprised to see Pinky standing there. His tricorn cap shadowed his eyes as he slowly tore his gaze from the planks to mine. I finally got a good look at him in the soft light of my oil lamp. His dark blue skin looked gray, his eyes nearly swollen, as if he'd been repressing tears all day.

He looks as broken as I feel inside.

Glancing outside my cabin, I caught a few of my sailors on watch, some of them laying out bedrolls on the deck. I didn't mind. We weren't in motion, and if it made them feel safer, that was all that mattered.

"What can I do for you, Pinky?"

"Can I come in, Leviathan?" he asked, hands balled into fists by his sides. His mouth was pressed into a hard line.

I stepped to the side and gestured for him to enter. As soon as he did, I closed the door. Pinky looked around, noticing the big cat on my bed and the clutter I didn't have the energy to tidy.

"I've never been in your cabin," he mused. "They say a man's dwelling reflects who he is inside. Is that true? Are you this put together inside?"

Put together? Ha.

"I have to be," I answered.

Pinky nodded, taking his hat off, his dark brows pinched together. "I'm sorry about your freshie, Levi. I gave you a lot of shit, but I liked her. I hope you're able to get her back."

I nodded, crossing my arms over my chest. "I'm sorry about Violetta," I said sincerely.

Pinky swallowed hard. "Vee's gone, but I'm not."

A few moments of comfortable silence fell between us before I asked, "Can I do anything for you?"

He sucked his teeth before looking me straight in the eye. "I've never been a leader. That was Vee's job. I learned a great deal about our enemies. I exposed their soft bellies for Vee to strike. It wasn't honest work, but I got the job done."

"I never liked how you did things," I admitted. "But I'd be

a fool not to see how you sacrificed your honor so your crew didn't have to."

Pinky took a deep breath and stood up tall. "I'm not fit to be a captain, Levi. Not like you and not like Vee. Let me put my colors behind you and exploit our enemies. Let me… let me *help*. For Vee."

I enjoyed the thought of putting Pinky to work. He fought dirty and did whatever was necessary for Violetta to get a leg up.

When I didn't say anything immediately, he blew a heavy breath out of his nose and said, "I need this, Leviathan. Give me orders."

"You will go back to the tunnels. Bliss and Wraith need someone with your skills. If you want to help me and help this cause, then you are going to find the navy's weakness for us to strike."

"Aye, aye, Captain," Pinky declared, squaring his shoulders to salute me. He placed his hat back on his head, standing tall as if new life had been breathed into him.

"In the morning." I said, stopping him as he turned to go. "Get some sleep. Eat something. That's an order."

Pinky looked over his shoulder, and I barely made out the glistening of his eyes before he nodded and left.

THE OCEAN ROARED FROM OUTSIDE MY WINDOW. MAE'S SIDE of my bed was cold. I kept unconsciously reaching over to her pillow, from where I would frequently pull her into my chest while we slept so I could feel her hair tickling my nose.

I missed her warmth in my arms.

I sat up in bed, burying my face in my hands. The muscles in my arms twitched and tightened from the exertion I'd put myself through.

I needed to fucking sleep, but how could I recover when it felt like a vital piece of me was gone? Without her, the nightmares clawed through my head, and I couldn't get rid of this ball of dread sitting on my chest.

I didn't realize how much I needed her to be able to sleep.

And those fuckers took her from me. My heart ached with how badly I missed her. I longed for her voice, for her little wheezes when she slept, for how her face flushed that pretty shade of pink when I riled her up.

I'd wasted so much of our time together battling my own problems.

And I was so *fucking angry.*

An ocean wave clapped the side of the ship, loud as a rumble of thunder. The sea was also in distress. I could feel it in my bones. A soul-deep unrest.

Crack! Crack! Crack! Each new wave was deafening, almost like it tried to get my attention. Another surge crashed into the stern of my ship, the water splashing and frothing against my window.

The fuck?

The sea was always calm in the cove where the ship docked, but this…. This was oddly aggressive. I got up and went over to my window where the waves splashed relentlessly, slapping hard against the rudder. Through all the droplets on the glass, I could barely make out a figure standing on the surface of the water.

The waves wove around her feet with every exaggerated gesture of her hands.

Glowing blue eyes met mine through the window as she pointed directly at me and curled her finger as if beckoning me to join her in the water. She didn't have any hair, and the moon left her face in shadow, aside from those striking eyes.

Under normal circumstances, I wouldn't have opened my window to join a strange magic-using woman in the ocean, but I had a feeling that she wouldn't stop slapping waves against my window and would keep me up until morning unless I obeyed.

The water in the cove wasn't deep enough to accommodate my leviathan form, but it was deep enough for a dive. I swung open my window and climbed out to dive into the big blue. She watched me intently with the moon behind her.

The wind whistled in my ears as I cut through the air, making sure my form was perfect before I hit the water. I'd done enough dives in my life to know that if I fucked it up, I couldn't walk straight for a week.

The ocean gave way as I plummeted into the comforting chill. It felt as if an old friend was embracing me. As soon as the water engulfed me, I willed a partial change to take over. My hands turned into webbed claws, and my eyes adjusted to the salt water. Gills cut into the side of my throat, allowing me to take a deep, comfortable breath.

A hundred feet in front of me, the figured dropped into the sea. Her form was draped in white fabric, arms adorned in iridescent black-blue scales. Her pallid complexion looked ethereal beneath the waves as she swam away from me like an angler fish.

Against my better judgment, I followed her into deeper water to where rocks jutted up from the surface. When they weren't hunting us, I occasionally saw sirens basking in the sun here before they disappeared back into the deep.

The sirens devoured sailors, but that wasn't their only defining trait. They still had their own hierarchy in the water. My crew viewed sirens as predators and something to avoid at all times, but I was sure fish viewed fishermen the same way.

I saw the sirens in ways that my crew never did.

The white-clad figure disappeared out of the water to climb on top of a rock. When I popped my head above the surface, I noticed pale shoulders, nearly the same color as her dress. Tattoos decorated her scalp, like the unique markings on tropical fish.

"Do you know how long I was trying to wake you, dragonling?" she asked, glancing over her shoulder to pin me with glowing blue eyes. The language she used wasn't Common. She was speaking Trill… like the sirens did.

I narrowed my eyes and climbed up the slippery rock to where she sat. "Do enlighten me."

"You've never prayed to me before, so I assumed you'd be easier to reach. Pity."

I looked at her blankly, unsure what she was referring to.

She released an exaggerated sigh and said, "*Cliohde, I want blood. Help me make them pay.*"

I recoiled completely. "*Cliohde?*"

"That's what you mortals call me," she retorted.

My mouth hung open as I strung together a few words to form a sentence. "What are you doing here?"

"I'm here to give you a gift," she said, rising from her spot to turn and look at me. She was long and slender, flat-chested like the merrow. The draping fabric gave way around her torso to display blue scales that looked a lot like mine when I was fully shifted.

I was suspicious. A goddess visiting me personally to deliver a gift? I didn't trust it.

"Do you think I haven't noticed you turn your back on your lineage?" Cliohde asked, her voice elegant and timeless. But it also sounded like a mother chastising a child. "To think that I gave you this human skin as a gift centuries ago to let you hide among your prey and protect your young, but now you let your prey hunt you."

I pressed my tongue into my cheek with annoyance. "What did you expect? We're at our weakest like this."

She sighed. "I know. I took away your venom and

expected your fangs to be enough." Cliohde dipped her head. "I underestimated the enemy, and they hurt my children. Let me aid you." She slowly reached out her hand to me, webbed with black-tipped claws.

I didn't take it. "I've done this without you. I don't need your help."

"It's not enough, Ronin. Do you want revenge?" She punctuated her next sentence by clicking her claws together with one hand in imitation of a mouth. "Or do you just like to hear your own voice?"

I ran my tongue over my teeth, glancing over my shoulder to my ship in the distance, and thought about the countless people depending on me to save them. The responsibility was heavy enough without being outmanned and outgunned by the navy. "What is it?"

"I'm giving you your legacy. Trust me," she pleaded, her voice much softer than before.

I took a deep breath, noticing how the waves lapped around the edges of the boulder. If trusting her meant having an edge to save my people, I would take it. I reached forward and grasped her hand.

Instantly, she vanished into moonlight, and agony erupted through me.

"Use it well."

It felt like a thousand ancestors had gripped me with talons, embedding pain and might within my flesh and making me whole again. The flood of power was dizzying but not unwelcome. My tattoo scorched my skin, glowing a deeper blue than ever before. It felt like a brand. A fresh wound.

A demand.

"Do not hide anymore. You will wear your legacy proudly," Cliohde commanded as the seawater drew over the rock and across my body like the fingertips of a tinkering artist

sculpting my flesh until it suited her. Like hundreds of sewing needles plucking at the threads of my being.

The first thing I did was fight it. *Get your fucking hands off me.*

A searing agony burst from my back, throwing me into another shift. A groan fizzled up my throat as I collapsed onto the stone, both hands flat against the rough surface of the rock.

I recoiled from her touch as I threw my neck back and shouted, my teeth forming into exaggerated points that cut into my lower lip. Blood dribbled down my chin and filled my mouth with the taste of rusted iron.

The salty water wove around my ankles like a preening feline, branding me with scales that were iridescent like my full leviathan form. Hardened like leather. I could feel my bones break and reform.

"Stop touching me!" I shouted, writhing as I tried to shake the ghostly touch off me. The hot sensation of panic overtook me as the unfamiliar pressure spanned my entire body.

Pain rippled across my skull as horns burst through my temples.

I tried to repress it. I willed it to go away. I begged the forceful hands to let me go. Then a hard, hot hand landed on my back as if willing me not to fight the transformation.

"Do you want this?" Cliohde's voice rumbled. *"Tell me again to leave, and I will."*

Fear welled up in my throat. I didn't know what she was doing to me, but I didn't believe she meant to hurt me. If this were before Pike, before Farlight Prison, it wouldn't have affected me this badly.

I wouldn't be hyperventilating at the sensation of fingertips.

But this was happening *now*. After all I'd endured, this was another test.

More questions fluttered through the air.

"*Are you ready to take control? Are you ready to lead?*" Cliohde asked.

"Yes," I answered. No more waiting. I was ready.

"*Then trust me, dragonling.*"

My eyes fell shut, and I surrendered. As the resistance melted away, so did the pain. It felt less like the prodding of fingertips and more like the cascading of water. The impact of landing on the hard surface of the ocean before sinking into its embrace.

My shirt tore into ribbons as wings erupted from my back. The small bones in my hands splintered and reformed, feeling exactly as they did whenever I would partially shift in the water.

The blinding discomfort ebbed to nothing as I experienced an overwhelming reprieve. I collapsed onto the water-worn rocks and lost consciousness.

9

RONIN MURDOCH

A LEVIATHAN'S LEGACY

Caw. Caw. Caw.

The intrusive noises of seagulls awoke me from my slumber. I blinked blearily, squinting under the sunlight before I realized I wasn't in my cabin. Hard, waterworn stone was smooth against my hands. Salt clung to my eyelashes.

Waves splashed against the rock, raining onto my bare back.

What the fuck?

I put my hands in front of me to push myself to my feet… but my hands didn't look like mine. Instead of large, square, calloused palms with wide, blunt fingertips, my fingers were now elongated and webbed with black-tipped claws.

Even in the water during a partial shift, my fingers would web together, but they never lengthened into claws—not unless I was full leviathan.

My eyebrows pinched together as I recalled last night.

Cliohde.

The backs of my hands were lined with black-blue scales running up my arms to give way to tawny skin on the undersides of my forearms. My hands flew up to my face, and I felt my familiar nose, but my canines were lengthened and pressed against my lower lip.

The shirt I had slept in hung off me in tatters, revealing my dragon tattoo, but it looked as if it had *bloomed*, decorating my chest with my leviathan's scales in a way similar to merrow markings. But mine were pronounced, not melted into my skin.

It wasn't only coloring either. They were textured like a snake's scales.

As I stood there, I looked down at my toes, easily two feet farther away from my eyes than usual. They looked like my hands, long and clawed. My pants filled out around meatier thighs, rife with much more pronounced muscle than I had before.

This is what Cliohde meant when she said I wouldn't be able to hide anymore.

I felt massive, and when I flexed my shoulders, something *else* moved. Startled, I looked over my shoulder and saw two wings pressed flat against my back.

I have wings?

As I touched them, the skin felt soft and fuzzy like moleskin, incredibly thin in parts like any ill-timed bump would tear a hole through them. My leviathan's wings were thick and leathery, but these felt much more fragile, like a middle ground between full dragon and the partial transformation I'd undergo in the water.

The skin reacted to the prickle of my claws, breaking out in something like goose bumps. My wings were outrageously sensitive, like the flesh underneath a cracked callus. I despised the very idea of anyone or anything brushing against them.

How the fuck am I supposed to greet my crew this morning?

I could hear the echo within the wooden walls as well as my door creaking open. But it wasn't noise, per se. It was more like electrical frequencies bouncing through the air to tickle my nose.

"Levi?" Andra's voice carried over to me from inside my cabin.

With a deep sigh, I ran my fingers through my hair and—

What the fuck? Horns too?

I was going to feel like a fucking monster the moment all these people laid their eyes on me. *Who wants to put their lives in the hands of a clawed, horned* beast?

Anxiety gripped my heart, the familiar sensation of fear whispering against my neck. I glanced over at the big blue miles and miles of sea beyond the reef. I could run—swim beneath the waves, never to be seen again. I could tuck my head between my knees and crumple into that pit of tarry despair.

That would be easy.

Every instinct and every worry I had was telling me to abandon them.

They wouldn't understand. You'd just be a monster, like the lies Cross told.

But the moment I turned away and ran, I would be failing Wesley and Mama. I'd prove Bliss right. I wouldn't be the man who Lucky put his faith in. I might as well be lining up my sailors to dance with Jack Ketch, like a hooded executioner.

Worst of all, I'd be failing Mae.

So I didn't run. I flexed my wings behind me and dove. The water cut around me as I outstretched them to part it. I kicked my feet, propelling myself through the sea as the fish and other wildlife around me darted away.

The ocean embraced me like a guiding force, and I could hear Cliohde's echo around me.

"Do not hide anymore. You will wear your legacy proudly."

I was done pretending.

The fear and anxiety still lingered inside me, but I'd made a promise to protect them. A promise to avenge what we'd lost. All those insecurities didn't matter. I was still the same man, but now I had the power of my leviathan in the palm of my hand at all times.

I would keep my promise whether the townspeople accepted me or not.

I swam toward *The Ollipheist*, slicing through the water faster than ever before. Before I could ram into my ship, I tilted my wings back and breached the surface. I flew up to the top deck, tucking my wings behind me to land directly on the planks.

Clad in the armor of my leviathan, I stood up straight as liberation swelled in my chest. Without a doubt in my mind, I felt freed of my fears. I was claiming my birthright.

Instantly, my entire crew jumped to their feet. Several shouts of surprise or terror rang out, and Andra darted out of my cabin, eyebrows crinkled with worry. Everything stopped and mouths hung open as they debated whether to attack me or talk to me.

In my human form, I was an impressive height, but now I towered over every sailor in attendance. Fear and disbelief were apparent on everyone's faces. Luckily, it was the time of day before most of the townspeople went out to get their rations or visit the injured, so I only had my crew and a few stragglers from Violetta's to answer to.

I cleared my throat and stated, "Good morning."

Andra recoiled before she asked, "Captain?" I didn't have to answer because realization filled her eyes, and she lowered her cutlass. "You know how to make an entrance."

I looked around at the rest of those gathered. "I know you lot have questions, and I'll answer what I can. For now, all you need to know is that I'm the same man I was before. I've always been a leviathan."

Most of my crew had seen me fully shifted, so even if this new appearance was a surprise, I didn't expect any pushback. The other sailors and the townspeople would require more convincing. My first stop was going to be Udine and the merrow.

Even though nerves racked my stomach and made my heart slam into my ribs, I maintained a cool demeanor. "Boats," I said, gesturing my sister over. "Walk with me."

Andra adjusted her hat and said, "Aye."

I sauntered down the gangway with Andra close behind me. I could hear the whispers. Doubts and concerns. I expected it, but I had to squash them quickly. People feared what they didn't understand, and that would only get worse if I locked myself away.

As soon as we were away from prying ears, Andra hissed, "A little warning would've been nice. I nearly took your head off!"

"I didn't get much warning either," I retorted. "I grew wings overnight and suddenly have oddly shaped feet." I kicked up my foot for emphasis, annoyed that my feet wouldn't fit into my boots anymore.

"Just like that?"

"No, Cliohde paid me a visit," I explained. "Told me she wouldn't let me hide my legacy anymore."

Andra sighed. "You know this war is fucked when the Gods get involved." She paused and looked up at me. "For the record, you still look like *you*, just extra toothy. You have the same nose and eyes. Same hair despite the horns."

I swallowed, offering her a small smile. "That makes me feel a little better. Thank you."

"I can't imagine being dropped into a new body without any time to practice operating it." Andra looked me up and down. "We've got to get you to Siggi. He needs to let your pants out." She put both her hands up. "I know you like the whole tight-pants look, but I don't want to see more of you than I have to."

I laughed. "Do you think he could fix my shirts?"

Andra shrugged. "Don't wear one. Show off that tattoo. Let's see who wants to question a dragon, eh?"

Down the hill from my cabana, I caught sight of a few merrow swimming in the pool I taught Mae to swim in. I tried not to think about her, knowing the horror Pike was putting her through.

It wasn't always Pike either.

Several of his crew often paid me a visit when he was off somewhere else. I didn't remember most of it, and I didn't want to. It'd be too easy to slip into that prison of helplessness, trapped in my own skin while they used me for entertainment. They enjoyed taking my power away in any possible way they could.

However, whenever I caught glimpses of myself in reflective surfaces now, I didn't feel helpless.

But deep inside, that fear lingered, that feeling of *I'm not safe* never far away. The last time I felt truly safe was when Mae stood beside me the morning before she was taken away.

As I walked up the hill, the merrow stopped to stare. Various townspeople did double takes. Thankfully, Andra acted as mediator, easing any tension between me and them. She'd put on a smile and crack a joke, indicating that if she could be comfortable in my presence, they should be too.

"Captain Ronin?" Udine asked, sitting up from a chair on my porch. Her eyes widened in complete awe. "Fascinating. I've only ever seen illustrations of partial shifts."

"You said Cliohde talked to you. What is she telling you?" I asked.

A smile spread across her face. "She's given us an edge. Come in. Siggi is already hard at work."

10

MAEVE CROSS

THE COMFORT OF RATS

THE DAYS—IF I COULD CALL THEM THAT—WERE A BLUR.

Hidden from the sun's warmth and the night sea illuminated by the moon, it was impossible to track the passage of time consistently on my own. When Nathaniel wasn't trying to draw information from me with various methods of torture or prattling on about being an *artist* in the ways of misery, I found comfort in the brig. Even the rats were some kind of consolation when they climbed up from the bilge to devour the crumbs I left out by my feet.

Would they nibble my toes off one day? Perhaps. But Freynir and I enjoyed the company. I understood what it felt like to be a rat in a cage. To have my tail twisted and little limbs stepped on by someone who viewed themself as superior.

It helps that Adams is afraid of rats. Fuck him.

When Ensign Adams wanted a toy to play with and decided to climb down to us, he'd turn right around if he heard a rat squeaking. As soon as Freynir and I realized that, we purposely spilled our porridge as a rat lure, much to Seymour's annoyance.

But even Seymour was relieved when Adams left him alone, too, complaining about how filthy we were before putting his sights on someone else.

No matter the time of day, it was always dark in the bilge, with only Seymour's oil lamps to keep it lit. Even when it was time for him to rest, no one relieved him. He'd take his lamp to a swinging hammock and sleep, never snuffing the flame. I had a theory that he was afraid of the dark.

That was when Freynir and I would have our most meaningless conversations. Usually about food. He'd tell me about how he missed mead and honey pastries, and I'd talk about Butcher's stew and how Ronin made the best bread.

Though Ronin disagreed. He didn't understand why I'd choose his bread over the baker's every time. It had very little to do with the actual food and everything to do with how much I enjoyed watching him make it. It was even better when I'd kiss him while his hands were filthy, and he'd keep himself from dirtying my clothes.

I adored how he'd get this wrinkle between his brows and grumble in frustration.

Gods, how I love to frustrate him....

I miss him so much.

Squeaking drew my gaze to the dark corner of the room where the rats wiggled their way up between the walls to steal crumbs. I grabbed a handful of bread crumbles and tossed it toward them.

Rats were a common nuisance on any ship. That was why *The Ollipheist* had Lieutenant Commander Lazlo as well as a few other mousers. I hadn't seen any cats on Pike's ship, but it wouldn't surprise me if his personality deterred any animals from staying on board.

"I used to feed a mouse in my bedroom," I said quietly as I listened to the rats chitter around my offering. "I named it Crumb."

Freynir looked over at me, one of his eyes a deep purple-black. Blue blood had crusted around his broken nose and where Adams had ripped out his piercings. The bruises had faded, but his injuries were still swollen and weeping, and I found myself watching him closer, fearing infection.

Elves and fae weren't as prone to infection as humans were, but they weren't impervious.

"Varric crushed it under his boot," I said before pausing with a quiet sigh. "I didn't have many friends then."

Freynir took his marital pendant out from under his collar and rolled it between his fingers. I noticed that he did that as a coping mechanism, as if he could feel her whenever he touched it. "I've always liked rodents. If our crops died or our usual game spoiled, rats were plentiful. We fed a lot of starving Skadians with them. Fed our wolves. Not ideal, but if the rats survive, so do we."

"There were times when the Skadian *prince* ate rats?" I asked.

"I eat what my people eat. What kind of leader would I be if I expected my people to do what I was unwilling to? So yes. Me and all six of my brothers," Freynir said. "I'm the eldest."

A hot feeling of shame welled in my chest. "I'm sure the poor starved, but we still indulged in smoked meats and fresh produce." I looked down at my filthy hands and scraped the dirt from under my nails. "There were times that the charities would petition Varric for food or blankets, and he'd deny them every time to keep the nobles happy."

Freynir made this deep noise in the back of his throat. "Elinora used to say the same thing about Edessa. The nobles were always at odds with the commoners."

"Elinora?"

"My *skelmis*," he said absentmindedly before tucking the pendant back under his collar.

Skelmis? He frequently used that term to reference his wife. "What does that mean?"

The corner of his mouth turned up, revealing one of his elongated canines. "My little trickster," he stated with a chuckle. "We first met during the Annual Monster Hunt, when all the kingdoms line up their best hunters for the chance to win the title. And gold, but I was always in it for the glory."

I remembered how he told me he was renowned for his prowess in battle. I leaned back against my bars and gestured for him to continue.

"But that year, I wasn't sent there to win the title. I was sent there to kill the Edessan princess, Rayna."

My lips parted in surprise. "I'm going to assume that you didn't actually kill her, right?"

He grinned.

"Right?"

He ignored my question and said, "Elinora was her court sorceress and personal bodyguard. She always wore these flowy robes that didn't cover anything. Very elegant and *very* transparent. Always blue. She looked lovely in blue. I thought she'd be easy enough to dispatch before I went for the princess."

The squeaking and chittering of the rats dissipated as they wiggled back to the lower decks, taking their treasures with them.

"I was... *deeply* mistaken," he continued before his grin widened. "I may or may not have said something rude to Rayna, and Elinora strung me up for the banshees."

"You need to tell me what you said," I demanded.

He tapped his chin in mock thought. "It's more amusing to let you speculate."

"Frey!" I whined. "Don't be a prick."

It was the first time I'd used a nickname for him, and I didn't miss the subtle fondness that softened his forehead wrinkle. "I thought you liked men who act like pricks. Look at your leviathan," he replied playfully.

I rolled my eyes. "He makes it up to me. Don't make me kick you again."

"Fine, fine," he chuckled. "Something about how they would be more useful as bait." He drew his braid over his shoulder to smooth out some of the flyaways. "Then Elinora made *me* the bait."

I laughed. "Serves you right."

"Oh, I deserved it. I was a prick. Still am, depending on the day." He flashed me another smile, but it didn't reach his eyes. "She was such a vicious woman, but she had a taste for finery. I'd lay all the finery of my kingdom on her altar if that would bring her back." He tilted his head back and sighed deeply. "I swear, if my brothers use primrose instead of snowdrops, I'll kill them for fucking up her altar. Snowdrops were her favorite Skadian flower."

"I'm so sorry, Frey."

He shook his head. "Don't apologize to me. I nearly put you through the same grief. How could I be so shortsighted?"

"That doesn't mean that you don't hurt. I'm allowed to feel for you." I paused and tried to lighten the statement with a "Despite my better judgment."

He cracked another smile. "Is poor judgment a character trait of yours?"

"Depends on the day," I retorted with a wink.

The hatch flew open, and Ensign Adams walked in. Dread instantly filled my belly, replacing whatever comfort I had felt earlier. The brig was silent aside from Seymour flipping through his book, shoulders so rigid, they touched his ears.

"I'm here for you, little girl," Adams stated, sighing contently when he realized there were no rats nearby. "We get to have fun with you tonight." He took the key to my cuffs out of his pocket and twirled it around his finger.

"Get out of here," Frey demanded, rising to his feet. "Would it kill you to fuck off?"

"No, but the admiral would have my head if I didn't take her out for her punishment." Adams walked past Seymour and unlocked my cell with one of the keys hanging behind Seymour's head. He tossed it on the table. "I'd be lying if I said I wasn't looking forward to it too."

Frey banged his fists against his cell door. "What did she do? Hmm? What the fuck did she do?"

Adams paused and looked over at Frey. "She was disrespectful. This woman needs a reminder that we own her."

"You don't own me," I hissed, pulling at my irons and rubbing my wrists raw on the uneven metal.

Adams grabbed my arm hard, nearly dislodging my shoulder again when he knocked me onto my knees.

"Get your fucking hands off her!" Frey shouted, smashing his draconite cuffs against the door.

"You've earned yourself a beating," Adams decided, taking a full step away from me to get to Frey's cell. "Prince or not, you'll learn that you're nothing more than property."

I heard the first punch land and then the sound of Frey hitting the dusty ground. Adams was a stocky man with hands the size of ham hocks. The Skadian prince was long and lean, but without his sword or ample room to move and dodge, all he could do was lie there and take the beating.

Frey coughed, curling in on himself to protect his organs.

"Hey! Get back over here to me! *Look at me!*" I demanded, flailing against the restraints.

"I'll save some for you, don't you worry," Adams said, kicking Frey hard in the stomach so he grunted and flopped over onto his back. He slammed his boot relentlessly into Frey until his coughs turned wet.

"That's enough," Seymour offered weakly, slowly standing up from his seat. "You don't want the surgeon to see him. Then I'd have to report you to the lieutenant."

Adams scoffed. "Soft bellied like you. All I have to do is knock into him by the half wall. You wouldn't want to be responsible for someone else's pain, would you?"

Seymour swallowed thickly. "...No."

"No, *sir*, runt."

"No, sir."

As Frey rolled over onto his side, his marital pendant slipped out from under his collar. He didn't have enough time to hide it before Adams saw it.

"What do we have here? Something nice and shiny, huh?" Adams snapped forward to grab the pendant when Frey mustered up all the energy he had to punch the ensign in his barrel chest. With his big mitt, he grabbed Frey's whole face and slammed his head down to the ground before he ripped the pendant off him.

"No!" Frey shouted, flailing as Adams smashed his boot directly onto his chest.

Adams lifted the pendant and dangled it in front of his face. "I like this. Some elf lucky charm?"

"Give that back! It's not yours!" I demanded, my cuffs clashing harder against the bars.

A smug grin stretched across his face as he stepped out of Frey's cell with his prize. "It's mine now. Be careful, little girl. Keep crying and I'll have my eyes on another prize."

Disgust churned in my belly.

"I'll share you with a few of my mates. You heal quick enough. The admiral doesn't have to know."

When he grabbed my cuffs, I spat in his face. "It'll be the last thing you do."

"Then what a way to die, with something pretty underneath me." Adams dragged me to my feet, tucking Frey's pendant into his pocket with my key. "But first, I'm curious how long you'll last tonight before you beg for mercy. I bet the sound of you begging is the prettiest music."

I flailed, trying desperately to strike flesh, but he laughed at me before dragging me away to the main deck.

11

MAEVE CROSS

A THOUSAND CUTS

EACH CUT HEALED AS SOON AS IT APPEARED. EVERY INJURY FELT fresh. I wasn't granted the liberation of numbness. Just pain. But I wouldn't give them the pleasure of knowing how bad it hurt.

My shirt was torn open, both my hands tied around the center mast. Every crew member was encouraged to slice me across my back. They woke sailors from their beds to partake in my torture. Even Seymour from the brig.

They were the most merciful in their cuts, which were shallow and quick like a papercut. I welcomed the pinch. It felt like a reprieve compared to everything else done by the sailors who enjoyed it, giving me deep wounds that lasted more than a moment. They would twist the knife and see how far it went in before it punctured a lung. I'd gasp on a breath before my body recovered.

I stared up at the sky, hoping to see the moon, but was only met with another moonless night. The stars seemed so far away as I choked down another whimper. My head swam with agony as I recalled the sweet embrace of peace that Death granted me when my body had met the limit.

But I was never granted that reprieve.

It felt as if Death had abandoned me. Thrown me to the wolves to *endure*. I was *made* to endure. I was *made* to suffer alone.

I chose this, though, didn't I?

All those years ago, I was the one who refused to cross over. My oath didn't bind me to this torture. I did that all by myself. If I had known the pain… the *suffering* I was destined to endure, would I have chosen the same path?

Tears beaded and spilled from the corners of my eyes as I gazed into the night. In all that darkness, I could see the moment Ronin stared down at me that first night, nothing but the moon and stars behind him. One of the many times his fingers clasped my chin to demand my attention, especially when I tried to lie.

Another cut sliced into my back, and I squeezed my eyes shut.

"Red is such a splendid color on you," Adams whispered with barely veiled glee. He dug in deeper as my skin closed around the blade before he ripped it out. Warmth flooded down my back as I muffled a noise of anguish.

Don't give him the pleasure of your cries.

I gripped my cuffs and held on to them for something to anchor myself, never slipping deeper into the dark.

I wouldn't let go. I wouldn't let them win. *Even if it hurts.*

I thought of the elation glimmering in Ronin's eyes when I came to his rescue. The tenderness etched across his face when he'd wake up beside me, one hand cupping my waist, fitting perfectly into the divot of my hip. I could feel his touch as if he were there with me.

"Stay strong, sweetheart."

I remembered the fire and passion, the lasting pain from each heartbreak, the beauty of everything in between. Everything that made him *mine*.

"I don't think anyone has ever owned me as completely as you do. You're mine, but I'm just as much yours." Ronin's voice echoed in my mind, and the memory of him engulfed everything. I could smell the ghost of cedar and seawater, and my heart didn't ache so badly.

I found comfort in the knowledge that I *would* see him again. I would endure *anything* for him. I would grin and bear it if it meant protecting what was *mine*.

I would choose this fate over and over again.

A thousand cuts, but all that was left behind were smears of blood. No broken skin. Only my own lifeblood saturated across my back and puddled at my feet. It quickly turned cold, covering me in a blanket of chill.

I steeled myself for more pain, letting my mind wander to my family.

The long nights where we would pass a bottle of rum around and tell stories of conquests. I thought of Luella's scary smile and Andra poking fun at Ronin. Gunny's swindling. The card games at Wesley and Isa's. Little voices and giggles waking Ronin and me up when the kids wanted to have breakfast.

My people.

I'd suffer over and over again to protect them.

"Enough, men." Nathaniel's voice snapped me out of my thoughts as my eyes shot up to him. "It's my turn. When you have a pirate under the knife, you have to make it *hurt*."

My upper lip curled into a snarl.

Unfortunately, Nathaniel knew his way around a knife, and every slice nicked the right nerve. My muscles spasmed as pain shot through my entire being. While the blood had grown cold, vengeance brewed in my belly, and that kept me warm. My nails bit into the ropes, and I succumbed to the pain.

I disassociated from the world and settled into a void of my own making.

In my mind, I wasn't on Nathaniel's ship. I was back home, wrapped in a familiar embrace. It wasn't Ronin's cabana or Wesley's homestead—it was *The Ollipheist*. The first place that ever felt like home. *That* gave me the strength I needed to survive until morning.

My tears had dried, and my throat didn't ache from repressed sobs.

He wanted to break me, but I didn't *let* him.

"I'm impressed," Nathaniel said as his men undid the ropes.

I collapsed onto the deck, completely exhausted. While my back didn't hurt anymore, my limbs were weary, and I couldn't bear the thought of standing. I could feel the phantom pain lingering in my muscles like an excruciating memory.

As with Varric's scalpel slicing my throat like he was splitting a seam, I could recall each cut with acute accuracy. I knew that whenever I curled up in my cell, I'd have nightmares about it.

An insult bubbled up to my lips, but I choked it down.

"I don't like the way you're looking at me," he stated loudly, getting the attention of every sailor on the upper deck. It took me a long moment to realize he wasn't talking to me. "You didn't partake."

I couldn't twist my head to see who he was addressing.

"No, Admiral," the voice of an older man answered.

"Why not?" It wasn't a genuine question. "Maeve is a traitor. She isn't worthy of mercy."

The voice replied, "I won't participate in torturing a woman for the fun of it. I can't stop you, but I'll have no part in it."

In response, Nathaniel's heavy boot landed on my throat. I choked, squirming underneath it.

"What is your name and rank?"

"Seaman Seymour, sir."

Seymour? His voice sounded much older than the petty officer in the brig.

"Well, Seaman Seymour, if I say, *Slit their throat in front of their family,* you do it. If I say, *Burn their house to the ground,* you obey. If I say, *Hold their head underwater,* you obey. I control who you kill, what you eat, and who you fuck." With every word, he pressed his boot harder.

No matter what I did, Nathaniel could physically overpower me. It filled me with unadulterated hatred. I'd never hated anyone, not even Varric, but I hated Nathaniel with a malice I couldn't hold back. I drowned in it.

"You made your point," I hissed.

Nathaniel's icy eyes came back to me again. "Oh, did I?" He looked back over at the sailor who had defied him. "Tie him to the mast."

I heard a shout of fear and collective gasps as Adams and one of the other sailors restrained him.

"Get your *fucking* foot off me," I croaked, squirming harder.

"I will have your respect," Nathaniel snarled at his crew, nearly crushing my windpipe. "Now, I don't care if this sailor is your friend, your father, or even your lover—you *will* participate, or I will have you thrown overboard to feed the kuru in the trenches."

"Fear is not respect!" I snarled.

Suddenly, his foot left me, and my head reeled as he hoisted me up to my feet.

His voice was eerily soft when he asked, "What was that, Maeve? You didn't bleed enough?" He took my unbound wrists and yanked them hard, bending my arms up at a painful angle until it strained my shoulders. "I've been kind to you, you disrespectful little girl. Do you know how long it's been since my men have had a woman? Varric wouldn't know the difference. You'd still be whole."

My upper lip curled into a snarl as fear licked at the nape of my neck. I looked around the deck, noticing the tight-lipped restraint echoed on several of the sailors' faces. But not one person said a thing. Not one person stopped him.

Nathaniel grinned that cruel smile. He took a handful of my hair and lurched my head back to whisper in my ear, "You're so much prettier when you're silent."

"Fuck you," I managed through my strained throat.

With only his grip on my hair holding me up, he dropped me flat onto the deck.

"Take her back to her cell, and while you're there, bring me the other Seymour. He'll get the first cut."

Rage erupted in my belly, boiling my bones, simmering my blood. Nathaniel's sailors might fear death, but I didn't have any such affliction.

Two men dragged me to my feet, locking my wrists in my irons in front of me. Behind them, Nathaniel smirked, and I *snapped*.

A wail tore from my chest as I flung myself forward, breaking their grasp on me as I went straight for him.

Shouts and gasps filled the air as I tackled Nathaniel to the ground, taking him completely off guard. I used my bound wrists as a vise against his throat, the irons digging into the soft flesh of his neck. He kicked his legs, trying to wrestle me off him with his hands, but I latched on.

His icy eyes were wide open, and for the first time, I saw *fear*. Like I'd sensed blood in the water, a frenzy came over me. He would pay for everything he'd done, and he'd do it by my hand.

I'd kill him for what he did to Ronin. For what he did to

his sailors. For what he did to his wives. For how he scorned *me*.

His hands closed over my wrists, and he used brute strength to throw me off him. The deck knocked the wind out of me, but I felt unbearably satisfied when I looked at him again.

Nathaniel choked as he clutched his throat. The two men restrained me again, this time with firmer grasps.

There he was. A spoiled, insignificant *boy*. And *everyone* saw it.

The bravado disappeared from his face as he looked around at our audience. *No one came to his rescue.* A smile pulled at my lips as I stated, "For a man who supposedly is a harbinger of death, you're awfully afraid of it."

Nathaniel's hands were still clasped over his throat, where a blue-black bruise was already peeking out from around his fingers.

"But you shouldn't fear death, Nathaniel. You should fear *me*."

Even if his eyes said otherwise, he shakily replied, "Like a python fears a bunny." He took a jagged breath, coughing hard.

I looked up at the rising sun, feeling its warmth cascade over my bones. I had survived the never-ending night and seen the light again. "You'll only be free of me in death."

Nathaniel gulped several times before he croaked, "Take her away, Adams."

"Yes, Admiral," Adams replied before he took me away to my cell. Leaning in, he sneered in my ear, "After a display like that, I might not have to hide you in my chambers. Rest well, Princess. You'll need it."

Fuck you.

My cell had never looked so welcoming, but then I glanced at the softspoken guard who sat at his table, and I felt guilty. Adams locked my irons to the far side of my cell but didn't touch me otherwise before he grabbed Seymour by the scruff of his neck and took him away to the upper deck.

Frey was still motionless on the floor of his cell.

"You alive in there, Frey?" I asked.

He groaned in response, pulling at his collar and sitting up against the bars. "Barely." One of his eyes was swollen shut worse than before, but he still noticed my torn shirt and the blood crusted across my clothing. "What the fuck did they do to you?"

"Took turns slicing my back open." My answer, though truthful, felt too nonchalant.

Frey looked at me seriously with his one good eye. "Are you all right?"

"No. Are you?"

"No."

"Then we're on the same page." I groaned and leaned back against the bars, utterly exhausted. "I'm going to take a nap. Let me know if anything good happens."

"Define *good* exactly."

"If the ship sinks or anyone kills Nathaniel in his sleep. Or if they finally give us a bucket of water to clean ourselves." I yawned, shuffling against the hard floor for any semblance of comfort.

Frey sighed. "I would kill for one of Skadi's hot springs right about now. They work miracles for injuries."

I made a noise of delight. "When this is over, you owe me a visit to one of those."

"I promise I'll take you and your leviathan to one of my favorites." He gave me a genuine, tired grin, all crooked because of the bruises on his jaw. "A naked one."

I snorted a laugh. "Flirt."

"It's just my personality," he retorted, coughing hard when he tried to laugh. "Get some rest. I'll keep an eye out."

My eyelids fluttered closed. "As long as it's your good one and not your swollen one."

I WAS AWOKEN BY A SOFT SOB FOLLOWED BY A CHUCKLE.

"He didn't even last until the twentieth cut. Weak. So are you, Seymour," said a voice I knew was Adams's. "We cull the weak."

"Please, let me grieve in peace," Seymour replied, voice warbling from repressed tears.

My eyes slowly opened, and I saw Adams looming over the smaller man to cage him against his table. His eyes were red, cheeks flushed, throat bobbing up and down.

"Look at you. Sniveling like a child." Adams's big mitt smacked Seymour upside the head. "I bet your father didn't have a firm hand with you."

"Hey!" I shouted, banging my irons against the bars.

Adams ignored me, all focus on the man in front of him. "I could show you a firm hand. In so many different ways."

"That's enough," Frey chimed in, standing up on shaky legs. "Leave him alone."

I smashed my cuffs on my cell again, hard enough that I could feel the bones in my wrists rattle. "Don't look at him! Look at *us*."

Adams glanced over at Frey and me. "You should be on my good side considering you'll be mine soon enough."

"*Over my dead body*," I hissed.

"If I killed you, how long would it be until you woke up?" he asked as he took two steps over to my cell, walking his fingers along the bars. "Right after a dose of vitrophine, that leviathan was so strung out that he didn't understand what was happening. He'd say your name. Sometimes he'd cry after he got a taste of my boot." He laughed. "Gods, he was fucking pathetic."

"Watch your mouth," I snapped.

There wasn't any light behind Adams's eyes as he said, "You'd fuck a monster—a pirate at that—but you think *I'm* unworthy? I'm a naval officer, Princess. You'll put my cock in your mouth, and you'll thank me for it like the monster-fucking whore you are."

Frey growled, "You'll keep your fucking hands off her, or I'll *cut them off.*"

Adams looked over at Frey with this overwhelming sense of entitlement. "I heard that Skadian elves have nipple piercings." He tapped his chin. "In fact, you have piercings on your prick, too, don't you? I could use more silver, Prince."

I watched fear contract Frey's pupils into vertical slits even if the expression on the rest of his face said otherwise. He swallowed, lips twitching as if he was torn between threatening Adams again or bending his neck in submission.

Adams took Frey's pendant out from under his collar, and I could smell a wintery hearth as rage physically jolted through the Skadian. Even if he didn't mean to berserk, the collar punished him for it. The draconite seared his throat, and Frey howled at the ripple of unrelenting misery.

Adams laughed boorishly at Frey's agony and said, "You're lucky that she's prettier than you are. Don't worry, she'll heal. Won't you, little girl?"

"Fuck you," I snarled.

Seymour stood behind Adams, completely frozen in terror and grief, but it boiled down to the same thing—helplessness. His mouth opened and closed, but he didn't say a damn thing.

Someone above us opened the hatch. "Ensign Adams! We need you up here."

Adams looked up the hatch and then at me. "I'll be back

for you." He turned, swiping his hand through Seymour's blond hair to ruffle it out of sorts, then finally left, climbing up the stairs to the hatch.

After a few beats, I asked Frey, "You all right?"

"No," he admitted. "I'm sorry, Maeve."

Dread thickened my throat, and I fought the raw tears that threatened to stain my cheeks again. "What are you sorry for now?"

"I don't know if I can protect you when he comes back." Frey lay there, and the stench of burning flesh filled my nostrils. He was holding on so tight, but at this rate, he was going to shatter.

"I don't need your protection," I replied. "I need you to survive."

Frey reached for his pendant, a broken sound choking up from his throat when he realized it wasn't there. "I don't think I can."

I puffed out a loud breath from my nose. "You don't get to break, Frey. *Get up.*"

He stared at me for a long moment before he pushed himself up, leaning heavily against the bars. "All right, *ylgr*. I'll try."

I'd never heard that word before. Not when Ronin and Siggi joked in Skaditung. Not when Frey muttered curses under his breath in his native tongue. "What does that mean?"

"I'll tell you when we get out of this alive," he promised, taking a deep breath before addressing the shaking guard. "Are you hanging in there, Seymour?"

Like a dam breaking, tears cascaded down Seymour's cheeks. "How am I supposed to tell my mama what happened? That I… I…."

"It wasn't you," I said with conviction. None of us chose to be here. Even if he had a part in what happened to me last night, it wasn't his choice. Nathaniel had a knack for taking that away. "It was Nathaniel. Using your hands. I'm sorry."

Seymour sat down at his table, softly sobbing before saying, "We were conscripted. My little brother, my father, and me. I'd never even used a knife before. Not like that. Not outside of skinning rabbits. *It felt nothing like skinning a rabbit.*"

Then he got up and went over to where he kept his trinkets and baubles in a small trunk next to his hammock.

"Tell me about your brother," I said softly.

He paused and pinched the bridge of his nose, trying to quell his tears. "He was sent on the siege. A scout. He's probably dead. He's only sixteen. He wouldn't last against pirates."

"You don't know that," Frey offered.

Seymour shook his head as he rifled through his belongings and found a small jar. "Robbie never knew how to use his sword correctly. He was always cutting himself." He turned to us and tossed it through the bars. It landed right at Frey's feet. "He won't need it anymore. It'll help with the swelling and hopefully prevent your infection from getting worse."

Frey leaned over and picked up the jar. "Thank you."

Seymour returned to his table. "Don't let them find it."

12

RONIN MURDOCH

CONSCRIPTS

After a little over a week of settling in and sleeping in a bed that suddenly felt too small, a semblance of normalcy started to form. We were still waiting for Luella and Bliss to come back with news of who had survived the siege, but I'd taken to my new role easily.

Anchorage Cove was open to refugees and those fleeing the attack, with Butcher and Conway handling rations, Udine and the merrow catering to the wounded, and Andra organizing sloop routes for whoever wanted to flee altogether. Isa also stepped in with her girls, taking in any children or mothers without their family.

With all the moving parts in Anchorage Cove, the children needed a home that was quieter. A place with a little more structure. Isa and Wesley's homestead offered just that. The farm required maintenance, and the chickens needed tending. On top of that, after all the rations were set out for the day, Conway made time to play with the children.

They were all quite charmed by the kind, milky-eyed man who liked to make toys from scraps he found lying around.

Meanwhile, Butcher found something for the adolescents to do, making space for them in the kitchen.

The families with small children set course for Lucky's Outpost with some of Lucky's crew to deliver the news. Some went to Violetta's Haven or Bliss's Colony. We could get them to safety on one of the two sloops or sole ketch we had available. With the families, I'd sent letters detailing what happened, what we needed, and how dire our situation was.

The correspondence would prepare the pirate colonies for war.

I was sure that some pirates would seize this opportunity to take advantage of the power imbalance, but loyalty ran hot through their ranks. While families went to safety, I hoped I'd be receiving reinforcements and supplies in return.

All we had to do was wait and then fracture whatever hold Pike had on Shipwreck Bay.

My crew and I stayed on *The Ollipheist* for the most part, the upper deck becoming a makeshift town hall where townspeople would come to me for help or grievances. The wings, horns, and fangs put a lot of people off at first, but the more they saw me, the more comfortable they became.

I wanted to be available for them the same way I was available for my crew. I wasn't going to be the absent leader. They were going to see me do anything and everything that I expected them to do.

And when night fell, I took to the ocean. My full leviathan form was easier to access than ever before as I scoured the shipwrecks that littered the ocean floor, scavenging supplies and gathering healing silt for the wounded.

All the work kept me so busy that I didn't have time to let the anger come back.

I didn't sleep much, but when I did, I dreamed of my Mae. But instead of seeing her broken and bloody like I used to, I saw her bathed in sunlight when I'd admire her before she woke up. I'd think of my brave, resilient girl.

The girl who made me feel safe.

Imagining her wide doe eyes and her cheeky smile was enough to keep me going. Even when I hadn't slept and people were demanding things of me. It would only get worse when I claimed the throne. I'd never be able to rest again, but that was the burden I had to carry.

The moments of silence were few and far between. The only reprieve I got was when I sank to the bottom of the ocean, surrounded by the familiar embrace of the sea. I loved the land, but I belonged to the sea.

With a heavy sigh, I left my thoughts to get back to the problem at hand. I sat at my desk in my cabin with a long list of items that we were running out of. For the twentieth time, I went through it. Medical supplies like gauze and antiseptic were high priority.

Several injured townspeople had succumbed to infection or blood loss. Some of them were too far gone to save. I'd seen enough injuries the past week for several lifetimes. After the town doctor fell to his wounds, we needed my mother's expertise.

But still no word.

"Cap!" Gunny exclaimed as he barged into my office, blueprints in hand. He had gauze fastened over his eye. He'd fought the infection and come out victorious, but even so, it was unlikely he'd ever see through it again. "I had a break-through!"

I leaned back against my chair, the discomfort reminding me that my wings were there. I still wasn't used to the new form, especially not when I saw myself in the mirror. But even if he was unfamiliar… my reflection felt right.

Like that was who I had always been underneath my camouflage. My kind had been hiding so long that the camouflage became us. While merrow showed their form proudly even on land, leviathans appeared completely human for survival.

"What breakthrough?" I asked, giving my gunner my full attention.

Gunny squinted his good eye before he recoiled, clearly remembering what I looked like before, and said, "I like your horns, Cap. Very regal."

Most of my crew had seen me at a distance, but never really close enough to clock the details. I made myself available, but even so, I knew many of my sailors were wary of me.

Who could blame them, really? I now wore the face of a monster.

"Thank you, Gun. Tell me about your plans."

"Explosives, Cap."

I crooked a brow. "You're going to have to go into more detail than '*Explosives, Cap.*'"

Gunny came forward and slapped the blueprints onto my desk. The numbers and lines were shaky, as if he'd struggled with determining how far the paper was from his pen. "Our edge. We use gunpowder to propel our ammunition, but what if I crafted ammunition with gunpowder inside? We don't know how many pirate hunters we're up against, but we could—"

"You want to expose gunpowder to molten metal to craft an explosive bullet?" I asked.

"I know how it sounds," Gunny said, putting both his hands up. "But I could enlist Ingrid's help. I'm not talking about lighting gunpowder barrels on fire. I'm talking about calculated explosions that could rattle their ships and break down whatever barricades they're building. Even to instantly dispatch a pirate hunter."

I pressed my tongue against my inner cheek. "I'm not keen on using this on people, Gun."

"Then we won't, but you have to admit that we need more firepower."

I hummed. "Not bullets. Too much of a possibility of taking your fingers off or damaging our pistols. You're on the right track, though. Maybe fill a bottle with it and have a fuse so there's enough time to get the gunpowder away from us before it combusts."

Gunny looked down at the blueprints, a thick haze of determination pinching his eyebrows together. "Aye, Cap!"

Right after he left, I heard a little commotion outside as my door was thrown open, Luella storming into my cabin.

She wore a vicious grin, looking me up and down. "Andra told me you looked different, but I didn't realize you'd look so glorious."

"It's nice to see you, too, Wraith," I stated, repressing my amusement. "Where are Bliss and Pinky?"

"About to walk in with a hostage," Luella replied, placing her hands on my desk to lean in closer and admire my horns. She didn't touch me, but I could tell that she wanted to. "I had to see you first, Levi. Gods, you're going to scare the piss right out of him!"

Pinky and Bliss dragged a screaming man into my cabin. Both pirates tried to repress their reactions to my massive half-dragon form, but I didn't miss the awe that unfolded in Bliss's eyes and the excitement in Pinky's.

"You wanna see what happens when you fuck with a leviathan?" Luella asked, shifting from foot to foot as they threw the man at her feet. She grabbed a handful of his hair, doing her damnedest to terrify him. "Hmm? You blow our town to dust and expect no repercussions?"

His face was bloodied, but he wore an embroidered barracuda on his scrappy jacket. No officer insignia, though.

When Luella stepped to the side, I stood up to my full height, and the pirate hunter got a good look at me. I flexed my wings and pinned him with a glare down the bridge of my nose.

At the sight of the barracuda, the anger came back full force. My hands clenched, and a tic formed in my jaw. I wanted to take his throat into my hands and *squeeze*. I wanted to make him pay for all the crimes right there and then.

"He's just a kid, Ronin." I could've sworn it was Mae's voice coming to me, cutting through the red haze to make me see who was in front of me.

That was when I noticed how young he was. The anger left me like a wave of water snuffing out a growing fire. He hadn't even lost the baby fat in his face yet. Guilt curdled in my stomach like milk mixed with vinegar.

Panic etched across his youthful face as he froze at my feet, absolutely paralyzed with fear. The blond hair at his temples was saturated with sweat.

Several people held the door open, crowding my doorway to watch what unfolded.

"No! No! Gods, *please!*" he screamed, growing more frantic the longer he looked at me.

I raised my eyebrows at Luella, focusing on the problem at hand. "Are you going to introduce us?"

Luella gave me the biggest shit-eating grin she ever had. "Pinky found a scout sniffing near the tunnels. The bastard was about to run back to his CO."

The pirate hunter continued to utter words of despair. "Please. Please. No. Gods, no."

"Good work," I said to Pinky before addressing the groveling young man. "You're going to answer a few questions."

He looked up, catching my gaze before he wailed, "Please don't hurt me! Please don't eat me!"

I blinked. "What?"

"You're going to rip me limb from limb! Devour me like you devoured all the children in my village!" He was distraught, sobbing violently. His voice undulated, turning shrill and cracking. "Like you burned my village to the ground!"

Is that what Pike had been telling everyone? The lies Varric filled everyone's heads with? That was one way to instill fear in your civilians to twist them however you needed.

I sucked my teeth and said dryly, "Oh, yes, because I eat people. But no one is going to eat you. As long as you answer my questions."

He nodded, snot and tears spilling all over his face. "Please."

"For fuck's sake, stand up and wipe your fucking nose." I glanced over at the door, where everyone was peeking in. "Would you close that?"

Luella nodded and went over to close it. "You heard Cap. Now git!"

The scout was utterly terrified as he stood up on shaking legs and wiped his nose with his sleeve. He couldn't be old enough to join the military, unless he was conscripted. Cross ignored the age limit laws when he forced teenage boys to join the service.

This kid looked significantly younger than Mae. All wide eyes and round cheeks.

It wouldn't be the first time Cross had mandated a draft. He and the lords of the surrounding villages were irresponsible with civilian lives, so far separated from the common people that I doubted they even viewed them as people at all.

"Sit down. What's your name, kid? How old are you?" I asked, gesturing to the chair across from me.

He stood there like a startled rabbit.

I sat back in my chair. "Sit the fuck down. I don't like to repeat myself."

Luella muffled a snicker as he sat down, hands trembling violently.

Bliss raised their eyebrows but didn't intervene. It seemed like they wanted to see what I was going to do with a hostage.

"I'm S-Scout Seymour…. I'm sixteen," he answered quietly. "I'm not a kid."

"You're not in the navy anymore. What's your first name?"

He ruffled a hand through unkempt blond hair, dirtied and bloody, dark brown eyes wide as he gulped repeatedly. "Robbie…. *Robert*."

"All right, Robbie," I said. "Tell me what you know."

He shook his head. "I can't. I can't."

Bliss chimed in. "We could stab him. That'll loosen his lips."

"I'm a fan of the teeth. Rip a few out," Pinky added.

The kid audibly sniffled, and I said, "You heard them."

"Well… they told me if I was caught, tell the pirates they have until the full moon to surrender before their people get hanged," he said slowly, rubbing his hands together nervously.

"Who?" I demanded. "Who do they have?"

He gulped. "There's a black man with a bandanna and a blonde woman with three fingers. The only one I know by name is, um, Lucky Bartram. My CO had been hunting him down for a while. A few others, too, but they were the only ones alive under the tavern."

Luella and I locked eyes. We both knew what happened.

"Fuck," Luella sighed. "They sent him on purpose."

"What?" Robbie asked, voice cracking, before he cleared his throat.

I gestured to him. "You. They gave you the message with

all intention of having us catch you. Shit. How long do we have?"

"Two weeks," Bliss said. "Two fucking weeks."

The kid stammered over his words. "Wh-What do you mean? They said that route was clear. I-I don't—"

I was done listening to him. "That means they know where the tunnels are," I stated. "We need a new path."

"We have what we need. Let's kill him before he makes it back to his—"

"I'm not killing this kid, Pinky." I glanced at the scout one more time. "He's terrified."

"So are our people. So are the refugees who had everything taken from them by him!" Pinky argued. "How do I know it wasn't him who lit the cannon that killed Vee?"

"Conscripts aren't allowed to use the cannons," Robbie offered weakly, shrinking under the scrutinizing gazes of both Pinky and Bliss.

"The people will want blood," Bliss stated.

"And so do I." I stood up, staring down at Bliss from the bridge of my nose. "We will get it when we take back Shipwreck Bay and give Pike a bloody death. Not by killing someone who hasn't grown into his skivvies yet." I cast the kid a sidelong glance. "Did Pike tell you that leviathans eat children and burn villages?"

He blinked, looking between all four of us. "My village was off the edge of the Ivory Keys. It was just me, my parents, and my big brother at our farm. A few neighbors. The nice girl my brother liked next door. Lord Pike said we were easy pickings for leviathans. Why else would my neighbors go missing?"

"Why would a leviathan go to the island of a known dragon hunter?" I watched doubt fill the boy's eyes before I said, "Get comfortable, kid. You're better off here anyway."

Two weeks. That was all the time we had before our families were dancing with Jack Ketch.

Over my dead fucking body.

13

RONIN MURDOCH

WE ARE ONE CREW, AND I'M THE FUCKING CAPTAIN.

I couldn't fucking sleep. It was even harder now because Mae's pillow didn't smell like her anymore. That springtime scent of cinnamon and berries was gone, and all I had left was a memory.

In time, memories fade....

I wasn't going to dwell, so I buried myself in work. We were on a ticking clock, and every passing moment was one that I'd never get back. It was one tick closer to failure. If I couldn't get to the hostages, I'd lose the morale of everyone in Anchorage Cove.

With Bliss watching me closely and their crew equally on edge, I was teetering on the line of a mutiny. Bliss was waiting for the moment to seize it. They thought I didn't know what they were planning, but Luella was in my corner, reporting back on every hushed meeting, every diverting of resources, every carefully placed rumor.

If infighting started, it wouldn't stop. People would die, both Bliss's forces and mine. Pike would solidify his foothold, and we'd never recover.

If I survived the mutiny, of course.

Even with my new form, I was sure a properly placed blade would end me in an instant. To make it worse, I hadn't heard back from any reinforcements. I'd sent families and orphans to pirate safeholds with whatever sloops I had available, but for all intents and purposes, I had to assume that I was doing this alone.

That everything I had right now was all I was going to get.

I didn't know what I expected. These were pirates, hardly bound to the same code of honor as I was. They would protect themselves before they helped anyone else. I'd even had a few of my own crew abandon their ranks to defect.

A blow for sure, but I wouldn't force anyone to fight for me. I wasn't Cross. I wasn't going to conscript soldiers and force them to lay down their lives for me. They would have a choice. Pike had many of these soldiers under his thumb, either because of fear or because he allowed them to act on their impulses.

Knowing where Mae was dragged up the repressed memories I carried from when I was Pike's prisoner. The *things* he did to me. That his crew did to me.

If they touched her....

No. Not *if*. I *knew* they'd fucking touched her.

The first thing I was going to do after I took Shipwreck Bay was plan for a full siege of the Ivory Keys. Then I would personally make Pike kneel in front of my girl before I took the light from his eyes.

If she's there.

It didn't matter if Mae had been taken to the Ivory Keys. I had to fracture Pike's army, or they'd overwhelm us before we got to Farlight Harbor. I *hoped* Mae was there, because I couldn't bear the idea that I'd have to wait even longer before I saw her wide eyes again.

Her pink freckled cheeks.

Her warm smile.

I missed her like nothing else, even if it became harder to recall the details of her pointed nose or her petal-pink lips.

The longer she was away, the blurrier she became.

But the way she made me *feel*… that never faded.

Absentmindedly, I wandered into *The Ollipheist* mess hall, where Butcher was preparing food for a midday meal. Townspeople came and went, taking their rations out to their families or friends. I hunched over, barely fitting through the doorframe with my wings folded behind my back.

Siggi had to sew together two pairs of my pants to fit my massive legs, as well as a vest I could button over my chest to house my gear because my lucky red sash didn't have enough fabric to wrap around my waist twice and knot. I still wore it looped through my belt, but it didn't serve its usual function anymore. My cutlass felt small against my hip, but that made it considerably easier to wield.

Even when I sparred with Andra to pass the time, I was a more formidable opponent than before. That fucking Skadian heir had gotten the best of me during the storm, but that would never happen again.

The mess hall was always bustling these days, full of bodies retrieving prepared food, bread, or produce to prepare for themselves. Conway worked dutifully by Butcher's side, placing satchels of vegetables and bread down where anyone could grab them while Butcher and his volunteers cooked for the next meal.

When I finally looked up, I noticed Gunny among the volunteers, wearing an eyepatch and struggling to slice vegetables for Butcher. His brow was furrowed in focus as he carefully gauged where the carrot was before missing it again.

I waited for them to notice me, listening to their conversation among all the humdrum of the mess hall.

"Don't get frustrated, Gunny," Butcher said, moving next to my gunner to slice and dice his produce for the stew masterfully.

"I don't know how you do this," Gunny admitted, bringing his knife down with a hard clack on the wooden cutting board.

"I don't know how you load cannons," Butcher commented, his voice a low hum. "Or come up with all those plans in your head. That's bloody spectacular to me."

Gunny shook his head. "This is all wrong. I can barely put a pen to paper anymore. I worked too hard on my penmanship for it to be messy. I can't give Cap messy plans."

"I'm sure Cap doesn't mind."

I didn't. As far as I was concerned, learning how to read and write was an accomplishment. As was surviving a piece of shrapnel embedded in the eye.

"I was the same way after I lost my eye. Had to relearn everything all over again."

Gunny made a noise of frustration as he missed the carrot again. "We don't have time for that, Butcher. Cap needs these plans. We need to get our friends back."

Butcher sighed and laid his knife down. "Cap is doing everything he can. As are you."

Gunny obviously didn't agree, as he slammed his knife into the carrot in a messy cut. "I can't chop a fucking carrot. What good is a gunner without his eyes?"

"You only need one eye to shoot." Butcher enclosed his scarred hands around Gunny's. "Besides, a gunner is more than his eyes." Slowly, he took the hand with the knife in it and brought it down into the carrot, neatly slicing. "Do you feel where the vegetable is?"

Gunny frowned but replied, "Yes."

"Like any recovery, you need to take it slowly. The rest of your body needs to learn how to compensate for your depth perception." Butcher took Gunny's other hand to show him where to slice next before moving the knife hand accordingly. "It's all right to go slowly. It may not be as fast as you want it, but this is a victory. Everything is a victory."

Something stirred in my chest as Gunny looked up at Butcher before taking his hands away from the older man to do it himself.

"This is a victory," Gunny sighed as he gently felt where he should make the next cut and smiled wide enough to show off his twisted tooth when it was successful.

Butcher looked down at Gunny with a fatherly pride before he glanced over at me and waved. "Aye, Cap. Good to see you."

Gunny's head jerked up, a flush blooming across his tawny cheeks. "Oi, Cap. I didn't see you there."

I stepped forward to the line and asked, "How are the rations? Do you need anything?"

Butcher clicked his tongue and squinted toward the cold box. "The fishermen have been a great help. Conway and the merrow have cultivated the garden. Isa's rugrats bring us eggs every morning. Shep has had a successful breeding season with the goats, so we should have milk soon. Cheese would be a nice treat. But we can feed everyone, just barely."

That was good news. "And yourself?"

"You look as exhausted as I feel, Cap." Butcher gave me a tired smile. "Hard work, but it's worth it. I can't let all these lads and lassies go unfed, now can I?"

"It's appreciated," I said. "When we take Shipwreck Bay, you'll be able to get some rest."

Butcher parted his lips to say something, but when the

entire mess hall went quiet, his eye focused on something behind me. I bristled, a hostility filling the air.

"And *when* will that be, Leviathan? After our own have danced with Jack Ketch? Are you already planning a plot of land for the funeral rites?" Bliss's voice rang clear across the mess.

Ah, fuck.

I turned around and met the golden eyes of someone who was imagining my death. Their mouth was fixed in a set line, a small number of their sailors fanned out behind them.

Of course Bliss waited until my mates hadn't accompanied me. I didn't have Udine or Pinky to talk them down either.

"Do you want to have it out here? Right now?" I asked dryly.

"You may be king by birthright, but I abhor kings. I follow my own doctrine, not a man who's hidden himself his whole life," Bliss snarled. They gripped the hilt of their cutlass and added, "When I take your life from you, they will know me as Bliss Thatcher—Slayer of Dragons."

I didn't reach for my blade. "You'd risk the lives of your crew—of *my* crew—for what? Because you can't share?"

"You led us here. *You* got Violetta killed. *You* got Lucky captured. It was *your* correspondence that got intercepted. I will not stand behind a man who damned us." Bliss drew their sword and pointed it right at me.

I crossed my arms. "Do you want me to say that I fucked up? Is that it, Bliss?" I straightened my back, walking a slow, steady stride toward them. "I can admit that I fucked up. Haven't you noticed?"

Bliss narrowed their eyes, a stray curl falling over their forehead.

"But I'm not the only one. *I'm* not the one who divided us at the first sign of danger. No. I'm here making sure everyone is fed and receives proper medical care. Including your people, because they're my people now. I'm the one planning a siege to take back Shipwreck Bay. And what have *you* done?" I didn't let Bliss answer. "*You* divert resources. *You* spread factless rumors. *You* plan a fucking mutiny."

Bliss took a step back as I approached them.

"Sure, I may have fucked up, but I'm doing *everything* in my power to fix it. What would you have me do instead?" I towered over Bliss, looking down at them from the bridge of my nose. "Indulge this? Because I have far more important things to do than play your game."

Bliss swallowed before sheathing their weapon. They turned on their heel, not saying another word as they tried to flee.

"I'd rather work with you, but try that again, Bliss, and I'll fucking kill you."

They didn't say anything, didn't even acknowledge me as they left. The crew they came in with stayed, watching me while their captain fled.

"I'm only going to say this once," I declared, authority dripping from my voice. "I will not tolerate a mutiny. I will not tolerate dividing us between who we put our colors behind. We are *one* crew, and I'm the fucking captain. It's Pike against us. If any of you disagree, then get on the next sloop and get off my island."

The crew members who had followed Bliss into the mess nodded and took a seat at one of the tables. Any source of animosity vanished with Bliss as I turned back to Butcher and Gunny. I flexed my shoulders and sighed, now thoroughly annoyed.

"That was well said, Cap," Butcher remarked, grabbing a satchel of rations for me. "You know that this old sea dog would've raised a cleaver in your name, right?"

"And this gunner," Gunny concurred.

A soft chuckle left my lips. "I appreciate it. Loyalty goes both ways. I'm indebted to you for how you've served *The Ollipheist* over the years. Never forget that."

Butcher smiled at me as I took the rations and left to have lunch with my mates and tell them about my latest brush with Bliss.

14

RONIN MURDOCH

CRAFTING A PLAN

Across from me, the conscripted scout had been restrained against the ballast in my cabin. We still hadn't fixed the door in the pit, but I couldn't risk him slipping out to alert his CO to our whereabouts.

As I stared at him where he was sitting there twiddling his thumbs, he didn't look remotely threatening. Not only was he slender and rather small for his age, but his cheeks were still round with baby fat. He had this childlike wonder in his eyes that hadn't been squashed by the horrors of war.

Not yet.

"You could save a lot of lives by telling me where they're keeping the hostages," I stated, startling him.

He looked up at me, appearing every bit as young as he was. He shook his head. "No."

"Make me wait any longer, and I'll use a blade to get the information from you." I glanced at my claws, noting how sharp they seemed. "But I'm sure my claws are better than a blade."

He gulped before straightening his back and steeling himself. "You're going to hurt the people I care about."

"It's a possibility," I said, straightening out some papers and Gunny's blueprints. "But if they stand down, I'll have no reason to shed blood." I paused, eyeing his fidgeting form. "Tell me something, Robbie—"

"*Robert*," he corrected.

"*Robbie*," I insisted, trying to get a rise out of him. "When the leviathans destroyed your town, did you see them?"

He frowned, averting his gaze. "No, but they said leviathans could wipe our memories—"

I threw my head back and laughed. "We aren't sirens. That's absurd. Just as absurd as leviathans eating people."

"But...." Robbie licked his lips, racking his brain for a response. "If my mind were tampered with, I wouldn't know. You could be doing it right now!"

I ran my hand through my hair, smoothing the strands down around my horns. "If I could tamper with your mind, I would've found the information myself. Your pirate hunters have imprisoned my family. Pike fucking kidnapped my girl. I have every reason to force the information out of you. But instead, I'm *asking*."

He twiddled his thumbs again, looking awfully ashamed. "Are you talking about Princess Maeve? I... I saw what they did to her before I was sent ashore."

My vision tunneled around him as my breath came out hot. "What did they do to her?" I snapped.

An intense look of fear constricted his pupils before he looked away again, his voice so quiet, it was nearly silent as he said, "They... clipped her wings. They did it to a few of my friends when I was recruited, and one of the ensigns did it to my brother when he found a jar of salve for me."

My claws sank into the soft wood of my desk.

"There was this one ensign who liked to brag about what he did to... you," the scout added quietly. "Was what he said true?"

A tic formed in my jaw. "That is none of your fucking business."

"I wasn't on board yet, but I'm... I'm sorry."

I rolled my shoulders, a muscle tense in my neck as an eruption of phantom touches cascaded down my back. I pushed it all down and uttered a sentiment through my teeth that I'd been holding on to. "My friends have died. My father was murdered in front of me when I was five fucking years old. Countless lives have been lost because of Pike and Cross. Your crewmates took advantage of me numerous times while I was incapacitated."

I didn't remember most of it, but I still *felt* it when I was alone.

The scout shrank down, unable to meet my scrutinizing gaze.

"You want to make it better? Pay retribution for the tyrant you blindly follow? Tell me where my people are."

Silence fell between us. It was so quiet that I could hear the waves lapping against the hull of the ship. I could hear the small chatter of my crew on deck. I could feel the sound tickling the tip of my nose as everyone went about their day, dreading whatever horror was to come.

Finally, Robbie looked up at me and said, "They're in the townhouses."

I leaned back in my chair. "What else?"

"The man with the bandanna... he can't walk. He was injured when we found him under the tavern."

I stiffened but didn't reply as he told me about Mama and Lucky. That they were beaten up but alive. Wesley's back was fucking shattered when the tavern fell on him. The pirate hunters had gathered the dead into a mass grave behind the bakery in what used to be wheat fields.

"What about Spider? A man with a spider tattoo on his neck?" I asked.

Robbie shook his head. "I don't remember anyone like that."

"Defenses," I demanded. "Tell me about them."

The scout hesitated, but then his lips parted when someone knocked at my cabin door. I huffed in frustration but got up from my seat and opened the door to find Bliss standing there, a frown fixed on their face and their arms crossed.

"What the fuck do you want?" I hissed.

Bliss brushed past me, eyed the prisoner, and said, "I'm here to discuss the siege."

I scoffed. "Like the Hells you are. You come in here after attempting a mutiny and expect to know *anything* about my plans?"

"Leviathan, be civil. I thought you wanted to work together."

I couldn't fight the roll of my eyes. "Get out of my fucking cabin."

Bliss blanched. "I am a *captain*. I will be spoken to as such."

I looked down at Bliss, and they met my gaze with a blazing one of their own. "You're wrong. At this rate, you're not even a cabin boy."

Bliss's mouth opened and closed as they struggled to produce a reply.

I silenced whatever retort they had in mind. "You proved to me that I can't trust you. Do you think you deserve to be in my inner circle?" I lowered my head until I was a breath away from their face, demanding Bliss's complete attention. "Prove to me that you belong here." I took a step forward, caging them in the direction of my door. "Until then, *get the fuck out*."

Bliss's throat bobbed before they broke my gaze and left without another word.

I slammed the door behind them, barely quelling my temper before I whipped around and demanded, "Defenses. Now."

MY CABANA LOOKED ENTIRELY DIFFERENT BEING OCCUPIED BY the merrow. Most of my things hadn't been touched, but with tridents and halberds lining the entryway and a handful of warriors curled up on the floor, sleeping, there was more life than I'd ever seen in my space before.

The guest room was being occupied by Siggi, who made it into an effective tailor shop. He was still working away on blankets and nets for the fishermen while I sat on my chaise with my advisers, preparing for the siege on Shipwreck Bay.

Luella had sketched a map for me on short notice, laying it across the table where I used to put my feet up and read a book while Mae slept upstairs.

"Four guard towers," I stated, marking the spots with a set of bones where Robbie had told me they were. "And here is where our people are being held." I took a dried bean and placed it over the townhouses.

"And you can trust his information?" Andra asked, leaning her elbow on the counter.

"It's all I have right now," I said. "And I have no reason to believe he'd lie to me."

Luella hummed. "All right, Levi. Let's say his information is right. They'll be expecting us on the full moon."

"That's why I wanted to call this meeting now." I glanced over at Udine. "Gunny said the grenados will be ready in a few days. I want the element of surprise."

"You want to stage an attack early?" Udine clarified.

I dipped my head in a nod. "We don't have reinforcements. Surprise is the only edge we have." I drew their attention back to the map. "I would have Udine and her warriors incapacitate the ships, keep them from leaving, and get rid of their cannons."

Udine pursed her lips, tapping pointed claws against her breastplate. "My warriors can't do this singlehandedly."

"I want Luella and Andra to lead the ground attack. We use the grenados to take the towers." I gestured to the town-houses. "I'll put these wings to use and fly directly to the hostages to set them free. Once that happens, I'll signal the full-scale attack."

"Even with all of our people, we're going to be outgunned," Andra said.

I frowned because I knew she was right. I pressed my tongue into my cheek, mulling over the other variables, but it all came back to the same thing.

We weren't enough.

The front door to the cabana opened, and Pinky stuck his head in, knocking as an afterthought. It was obvious that he had been listening in, as he said, "Can I come in?"

I nodded and gestured for him to stand next to me. "Eavesdropping, are we?"

"It's what I do best," Pinky admitted.

"What do you have to say?" Udine asked, her crescent-shaped pupils contracting and dilating as she sized him up.

"I listened to scouting parties as they trekked up and down the forest paths around the tunnels." He tapped his blue-toned lower lip. "And most of them *hate* Pike as much as we do. I heard whispers of doubt, anger about their friends being brutalized on board the ships, even casual jokes about defecting. Disloyal soldiers don't lay down their lives for their commanders."

That solidified all my suspicions about the pirate hunters.

"When they were with their COs, they acted like the perfect soldiers. Pike has a track record of thinning his ranks and instilling those left with fear. The COs use the exact same tactics. But when these soldiers are with their peers, you hear how they really feel."

Udine concurred, "It's true. Several defectors joined my ranks at the Colony when we took Fisherman's Gully. Give them a taste of true freedom, and they'll never go back."

"When Pike captured most of the crew," Andra recalled, "Pike himself wasn't in the brig. There were a few pricks, but for the most part, the cabin boys tended to us. There was even this lieutenant who deterred some of the abuse that would've otherwise occurred."

A tic formed in my jaw as I wondered why my calls for help weren't loud enough or worthy enough for attention. I pushed down the thoughts, focusing on the plan.

"So let's give them the opportunity to be disloyal," I decided. "Let me see if Robbie will give me the names of the commanding officers. I'll go for them after I free our people." I made direct eye contact with Luella. "Get this plan out to everyone. We're getting our home back."

Pinky grinned and stood up straight. He saluted me and said, "Fuck yes, we are! Call, and *The Violet Queen* is at your service."

The band of anxiety in my chest started to loosen, and for the first time, I thought...

We can do this.

15

MAEVE CROSS

ALONE

The week dragged on. Several days of watching Frey's infection get worse. Of withstanding Adams coming down to the brig to toy with Frey, Seymour, and me. Ever since I attacked Nathaniel, there were strict rules on not letting me out of my cage unless completely necessary.

That didn't stop Adams, though.

Frey was regularly taken from his cell to entertain Nathaniel, and Adams liked to sit there beside Seymour and watch me. Waiting for the opportunity for more.

On a particularly awful day, Adams got orders to wash me. The first time, he kept his hands to himself. The lieutenant was nearby, averting his eyes from me to watch Adams closely. His hand rested on the hilt of his sword, and I wished he would kill the ensign and be done with it.

But he didn't. He let Adams gawk at me until I felt filthier than I did before I got into the water.

The fact that the lieutenant was a bystander only emboldened Adams.

That led to one of the ensign's favorite pastimes—

flaunting me through the barracks. Usually after that lieutenant had turned in for the night.

Even as I leaned against the bars after a night without torment, I wasn't free of it. I could still feel the fingers on my skin. His breath on my neck. I could hear the other sailors commenting on my body, warning Adams that Nathaniel would kill him if he went too far.

He merely replied that he was sure the admiral wanted them to put me in my place. But to be safe, they'd have to wait until the admiral was busy with disembarkment before they could take what they wanted from me.

They did this to Ronin too. They called him a *filthy creature* only worthy of being *used*.

I'm going to kill them all.

The phantom hands in my hair still pulled. The lashes on my back were gone, but I still winced as if the whip cracked in my ears. My wrists were rubbed raw again, the irons biting into my skin. I tasted the blood in my mouth even if my lips weren't split anymore. I fought the dark thoughts, trying hard not to slip into the trenches.

It only got harder.

Tears had left tight salty trails down my cheeks, my dirty blouse wet from lying in the showers.

"Will you ever marry him? Your leviathan?" Frey asked me, snapping me out of the circle of the Hells I'd begun to sink into.

I glanced over at him. His shirt had been torn open to reveal the place where one of his nipple rings had been ripped out, leaving an angry gaping wound on his chest. Blue blood streaked against the fair skin, and under it, I could see feathering veins bulging and purple.

Nathaniel had refused to see me after I attacked him on deck, so all of his attention went to Frey. He didn't like to talk about what happened when Nathaniel called for him, but his wounds spoke loudly enough.

His face was all clammy, his usually purple-toned lips as pale as his hair. I knew he was on the path to a severe infection and had to be running a fever. Seymour's salve wouldn't be enough to save him if it got too bad.

He could barely keep his eyes open most of the time.

"We never talked about marriage," I replied, leaning my knotted hair against the bars. A helpless smile pulled up the side of my mouth as I thought about Ronin and the way he'd pinch my chin between his fingers before he kissed me.

More tears spilled down my cheeks. *Gods, I hope he's alive. I hope he's not shutting everyone out. I want him to be all right.*

My voice cracked when I added, "I'd like to. But I'm... I'm different now. I don't know if he'd still want me."

"Different how, Mae?"

"This rage. It's consuming me. I can feel it changing me."

"Then let it," he replied.

"What if it turns me into a monster?"

"Being monstrous is subjective, Mae. It'll turn you into a survivor. If your leviathan can't see that, then he's not the one for you." Frey looked over at me, utterly exhausted and fighting drooping eyelids. "I'm not familiar with Farlight marriage customs. Tell me about them."

"I'm not a good study. The only time I've been married was against my will."

He made a noise of disgust. "Pike likes to call me *barbaric*. He thinks Skadians are animals because of our practices." Frey stroked his braid, trying to tame the flyaway strands.

I could hear the rats squeaking in the corner of the room again.

"If I fall unconscious, don't let them eat me," Frey requested. "I don't want to join the afterlife with rat bites taken out of me." He groaned, eyelids fluttering shut.

"Don't fall asleep," I said urgently, sitting up straight. "Come on, Frey, stay awake. Keep me company." I gulped, not knowing if he'd wake up again if he succumbed to sleep.

Slowly, he opened his eyes. "Do you think Death will be kind to me, *ylgr*?"

I turned to Seymour, sitting at his table, back completely rigid. I shouted, "What are you doing? Why hasn't the surgeon seen him yet?"

The guard's light-colored eyes were wide as he fiddled with his fingers. "I can't."

"What the fuck do you mean, *you can't*? You *won't*." I struggled up to my feet, dragging my irons up the cell bar with me.

Seymour refused to look at me even when I kicked the bars hard enough to feel the impact on the bottoms of my feet. "I… I've reported it, but he won't come. Not for a Skadian dog."

"Fucker," Frey groaned.

"Godsdamnit!" I hissed, kicking the bars again.

Frey shushed me and fell slack against the bars. "I need to rest my eyes. Just a moment."

"What is your braid for?" I asked, causing Frey to sleepily look at me again. "You're always preening it."

"My marital braid," he answered before he chuckled weakly. "Elinora demanded that I wear my hair like this or I'd never see her tits again. She didn't have to threaten me. I would've done anything she asked."

He groaned again, body trembling violently as he tried to keep himself upright.

"If you ever get married, *ylgr*, there're these two weeks in Skadi when the snow melts and the flowers bloom. Brief and beautiful. It makes all the cold…." He trailed off, blinking hard. Sweat beaded along his brow, dripping down his cheeks. "Fuck, why is it so hot in this fucking place?"

"He has a fever, Seymour. It'll take him if he can't get help," I implored. "Please. We can't let him die."

Seymour got up and strode over to Frey to touch his sopping-wet brow. Given all the injuries Frey had suffered since the moment he was trapped here, an infection wasn't surprising. I'd seen Enya treat enough infections on *The Ollipheist* to know they can happen suddenly, and they'd claimed countless lives at sea.

"Shit," Seymour said. "I'll be right back." He turned and darted up the steps to the hatch.

"It's bad, isn't it?" Frey asked.

"You'll die," I replied.

Frey choked on a laugh. "You're blunt."

"It's part of my charm," I said weakly. "Come on, stay with me. You need to tell me what *ylgr* means."

"She-wolf," he murmured. "It means she-wolf. Viciously loyal and protective of their own. Like you. I would have liked to be your friend one day."

"You are my friend. Even if it's in poor taste." I gulped, emotion forming a lump in my throat. "That's not a free pass to die, Frey."

He grinned before his head lolled back, and he fell slack against the bars.

"Frey!" I shouted. I kicked the bars again, but he didn't stir. "Don't leave me here alone." Fresh tears welled in my eyes, and a sob retched from my chest. A wail broke through my throat. "Please, Frey. Don't do this to me. I can't be alone again." I looked up at the hatch and screamed, "Help! Help! *Please!*"

Right then, the weight of my failure hung on my shoulders. When Varric burned everything to the ground, my friends would be ash, but I would rise again. Everyone else.... They weren't like me. They were fragile. They would bend and crumble and *break*.

Why is everything so heavy?

The weight bore down, pressing on my chest. My mind raced, vision tunneling and blurring. My heart hammered, and I couldn't control my breathing.

Panic had its grip on me, and I was *drowning* in it.

I kicked. I thrashed. I *screamed*.

I'm alone. I'm alone. I'm alone.

The only solace I had being trapped in this fucking cage was that at least I wasn't alone. I had a friend, as flimsy as that title may have been for Frey. He stuck me here. He hurt the people I cared about. He'd been someone I'd vowed to kill.

But in this dark, lonely, dirty place, he wasn't a point of misery. He had become a friend.

I felt utterly helpless as I thrashed against the irons, banging them on the bars over and over again. My wrists were wet with blood oozing down my arms, but I couldn't feel the pain.

My throat became raw as I screamed for help again, but no one came.

No one came.

It didn't matter what Adams had put me through. It didn't matter that Pike had tormented me until I almost broke. I was overcome with pure fuming *rage*. It spilled over into my belly and ran through my veins.

How many times had someone called for help, but no one came?

How many times had *Ronin* begged for help to be cast aside because he was a "filthy creature"?

Did anyone ever come to his rescue, or did they use him until he had nothing left? *How many fucking times did they hurt him?*

Black spots dotted my vision.

Helplessness dropped me right back into Fisherman's

Gully when I was only a child, unable to save anyone from Varric's massacre. So many innocent people died, and I couldn't help them.

After my wedding, Nathaniel's hands closed around my neck as he strangled the life out of me. I was powerless to stop him.

I could see the cannonballs tear through Shipwreck Bay. I could hear the screams. I could feel Ronin's arms around me, keeping me grounded. I watched the beam fall on top of Enya and Wesley. I felt the hot spray of Violetta's blood when she was killed.

I couldn't do anything.

And I can't do anything now.

"Help! Help!" I sobbed, sinking slowly to the ground. I muttered the word brokenly over and over again. I didn't know what else to say.

But no one came.

16

MAEVE CROSS

THE BOOT ON YOUR NECK

ALL I COULD DO WAS WATCH FREY'S CHEST SHALLOWLY RISE and fall and hope that he didn't stop breathing. Even under the dull yellow light, I could see the lilac flush deepen the lavender of his skin.

When Seymour came back, there was no doctor with him. No medicine. Nothing but sorrow in his eyes. Those bastards would let Frey die because it gave them something to lord over. They'd never have Pike's power, so they'd take whatever they could.

Tormenting Frey… tormenting me…. It made even the cabin boys and lower-ranking officers like Seymour feel like *big men*, but I saw them for what they were.

Deplorable, pathetic little boys pretending to be gods.

Their last mistake.

My eyes felt dry, and I couldn't remember the last time I'd blinked.

How long have I stared at Frey? Hours? Days?

I feared that if I looked away for only a moment, it would be the moment the fever would take him.

Frey doesn't get to die.

He didn't deserve what they'd done to him, but after everything he'd done, all the pain he'd caused, he didn't deserve peace either. I'd drag him back from the Hells myself.

Even if he'd grown on me during our time together, that didn't change the fact that he would get *no* peace until he paid his penance.

Only then would I *let* him rest.

Only then would he be allowed to join his wife in the afterlife.

Not a moment before.

An announcement from the upper deck roused Frey, eyes fluttering open before they closed and he slackened onto the floor again. "Land ho!"

Fuck. Disembarkment.

When Pike and all his high-ranking officers would be too busy to stop Adams from stealing me for one more awful round of humiliation. But that also meant there would be no one there to stop *me.*

I tugged on my irons, not looking away as I asked Seymour, "Aren't you going to do anything? You know Adams is coming back for me."

"What could I do?" Helplessness echoed in his voice.

"Anything. You sit there and you put your head down, but you never do anything."

He was quiet for a long moment, flipping a page in his book. "I can't. I don't have the keys for your irons. I can't wield a sword to save my life. You can't die, Princess, but I can."

Frey's chest rose and fell, and I counted each breath. They were shallow but even.

Seymour turned another page, the noise of scratchy paper filling the room. But it was rougher than before, like a flick and scrape. A crinkle and *rip* in the corner of the page. It was as if he didn't know what to say, so he anxiously abused his book instead.

I could see that helpless plea shining in his eyes, that prayer for strength on his lips whenever he wanted to do something. *Say* something. But he didn't need strength to fight his fear—he just needed courage.

Seymour's reactions were all in the details. A subtle shake in his hands or the tremble of an eyebrow. When Adams was breathing in his face, his chin would quiver. It was a learned reaction.

Like the moment I'd swallow tears after Varric reprimanded me because if I let myself cry, that was another thing to be held against me. That was one more reason that I was weak and *ruled by emotion.*

But I was a girl, and an *emotional* response was expected, invalidated, and dismissed. Boys had it beaten out of them by lesser men.

Bitterly, I replied, "Ah, yes. *Death.* But what's the point of living if there's nothing to die for?"

From the corner of my eye, I saw Seymour stand up, slamming his book down. "My father died for something! But that doesn't matter because he's dead. He's gone. My brother has likely died at the hands of pirates! My mother needs me to survive—"

"I die over and over again," I mused. "I'm pushed to the brink constantly for the amusement of men. My death used to matter, but now it's another way to torture me."

"...I'm sorry, Maeve. I'm sorry that I'm not you."

I hummed. "Don't be sorry. Count yourself lucky that you can only die once. I wouldn't wish this on anyone, Seymour. But know this." I paused, rubbing the raw parts of my wrists. "I would trade myself for you in an instant."

"*Why?*" he choked out. "I... I cut you, Maeve."

"You did," I said. "Sometimes a boot on your neck makes you forget what a full breath feels like."

"I... I...," Seymour stammered, the words not forming on his tongue.

The hatch above us opened, and my entire body went cold at the sound of Adams's voice. "Sorry to interrupt. I found a nice quiet place for us, Princess."

"There's the boot now," I murmured.

One. Two. Three. I started counting Frey's breaths again, my back growing rigid as Adams's heavy footsteps got closer to me.

The door of the cell clicked open, and then a thick, clammy hand clenched around my jaw, jerking my head to meet Adams's eyes. "Look at me. It's the last chance you'll get to before I take what I want from you."

Always with the taking.

I widened my eyes and tilted my head to the side, looking over his appearance thoroughly. The crooked nose. The split lip. Sun-scorched skin as if he'd never taken the proper precautions to protect himself on deck. Frey's marital pendant hung from his neck, taunting me.

That doesn't belong to you.

"How could I forget such a hideous face?" I asked sweetly.

Adams blinked, and it took him several moments to fully realize what I'd said. "Says the monster-fucker," he snarled, slapping me across the face with the back of his hand.

The taste of metal filled my mouth. "And he's more of a man than you'll ever be."

"I'll do something to that mouth."

I stared directly into his eyes, not faltering for a moment. "You have one more chance to leave, Adams."

"Threats sound so precious coming from your lips, little girl," he chuckled, unlocking my irons and yanking me to my feet. Then he relocked my hands behind my back and pulled me out of the cell. "I have some friends joining us. That won't be a problem, will it? I wouldn't want anyone to miss the opportunity to know what a princess feels like."

I swallowed my reaction, remaining as impassive as possible.

"Pretend to be defenseless. It's your greatest weapon," Luella had told me once during one of our sparing sessions. She taught me many lessons on how I'd never overpower an opponent, but I could outsmart them.

I glanced at Frey one more time, silently promising, *I'll be back for you.*

"That's enough, Adams," Seymour demanded, stepping in front of us.

Adams laughed. "And what will you do about it, runt?"

I thought Seymour was going to wither under Adams's scrutinizing glare, but both of his hands came out to shove the ensign back. The larger man gasped in surprise at the weak push, but he let me go, knocking me backward onto the hard planks to fist both hands into Seymour's jacket, pinning him against the wall.

"When she's gone, you'll be my new toy. No one will save you," Adams promised, backhanding Seymour across the face.

No one will save you....

Fuck you.

He dropped Seymour to the ground and turned to pull me to my feet again. "Gather yourself, Seymour. I'd hate for you to look disheveled for disembarkment. The admiral hates that."

Seymour averted his eyes from Adams, head dipped down low in subservience. Adams pulled me past the young officer, my hands still bound behind my back. But as I passed him, Seymour placed something cold in my hand, curling my fingers closed around the small object.

My key.

17

MAEVE CROSS

BROKEN GLASS LIKE GLITTERING STARS

My breath caught, hope warming my blood. Seymour didn't look at me, the side of his face already swelling as I was pulled up the stairs and onto the deck. We moved past the barracks, and then Adams pulled me down a hallway in the middle deck. Oil lamps lined the walls, only half of them lit, and I clutched that key like it was a lifeline.

I didn't keep my head down as he led me down long narrow hallways to the stern of the ship. The lights barely illuminated the darkness. The planks gave my toes splinters, nipping the soles of my feet.

He continued to clasp the nape of my neck, leading me like a lamb to slaughter. But, as we passed hardly any other sailors, the key felt heavier and heavier, my palms slicked with sweat.

Wait. Wait for your moment.

He brought me down to a storage room full of barrels and crates in a lower deck. A line of other men waited outside. I recognized all of them. They'd laughed at me when Adams splintered my ribs under his boots. While his putrid breath kissed the back of my neck, they made crude comments about my body.

They baited me with brags about what they did to Ronin.

My Ronin.

As my knuckles turned white, they demanded my submission. They told me women were bad luck, but only if they got ideas. There had to be fifteen of them, staring at me, taking pleasure in my torment.

They humiliated me.

They abused me.

They hurt the man I loved.

And they will pay for it all.

When I saw Ronin again, I'd gift him with the knowledge that they died screaming.

"You'll all get a turn, but I get her first," Adams said as another man opened the door for him. Adams's nails clipped the soft skin on the back of my neck as he shoved me forward with enough power to send me stumbling inside, knocking my breath out as my stomach collided with a barrel.

An oil lamp was perched on the barrel, casting long shadows all over the room.

Rage spilled into my chest, spitting up from my stomach like boiling water over a fire. I got back to my feet and turned around to watch the other men close the door, telling Adams to have fun.

The door locked with a click.

"Finally, we'll have some privacy. Now where is that key?" Adams patted his pockets, jolting slightly at the soft squeaking in the corners of the room from the rats. I watched him try to settle himself as his eyes darted around the space, searching for pests in the darkness. He rubbed one of his arms in a self-soothing motion before turning his attention back to the missing key.

My lips twitched as I loosened my grip on the key, then unlocked one of my wrists. The hand that was still bound curled around the free loop. I leaned against the barrel and watched him flounder as he looked for my key.

He muttered a curse under his breath and stopped his search. Adams approached me, stroking the side of my face with a grimy fingernail. "Don't look so sad, love. We'll make it worth it, won't we? I guarantee you'll enjoy it more than your leviathan did. At least you'll remember."

"How many times did you hurt him?" I demanded.

Adams cackled. "Hard to keep count."

I tilted my head to the side, observing the wrinkles around his mouth. His crooked nose that I'd broken more than once at this point. My hands twitched behind my back. "Tell me. Tell me how many times you hurt *my* leviathan."

His eyebrows came together in confusion. "It doesn't really matter, does it? We'll hurt you twice as many."

I could feel the rage rise within me, growing hot. "It does. I need to know how many ways I should make you bleed."

He threw his head back and laughed.

"Go ahead. Laugh," I said. "You're under the impression that I'm trapped in here with you. But really, you're in here with *me*."

At that moment, I dropped the key. It clinked on the planks and stole Adams's attention. His eyes grew wide, and I swung my hand back, gripping the metal cuff hard as I brought it toward him. It collided with his face and knocked out several teeth.

He recoiled in shock, a shout of pain leaving his lips as I pounced, knocking him flat onto his back. I didn't stop swinging, not even as his blood squelched under my knuckles.

Frey's pendant peeked from under Adams's collar, and I seized it. "This isn't yours," I snarled.

He cried out weakly for help beneath my flurry of violence. He tried to fling me off him, but I snatched my key from the floorboards and thrust it into the soft spot in the side of his neck. It was small but sharp around the rusted edges. There was a ruckus on the other side of the door as the men rushed to open it.

Adams reached for his throat, gurgling and choking on his own blood. He flailed, ripping the key out in a panicked frenzy. It didn't take long for him to bleed out, that sunburnt skin drained of all color. Then, slowly, the panic ebbed away from his features, and he ceased making any movement at all.

I rose to my feet as the door flew open. There had to have been six or seven men standing in the doorway, horrified at what was left of Adams.

"Get her! Get her!"

A manic laugh spilled from my lips as I grasped the oil lamp from the barrel behind me and hurled it directly at the men in the doorway. The glass exploded like glittering stars, the oil splattering across all of them. The fire caught like an inferno, and the swelling of screams sounded like music.

Oil and fire cascaded across the floor like a wave of frothing sea. A musical chorus of chittering rats reached its climax as they came out of the dark, equally as panicked as the men behind the wall of flames.

As the fire ate them up, I walked through it. It nibbled on my clothes and scorched my skin, but I was reborn. The men dropped to the floor, desperately trying to put it out as I stepped over them.

I grasped lamp after lamp and threw them behind me into the growing blaze.

My heart was in my ears, the very heat of the flames *roaring* inside me. I *was* the fire, devouring everything in my path. Smoke wafted through the floorboards to the upper deck, engulfing the close quarters in a thick haze.

I grasped Frey's bloodied pendant in my hand and ran as fast as I could to the brig. Noises of panic filled my ears as fire devoured the wood.

"Abandon ship! Abandon ship!"

I swung the hatch open to see Seymour trying every key he had to unlock Frey from the cell wall. He coughed, folding his jacket over his mouth, visibly blanching when he saw me. "You set the ship on fire!"

"Are you ready to get the boot off your neck?" I asked, walking directly into Frey's cell.

"He's not waking up," Seymour said, shaking Frey, but he only winced, not opening his eyes.

"Move," I commanded. I grasped the collar and the draconite shattered almost instantly, whispers of the trapped spirits thanking me before evaporating above us. The cuffs were made of the same material, so they were also destroyed easily in my grip.

"That's why they didn't want you touching it," Seymour realized, mouth agape.

I grabbed both of Frey's shoulders. He was saturated with sweat and still burning up. "Get up."

Slowly, his eyes fluttered open as he deliriously whispered, "Were you crying over me, Princess?"

"Get up," I ordered, shoving at his shoulders, the lavender skin slick with sweat and grime. Smoke flooded into the room, and I had to repress a cough as the fire began to eat through the wall.

"Leave me," Frey murmured as his eyes fluttered closed again. "I'm finished, *ylgr*."

"Look at me!" I demanded, grabbing his face to forcefully jerk his head up to meet my gaze. "If you die, I will go to Death's domain and *drag you kicking and screaming* off their fucking boat."

"Don't threaten me with a good time," he coughed out as the smoke thickened.

"Stop flirting with me and get the fuck up." I dangled his marital pendant right in front of him. "Don't you want this back?"

Frey's yellow eyes flashed to the pendant and then back to me with newfound determination. He nodded. "Help me."

I fell to my knees and got him to curl one of his arms around my shoulders. "Seymour! Other side."

Seymour didn't hesitate, helping me hoist Frey to his feet. The flames devoured the brig as we climbed the steps up the hatch. The fire wreaked havoc on the upper deck as the chain of command fell apart. Officers abandoned their posts, and cabin boys struggled to find a rowboat.

Several men were thrown overboard to make room for Nathaniel on one of the boats. "Get Maeve! Find her!" he ordered.

I looked over the side of the half wall, loving the cool, salty breeze as the moon shone down on us. Seeing the Ivory Keys port on the edge of the horizon, I took a deep breath. We could make that swim. It wouldn't be easy, but we could let the waves do most of the work.

As Seymour and I carried Frey to the side of the ship, I caught the gaze of the lieutenant. The one who protected cabin boys and stopped Adams from assaulting me several times. He stared at me for a long moment before turning his back to me as if saying, *"Go. I didn't see anything."*

Without waiting another moment, all three of us jumped overboard.

18

RONIN MURDOCH

A CALL TO ACTION

WE GATHERED OUR FORCES. ALL AROUND THE COVE, townspeople—various crews, young and old, bakers, and fishermen—lined up for orders.

We stood as one. Merrow, pirates, former soldiers, refugees—it didn't matter.

My gunnery crew dressed them in our gear. Sashes and thick leathers. Cutlasses and pistols. Siggi fashioned a pin for us as something like an insignia, a dragon crest like my family coat of arms. My throat thickened as I remembered the moment when Siggi presented it to me.

It wasn't the same, but it was *mine*.

Pinning the embroidery to my vest made everything real. For better or worse, I represented every single fucking thing that opposed the monarchy. I was going to lead us on a charge to get our home back from the clutches of tyranny.

We would either fail and die, or we'd rise.

But from where I was standing, there was only one fucking option.

I watched Luella, Andra, and Udine wind through the ranks throughout the cove, handing out the coat of arms—an unspoken request for loyalty, but a choice like everything else. I'd never force a sailor to join my ranks.

I wasn't asking for mindless soldiers. I didn't want puppets or pawns. My fighters believed in the message of rebellion. They believed we deserved better than to be cast aside as criminals. The nobles were going to learn that they were only as strong as the promises they'd kept.

It felt as it did before I'd command the seizure of a merchant ship. Fear was our greatest weapon, so a few sailors would outfit themselves with razor teeth or wear jewelry made of bones. Ash around their eyes or a berry stain over their mouths. Anything to intimidate a ship into surrendering.

Most of the time, it worked. I never spilled blood unless necessary, and I intended to do the same today. But it didn't matter what my intentions were. Casualties, both the pirate hunters and those under my charge, were unavoidable.

I looked around the cove from the top deck of *The Ollipheist*, and I knew this would be the last time I saw some of their faces. These people were pledging their life to me, and by the fucking Gods, I was going to make it count.

Down the pier, I caught sight of the last person I wanted to see weaving through the bodies to the gangway.

Isa.

In truth, I'd been avoiding her. Andra and Luella still stayed with her to help with the orphaned children in the night, but I made myself scarce. I knew she didn't want to see me. Not when she blamed me for Wesley.

I blamed myself too.

By now, she would've heard the news that Wesley was alive. Andra tried to convince me to speak with her, but I couldn't. I didn't want to make promises of bringing Wesley back that would be empty if I failed.

Isa maneuvered up the gangway, eyes locked on me. She

wasn't dressed in her usual attire—a long skirt and a comfortable blouse to keep up with the kids. No, she wore leathered pants, a sash housing a butcher's knife, and one of Wesley's bandannas wrapped around a coarse poof on top of her head.

Fuck no.

"You're not coming," I stated before she got up to the deck.

"I'm getting my husband back," Isa declared, climbing onto the deck. "Why didn't you tell me he's alive?"

I narrowed my eyes. "I'm respecting your wishes to stay away."

Isa gave it back to me immediately. "That's bullshit, and you know it."

With a quick glance around the deck, I repeated, "You're not coming."

"Gods, you're such a prick! Why are you always such a prick?" she asked with exasperation. "I'm going with or without your approval. I thought you should know—"

"*You're not coming!*" I shouted, straightening my back to tower over her more than usual. My wings fluttered as a flush of anger came over me. At her or myself, I couldn't be sure. "I will not be repeating myself again, Isa."

She reeled back in surprise before pressing her tongue into her cheek, eyes set and blazing. "You did *not* raise your voice at me."

I shut my eyes for a moment, calming myself with a heavy breath before I finally said, "Wesley will have my fucking head if anything happens to you. He ended up in that position because of me, and I'll be damned if you get hurt too."

Her eyes softened. "I won't get hurt."

"Do you realize how quickly this could all go sideways? I will not leave your children without their parents." Then I admitted, "I didn't tell you because it would be so much easier to bring your husband back than give you false hope."

"What I said to you was unfair. I know that. But I heard Wes was hurt—hurt *bad*. I need to be there, Levi." Isa turned away with a sense of finality. "He's my one and only. I'm sure you understand."

I did.

"I can't change your mind," I said, realizing it was true. "But if you're dead set on this, you will not leave Luella's or Andra's side. Do you understand me?"

Isa smiled softly, the sides of her two-toned lips pulling at the corners. "They're the ones who told me to clear it with you first. For the record, those pirate hunters are going to lay down their weapons the moment they see you."

"I hope so," I murmured. "Now get out of here before I have you thrown into the pit for safekeeping."

Knowing I was completely serious, she turned on her heel and darted down the gangway.

I glanced up at the sky toward the sun sinking on the horizon. Night was quickly approaching, which meant it would soon be time to strike.

My forces gathered around *The Ollipheist*. In the orange light of the setting sun, I gave one more call to arms. We were an army of barely a few hundred, but it was enough.

It had to be enough.

I cleared my throat as Luella and Andra came to either side of me. Nearby, Udine was awaiting my final order for her warriors. Eyes gazed up at me from the pier and the hill around the cove.

If this is the last thing they hear, make it count.

"The tyrants of Farlight Isles have chased us for as long as I can remember. They cage us to the far corner of the Isles, and when we make it our slice of paradise, free from the monarchy, Pike takes it from us."

The crowd murmured in agreement.

"They've conscripted us. They've killed our families. They've pushed us to the point that we have nowhere else to run. I say *enough*. I'm done running. I'm done hiding. I'm done letting these bastards take whatever they want without consequence," I stated, voice growing louder as hums of approval bolstered my spirit.

"Enough!" some called out, raising their fists.

"Today, we show them who they're fucking with. They took our home, our people, and today, we pay them back by taking Farlight Isles, starting with Shipwreck Bay. Are you ready to stand up?"

Rallying cries tore through Anchorage Cove.

I looked at my mates, at Udine, and we shared a look of understanding.

No more talk.

It was time for action.

With my wings outstretched, I launched toward the sky.

19

RONIN MURDOCH

SURRENDER OR DIE

THE WIND LAPPING AT MY FACE, I CUT THROUGH THE AIR AS easily as I cut through the water. My hair whipped back and forth as I was met with an overwhelming sense of freedom. It was one thing to be in the water, embraced by the waves, but it was another altogether to be untethered from the ground, from the sea.

As I flew above the towers, exactly where Robbie had shown me, it was tempting to take them out before my ground force got here, but that would alert them. I had to do this quietly to give my people the best advantage.

I couldn't count on reinforcements.

This would either solidify me as the leader, or it would shatter any faith they had in me.

A waxing moon cast my shadow on the ground below me. I could feel a subtle pull, but not as strong as when it was full and round in the sky. Orange flames from torches gave away the positions of the guards lining the towers.

My forces hid in the dark, unseen by the pirate hunters. They were waiting for my signal. Torches and oil lamps lined the port town, where I could see the wreckage in piles along the roads as if they were starting to clean it up to make room for more towers.

Mass graves were dug in the farmland behind the town. From my vantage point, I could see the uncovered bodies. Lives lost pointlessly to maintain Cross's iron grip on the Isles. It made me sick.

Most of the town still lay in waste. A few houses and abandoned businesses stood among the debris like a farm untouched by a hurricane. Floods and violent winds swirled around them, destroying everything in their wake but the lone structure.

But even if it looked untouched from a distance, I knew the floor was rotted. Precious things inside had been damaged beyond repair. Like I was. But like that lone farm, I had to be a beacon of hope that we could recover. That the damage could be mended.

A beautiful lie.

Whatever had happened to me couldn't be fixed. I'd never be the same man I was before, but I'd do everything in my power to fix what *could* be salvaged. I'd build them up stronger than before, even if I remained the same damaged casualty of the storm.

This wasn't about me.

Mae had come to that realization a long time ago. Her light had rekindled some of the fire that smoldered inside me. My sole purpose was to make a world that Isa and Wesley's children could thrive in. A world that young men like Robbie didn't have to give their lives to maintain. A world that wouldn't take fathers before they had the chance to see the men their boys turned into.

If it killed me, so be it. I would die on my own terms, not tied to a table at Varric Cross's mercy.

The line of townhouses came into view. Robbie told me they had recently moved the hostages to the one with the garden terrace. Conway and Butcher's home. I tucked my wings behind me and landed with an impact.

"What was that?" I heard beneath me like whispers tickling my face.

In the water, I could feel the electrical impulses of anything around me, and while it was somewhat muted on land, those senses still gave me an edge. I didn't wait for them to find me. I went to the door of the terrace and tore it open.

The wood flew off the hinges as I tossed it behind me.

I'll pay Conway for that later.

A flurry of startled gasps rang through the air as I charged down the stairs. In the familiar common room, numerous people were on their knees, arms bound behind them. In a panic, the hostages looked up at me, and I caught both Lucky and Mama taking advantage of the momentary distraction to break from their bonds.

My mother was bound in ropes, but Lucky had more secure binds, cuffs that were made of some type of metal glittering black and blue.

Draconite.

Wesley was laid out on his chest, writhing in pain as he fought to look up at me and see what the commotion was. My heart clenched with a mixture of worry and anger. I wanted nothing more than to fly him out of this immediately.

But I couldn't. Not yet.

I could sense four hunters nearby, all reaching for their weapons. They balked, looking up at me, taking in my horns and wingspan. I flexed my shoulders and stared down at them, rising to my full height despite the low ceiling. The men shrank, hands shaking in fear around the hilts of their infantry swords.

"Surrender or die," I commanded through my teeth.

One of the hunters shrieked, "Monster!" before drawing their sword to slash through me.

I gripped it in a leathered claw, barely feeling the impact. I was sure it had nicked my palm, but a soaring sense of power came over me as I ripped it from their grasp while using my other hand to clasp their throat and hoist them up into the air.

"I don't repeat myself," I growled, killing them in an instant. I dropped their lifeless body onto the ground before turning my attention to the rest of the hunters. While I had their attention, Mama had broken out of her ropes and disarmed one of the other hunters.

She kicked them in the back of the knees, holding the blade to their throat. "Keys, now."

I narrowed my eyes at the remaining hunters. "*Now.*"

They tossed the keys to Mama, and she kicked them over to Lucky, who got to work unlocking himself as well as the other magic users who wore the same binds. After that, they slowly got to their knees, surrendering.

"Smart," I commented. "Tie them up."

One of the hostages obeyed instantly, not questioning me at all.

Mama looked up at me, eyes filling with teary emotions as she came forward and embraced me.

Any other time, I would've flinched, but I was relieved to see that she was all right despite the bruises that lined her face. At that moment, I forgot about my new form. She gazed at me the same way she always did.

"My boy," she sobbed, reaching up to cup my face. "Look at you."

I gave her a sheepish smile as I returned her embrace. "Get ready, Mama. We're taking this place back."

Several of the hostages were already disarming the soldiers and gathering weapons from around Conway's kitchen. Lucky rubbed his bruised wrists, not wasting time in getting over to Wesley and rolling him into a more comfortable position.

Wesley cried out in anguish, "Sit me up. Sit me up. I can't lie down." He squeezed his eyes together, finally falling slack in relief as Lucky leaned him against the wall. "Levi?"

"In the flesh," I said.

Wesley's eyes snapped open, and he looked me up and down. "What the fuck, mate?"

"I don't have time to explain, but I will."

"I can't walk," Wesley panted, sweat beading along his brow. "I-I can't *fucking* walk." The pain in his voice was palpable as he sat there, utterly exhausted in his misery.

"I don't need you to walk. I need you to stay alive," I demanded.

"Isa?" he asked.

"Alive. She's coming for you. I couldn't stop her," I said.

Tears spilled from the corners of his eyes in utter relief. "I don't suppose you could."

I turned my attention to some of the other hostages. "To get out of this alive, I need you to stand guard. Make sure these fuckers don't get away. Watch my friend."

One of the older townspeople said, "Aye. You can count on me, Captain Leviathan."

Next, I addressed Lucky, who was looking at me with a wide wolfish grin. "Are you ready?"

"To make these fuckers pay? Always," Lucky concurred. He stood up straight and murmured words of Antediluvian, delight etched all over his face when magic sparked between his fingers. "What are my orders?"

"Wait for my signal. We're going after commanding officers," I said.

Mama and Lucky shared a look before she said, "Good. I never forget a face."

"What's the signal?" Lucky asked.

"You'll know," I replied, turning to the front door and leaving as quietly as possible, closing the door behind me.

I listened closely to the pirate hunter conversations in the distance. A few dozen of them were crowded around a lopsided, almost fully completed structure in the center of town.

As I got closer, I knew exactly what was being built.

Gallows.

A bead of rage ignited in my chest as I sauntered toward the elevated stage, drawing the attention of a few pirate hunters here and there. I walked up each step with a heavy thud as eyes turned to me and shouts erupted all over the town.

I raised my claws and sliced through a cracking pillar meant to support the weight of everyone who would be hanged. The wood splintered and broke, crashing onto the ground. Over my years of pirating, some of my friends had been captured and hanged as examples, so this was cathartic for me.

I remembered being a teenager, hiding in a crowd, unable to do anything but say goodbye as sailors younger than me danced with Jack Ketch. The first time I'd seen gallows, against my mother's orders. Pirate hunters cheered when they kicked and squirmed, fighting for their lives. They didn't care. They just drank and fucked the bounty away.

That wasn't the last time I'd lost friends to hanging.

I couldn't do anything about it then… but I could now.

Leisurely, I continued my ministrations, waiting for hunters to surround me. Words of terror fluttered in the air along with sounds of concern and disbelief. They didn't know how I got into their camp. They didn't know what to do with me.

I noticed a few long coats shove their way through the

gathering crowd. *Commanding officers.* They moved with a sense of entitlement but paused the moment they saw me standing up here, all wings, horns, and teeth.

They could pretend to have control over the situation, but the fear in their eyes gave them away. The commanding officers—three or four of them—stared among themselves, daring one another to address me first.

"Surrender or die," I stated simply, my booming voice carrying over to the stragglers who were smart enough to keep their distance.

"What are you doing?" one of the commanding officers shrieked, taking a step back into the crowd and putting several men between them and me. "Kill it!"

The hesitation was loud.

"Why do something your superiors refuse to?"

"There's only one of it! Kill it!" another officer demanded.

More hesitation, and one of the officers shoved a soldier onto the steps. A boy nearly the same age as Robbie. The kid stood there, shaking as he reached for his blade, doubting his orders.

I looked over him at the officer. "Coward," I accused. I unclasped my vest and laid it on the stage, followed by my trousers. "I'll repeat myself *one more time.* Surrender or die," I commanded.

My dragon tattoo blazed as I called my leviathan forth. I extended my wings, flying into the air as it materialized completely. The massive beast enveloped me, shaking the ground as I landed back on the stage, letting it splinter beneath my feet.

As soon as I shifted, I knew I'd only be able to hold my form for a short period of time. Longer than I'd been able to before, but my power was still limited.

I threw my head back and *roared.*

On cue, screams erupted from the ships docked at the

port. Cannons splashed into the water as Udine and her merrow warriors rendered them useless. A horn blew in the distance as each of the towers collapsed in a haze of fire at the edge of the tree line.

Inside the townhouses, Lucky and Mama led a charge of hostages against their captors.

Some of the commanding officers shot their flintlock pistols into the crowd. A few of the bullets hit me, leaving small divots in my flesh, but nothing compared to how a cannon would've torn through me.

"Kill it! Kill it!"

More bullets flew into the crowd, hitting their own men as they tried to flee. Chaos bolstered the panic. I could hear the terror as soldiers went to their injured friends, enraged at their commanders.

It was the final straw.

As my forces came through the forest to the edge of town, the pirate hunters turned on their officers. Some of the hunters came after me, but a swat with my claw sent them flying. Exhaustion racked through me as I struggled to hold my form.

My leviathan slipped through my fingers as I shrank down into my half-dragon form again. I grasped at my chest, veering back to force myself onto my feet, refusing to show weakness even if it drained me.

A handful of soldiers came back at me, but I gathered my gear, ripping my cutlass from my vest. I met each of their attacks, holding them off as my forces flooded the town. We weren't many, but we were mighty. I used brute strength to shove my attackers off the stage, then took the brief reprieve to pull my trousers on, clasping my vest to my chest.

In the distance, I caught sight of Luella's red hair as she fought like a storm, Isa next to her. Andra wasn't far away, joining Mama to fight by her side. Blood muddied the cobblestone roads. Some of the pirate hunters shed their coats and were attacking one another.

"I won't play this game anymore!" one of the young men shouted, turning on the commanding officer who'd shoved him at my feet.

The officer didn't hesitate to kill him, but his treason emboldened several others.

But even with the infighting, they still outnumbered us.

Three men were rushing at Luella and Isa. A guttural shout came from Luella as she shoved Isa out of the way, taking a sword to the arm as she used her other one to keep Isa behind her. The crimson of her hair blended with the blood that flowed onto the cobblestone.

Men crowded around Mama and Lucky, and even with his magic, there were too many.

A cannon that the merrow hadn't dispatched rang out, hitting a cluster of people who became red mist and a tangle of limbs.

We weren't enough.

Boom!

Boom!

Boom!

It became a repeat of Pike's siege as a haze of helplessness swallowed me. But I couldn't let it. There had to be *something*. *Anything*.

I scanned the chaos, noticing a lieutenant trying to flee. His coat was longer than the others, and he was wearing a hat that dictated a rank far above everyone else's. I locked in on him and evaded other pirate hunters, propelling myself into the air.

I landed in front of him, cutlass drawn and ready to kill.

The lieutenant reeled back, looking between me and the carnage behind him. He steeled himself against my stare as his shoulders relaxed. He drew his sword, looking awfully smug. "It was a good attempt," he stated. "But you'll make a splendid trophy for my admiral."

"Is this worth dying for?" I asked. "You could surrender."

"I would die for the glory of my king. For the glory of Farlight Isles," he replied without missing a beat, as if he'd repeated the phrase over and over again in the presence of Cross.

He swung his sword, and I met it in a flurry of sparks.

"You would die for a leader who wouldn't remember your name after your sacrifice?" I inquired, swinging my cutlass and connecting with his blade.

He blinked but didn't reply as he tried to hit me again.

"You would fight for a leader who would never do the same for you?"

With a thick swallow and sweat beading on his brow, he fought to keep up with me.

"Why waste that talent when you can fight for *me*?"

His eyes glistened with doubt, his strikes faltering.

Suddenly, more cannon fire exploded from the distance, startling me as the lieutenant's eyes widened.

"Wait," he gasped as he blocked another strike.

I paused, and he dropped his sword in the dirt. I glanced over my shoulder toward the sea and saw a line of unmarked ships.

Ketches. Sloops. Smaller vessels like I'd see all over the Isles.

Reinforcements.

"I surrender," the lieutenant pleaded, putting both of his hands up as I looked back over at him. "I surrender."

A wave of emotion gripped me as I sheathed my sword. "Tell them that," I ordered, gesturing to the fighting that still ensued in the middle of town. I hoisted the lieutenant up into the air, outstretching my wings as he shouted in fright.

I dropped him onto the stage, then landed next to him.

"Stand down!" He scrambled up to his feet. "Stand down!"

As the reinforcements crowded the port, pirates of all creeds flooding the beaches, the pirate hunters laid down their weapons.

We'd won.

Finally, we won.

MAEVE CROSS

OUT OF THE PAN AND INTO THE FIRE

THE IMPACT OF HITTING THE WATER MADE ME DIZZY, THE waves pushing and pulling us against the ship. Frey slipped from my fingertips, sinking into the depths. Seymour split off, hitting the hull hard, the current churning like a meat grinder.

I could feel the fleeting gaze of the Reaper. The cold breath of Death. But I wouldn't let them claim either Frey or Seymour.

My lungs burned from the lack of oxygen as I kicked through the waves, one hand grasping Frey's as he sank and the other curling around Seymour's collar. I dragged them up to the surface with all the strength I could muster.

Adrenaline exploded through my system as all those swimming lessons came back to me. Ronin taught me how to hold my breath and let the waves do the work for me. He may not have saved my life when I drowned all those moons ago, but he saved my life when I dove off Nathaniel's ship.

Frey's wet braid slapped against my shoulder as he leaned heavily against me. Seymour regained his sense quickly once we breached the surface. He kicked his legs and propelled himself to the other side of Frey, and we worked together to drag the Skadian prince to the beach.

Gunshots echoed through the air as Nathaniel's voice boomed. The smell of acrid smoke flooded the sky as his ship burned and sank. Frey was horribly exhausted as he crawled across the sand, desperately holding on to his consciousness.

"Get up," I hissed, pulling Frey's arm across my shoulders. My legs shook, but I couldn't let the exhaustion get to me, not with the sound of gunshots and danger close by.

Nathaniel's voice carried over the water, and by its frenzied cadence, I knew he'd spotted us.

"I know a place we can go," Seymour said, gasping and struggling under the weight of his saturated jacket. He shed the sodden garment and then helped me with Frey despite his waterlogged trousers.

A rapid series of gunshots rang out, and on instinct, I spread my arms as wide as they could go and tackled both Seymour and Frey to the ground. "Get down!" Pain ripped up my back. I scrambled to my feet, biting down the agony as I tried to help Frey stand up again.

"Oh fuck," I hissed through my teeth, splaying my hand over my stomach where bullets had exited. Blood flooded down my legs. As resilient as I was, this was too much. My eyesight became fuzzy as I dropped to my knees, darkness eating at the corners of my eyes.

"Mae!" Frey grunted, struggling to his feet to grab me by my arms and hoist me up. But he wasn't strong enough. His body had been beaten and pushed past its limit.

The familiar chill of death licked at the nape of my neck, and I knew the Reaper wasn't far away.

"Mae! Get up! Come on, we just got off the ship. Only a little farther!" Frey demanded as both he and Seymour tried to carry me.

Nathaniel's voice got closer, accompanied by more gunshots.

"Seymour can't carry us both, Frey," I muttered through blood-streaked coughs. "I'm fucked."

"I'm not leaving you!" Frey hissed, trying and failing to support my weight.

All I could do was crumple back to the ground. The gunshots had killed me, and it was only a matter of time before Nathaniel took all of us.

With all my strength, I slapped a hand onto his shoulder. "I can't die, Frey, but you can." I glanced at Seymour. "I didn't drag your asses off that ship and out of the ocean to get you killed."

Pain pinched Frey's eyebrows together as both he and Seymour were forced to duck under another onslaught of ill-aimed bullets. "I need to save you, Mae. I promised."

"Little late for that. Find Ronin. He needs all the help he can get."

Frey tried to get me to my feet again, but it was no use. I was growing cold quick, and I wouldn't last long.

"He's going to kill me the moment he sees me."

A pained laugh racked my chest. "He might." I wheezed and coughed. "But you owe me this, Frey."

The Skadian prince stared at me for a long moment, an expression of helplessness unfolding across his face. "You have my word."

Seymour pulled Frey to his wobbly feet and said, "I know where we can find a boat."

Both men looked at me, and I sank deeper into the sand. The grit got stuck in my teeth. "Go. *Please.*"

I didn't have to say it again. They were gone, and the pain ebbed away into the peaceful reprieve that I couldn't help but miss. I didn't know where I'd be when I woke up, but I knew that when I did, the reprieve would be over.

Death was nowhere to be seen, but I still embraced whatever fleeting peace I had for however long the realm would let me.

ONE AT A TIME, MY LIMBS GREW HEAVY, A REMINDER THAT I was back in my body again. I felt something cold against my back, like a metal slab. My wrists and my ankles were bound in leather, limiting my movement as I tried to thrash my way out of it. The scent of blood was thick in the air, and I didn't know if it was mine or not.

Voices surrounded me, and I could instantly place them as Varric's and Nathaniel's.

"She *destroyed* my ship, Cross! She will pay for it!" Nathaniel snarled, and I heard an impact of metal on metal.

My eyes slowly opened, met by too-bright light as Nathaniel slammed a short dagger onto a silver plate atop a desk that was laid out with instruments I recognized from Varric's study back at Farlight Castle.

The ceiling was a flaking mural of golden filigree. As if once upon a time, someone had painstakingly painted their love of flowers only to be forgotten. Neglected. But the ghost of whoever lived there before still haunted the halls, horrified by what their haven had turned into.

Who painted it?

Varric was unmoved by Nathaniel's aggression, a velvet robe flowing off narrowed shoulders. "The fire started in the stern. Tell me why my daughter was in the back of the ship."

The younger man froze, icy eyes flickering from the blade up to Varric's unrelenting stare.

"Tell me why you bring Maeve to me, riddled with bullets and covered in blood—"

"She escaped! How else was I supposed to—"

Varric muttered in Antediluvian, and Nathaniel's voice was instantly silenced like an invisible thread had knit his lips closed. "Do not interrupt me, *boy*. My daughter is drenched in filth. So much of it that the ocean herself couldn't wash it away. I warned you to not let harm come to her—and *look at her*."

Nathaniel gulped thickly, eyes gleaming with thinly veiled terror. Then Varric's amulet stopped glowing, and Nathaniel's lips parted.

"You are permitted to speak, but choose your next words carefully."

The lord reeled back, scoffing loudly. "I have an army, Cross. Don't forget who you speak to. You need me."

A gray eyebrow arched, and Varric tilted his head to the side in a way that chilled me to the bone. Then he laughed. A barking, mocking laugh. "I don't need you whole, boy." Another Antediluvian phrase left Varric's lips as his amulet glowed. He drew his hands up like a puppeteer manipulating a marionette.

Fear blew Nathaniel's eyes wide open as his hands drew up without his control. He reached for his own blade and brought it up to his throat, carefully nicking the side of his neck. A single ruby-red droplet slid down.

The next words Varric spoke also left Nathaniel's mouth at the same time in perfect synchronicity.

"The moment you exhaust your use, I'll bleed you like a pig. I've tolerated your compulsions, but you're under the impression that you're untouchable. You, Nathaniel, are temporary. You may have armies, but don't forget who has *power*. You are merely a body I can puppeteer."

In an instant, Varric released Nathaniel, and he clattered to the ground, grasping at the bleeding wound in his neck.

Nathaniel panted like a trapped animal, huffing, "My father—"

"Views you as a failure just like I do," Varric finished. "Let me tell you what I expect from you if you value your free will."

Nathaniel swallowed, barely maintaining his composure as he got to his feet. "Yes, Your Majesty?"

Varric glanced over at me, those stormy eyes meeting mine before he ordered, "You will put Maeve in one of your finest rooms. You will dress her in your finest silks. You will feed her your finest dishes. And you will not lay a finger on her. Do you understand me?"

"I understand," Nathaniel croaked.

"Be gone, then. Maeve is my most prized possession, and I'll be damned if any harm comes to her. Not by you, and not by your crooked men," Varric commanded, turning his back to Nathaniel and grabbing a tray of his instruments before coming toward me.

Always a possession....

Varric's words confused me, making me feel this odd combination of feeling worthy of his attention and hating it. It brought me back to when I was a child—butting heads with Varric, but at the same time, wanting him to love and approve of me.

I was always vying for his approval back then, and it appeared that even now, I still wanted it. I craved that moment of elation when my father told me he was proud of me. It was something I never had. Even as I stared at this evil man, who *stole* me from a loving family, he was still the closest thing to a father I'd ever had.

For a split second, it looked like Nathaniel entertained the idea of sliding his dagger into Varric's back but thought better of it. He left, slamming the door behind him.

"Welcome back, Maeve," Varric said, sitting in a chair by my side. He still wore that crown, the white gold embedded in his silvery curls.

At the edge of the tray, I noticed a familiar blue vial of vitrophine clicked into a syringe. He picked it up and injected it into my arm. "This should help with any pain," Varric said, laying it back down on the tray.

My mouth moved to say, *"Thank you,"* but I swallowed it down. I wouldn't thank him for the Hells he was about to put me through.

"What happened to you on Nathaniel's ship, Maeve?" Varric asked.

I narrowed my eyes. "What do you think happened to me?"

He picked up an instrument to prick my arm to see if I'd react. I winced, and he put it back down. "I didn't want that."

Emotion filled my eyes as my chest tightened. I averted my gaze, not saying a word.

He hummed and opened a journal, then ticked a few things before turning his attention back to me. "Perhaps if you had obeyed, none of this would have happened. Subservience would have saved you all this pain."

"Burn in the Nine Hells," I hissed. "If you wanted a daughter to bow her head, you shouldn't have stolen me."

"Any treasure comes with a price. Tell me if you still feel pain."

Before I could reply, he pricked my arm again, and I flinched.

"Not yet," Varric murmured. "You have been the greatest challenge, Maeve. Constantly disrupting my plans. Right before I had my leviathan prize, you plucked him away. Then I have a Skadian heir with an entire kingdom hunting for him eating out of my palm, and you release him."

I fought a smile. "You can't find him," I stated matter-of-factly.

He frowned, tapping his fingers against the metal tray.

I huffed a soft laugh. "Good. You won't be getting anything out of me either."

Then a smile curled the corners of his mouth like he was a cat who had caught the canary. He tilted his head to the side and asked, "What am I supposed to tell his wife, Maeve?"

His wife? "What?"

Varric leaned forward, smiling in a way that told me he knew so much more than I did. "Yes, his wife. High Sorceress Elinora. I was going to get her to agree to close the gap between Algar and Farlight for the return of her husband."

"She's dead."

"Oh, yes. He thinks that." Varric turned around with a flourished wave of a spindly hand. "Who am I to correct him?"

All that grief Frey carried with him was for nothing. He suffered. He was misled.

All for *nothing.*

Varric used him.

"You bastard," I muttered.

"You can find a better insult, surely," Varric commented. "I went through all the trouble of having Thallan poison the sorceress to bargain my antidote. But instead, Thallan dropped the antidote and gave me a very testy, insubordinate prince."

"Does she know what Nathaniel did to him?" I asked.

Varric's eyes flared, something sounding akin to a growl leaving his lips. "Tell me."

As I lay there, I told Varric everything I witnessed happen to Frey. In gruesome detail. I documented every piercing Adams ripped out. His broken ribs. His fever that almost claimed him. How we suffered side by side.

I left out the part where he became my unlikely friend in a cold place, but by Varric's gaze, he could tell I'd grown fond of Frey.

"I will handle Pike after we're finished," he vowed. "Does this still hurt?"

He pricked me again, and I flinched. The anesthetic wasn't working on me. Varric went back to the desk and opened a drawer for more vitrophine. He tried another vial, injecting me with it. My head went light for a moment, but then it was gone in an instant.

Varric looked down at me and sighed. "Your blood filters it out." He hung his head, sitting back in his seat. "I regret what comes next."

Panic flared in my chest as I looked around the unfamiliar room, searching for a distraction. "Where am I?"

"The Ivory Keys. You know Farlight Castle too well. I can't handle another prison break before I get what I need from you." Varric took a needle and jabbed it into my arm, pulling the plunger to fill a vial with blood. "I hope your power is in your blood."

I tensed as he took the vial away to examine it. "What do you want from me?"

"If I can't have your powers by will, then I will take them by force." He placed the blood into a larger piece of alchemy equipment, but as soon as he did, it turned to dust.

No, not dust. It turned into *soot and ash.*

His shoulders slackened. "I will spare you every mercy I can. Despite your disloyalty, I don't wish you more suffering."

As I gazed over his tray of instruments, I knew what was going to happen next. "Please—"

"I'm sorry, Maeve, but I will take what I need." Varric gathered a pointed instrument from the tray. "Do you remember when I told you that one day, I was going to find out what was behind your eyes?"

I stiffened, my breath coming out in fast pants.

"This will not hurt me as much as it will you, but it gives me no pleasure."

My screams echoed through the walls as agony swallowed me.

PART II
A PRETTY CAGE AND A RUINED CITY

MAEVE CROSS

A NEW CAGE

I stood there in front of the mirror in my new cage.

Varric sat in a lounge chair beside me, watching as he ordered the barber to snip my hair away. He carefully snatched clumps of my hair to take with him for more experiments when the handmaidens weren't looking.

I refused to let the tears fall, my lower lip trembling.

"It was time for a change, Maeve," Varric said. "You look lovely with short hair."

My upper lip curled as my hands became fists. Finally, tears streamed down my cheeks. I couldn't hold them back anymore. More of my brown ringlets fell to the ground, completely altering how I saw myself.

"It's only hair, Maeve. Don't make a scene."

I could still feel the cut of Varric's scalpel. The needles where he'd plunged a thick syringe into my hip for my bone marrow. The piece of bone he shattered in my hand with a hammer before it came back together again.

When he dropped each new sample into the clear liquid swirling in a glass vessel, it turned to ash. With every piece of me he carved away, it felt gone forever, even as it reformed before my eyes.

Green velvet finery draped my figure, my irons replaced with ornate silver chains that served the same purpose. My freckled skin was scrubbed clean thanks to the handmaidens, right before they stuffed me into a corset, pulling the strings until every breath was shallow.

With purpose.

The tighter the corset, the less likely I was to fight back.

I flinched away from every touch, but the handmaidens didn't divert from their orders. Even when tears tracked down my face and I begged them to leave me alone, they didn't listen to me.

Needlelike hairs stuck to the nape of my neck. I didn't recognize myself anymore. Not with how much I'd changed. I looked prim and proper, the way I did before I stowed away, in a gown with freshly trimmed hair, jewelry dangling between my collarbones.

This was a fallacy. I was *never* this girl.

The honey in my eyes was dulled even if they were clear and glossy. My arms had lost some of the visible muscle I had, freckles faded from lack of sun. They painted red stain on my cheeks and lips because otherwise I was pale and lifeless.

My appearance was carefully coordinated. No one could see the scars I wore within my soul. I was unmarked on the outside, but the inside was full of bruises. Holes. Like I was a loose thread, waiting for the moment to unravel completely.

But Death was a talented tailor.

The longer I stared at myself in the mirror, the more I found myself asking...

Who is she?

"Stop touching me," I hissed through watery breaths.

The barber stepped away from me. The only person in

this fucking tower who had listened to me yet. He held his scissors up and waited.

"Finish it," Varric demanded. "Gods, Maeve. Don't be so hysterical."

Hysterical? I'll show him hysterical.

Rage boiled in my bones as my fist shot out, cracking the mirror, which sliced into my hand. Handmaidens gasped and fled from the room, but the barber remained, eyes wide, waiting for instruction.

"Leave us," Varric ordered.

The guard and barber left, looking spooked at my outburst. I stared down at my hand, at the glass embedded in my knuckles. For a moment, I felt normal. Like I wasn't gifted with unnatural healing.

My hand shook as Varric came over to cup it in his.

I tried to pull away, but Varric was stronger than he looked. He had aged considerably since I'd last seen him, with loose jowls and deeper wrinkles. Even his hands had more sunspots, the thin skin giving way to skeletal fingers.

But he didn't let go of me. He held my hand tightly as he plucked a jagged piece of glass from my knuckles and watched the skin stitch itself back together.

"Do you want to see the sun again? Do you want to feel the warmth of it? Do you want to smell the sea?" Varric asked, grasping my chin and drawing my face up to look him in the eyes. Even if his skin had aged, his eyes were full of clarity, like a vindictive soul trapped in a weakening body. "Behave."

"Never," I hissed, finally ripping myself away from him but unable to get much farther from the bed, where my silver chains were connected.

"What a pity," Varric sighed, pulling away to move toward the door.

I tried to pursue him as rage darkened into malice inside

me, but the chains didn't give me much clearance, leaving me trapped.

He opened the door to address the guards outside. "Don't mind my daughter. The pirates did quite the number on her," Varric said before lowering his voice. "Between us, she barely knows reality from her delusions. Be kind to her."

My upper lip twitched into a snarl. With that carefully placed lie, he successfully invalidated everything I could possibly say.

"Replace that mirror. I wouldn't want the poor thing to hurt herself."

I stared at myself in the shattered mirror and touched my hair. I hated it.

Tears spilled down my cheeks.

I don't recognize myself.

Fuck this.

Fuck you.

My nostrils flared as I swallowed a bout of white-hot rage. I glanced down at the haphazard pile of bloodied glass shards and snatched one, tucking it into my corset before the guards took it away. It wasn't much, but I'd slice Nathaniel's throat before he touched me.

Before *anyone* touched me.

I looked around my room, feeling like a rat trapped in a cage. The bed was made with fresh linens. There was one window, locked with dusty shutters. The wardrobe was filled with robes and expensive dresses. It was a wonderful ruse to fool anyone into thinking I wasn't taken to Varric's study every night and subjected to ever-increasing horrors.

No one would be able to tell that he'd taken my eyes just for them to become ash on his table. No one would know how much he'd stolen from me. Every time he took a piece of me, it would return good as new.

But I still knew how it felt to have it taken.

Just like during my youth, Varric always found a way to take things from me and fool everyone else into thinking he'd given me the world. He even fooled himself.

I was really sick of having everything taken from me.

My home, my friends, my love. All of it was gone. What was left?

Me.

No one is going to save you....

The intrusive thought filled my mind, but I reminded myself that Ronin couldn't save me without turning his back on everyone else. I could forgive him for choosing our family, but I could *never* forgive him for choosing me.

I didn't need anyone to save me.

I gulped hard, wiping the tears from my cheeks. I would get out of this, but it gave me the unique opportunity to figure out what Varric was planning. Then I'd get back to where I belonged. To my family and the man I loved with everything in my heart.

Out of the corner of my eye, I saw something move. I sought it out, only to see a hole in the wall and movement of something behind it.

"Are... are you all right?" a soft voice asked, all whispery and feminine. "I-I can hear you crying, and... I-I just wanted to be sure," she stammered.

I stepped away from the mirror, following the voice to the hole in the wall. It was right behind my bed, not hidden by the flat headboard.

"I-I have guards outside my door, too, but I-I—" She took a deep breath, trying to quell her stuttering. "There aren't many other women in the castle aside from the handmaidens. And they aren't allowed to speak to me."

"Who are you?" I asked quietly, trying to get a good look at her, but all I could see was her shadow.

"Penelope Bristol." She quickly corrected herself. "I-I mean Pike! Penelope Pike."

Nathaniel's new wife. The realization filled me with dread. "Are *you* all right, Penelope?"

She laughed nervously. "I-I asked you first."

"I'm probably as all right as you are," I answered. "I'm Mae."

She gasped, and there was a clatter on the other side of the wall. "I can't talk to you."

"But we're already talking."

The fear in her voice was palpable when she said, "He's coming. I *can't* talk to you."

Through the wall, I heard the door slam open. Penelope made a noise of shock as I heard a loud bang. My heart raced, and I pressed my ear to the wall.

"Did I hear you speaking, my sweet?" Nathaniel asked. His voice was full of false tenderness, and I heard a feminine gasp of pain. "Making new friends, are we?"

"No. No. I-I was only speaking to myself," Penelope replied, her voice trembling.

A thickness rose in my throat.

She was terrified.

"I require your services in my bedchamber tonight," Nathaniel told her. "Remember what happens if you refuse."

She emitted a soft cry. "Y-Yes."

"Don't cry yet, darling. It takes the fun out of it." No kindness in his tone. "Tonight, I expect you to service me in front of the court. I crave an audience."

"Please. Not again. I-It's indecent," she whispered, voice shaking as it got caught on the consonants.

"Consider it punishment for *lying*. Then everyone can see how *indecent* my pretty wife can be."

Penelope sputtered, "I-I-I—"

"Shh, I expected as much. It's in a bird's nature to sing."

She made another noise of pain.

"But you only sing for me. The woman in the next room is not your friend. She will turn you against me. I am the only one who can protect your family. Without my coin, they *drown*. Do you want your little brothers hung by their toes like debtors? Bled like suckling pigs? Or what about Caine? You'd like to see him again, wouldn't you?"

She didn't say anything, but I could hear her panicked breathing.

"That's what I thought." His voice lowered. "Then *be good*."

I listened closely to the heavy footsteps leaving, the door closing and locking behind him.

"Penelope?" I asked softly.

I heard a ragged intake of breath followed by a muffled sob.

"Pen… Penelope?" I tried again, my heart aching more deeply the longer I listened to her cries.

"Please," she pleaded. "L-Leave me alone."

So, I did. I pressed my palm against the plaster and listened to her cry, wanting nothing more than to take her away from this place.

I will save you, Penelope.

22

RONIN MURDOCH

THE AFTERMATH

THE FIRST THING WE DID WAS CLEAR THE BUILDINGS.

We took pirate hunters into custody in a makeshift cell block within one of the numerous empty barns. I didn't know what happened to the livestock, whether they were slaughtered or ran into the thicket. Either way, food was a priority.

I could coordinate supplies with Conway and Butcher's help. Scavenge the ships. Put the fishermen to work off the reefs.

Nothing about this was easy, but it was possible.

Some homes stood the test of the siege, while others were reduced to rubble. Most of the homes, like this one, were somewhere in between. I stared up at the holes in the ceiling through which cannonballs had crushed precious keepsakes. Rainwater flooded parts of the kitchen.

Out of the corner of my eye, I noticed children's toys covered in soot and muck.

I swallowed a lump of pain. Lives lost. Innocents wiped from this world much more easily than they were brought into it. *Fuck*. Slowly, I stepped toward a wooden boat, a stuffed bear saturated in filth. A trickle of despair licked at the back of my neck.

Then I heard something. A muffled *tap, tap, tap* beneath a collapsed bookshelf. I moved quickly, clutching the bookshelf with my claws and lifting it clear of a concealed trapdoor.

"Is anyone there?" I asked, hope swelling inside me.

The hatch clicked and rose.

"You can come out. It's safe," I promised, curling my fingers around the wood to lift it all the way. A smile pulled at my lips, and I tried my hardest to look approachable.

Round blue eyes met mine, and the small child let out a noise of surprise and a shout of fear followed by wailing and tears. They couldn't have been older than six. Just a little thing.

"No, no, no! It's okay!" I tried to soothe them, looking back at the toys and scrambling to grab one. I presented them with the stuffed bear, and they hesitantly accepted it. "I'm not going to hurt you."

They rubbed their nose. "Why do you look like that?"

I held out a clawed hand to help them out of their hiding place. I knelt down as much as I could to seem smaller than I was. "Well, I'm a leviathan."

"You're scary."

"I know," I said softly. "I had to be scarier than the pirate hunters."

"I bet you scared them good." They blinked, tilting their head to the side. "Where's my mama? Daddy? They tried to find food for me. I'm so hungry."

"I don't know," I answered honestly. "We'll find them."

Behind me, I heard shuffling. I glanced over my shoulder to see Pinky. He was caked in blood and muck, but when he saw the child, his eyes softened. "Hey, little one."

"Would you take them to get something to eat? I can hear their belly rumbling from here."

In response, their stomach grumbled loudly. I smiled and guided the child toward Pinky.

"Of course, Levi," Pinky replied, gently placing his hand on the child's shoulder to guide them out the door and to the other survivors. "But there's something you need to see in the field behind town."

His tone told me I wasn't going to like it.

I dipped my head, standing up to my full height.

The child's eyes widened, noticing my wings. I could see a million questions light up their eyes, but before they could ask, Pinky led them away. "Come on, you. Cap is a busy man."

As I traversed the cobblestone streets, I watched my sailors find more townspeople who had hidden in their cellars and attics. Neighbors, friends, and families were reunited. Relief rang through the town with the hope that they could rebuild.

It wasn't difficult to find what Pinky wanted to show me.

My gunner knelt beside a pit dug into a field where crops were once grown for the farmers' market. Grayed limbs were tangled together inside it, bodies of all the casualties that occurred when Pike took Shipwreck Bay. I hardly recognized a few of the faces with the light gone from their eyes.

When you see one body, you've seen them all.

That didn't prevent the pain that unfurled in my chest as I remembered them for who they were. People I'd buy goods from or tavern-goers I'd gamble with. After all the loss I'd endured, I would have hoped it'd get easier, but it never did.

My chest tightened, my heart hardening into a stone when I focused on Gunny. His back was shaking, silent sobs racking his chest as he reached forward and moved an arm out of the way, revealing a spider tattoo on a pallid, blood-smeared neck.

Spider had been on my crew so long that I'd forgotten a time without him. I took him in as a cabin boy when I grew into my captain's coat. He was eager to serve and eager for freedom. He had deserted the navy, as many of my crew had. Quiet as a mouse most of the time, but he had a heart of gold and went out of his way to take care of the cabin boys.

He welcomed Gunny with open arms and became one of Mae's early friends when she first came aboard.

I curled a hand around Gunny's shoulder. "I'm sorry, Gun."

He shook his head, voice trembling as he said, "He was right next to me, and then he was gone, Cap. Why didn't anyone find him?"

"I don't know," I said, looking over Spider's injuries. His body was covered in soot, blood caking his chest. Those wounds wouldn't have killed him instantly, but they would have eventually. His eyes gazed emptily at the early-morning sky. I didn't know how long Spider must have lain in the debris, waiting for help for it to never come.

I swallowed hard, fighting the dark spiral that threatened to claim me, because I knew exactly what that felt like.

"He must have been so scared," Gunny cried as he wet the base of his shirt with saliva to wipe away the grime on Spider's face, closing his eyes. "He needs a proper burial."

"They all do," I replied. "We'll give him the respect he deserves."

Gunny nodded as tears left tracks in the dirt down his face. "I can't lose any more friends, Cap." He pulled his knees up to his chest, staring at Spider among all the bodies. "I can't."

I squeezed his shoulder in a gesture of comfort. Guilt sat

heavily on my chest, and I hated that I put anyone in this situation. "I'm sorry."

With red eyes, he looked up at me. "I don't blame you for this. I know you're doing the best you can."

Emotion welled in my throat, but I repressed it, doing my damnedest to remain strong. But when I gazed at all those empty faces, it got so much harder. I took a deep, shaky breath and asked, "Do you need anything else?"

He shook his head. "Quiet."

I obeyed his wishes, leaving him to grieve in peace. All this loss bore down on my shoulders, making them slouch downward. This wouldn't be the first time I'd arranged the funeral rites, but it was the first one of this magnitude.

I'd never seen so many bodies at once.

Sickness crawled up my throat, and I turned off the main path and fought the urge to retch my guts out. When I was out of sight, I turned down an alleyway, leaning heavily against a townhouse to gather myself.

I braced myself against the brick with one arm, clenching my eyes shut as my mouth watered. I steeled myself with shallow swallows, breathing short and fast through my nose until the wave of nausea passed.

My eyes welled with tears, but I blinked them away, refusing to cry, refusing to succumb to the awful sensation of loss. Part of me held on to the hope that we'd find Spider or even Violetta in the wreckage, clinging to threads of life. But now that I'd seen Spider's body and found Violetta's jewelry decorating various pirate hunters, I had to accept that they were dead.

And now my mates were lying in the infirmary, facing permanent injuries.

No one was getting out of this war unscathed.

But I would hold this loss, this burden, this responsibility until the day I died.

"I was beginning to think you didn't have a heart, Leviathan," Bliss mused, pausing at the entryway of the alley.

I swallowed once more, ignoring the churning in my belly. I pinned them with a withering stare. "Is there something you need?"

Bliss didn't look at me as they glanced behind themself at the sailors and townspeople wheeling the dead to the back plot. Several of our people had already started digging graves in the cemetery, preparing for families to claim the bodies of those lost.

So much death. So much crimson.

"It might not feel like it, but this is a victory," Bliss said. "You led us to our first victory."

I remained silent, waiting for Bliss to finish their thought.

They exhaled, crossing their arms as they said, somewhat uncomfortably, "I hate to admit wrongdoing, but I regret my actions."

I knew that was the closest thing I'd ever get to an apology. "I appreciate that."

"I care for my own, Leviathan. I protect what I hold closely, but… this is bigger. This means something."

"You want in," I stated.

"*I want in,*" Bliss concurred. "I want to be part of something bigger."

I straightened my back, tilting my head to the side. "What I said still stands. You want in? Prove to me that you belong here." I stepped past Bliss to the side street. "If you don't mind, I have funeral rites to prepare."

Bliss's hand shot out to grasp my arm, stopping me in my tracks. I recoiled instantly, despising the sensation of *anyone* touching me. Especially the person who had pushed back every step of the way.

I glared at their hand, and they removed it.

Putting both their hands up in surrender, they stated, "Let

me handle this for you. I lost countless sailors when I took Fisherman's Gully. I will prove to you that I deserve a seat at the table."

I sized Bliss up, looking up and down their stout physique. Blood still stained their garments from the battle. The round frames of their glasses didn't soften the determined gleam in their golden eyes. "Take Pinky. I also want all stolen jewelry and heirlooms reclaimed from the pirate hunters and given back to the families."

They dipped their head down. "Consider it done, *Captain*."

Their answer satisfied me, and as I stepped into the pathway fully, I called over my shoulder, "Report to me when you're done."

I STOOD OUTSIDE THE DOOR TO THE INFIRMARY.

It was an outfitted chapel that was big enough to house our wounded. I stared up at the steeple, a monument to those who followed the monotheistic God. One benevolent being who called all the shots. It was the same doctrine Pike followed, but he had priests wearing red robes and reading from a mistranslated holy book.

"Those who vex me will go into the next life dishonored and coinless..."

Conveniently mistranslated to put Pike and the nobles on a pedestal.

Anyone who knew any better knew it really said, *"Those who vex the coinless dishonor me far into the next life."* But who could blame them for falling in line when all they heard was the mistranslated text?

Faith wasn't a bad thing unless it was misplaced, and I

rather liked the way the Shipwreck Bay Chapel cared for the community.

Isa and Wesley got married here.

He insisted that I wear my finest clothing and my golden jewelry. This was back when I wore an ear piercing before it got ripped out during a raid. I reached up and touched the scar on my earlobe that had long faded.

So much had changed.

I remembered Wesley pacing back and forth, nervously reciting his vows so he wouldn't forget them. Maya was a few years old, and it was my job to make sure she scattered flower petals down the aisle. That little girl held my hand all day and babbled at me.

There weren't many opportunities to be around children as a pirate, so I did my best to not offend the little tornado. As much as I adored Maya, she stressed me out during the entirety of the wedding, but my discomfort was worth it to ensure that Isa and Wesley had a wonderful evening.

I thought I didn't want children. I'd be Uncle Levi, and I'd be happy with that fate.

But then I met my match in Mae.

As I looked back, I thought about how young we all were. Andra and I often competed for women. It was a game. We gambled with hearts as frequently as we gambled with coin. But when Isa walked down that aisle, and Wesley forgot all of his vows because he was so struck by her, I wondered if I'd ever have that.

Mae and I should be getting married in that chapel.

It shouldn't be housing countless injured. Wesley shouldn't be bound to a bed because his back was shattered. Isa shouldn't be kneeling beside him with tears in her eyes. My mother shouldn't be tending the bloodied and maimed sailors.

Luella shouldn't be lying in that bed after getting between Isa and a pirate hunter.

At the very least, if I was going to be here, Mae should be with me.

Gods, it would feel so much easier if she were here. My chest ached as I mourned everything I wanted. It carved out a piece of me to lay to rest like all the pieces that grieved the people I lost.

How much more was left of me?

I dreaded walking inside. I dreaded seeing my friends injured beyond repair. I dreaded seeing bloodstained white sheets covering the faces of those who'd succumbed to their wounds.

"By the way, I like the new look, kid."

I glanced over my shoulder to see Lucky with a bag full of supplies hanging off his shoulder. Despite our complicated history, I was relieved to see him. Bruises lined his temples, there was dried blood on his hands, but with his wide smile, he looked awfully radiant.

Thrilled to be alive.

"Help me, would you?" Lucky held out one of the bags of gauze and supplies that our reinforcements brought in.

"Aye," I said, taking it.

"Come on."

He opened the door for me, and I felt a wave of relief knowing I wouldn't be walking in alone. My mother was doing her rounds, not getting a lick of sleep because she knew people needed her more than she needed rest.

She took the supplies from us and hurried off, telling me where Wesley and Luella were and promising to speak to me later. Frankly, I was talked out, but I only nodded before Lucky and I went down the hall to the private room that they were being kept in.

I paused, reaching out and grabbing Lucky's arm before we went inside. "I'm going to need ships. A lot of ships."

He pursed his lips. "I don't have enough men, time, or materials to build galleons."

"What about ketches?"

He considered it. "If you can get me the manpower and three or four months, I can build a small fleet from scraps. Maybe even grow some lumber once my magic is rested. What comes after?"

The timeframe was less than ideal. I wanted to leave weeks ago, but a few months would be a sacrifice I'd have to make. "I want the Ivory Keys."

"The Ivory Keys or Pike's head on a stick?"

"Both," I replied.

Lucky grinned, looking pleased. "Then I'll start the plans." He glanced at the door. "But family has to come first. This is a victory. Let's enjoy it tonight."

I'd been working nonstop, but a night to celebrate our victory was worth the rest.

When I opened the door, Wesley smiled at me, and I could breathe easier knowing I had my best mate back. Beside him, Luella—pale-faced and bloody—gave me a wave with her good arm. Isa sat up beside her husband, genuinely happy to see me.

My feet moved before I could think about it, and I grasped Wesley's arm and leaned toward him in a familiar embrace.

He chuckled softly and clasped my arm back. "It's good to see you, too, mate." He looked over my shoulder. "And you, too, Lucky."

Lucky tipped his hat. "Alive to see another day."

I pulled away from Wesley, so relieved that he was here, alive. It felt like second nature to sink into the chair beside him as we caught up on everything that happened. Isa nodded along, preening her husband lovingly.

She was hard at work tidying Wesley's waves after weeks of unkempt tangles. He leaned against her chest as she whispered, "Let me take care of this for you, baby. I even brought one of your favorite bandannas."

With deep circles under his eyes, he gave her a radiant smile as if her tinkering alleviated all of his aches. "You know how to take care of me."

"Of course," Isa replied, using a generous coating of a pale salve that melted in her hands. Her face was dotted with blood and grime, but Wesley looked at her like she was the sun, the stars, and the wind whistling in his ears. "Let me take care of you before the kids tire you out."

He chuckled. "What I wouldn't give to hear their laughter right now."

"You say that now," Luella teased, and then she glanced over at me. "Hey, Levi. You see my wife anywhere?"

"Probably ordering the ship crew around," I answered.

"I love it when she's demanding," she replied.

Luella chimed in with stories of her own to catch Wesley up, like when she caught Robbie and scouted Shipwreck Bay with Bliss and Pinky.

While we didn't have drink or games to fill the time, we didn't need them. Lucky sat with us, smiling like we were his long-lost children. In a way, I supposed we were. It wasn't the perfect evening without Mae, Andra, Mama, or the kids, but we rejoiced because we were alive.

23

MAEVE CROSS

THE WOMAN IN THE MIRROR

I PLUMMETED DOWN INTO DEATH'S REALM AGAIN, A FINAL reprieve from Varric's blade in my gut as he fished around my insides. At some point, the pain was so potent that I succumbed to it completely.

This time, I spotted Death guiding souls gently into their rowboat to lead them into the next stage of the afterlife. The peaceful void was welcome, but as I gazed at Death's rowboat full of souls, I anxiously looked for Ronin, or any familiar face. I found none.

"Your family lives," Death reassured from behind me. "For now."

My shoulders slackened. "How are they? Do you know?"

Death gave me a warm smile, the skull flittering back and forth from under the hood of their robe. "They won."

I released a heavy breath even though the next one didn't fill my lungs the way it would have in my mortal form. "Thank the Gods."

"No need to thank us. We gave you the tools, but the craftsmanship is all you," Death said before adding, "I found something that might interest you. From your past life."

That intrigued me. "What did you find?"

"Watch," they replied.

Instantly, the realms split into mirrored shards, memories I remembered and some I didn't. The ground gave way into an abyss. At this point, I'd grown so accustomed to the darkness that I welcomed it with open arms.

The blurred images came together, enveloping me in a blanket of the past.

Farlight Castle came into focus, its walls bending around me to place me where it wanted to. Tapestries of leviathans hung from the walls, and the bustling of the staff filled my ears. It was right before a charity event.

I recalled that the Murdochs hosted one every year to support the local orphanage. A practice Varric got rid of the moment he took over.

A sentry strode through the halls, a longsword on her hip. The armor she wore sparkled with gold and blue, freshly polished. Her dark hair was braided under her helmet, pinned neatly into place. Across her back was a shield carved with the same coat of arms that decorated the walls.

She paused, looking back behind her suspiciously. The sentry didn't look like me. She wasn't freckled or brown-eyed. She was rather tall with wide shoulders accentuated by her armor.

But it didn't matter what her appearance was. She was me. Well, a version of me.

My eyebrows came together. Though I was completely on guard, I didn't grab the hilt of my sword.

Suddenly, two boys jumped out from behind a potted plant, one dark-haired ten-year-old and one blond thirteen-year-old. I knew them as Aiden and Martin. Two rambunctious little scamps. I was the only one on the sentry guard who'd indulge their games.

They also teased their younger brother, who was too small to keep up with them even if he tried.

I repressed a smile, not remotely surprised.

"Did we scare you?" the older one, Martin, asked.

I placed a hand over my heart and feigned shock. "You can't sneak up on me like that!"

The two boys laughed gleefully. "See, that's how you do it, Ronin! You can't announce yourself. You just jump out."

I turned to look at the youngest boy, who was wide-eyed and rocked on his heels, a dimpled smile stretched across his face. I wagged my finger, saying, "But don't frighten the wrong person."

It was jarring to see him like this. Just a happy little boy, clueless at the horror he would endure only a few months later. I knew him as a man, full of wounds that hadn't healed properly. This child was a stranger, but my heart ached to protect him, to save him from the pain he was doomed to suffer.

"Now, get out of here! Some of us have work to do," I teased.

As all three of the boys ran off, I shouted, "And put on those clothes your mother picked out for you!"

When they were out of sight, I walked to the desolated part of the castle where the court sorcerer—Varric—kept his study. I had been tasked with retrieving him for the event.

While the king's father had accepted the sorcerer willingly before his untimely death, there was something about him that put me on edge. I never liked him, though I tolerated him.

Now I realized I should never have tolerated him. I should've followed my instincts and rejected him, but my superiors told me not to make a scene and never to question the royals.

His door towered over me like an imposing force. A dark energy pulsated from the room. It was a sickly, cloyingly sweet sensation that made my stomach churn. It felt like rot. The sweet smell of a dying person's breath before their sickness took them.

I could hear Varric speaking to someone, and the returning voice echoed inhumanly. I leaned into the door but couldn't make out what they were saying.

I had a bad feeling, but I never ran away from danger. Slowly and as quietly as possible, I twisted the doorknob and opened it enough to sneak inside the dark room, where I caught sight of a large mirror. It looked like the one I'd seen in Varric's study many times, but this time it glowed, a figure within it coming in and out of focus.

"You need to get rid of the guards, love," the figure murmured, and Varric reacted to her voice as if she were touching him. He clearly reveled in it.

"All in due time. I only need Samuel Pike to weasel his way into the king's good graces," Varric replied softly. It was a tone I'd never heard from him before. He touched the mirror as if aching to caress the figure inside.

"Remember that this is your last body. You cannot afford to fail again," she warned. "You don't have another grandson."

"I'm well aware. I will not fail again. Not until we can walk among the ashes together. We will make them pay for what they did to us. For taking you away from me," he promised. "My queen."

"Then prove it to me. Harvest the children," the figure demanded.

I took a slow step backward, all my suspicions confirmed. I needed to get to the king quickly. The image of the Murdoch boys filled my mind. I wouldn't let Varric hurt them.

They were under my protection.

Get out. Get out now.

My armor creaked, and the figure's intense eyes darted up to me.

Godsdamnit!

"You have ears, my King of Ashes," her voice echoed, wrapping around me completely.

I spun on my heel and was darting toward the door when a familiar rush of magic seized me. Varric spoke Antediluvian words, and I lost the ability to run. Panic overtook me as all my muscles went stiff, and he suspended me in the air. Underneath his robes, something glowed blue.

"You foolish girl!" he hissed, dragging me back into the room to hold me right in front of the mirror. The air was sapped from my lungs as the magic forced its way down my throat, cutting off any breath.

The figure tsked. "Don't kill her. They'll notice if one of theirs goes missing. You're cleverer than that."

Varric tilted his head to the side, those stormy eyes filled with a wisdom that far surpassed his physical age. "You're right."

Another spell left his lips, something pulsing under his robes as I collapsed to the ground, dazed.

Varric straightened his robes and addressed the mirror once again.

The figure recited, "May ash rain above you."

"In your name," he returned, a brief sadness overcoming his expression before the figure vanished and it fell from his face.

On the ground, I stirred, grasping my temple. Varric looked down at me, no emotion behind his eyes. I jumped, startled at his proximity.

"You had quite the fall," he commented. "Are you all right, Sentry?"

I blinked, trying to recall what had happened before I walked down the hallway. How did I get into Varric's chambers? I didn't remember. He had taken the memory from me.

"Oh, I apologize, Court Sorcerer," I said, getting to my feet.

A sickness stirred in my belly, warning me that something was amiss, but I didn't know what it was.

"You should knock before you enter. That would've given me time to warn you about that crate on the floor," he stated, gesturing to a box that had tumbled to the side. "Is there something you needed?"

It felt wrong. Everything felt wrong, but I pushed it down and said, "The king is requesting an audience with you in the Great Hall before the event tonight."

Varric turned his back to me. "Ah, then tell him I will be there shortly."

"Right," I said, deeply put off as I made my way to the door. "Good day to you, sir."

The memory slipped away from me, vanishing into the ether as Death's realm came back into focus. Death stood before me, scythe strapped to their chest.

"Who was she?" I asked. "That figure."

Death tapped their chin, its hue a rich brown, contrasting the moonlit skin around their mouth. "A missing soul."

"That's all?"

"Very few evade Death. Even fewer can suspend their consciousness in a *between place*. She's who you need to find, Maeve. I need you to seize her soul for me."

She's Varric's weakness.

"I can try," I said. "Can I stay a little longer?"

Death nodded. "You can, but not forever." They turned to leave me to my own devices.

"Wait."

They paused. "Yes, child?"

"Can you show me something beautiful?" I asked, my heart aching so badly that I needed something to make me feel whole again.

Death tilted their head to the side, blinking slowly like a feline would. Even with the skull echoing through their dual-toned skin, there was something of a catlike curiosity about them. I thought about the times Lieutenant Commander Lazlo curled up in my lap and stared up at me. Ronin would watch like he wanted to save a portrait of me with his cat forever. He would knock the breath out of my lungs with his smile. I'd do anything to see those two dimples again. He would reach across my lap to pet Lazlo, but not before pinching my chin between his thumb and index finger to kiss me.

Gods, I missed him.

I missed his smile.

The way he felt.

The way he looked at me.

How he made me feel loved.

If he could kiss my trembling hands one fingertip at a time and brush my hair from my face, he'd take all the pain away. Even when I healed, the ghost of a blade shadowed my skin. I'd feel it until the day it took me away forever, but with only the brush of Ronin's lips, I'd forget it, even if just for a moment. He'd erase the torture, the soul-deep bruises. He'd soothe them all with the salve of his big hands.

I wanted to know what home felt like again.

"Can you… show me Ronin again?" I asked, throat feeling thick as I swallowed down watery heartbreak. "Not when he was a child. Like he is now."

Maybe when my heart broke this time, it wouldn't be because Ronin shut me out; it'd be because I couldn't bear being away from him anymore.

Death parted their lips, but I cut them off.

"Please."

"I can't," Death said quietly.

A sob broke from my lips. Seeing Ronin in the past had made me miss him more terribly. "Why not?"

"Your body is alive, Maeve. This vessel lives. I can't show you memories from your current life."

"I don't understand," I croaked. "I'm dead right now. I've died countless times since I last saw him. Why can't you show me something beautiful? Just once. I'm sick of seeing the dead. *Feeling* dead."

Death averted their eyes, and I couldn't tell if they pitied me or if I had annoyed them. "It's time to go back."

I shook my head desperately. "No. Please. Not yet."

"I will see you again," Death said, raising a moonlit hand to cup my cheek. "Goodbye for now."

As the ether surrounded me to lift me back into the land

of the living, I stepped out of their cold touch. "You made me your champion, but you've still damned me like everyone else has."

When I came back into my body again, Varric was muttering to himself, "Nothing. All ash."

He picked up the scalpel and sliced into my belly, repeating the cycle again.

And again.

Until I had nothing left.

At some point, I stopped fighting it.

24

RONIN MURDOCH

FUNERAL RITES

After burying countless sailors during my career as a captain, I thought funeral rites would get easier one day, but it never did. As I gazed upon the fresh graves as far as I could see, I saw all my failures.

There wasn't a single dry eye in the cemetery as visitors grabbed seashells, flowers, sea glass, or unpolished gems from a cache that Udine and the merrow had arranged. They laid them on the rich dirt adorned with a wooden plaque that listed the names of the fallen.

The small ornaments changed the cemetery into a treasure trove of color, bringing life into the field as a way to celebrate the full lives they'd lived, not the emptiness they left behind.

A hard lump formed in my throat, but I had to remind myself that Pike would've come for Shipwreck Bay with or without me here to defend it. As painful as all the loss was, it could've been a lot worse.

But I would honor each of them the way they deserved to be remembered.

I couldn't go to every service—it just wasn't possible—but

I still walked along the rows, laying gold coins beside the other offerings. A few of them were only adorned with my coin, but it was an injustice to leave them naked.

Taking my time, I paid my respects, offering my condolences to any family I passed. It was a long afternoon that hung heavily on me. A weight I would carry regardless of whether my knees buckled.

Bliss kept their word, creating a manifest to account for every lost soul, and families claimed their loved ones. Lucky and Bliss took possession of their fallen crew members, wrapping their bodies to ensure that they were safely returned home on the next ketch.

Slowly, I came up to Edgar Rivington's grave. I almost walked past it because I knew him as Spider. At the base of the wooden plaque, dusted with dirt, there was a set of bone pieces. Carved knucklebones and hooves.

Gunny was here.

I recognized the set as the one Gunny carved when we set course on that ketch to gather the monarchs. He always needed something to do with his hands, or he'd pick at his cuticles until they bled. There were times on *The Ollipheist* that I'd hear Spider chastise him for getting blood on his cards.

Gunny took up whittling shortly after and took great joy in carving a variety of things. Game pieces. Little animals. His name on the floor under his hammock. I remembered accidentally kicking over a little box full of trinkets when I was doing rounds.

Spider looked at me like I'd kicked his favorite puppy.

It wasn't until later that I learned from Luella that Spider never had much. His family was too poor to afford toys when he was a boy. Despite that, he always gave when he could. So when Gunny took it upon himself to make up for all those missed holidays, Spider finally had something that was only *his*.

I didn't know the man well. The ship was too big, and our differing ranks never allowed for much overlap. But from what I did know of Spider, I liked him. The gunnery crew had nothing but good things to say about him. And I remembered how Mae smiled when he'd chat her ear off during her rounds on *The Ollipheist*.

He'd be missed.

I reached into the pouch tied to one of my belt loops and plucked out a golden coin.

"I'm sorry I didn't know you better," I said as I placed my offering beside Gunny's.

Down the row, I noticed my mother standing in front of Luther's grave. She patted Butcher's arm as he and Conway paid their respects before leaving. When she turned, I waved at her.

With everything that'd happened, both of our plates remained full. We hadn't had the opportunity to talk, and with the cemetery thinning out, it seemed like a good time.

Mama dipped her head and came toward me, her fair white hair tied up with one of Wesley's bandannas. I knew that when she wasn't tending to the injured, she helped with the kids and all the extra hands at the homestead so Isa could be with Wesley.

None of us wanted him to be alone.

It was hard enough to recover from a back injury. It was even worse to do it while confined in a bed by yourself. Mama wasn't optimistic about Wesley's chances to walk again. She hadn't told him, but he already knew. It helped that Isa was prepared for the worst.

Andra and her nieces were at the homestead right now, helping Isa move furniture and fix up their bedroom to make it more accessible for him while he healed. Regardless of how long it took, Isa was ready.

When I visited, which wasn't often, it was a full house. Conway rocked Isa's chunky baby, Braxton, and played with the orphans as they did their damnedest to contribute. Whether it be gardening or helping Ellie with the chickens, they helped because it made everything feel normal.

Dina and Ellie—the youngest daughters—wanted me to fly them around, mystified by my wings. Maya liked my company while she wrote, pausing every once in a while to ask me if Wesley would like the story she was writing for him.

Then there was Lissy.

While a piano could accommodate my new strength and massive hands, my violin was too dainty. I knew that if I tried to play, I'd snap the strings, and my fingers were too big to carefully string it with new gut.

I really didn't want it to collect dust on my shelf, so I promised Lissy I'd teach her the violin like I taught her how to play piano. Her eyes rounded when she took the instrument from me. She vowed to keep it safe until I wanted it back.

"That all depends on you," I told her. "If you fall in love with it like I did, then it's yours."

I could see it meant the world to her, and that was payment enough. Plus, I was sure Isa appreciated all the new noise in her house. I was still Wesley's older brother, and I'd do whatever I could to irritate him until the day one of us died.

"Can I hug you?" my mother asked as she approached me. "I could use one."

I appreciated the ask. My aversion to touch wasn't as bad as it was, but every once in a while, I'd recoil at the phantom sensation of unwanted fingertips. "Come here," I said, reaching one arm around Mama's shoulders to bring her into an embrace.

She released a ragged sigh and pulled back to ruffle my hair. She had to get up on her tiptoes, so I bent at the waist to make it easier. Then I pecked her on the cheek like I used to before our lives fell apart.

A somewhat awkward silence fell between us, and I didn't know where to start.

"Andra told me Cliohde did this," she said, gesturing to my new form as she broke the silence.

"Practically pulled me out of bed in the middle of the night," I replied before I recalled something I noticed the day I rescued her. "You didn't seem overly surprised to see me like this."

Mama shook her head. "No. I saw illustrations when I was the tutor's assistant all those years ago. The Murdochs had a very extensive catalog of the family tree." Then she frowned, a blaze of anger coloring her cheeks pink. "Until Varric scorched the library. I could see the smoke from Albatross's pier. Then the rumors started, and no one could dispute them because everything was gone."

"You saw illustrations of this?"

"Your grandfather hated me, but he talked about how armies used to tremble at the mere sight of the men and women before him. I was curious, so I perused the catalogs. I never thought I'd see you like this, but you're an extraordinary man. Of course Cliohde took notice."

The pride in her voice caught me off guard. But she usually started with a compliment before she said what she wanted to.

"You haven't decided what to do with our prisoners," she stated.

"No, I haven't."

"They're going to want blood, Ronin." She searched my eyes. "And I know a piece of you wants that too."

I looked away from her. "I don't *just* want blood, Mama. I want to watch them choke on it."

But then I'd be no better than Pike or Cross. No judge. No jury. Just executioner.

My shoulders came up around my ears as tension squeezed my spine. Then I released a heavy breath, taking that tension right out of my body. "I hate what they stand for. What they represent. But it wouldn't be right, even though it'd be so much easier to kill them all."

"The crown is heavy for a reason." She straightened her back. "If you want the Ivory Keys—if you want *Mae*—then you need to show them that change is possible."

"I've shown mercy before and let Varric live," I recalled, looking directly at her. The warning bells had been ringing and the guards were flooding the dungeon, but I still let Varric walk away when he wouldn't have given me the same courtesy.

"Just because Varric squandered it doesn't mean it's not valuable. These people don't know anything else. Mercy is a gift." Mama patted me on the arm. "We won the battle, but now we need to win the war."

The whisper of an autumn wind blew around us, indicating that the seasons were going to change.

Has it really been that long since I've seen Mae? Since I've gotten a moment of peace?

"You're a good man, Ronin. You'll do what needs to be done. You always do," she said before turning around in the direction of the town. "I have to change Wraith's dressings. She's been up my ass about getting out of bed."

My mouth twitched. "Sounds like Wraith. How's her arm?" I'd seen Luella in bed, grouchy as all Hells, but I hadn't gotten a good look at her injury.

Mama shrugged. "Nasty slash, but elves rarely get infections. I'll let her leave if it looks good. Then she can be up *your* ass instead."

I chuckled. Luella needed to work like she needed to breathe. "Tell her she can find me at my cabin. I've got plenty of work for her."

She returned my laugh before asking, "Will I see you at Violetta's pyre tonight?"

"I'll be there."

Mama gave me a gentle smile and patted me on the arm before going down the row to pay her respects to another friend. And I continued on my own path, leaving offerings until every grave was adorned with a little gold.

25

RONIN MURDOCH

MERCY IS A GIFT

Pinky had arranged a lovely service for Violetta on the beach, not far from the tunnels, exactly how she would've wanted it, with expensive bourbon and her favorite flowers. Her body was perched on top of lavender and purple peonies that smelled fragrant and would cover the scent of the pyre when they burned.

I was early to the service, grasping Pinky's shoulder in a show of camaraderie and support.

"Thank you for being here, Levi," he said, wiping away some smudged kohl from the corner of his eye.

"I wouldn't miss it," I replied, taking a small leather pouch of coin from my vest to put it with the other offerings. I noticed fine jewelry, her feathered hat, and a long wine-red feathered robe. All her favorite things, several of which I'd recovered from what remained of her ship on the ocean floor or Pinky requested from the Haven.

"She'd do anything for coin," Pinky chuckled.

The corner of my mouth tipped up. "I know."

Despite the extensive damage the cannonballs and explosions had wreaked on her body, her face was wiped clean, eyes closed, her lips painted her shade of red, and she was dressed in a lavish violet gown. Subtle signs of decomposition showed—sunken eyes and stiff muscles—but her blood-curse slowed them, making her appear more freshly dead than she would have otherwise.

"Vee never had the chance to enjoy it," Pinky said as a few other people trickled in. "She always said it was too nice to wear. I couldn't think of a better occasion than now to send her off in it." His voice became watery as he released a heavy sigh.

"Do you need anything?" I asked.

He shook his head firmly. "No tears tonight, Levi. Tonight, we celebrate who she was. We tell our favorite stories. You can even tell that one where she charmed you into bed and robbed you blind."

I blinked, pressing my tongue into my cheek before chuckling, "No."

Pinky took that moment to laugh and then replied, "I thought you'd say that." He gulped, expression turning serious. "But in all seriousness, thank you."

"I already told you—"

"No." He put up a hand. "For giving me purpose. For not letting me wallow. Anything you need, Levi—I will be there. You have me. You have *The Lilac Queen*'s crew."

His request invigorated me, refilling me with a sense of certainty. "I will need you."

Pinky smiled and said, "I know. Walk with me."

I dipped my head, following beside him as he greeted the new guests. In fact, I stood nearby all night. Out of all the nights, this was the one that Pinky needed company most. He didn't say it outright, but I knew he appreciated it.

Lucky and Mama joined the service, as did Bliss and a handful of their crew. I chatted with my mates for a little while, sharing tales of Violetta's conquests and her clever schemes. There was laughter and tears of joy as we remembered all the best parts of Violetta.

After hours of stories and glasses filled with her favorite bourbon, Pinky lit the pyre, and we said goodbye to a friend, an ally, and one remarkable woman.

I LAY ON MY STOMACH WITH MY WINGS FOLDED BEHIND ME. I'D spent most of the night tossing and turning, dreaming of what it would be like to hold Mae again. But her pillow didn't smell like her anymore. It felt as if the longer she was gone, the more she disappeared.

Like I was losing that piece of me she carried forever.

I had small reminders of her all over my cabin. Her untouched toothbrush. Her linen shirt that still had a few buttons missing. The hat she wore the day she was stolen from me, still crushed and caked in dried mud, that I found shortly after we took Shipwreck Bay back. Her brooch in my desk drawer.

It wasn't enough. It would never be enough until I had her cradled in my arms.

Maybe then I could finally rest.

But there was no rest for men like me.

I gave up trying to sleep and sat up, swinging my legs off the bed before burying my face in my hands. I didn't want to wait anymore. I didn't want to hope that Mae would make her way back to me.

Cross and Pike were doing Gods knew what to her.

I tried not to think about it because whenever I did, it made me fucking furious. Mae was suffering, and I couldn't do a godsdamn thing about it without ships and without soldiers.

Not until now.

One battle had been won, but I'd lose the war if I didn't act.

Fuck it.

Across my cabin, the scout still slouched against a ballast. I had planned to move him to the makeshift holding cells with the other pirate hunters, but I didn't want anything to happen to him. He'd given me the valuable information I needed to come out ahead. I wouldn't throw him to the wolves.

"Get your ass up, Robbie," I ordered, getting to my feet to untie him.

His head rolled groggily as he slowly looked up at me with bleary eyes. "What?"

"Follow me," I demanded, dropping his restraints and walking to the door to my cabin. "This is happening now."

The kid struggled to his feet, wobbling back and forth. "What's happening now?"

I didn't answer as I flung the door open. It was the wee hours of the morning, the moon glowing across the ocean. The few of my crew who slept on the deck roused, getting up to stand at attention.

"Captain?" they asked.

"You're permitted to follow me to Shipwreck Bay, but I do not require it," I stated, not waiting for a response when I hustled down the gangway, Robbie close behind me.

There were a few murmurs as some of my crew gathered up oil lamps to follow, while others remained on deck. It didn't matter much to me. Shipwreck Bay wasn't a long walk, especially since I wasn't avoiding paths that were occupied by pirate hunters only a few days ago.

"Where are we going?" Robbie asked, trying to keep up with my long strides.

Now that he was beside me, I took note of how gangly he was. His round face and big eyes betrayed his age. It infuriated me to think about all the young men Cross conscripted who died for a war they didn't understand. Children snatched out of the cradle. Bred to be cannon fodder.

I'd had enough, and I wasn't going to wait for Pike to send reinforcements.

The closer I got to Shipwreck Bay, the more of my people followed me there, a line of yellow-orange oil lamps unspooling in the dark. Various sailors from Violetta's Haven, Lucky's Outpost, Bliss's Colony, and small corners of the Isles where word had traveled took notice of me and had also come to join the large group.

The merrow warriors stood guard around the surviving pirate hunters as they slept. We were keeping them locked up in one of the now-empty barns intended for livestock until we decided what to do with them.

Udine was nearby, keeping a close eye on town, and noticed me immediately. "Captain Ronin," she greeted me. "What is the meaning of this?"

As usual, she was clad in flowy fabric that complemented her strawberry blonde hair and adorned with her sea glass breastplate. But even if she kept her appearance tidy, exhaustion rang through her. Like many of my inner circle, Udine was waiting for the next orders, waiting for the other shoe to drop.

"Let me in," I ordered at the mouth of the barn.

The merrow looked to Udine for confirmation, and she nodded. Then the lead merrow muttered under their breath, "They've been talking about a prison break."

Of course they were. "It would surprise me if they weren't."

They opened the door, and I stepped inside. Several of the pirate hunters stirred awake, some of them gasping in terror when they saw me. A few of them had grouped together, hands clenched around makeshift weapons constructed from wood splinters and rusted nails.

The lieutenant who had called for the surrender was among the conspirators, but that didn't surprise me one bit.

"I wouldn't do that if I were you," I said, throwing the door open wide to reveal the massive group I'd gathered. "Not if you value your life." I gestured to the merrow warriors behind me. "Take any weapons."

The merrow fanned out, armed with halberds as they disarmed the prisoners.

The lieutenant clenched his hand around a splintered chunk of wood and shouted, "If you're going to kill us, Leviathan, get it over with! Don't toy with your food."

Again with the eating people thing.

I arched a brow as the pirate hunters looked around at one another. I could smell the stink of fear in the air and hear the whispers behind me as the sound waves tickled my nose. "I don't know what Pike or Cross told you about me, but I would never kill surrendering men."

The merrow encircled the lieutenant as he refused to give up his weapon. "I don't believe that. Not when you've taken one of our scouts and razed the corner villages of the Ivory Keys to the ground."

I glanced over my shoulder at Robbie hiding in the crowd. I beckoned him with two fingers. Hesitantly, the gangly young man approached, stepping up beside me. Gasps rang out, and I could only assume that meant that they'd thought I killed him.

Or *ate him*, by the sound of the rumors that were floating around.

"I've never been to the Ivory Keys. Not yet. Let me lay a few things out to you. Believe me or not. I don't give a shit," I stated.

Several of the pirate hunters tensed, twitchy as they looked from me to the crowd behind me. I could see the temptation to run written on their faces, but with merrow waiting to attack, it would be the last thing they did.

"It should come as no surprise to you that my name is Ronin Murdoch. Yes, *that* Ronin. No, I don't eat people," I said, waving my fingers with irritation. "No, I can't get into your head and warp your memories."

The murmurs behind me grew silent as they gave me their full attention.

"I've never laid siege to a town. I've never murdered an innocent. Anyone claiming otherwise is lying." I gestured to my horns. "My appearance is a gift from Cliohde to disprove anyone who questions my lineage. I am the rightful king to the throne, not the usurper, Varric Cross."

I looked directly at the lieutenant, whose grip on his weapon faltered.

"My offer to you on the battlefield still stands. I'm going to give each and every one of you the opportunity to take your lives back. Pike has lorded over you. Conscripted you. Taxed your farms to the point that you can't survive. He has stolen your daughters and your sisters and silenced anyone who dared speak their names."

Several of the pirate hunters exchanged glances, whispering doubts and uncertainties to one another.

"This is your chance to carve a future for your families. Pike doesn't deserve your loyalty—"

"And you do?" the lieutenant demanded. "What's stopping you from using us? We know Pike. We know what to expect."

"He's conditioned you to think this treatment is acceptable. I want you to take a good, long look at the brave souls behind me," I said. "Can't you see that you're the same? The only difference is that they said, '*Enough.*'"

The lieutenant dropped his weapon and glanced around at his peers. "If we say no?"

"*You* don't speak for the people behind you." I looked at the other pirate hunters. "If you say no, you'll remain prisoners for the duration of the war. Then you will stand trial for treason."

Another pirate hunter spoke up. "And if we say yes?"

The corner of my mouth twitched. "Then I will prove to you that your loyalty is well-placed. When this is over, you will be pardoned, and then your lives will be yours."

Robbie finally chimed in after standing beside me in silence, asking, "Who do I report to?"

"I will give you the night, and if you decide to join the winning side, you will report to Commander Lucky Bartram. Perhaps you'll see some familiar faces under his charge." Lucky had a reputation for recruiting defectors, which was one of the many reasons he had numerous bounties on his head in the mainland.

I turned to the mass of people behind me. "Get some rest. The work is far from done. I will not wait for Pike to send more men. We will take the fight to them."

A roar of cheers came from the crowd.

I gazed upon all the faces staring at me in disbelief and uncertainty. "My mercy is a gift. This is your chance to change."

The merrow locked up the barn as I left the pirate hunters to ponder my ultimatum.

"You're letting them *live*?" Bliss asked, eager to argue with my decision, but I cut them off.

"For now."

"This is a mistake," Bliss replied, crossing their arms.

Udine cleared her throat and said, "Mercy is rarely a mistake. But do you think it'll be enough?"

I dipped my head. "I think it will be, yes. To show them that I'm not Pike. I'm not Cross. I'm worthy of their loyalty. The fight is all they know. It's all they've been told. They've never seen the other side."

Bliss slouched their shoulders. "I want their blood saturating my hands, Leviathan."

"Blood always grows cold. It won't keep you warm like you think it will. They will pay their penance, Bliss. But it will be with redemption, not their lives," I said firmly. "I will satisfy my bloodlust with Pike's head on a fucking stick."

Bliss released a heavy breath. "What if they fight?"

"Then their lives will be forfeit." I glanced back at the doors. "It might be a problem with a handful, but I think more of them want to take their power back from those who stole it. I'm going to give them that chance."

"What if they run?" Udine asked seriously.

"Then they better run fast and pray to their God I don't catch them. I've led them to water. Let's see if they drink."

MAEVE CROSS

THE DARK NIGHT OF THE SOUL

CHAINS BOUND MY WRISTS TO MY BED, WHERE I WAS CURLED into a fetal position. I held my knees to my chest, stifling my own sobs. I could feel my spirit waning, and I didn't know how much more of this I could take.

I wanted to be strong.

I wanted to fight.

But every struggle cracked my soul.

My eyes fluttered closed over my wet cheeks, and I hoped my dreams would be kinder to me than reality. Better yet, I hoped I would fall into a dreamless abyss. I wanted some quiet. Before I fell asleep, I could hear Penelope crying herself to sleep like I was.

We were two sides of the same coin.

The bride who ran and the bride who couldn't.

But it appeared that all roads led us here, imprisoned in the Ivory Keys.

This dreamworld flowed around me, familiar and illusive. I knew I was in Ronin's cabin, but the words on the spines of his books were blurred. A foggy white light encompassed everything, like the moment after waking when I hadn't yet blinked all the sleep sand from my eyes.

I reached for his bed, always unmade. It didn't matter if he'd make it or not, we made a mess of the furs regardless. As I ran my hand over his pillow, I could feel the down feathers poking through the linen, a perfect imprint of his head.

The lump in my throat thickened because even in my dreams, I couldn't see him. I sank down onto the bed, desperate for the scent of cedar and seawater, but there was nothing. A sob broke from my chest as I lay there in the sanctuary of my mind.

I'd always loved Ronin's cabin and how it smelled like him. I missed him even more when I thought about how he backed me against his bookcases and dared me to lie to him again. This cabin was a source of excitement and comfort because it was ours.

Even when I was nervous or when he maintained that chasm between us, this cabin was safe. It was out of the sight of the crew, and he could show me who he was under all the layers of pain and scars that felt too stiff.

I remembered cutting his hair in the wet room, giving him back a piece of the control he lost when Pike captured him. I felt safe when he held me in this bed, knowing we could stay strong together.

His cabin on the ketch was too small, even if we shared many wonderful memories there.

The cabana held the memories of heartbreak. It was where Frey broke in and shattered any illusion that we were safe there.

But *The Ollipheist* was the first place that had ever felt like home.

I turned my face into Ronin's pillow and let myself fall apart.

"What are you doing here, sweetheart?"

He wasn't real. I *knew* he wasn't real. My mind conjured him up to comfort me, but that didn't matter. I leapt out of the bed, flinging myself as hard as I could at him, desperate for his touch to soothe the burning in my throat from my tears.

I fell through him like he was an apparition. I landed on my knees, and all the pain crested inside me. I turned around, staring up at him.

Ronin stood there, his face blurred like paint swirling in a glass of water. Had we been apart so long that I couldn't recall what he looked like? The memories faded and waned, but I couldn't....

I can't do this.

The memory of him wasn't a comfort. Not if I couldn't touch him. Not if I couldn't bask in his eyes like they were the warmth of the sun breaking through the clouds. Not if I couldn't *see him.*

"Don't cry, love. I hate it when you cry," the memory of his voice said, but even that was warped. Like my ears were clogged with water and he stood above the surface, everything I remembered obscured.

Can I really not remember the man I love? Has it been too long? Am I too broken?

"I miss you," I whimpered, barely able to string the words together.

"What are you doing here, sweetheart?" he asked again.

"You're not here," I murmured, overcome with how badly it hurt.

A big hand entered my peripheral just like how I'd imagine he'd pinch my chin to demand my eyes. But he couldn't touch me. "No, I'm not. But if I were, what would I say to you?"

"You'd tell me you love me."

A warm chuckle soothed the recesses of my mind. "Of

course. But that's not why you brought me here." He took on that tone that I loved and hated. That condescending asshole tone that I'd do anything to hear again. "Why are you letting them in?"

I furrowed my brow, unsure what he meant.

"Don't make a scene, Maeve," Varric's voice echoed.

"Like a python fears a bunny," Nathaniel hissed.

"A monster-fucking whore," Adams whispered.

"My girl would be making those fuckers regret kidnapping her," Ronin said.

My shoulders slumped, and I shook my head. "It's easier not to," I admitted. When I slouched on the table, it didn't hurt as much. If I kept my mouth shut, other people wouldn't get hurt for it. I thought back to Seymour, Frey, and even Penelope.

"I'm not saying it'll be easier, but you *know* a few of Varric's secrets. You've seen the journal he keeps his notes in. You even had Nathaniel terrified of you when you went after him," Ronin replied with conviction. "Make them suffer for everything they've done to you."

The tears dried. "I know the woman in the mirror."

"You're still here, Mae. And you're the strongest fucking woman I know."

A watery smile pulled the corner of my lips because that sounded exactly like how Ronin would say it.

"It's time to wake up, Mae," Ronin said, and his hands came around me as if he wanted to embrace me but couldn't.

I got to my feet as the light blurred like the sun had crested a wall of fog.

"And sweetheart?" Ronin asked before the dream sanctuary vanished. *"Make a fucking scene."*

MAEVE CROSS

SING, SONGBIRD

Ever since Nathaniel taunted Penelope through the wall, she hadn't talked to me. I could only listen to her soft sobs before a guard escorted her away. She would try to talk to them, but they'd silence her.

She wasn't permitted to speak to the handmaidens.

Or the guards.

Or anyone in passing.

How lonely....

Some nights I'd heard her sing to herself. I'd pressed my ear against the wall and traced the cracks along the plaster, hoping that she knew she wasn't alone. Her voice trembled and echoed in her small room.

Her bed would creak as she bounced on the mattress, letting herself fall into the song with everything in her soul. It was beautiful. I wondered if it was the only time she felt free. But if, Gods forbid, she was too loud… the guards were permitted to silence her with a cane.

Penelope was only allowed to sing for Nathaniel's pleasure. Her body wasn't hers. Her voice wasn't hers. Her spirit was the only thing she possessed.

She was a songbird trapped in a cage and punished when she sang. I wanted to tell her how much I loved her voice and how it made me feel less lonely. That she gave me a kinship through a wall of plaster.

Nathaniel came at all hours of the night, and I wasn't going to be responsible for him hurting her. If I said something, I knew Penelope would be the one to suffer for it. Maybe I could do something to deter his visits.

I vowed to make him pay. I would make him feel every anguish he inflicted on her.

Patience.

Varric had taken a break from his experiments because nobles were coming to check in on his progress. They insisted on my attendance to see if I was as broken as Varric claimed.

I would make him regret taking me from Fisherman's Gully. And this was my chance.

"Make a fucking scene," Ronin's voice whispered in the recesses of my mind.

I looked at myself in my new floor-length mirror. My mirror shard stayed between the mattress and the bedframe, close enough to reach, but hidden enough that no one would find it.

The handmaidens rushed into the room with gowns and corsets and new underthings. Silver entrapments for my wrists. They were so concerned about me making a break for it, but that wasn't what they should be worried about.

Most nights, I ate alone in my chambers. Never with silverware because they feared that I'd use it for an escape, so I stashed chicken bones with the intention of sharpening them into lockpicks or a needle blade. I'd hide one at a time. Something they wouldn't notice.

Then I'd practice picking the locks around my wrists. I'd

broken everything I'd stuck into my lock, but I wasn't going to give up.

I was going to get out of here, and when I did, I'd take Penelope with me.

Leaving Nathaniel in a puddle of his own entrails.

I stared at myself as they tightened my corset until my breath strained, then draped green velvet over me with wide bell sleeves to hide the chains. My short hair was braided along a diadem to give the illusion that I wasn't a prisoner. It was enough to fool the nobles, but silver or iron, they were still shackles.

"The guards will be here momentarily to take you away."

Playing the part of the traumatized daughter, I dipped my head, not saying a word as I went to sit on my bed. When they left, I tucked my hand under the mattress, nicking my fingers as I grabbed the shard of glass and tucked it into my shoe. Then for good measure, I took one of the needles I'd lifted from the tailor and wove it in between the threads on my pillow.

Varric would search my room after I dispatched Nathaniel, so I had to be one step ahead.

"Come now, Princess Maeve," a guard said as the door opened.

One guard was positioned on either side of me as they led me to the dining hall. As we walked, I noted the corridors. I learned where the bedrooms and the servants' quarters were. Unfortunately, the Ivory Keys Fortress was sprawling. Guards at every corner, though whether the additional security was for me, I couldn't be sure.

The glass crackled under my heel, slightly cutting into my skin. I was careful not to put my full weight onto that foot. I kept my expression completely neutral so no one would know how much blood pooled inside my shoe. The pain was fleeting. Nothing compared to what I'd endured so far.

The labyrinth of rooms wouldn't be easy to navigate when I escaped, but the long hallways made a square shape with a courtyard in the middle that obscured slightly when I passed a latticed iron portcullis. It closed vertically, operated by an internal winch.

I bet there was another one for the main entrance.

A wayward idea crossed my mind as I recalled how Frey fought back at Shipwreck Bay. How he *blinked* to propel himself forward. If the gate were closed, could he *blink* his way inside?

It was a pointless musing, but I hoped my friend was all right. I didn't know if he was able to survive his infection or if the sea had claimed Seymour and Frey.

Or if Ronin killed him. I wouldn't put it past him.

I shook the thoughts away as servants held the doors to the dining hall open. A long table was the focal point of the room, Varric already seated as the guests came in.

Some of the nobles I recognized from various events as a child, but most of them I didn't. All of them had that same greedy hunger in their eyes. For power, gold, or blood. The same gleam of cruelty I'd seen in Adams's eyes, but he didn't come from money. He had to be more secretive with his malice. He couldn't bribe his problems away.

They sat me near Varric, my silver binds locked behind the chair with enough clearance to reach my plate and maybe those on either side of mine, but nothing else.

"You look lovely, Maeve," Varric commented.

Go fuck yourself.

I didn't reply, sitting pretty like a good daughter as the rest of the nobles trickled in, filling the remaining chairs. I looked down at my empty plate when a sparkle caught my eyes.

I glanced up, taking note of an ornate rapier—

Like a punch to the gut, I could feel how it had pierced

through me, knocking me against the windowsill before it was ripped out of me. I remembered how it felt when I fell through the air, giving my life so Enya could go free.

Samuel Pike.

He looked older, but he still had that same gleeful gleam in his eye that Nathaniel had.

"Ah, you must be the ever-illusive Maeve," Samuel commented, taking a seat across from me. "You may look like a princess now, but all I see is a pirate's bitch."

"*Watch your tongue,*" Varric hissed.

"A better choice than your son," I retorted.

Varric shot a withering glare at me while Samuel balked. "Do not mind my daughter, Samuel. The leviathan took her mind." Then he muttered, "Know your place, Maeve."

My place. Under a boot. That's where they'd have me.

The corner of Samuel's mouth twitched as he glanced at the other nobles, as if he knew Varric was lying, but he didn't correct him. "I'll forgive the poor thing. Where is my son?"

As if on cue, Nathaniel walked through the doors with a small woman on his arm. She looked at the floor, avoiding any eye contact with anyone. Her gown covered her arms and came up to her neck, but when she moved her head, bruises peeked out from under the collar.

Her hair cascaded down her back like fire, an orange-red hue that complemented soft blue eyes and an ivory complexion. Her skin seemed so transparent and crystalline that I could see the blue veins showing through.

Penelope.

She obeyed every gesture of guidance, going to where Nathaniel pulled out the chair for her across the table from me.

"Nathaniel," Varric greeted him. "How about you take a seat on the other side of Maeve?"

He paled, glancing at the open chairs beside me. "Next to—"

"Sit down, boy," he snapped.

"Yes, Your Majesty." Nathaniel didn't argue again, placing one hand on the nape of Penelope's neck to direct her beside me.

He tried to sit her between us, but Varric said, "No, Nathaniel. *You* sit beside my lovely daughter."

Then Varric arched a brow at me as if daring me to do *something*. A coy smile curled the sides of his mouth as Nathaniel sat beside me, looking awfully uncomfortable. My fingertips twitched for the glass in my shoe, but I waited.

I will wait for the right moment to end Nathaniel's life. Right in front of his father. Right in front of the nobles. I will make an example of him.

"Forgive me for our tardiness," Nathaniel said before he glanced over at me. He gave me a sickly-sweet smile and gestured to Penelope. "She likes to hide in her room. Poor thing."

I didn't react, looking past him at Penelope. Her shoulders were taut, pupils contracting in fear. We looked at each other for a long moment, a sort of kindred understanding unfolding between us. Then Nathaniel got in the way, obscuring my view of her.

My oath remained true. *I will get you out of here.*

The first course was brought out, and I slowly sipped the soup. This was the one chance I had to bring Nathaniel's guard down. I would put him under the illusion that I would behave.

"I heard you lost contact with Shipwreck Bay," Samuel stated, pausing to take a spoonful of soup, but not before looking at Nathaniel with disappointment that only a father was capable of.

I fought the urge to smile, a giddiness filling my belly.

Death hadn't lied to me when they said Ronin had won. Pride bloomed inside me. Ronin did his part, and I would do mine.

"When I let you take control of our fleet so I could manage the bureaucracy, I thought you could handle it." Samuel sighed.

Nathaniel swallowed tightly, replying, "A brief setback—"

"If you cannot hold the pirate safehold, I'll take it myself," Samuel interrupted.

Varric made a loud throaty noise. "I assure you that Nathaniel is doing what he can. The pirates are crafty. Look at how they've rendered my daughter thoughtless."

Hmm.... Varric wants Nathaniel to stay in charge. Easier to manipulate?

"Now, that is not why you're here," Varric continued. "I have a meeting with the Edessan Sorceress and the King of Skadi. They are offering to merge the Islands with Algar again for the return of the prince."

I need to be at that meeting. I need to warn them. Frey is long gone, but who knows what lies Varric will spin to get their allegiance?

Varric leaned back as the servants cleared the first course and replaced it with the second. They hesitantly set a fork and spoon on either side of my plate, informed enough to not grace me with a knife.

"And I'm assuming that during the small window, we stage our land invasion," Samuel mused.

Something flickered in Varric's eyes as he replied, "We eradicate the Guild of Sorceresses first, starting with the Grand Sorceress. She's the one who damned the islands all those years ago. She'll do it again."

I watched his body language closely as he hissed the words, usually in complete control of his emotions, but this was different. This was a crack in the mask. I thought back to the memory that Death shared with me. The mirror with a black frame and golden detailing. The apparition of a woman whispering ideas in his ears.

Was that a calling mirror like the one Nathaniel had?

Did Varric bring that here with him?

Could I get a message out?

"Thallan served their purpose. A few of the kingdoms are destabilized, and it would be the perfect time to strike," Varric continued. "They will bend to us, or they'll die for us."

Samuel nodded, as did several of the other nobles who blindly agreed with him.

Nathaniel sat up, startling Penelope as he stated, "Now, since that is sorted, I have arranged some music." He squeezed her shoulders, and she flinched either from bruises or fear.

She stared up at him, and his grip tightened until I was certain she'd have pale imprints from his fingers.

"She hasn't finished her meal," I said, a bite in my tone. "Surely you'll feed your wife first."

Penelope shot me a look of gratitude, but Nathaniel squeezed harder until those imprints undoubtedly turned to more bruises. "Any good wife will please her husband above herself. Isn't that right, darling?"

She nodded, getting to her feet. Disgust churned in my belly as Nathaniel made her into a spectacle for the guests. She parted her lips and performed a similar song to the one she sang at night, but it lacked the joy I usually basked in.

I looked along the line of nobles. The men at the table who remained silent despite her obvious distress. To them, Penelope was an item to use for their enjoyment.

"Sing louder," Nathaniel ordered as tears collected in the corners of her eyes. It clearly wasn't good enough, as he took a short blade from the inside of his jacket, pointing it up toward her jaw. "Louder, songbird."

No one did a damn thing.

Rage boiled inside me.

They acted as if this was normal. Penelope clenched her eyes shut and came to the same conclusion I had so many nights ago.

"No one is going to save me."

Over my dead body. She had me now.

I glanced at Nathaniel's hand where it rested on the table near me and grasped my fork. When Penelope's voice warbled in panic, I slammed the prongs into his flesh. Gasps rang out as Nathaniel *screamed.*

He bent over in pain and desperately tried to remove the fork.

I kicked my shoe off and grasped the shard of glass with my other hand, then rose up as far as I could go and slashed. He veered to the side just as I aimed for his throat.

Instead, I got the side of his face, slicing upward toward his ear. Blood cascaded down his face and saturated my hand. This time, I wasn't covered in my own blood. It was *his.*

Funny. Even though he acts like he's above everyone else, he still bleeds red.

He grabbed at his face, falling backward onto the ground.

I snarled, *"Sing, songbird."*

Guards came to my sides, unlatching my binds and hoisting me up into the air. Samuel went to his son as Nathaniel writhed in pain on the ground. Penelope looked down at him and then back at me again, shock and relief clear as day in her gentle eyes.

"Check her for weapons!" Varric ordered. "Call for the nurse! Now! Now!"

The guards patted me down as chaos unfolded. The nurse took Nathaniel away, and his father stood up, shooting daggers at me, but I couldn't help the grin that stretched across my face. The elation in my stomach.

"I want her hanged," Samuel ordered. "Your traitorous daughter is in my home and mutilated my son!"

"Please, Samuel. That is pointless." Varric glanced at me and said with an air of ease, "Don't you see? Your son defied me. *He* lost the Skadian prince and brutalized my daughter against my direct orders. This is what happens to those who defy me. Isn't my darling Maeve a beautiful attack dog?"

A heavy weight slammed into my chest, snuffing out the flames of my victory that Varric stole for himself. My lips parted as my mind raced.

Did I do exactly what he wanted? Is he manipulating me even now?

"My daughter is an extension of myself, Samuel. And before you consider hanging her or committing her to the dungeons, let me explain to you *why* she is my right hand."

No. No, I'm not!

Before I could say as much out loud, he grasped a blade from the guard's sheath and plunged it deep into my stomach. A soundless shout left my lips as he tore it upward, blood pouring down my dress and puddling at my feet.

The guards released me, but I didn't crumple to my knees as my body healed, knitting my flesh like a trained seamstress. My hands were slick with blood as I looked up, catching eyes with the nobles who stared at me like *I* was the spectacle.

"Maeve Cross possesses immortality," Varric announced. "I have every intention of sharing her gift with you, but I have not yet figured out how to extract it from her."

Samuel stared at me, lips parted in awe. For a man who seemed privy to all of Varric's other secrets, it surprised me that he didn't know about me. Then again, *I* hadn't known about me either.

"She doesn't need my control because she already acts in my best interest. My most valuable possession. She is the final step for complete control of not only the Isles but the world," Varric continued. He looked at me, a cold storm clashing in his eyes before he addressed the Houses again. "I've extracted the magic from leviathans, and I plan to do the same to her. But she is a different creature altogether. I will reward your loyalty as I always have."

As all the nobles stared at me, I felt cold.

How many pieces of me will he give to them? Will I have anything left?

The message was clear.

Bend the knee.

Reap the rewards.

MAEVE CROSS

THE SEED OF SPITE

Varric watched as the guards tossed my chambers. They tore drawers out of the wardrobe and upended the desk. Everything clattered as they searched for contraband, any bits and bobs that I'd been hiding, while two other guards held either arm firmly behind my back.

"Where were you hiding it, Maeve?" Varric demanded.

"I don't know what you're talking about," I retorted.

"Get the handmaidens. I want her stripped down to her underthings," Samuel shouted, standing nearby in the doorway. The man was fuming, but Varric had given him another promise to earn his way into Samuel's good graces again.

After being trapped on Pike's ship with Adams and other disgusting men stripping me down naked and humiliating me on the floor of the showers, having the handmaidens undress me felt oddly pleasant in comparison.

They were careful as they unbuttoned my gown and smoothed down the wrinkles. The guards acted like I was a loose cannon ready to fire at any unexpecting servant and fly off the ropes. Every little movement had them jumping to grab their weapons.

The smile on my face didn't help.

I was giddy as all Hells for maiming Nathaniel, though I would've preferred to get his throat instead of his cheek. And as I looked at Samuel, I remembered how he murdered me— or an old version of me—during the coup.

In my previous life, Samuel toyed with me and the other sentries. Observing us. Commenting on our bodies to his son. Occasionally, I'd see Nathaniel join him for gatherings involving the other dukes and duchesses of small, isolated villages. It was hard to imagine that nine-year-old becoming the Nathaniel I knew today. He was always so quiet. Never looked anyone in the eye. Flinched when Samuel moved too quickly.

Nathaniel was just a child who needed kindness.

But when an awful man with an inflated ego whispered in his ear all day and night, any young boy could become a monster. They become their fathers. That cycle of violence and evil would repeat over and over again until something was strong enough to break it.

It was too late for Nathaniel now. He was no longer deserving of kindness.

The details of my first death came back to me. Samuel had speared me in the belly with his rapier. Pinned me against the windowsill before shoving me through it to fall several stories. The impact shattered my bones. I was still alive when I hit the ground before I grew cold.

I died the same way I lived my life. For someone else. *Alone.*

As the handmaidens wiggled me out of my remaining shoe, I nearly tripped and made a sudden motion toward Samuel as I caught myself. The man nearly jumped out of his skin.

"Oh, did I frighten you?" I asked coyly as the strings on

my corset were loosened and I could finally take a full breath in.

"Like a python fears a bunny," Samuel snarled.

"Nathaniel said the same thing. How'd that turn out for him?"

The man's hand shot out and slapped me hard across the face. I recoiled, but I was unable to stop that laugh from bubbling out of my throat. My shoulders shook from how I laughed, blood dribbling onto the floor.

"She's mad, Varric. We need to lock her in the dungeons like the rat she is," Samuel spat. He circled me. "She looks like a lady, but she's nothing but a bottom-feeder."

"A bottom-feeder?" I retorted, no longer tasting blood as my lip healed. "Says the lord who had to lie and scheme to stomp on the necks of the hardworking people he exploits. Do your servants hold your prick when you relieve yourself too?"

The air cut around Samuel's hand as he threw it back to strike me again.

Go ahead and hit me. You can't leave a mark on me.

"Ungrateful little—"

Varric sighed. "If you're letting her get to you, Samuel, you're not fit to be in this room."

"Control your daughter, then," he argued. "A woman will learn her place with enough cracks of the whip."

"Lord Samuel isn't himself," Varric said calmly. "Escort him out of these chambers immediately."

"I will not—" Samuel shouted, but his own guards surrounded him. "I am the *lord*! Don't touch me."

"And I'm the king. Speak more slander, and I will have you imprisoned. You forget *your* place." Varric snapped his fingers, and the guards closed in around their lord. "I sit at the head of the table. You would be nothing without me, Samuel. Don't ever forget that."

A heavy silence fell between them, but Samuel stopped arguing and left the room without force.

I looked up and caught the brief visual of a mad gleam in Varric's eye that matched my own. A complicated feeling expanded in my chest when I realized he was... *proud*, even if he said otherwise.

My entire youth, I ached to receive that look in his eye. I wanted him to be proud of me. But that was before I knew what he'd done. That spiteful seed inside me unfurled to reveal a blossom—some piece of me that craved fatherly approval.

How could I?

Hot shame welled in my chest.

The handmaidens removed my corset, leaving me in a loose chemise and bloomers. They started to undo the ties on those, too, but Varric stopped them. "Enough. There is clearly nothing on her. Where were you hiding it, Maeve?"

"In my shoe," I said, standing up straight.

"You're cleverer than they give you credit for," Varric mused. "Toss the room. Check the undersides of drawers."

I narrowed my eyes, standing still as the guards ripped out the drawers of my wardrobe, tossing clothing everywhere as they looked at the bottom to see if I'd stuck something there. But the search came up empty.

"Under the bed," Varric ordered.

Nothing.

"Behind the mirror."

Nothing.

I watched Varric's face closely as a smile curled the side of his mouth. "You're smarter and more resilient than you were when you were a child, but you're still that same little girl who hid books under your mattress, aren't you?"

Desperately, I tried not to give anything away, but the

unconscious twitch in my eyebrow was enough. He tilted his head toward the mattress, and the guards flipped it over, revealing chicken bones, glass shards, iron nails I'd pried from the bedframe, and another needle I'd lifted from the tailor.

"Did those pirates teach you to lockpick too?" Varric asked.

"You can teach yourself anything if you practice enough," I replied.

The guards gathered my stash, and the handmaidens got to work trying to piece my room back together.

"It's a shame it had to be like this, Maeve. You always had such wasted potential."

I narrowed my eyes. "Is it only wasted if you can't benefit from it?"

The corner of his mouth twitched. "As much as I enjoy verbally sparring with you, we have what we need. Leave this mess for Maeve," Varric ordered, and the handmaidens instantly stopped cleaning up. "It'll give you something to do."

He turned around, and the guards locked me to the bedframe with my chains again.

Finally, everyone left my room, leaving me in my underthings, but they were considerably more comfortable than the corset and gown. I turned my attention to the mattress on the ground, stained with little grease splotches where I'd hidden my bones to dry out.

But Varric did exactly as I expected him to. He underestimated me. I *wasn't* the same little girl who hid things under my mattress. I was better now.

I huffed and pushed the side of it back onto the bedframe before collapsing onto the down-filled mattress. Folding my arms under my head, I couldn't stop the smile from washing over my face again. Nathaniel would be in the infirmary for quite some time. It would at least give Penelope a break from his torment.

That was enough for me to feel satisfied.

After a few moments of silence, a quiet knock rapped against the wall.

"M-Maeve?" Penelope's soft voice asked through the hole in the plaster, stammering over the first letter of my name. While Nathaniel had reprimanded her for her stutter many times, I found it endearing.

She thought out her sentences thoroughly before she spoke. I'd been around so many men the past few months who said whatever awful thing came to their lips first. Half the time, it wasn't even a creative insult, so I found her thoughtfulness refreshing.

I jumped up in the bed, excitement pattering in my chest. If there was one person in the whole blasted castle I wanted to talk to, it was her. "Yes?"

She was quiet for a long moment, but I could hear her lips smack together as she struggled to form the words. That must be frustrating. To have quips and responses ready, but not to be able to get them past your lips.

"I-I'm sorry," she whispered. "Talking is… hard."

I leaned against the wall. "I'm not going anywhere. Take your time."

She exhaled in relief, and then she strung together a sentence. "N-No one has e-ever stood up for me be-before." She swallowed a few times. "Thank you."

"Don't thank me," I stated. "I hope his blasted face gets infected."

She replied with a timid laugh. "I-I hope half his face falls off."

I returned her laugh. "Me too."

A comfortable silence fell between us, but I wasn't ready

to stop talking. Penelope had this kindness in her voice that lightened the burden on my shoulders.

"Your stammer," I said, wondering briefly if I was sticking my foot in my mouth again. "You don't seem to have it when you sing."

Another moment of silence passed before she said, "I-I don't have to think about it when I sing."

"There's this man I know," I murmured, the lump in my throat growing thicker with longing. "He buried his emotions deep inside, but whenever he played his violin, I knew exactly what he was feeling."

What I wouldn't do to hear Ronin play his violin one more time....

"Do you play too?"

I chuckled. "I love music, but I don't have a rhythmic bone in my body. The only time I could dance was when he was leading." My chest ached, and I had to clear my throat in hopes that the emotion in my voice wasn't too thick.

"Do y-you miss him?" she asked.

My voice cracked when I said, "Like nothing else. I'd never known love until him."

"What's it like? To be in love?"

"It's like the sweetest agony," I replied before I looked down at my chains. I reached into my pillow and felt for the needle. When I had it, I poked it inside the lock. I wriggled it around in the keyhole and heard it when I hit the pins, like I always did, but even still, I hadn't found a way to unlock them yet.

But I would.

I hit more resistance and stopped, refusing to break my only tool of liberation.

"I… I think I know what you mean," she murmured.

"Do you?"

"The neighbor's boy, Caine." She paused and released a

mournful laugh. "Well, he's not a boy anymore. I never told him how I felt before he was conscripted. Hells, his whole family was conscripted." That laugh grew louder, but it wasn't from joy. It was bitter. "I'd only ever kissed him, because his brother kept walking in on us before it could progress further. I wish I knew what..."

"What?" I asked, trying to encourage her to tell me.

"I-It's foolish," she murmured, but it wasn't because she didn't want to tell me. Her tone took that sound of shame that I was all too familiar with.

"You don't have to be ashamed. Tell me."

"...what it felt like to be touched with love." Her voice cracked, longing curling at the corners of her words.

My heart shattered in my chest.

I'm so sorry, Penelope.

29

RONIN MURDOCH

A FAMILIAR FACE

My wings folded around me as I cut through the water. Udine and the merrow swam alongside me as we scoured the ocean for scraps. During the siege, Pike had sunk every pirate vessel docked at the pier.

The Lilac Queen—Violetta's man-o'-war.

The Marauder—Bliss's galleon.

The Dryad's Promise—Lucky's brigantine.

I could see the figureheads scattered in the silt and gathered the waterlogged debris. I scavenged whatever I could and swam to place them in the nets for the fishermen up top to pull up. Once the wood was dried out, it could be used for the next generation of ships, holding the spirits of everything we lost.

It would make us stronger.

Several of the pirate hunters had taken the deal. While we were on high alert, many of them jumped at the opportunity to make a difference. They wanted to go home, and if I kept my promises, then they could have the chance to make a better life for themselves without having to flee their homes or families.

Lucky had them learning under the surviving boat makers, building the skeletons of new ships. We put the others to work rebuilding homes and businesses. It'd never be the same, but I had faith that we'd flourish like the merrow.

Sometimes a forest needed to burn to grow back more beautiful than before.

Fish scattered as I dove into the hull of one of the ships, gathering personal effects for a few of the sailors. Anything to raise morale. I found a few sets of bones in ruined velvet pouches. A chess set. Little whittled figurines. Even weapons that I knew Gunny and his gunners could restore with enough work.

If no one claimed the chess set, I'd bring it to Wesley so he'd have something to do during his long recovery. He was in pain most days, relying on a small ration of opioids to sleep. It caused him pain to lie down, and his legs were too weak to try standing. Isa propped him up on pillows for a wink of relief.

Townspeople were slowly moving out of Anchorage Cove to reclaim their homes or rebuild what they'd lost. A sense of normalcy had returned now that they weren't afraid of pirate hunters storming the shores again.

If they did, we had enough numbers to keep control and enough of their people to convince at least a portion of Pike's men to switch sides.

If Pike hadn't wrung his people dry, they'd blindly follow him, but he'd burned too many bridges while I built them. And I hadn't given them a reason to think I wouldn't keep my word.

I was many things, but I wasn't a man who made idle promises.

Udine swam up next to me, her sea glass armor glittering

like jewels. The light reflected off her, catching on the scales that decorated her tail.

Merrow and sirens were alike in several ways, but while sirens could fly above the water to land on ships, the merrow lacked wings. Sirens were rarely colorful, mainly oil-slicked or gray to blend in with the water like a deep-sea fish. Merrow were built for the shallows and emulated reef fish.

I'd never swum beside either of them. Not unless I was chasing the sirens back to the trenches. The final resting place of the leviathans, as well as the sirens, the kuru, and the merrow. We all shared the belief that Death came into this realm through a doorway at the bottom of the trenches, guiding our souls into the afterlife as a favor to Cliohde.

When I was in the water, I was alone. In theory, I could give a land dweller a breath of life to join me temporarily. But I'd only ever used that skill to prevent drowning. Like the time Wesley got swept up in a riptide when we were kids, and I kept him alive.

Or when Mae fell off the ship, and I tried to give her a breath of life. I'd never even considered bringing her deep into the water with me. But it was peaceful to have company during a swim.

My heart squeezed in my chest as I gathered more scrap wood and metal. *I'm going to get you, Mae.*

Udine swam deeper into the dark, beckoning me to follow her as we worked together to drag up chests and wardrobes. Unfortunately, even in the water, cannons were fucking heavy. Those bastards were going to stay at the bottom of the sea until I shifted into my full form. We'd have to come back later. I made note of where they were located.

The merrow and I had been at this for hours, and it was almost time to take a break.

The sea always revitalized me, but even that had its limits. I was done, and we'd made progress, so that was enough for me. I swam up to the net and noticed that it hadn't been brought up again.

Odd.

Warning bells went off in my head, and I glanced at Udine, nodding toward the surface. Something was awry. I shot up, breaching the surface of the water and arcing my wings to land on the pier.

Instantly, I heard yelling. There was a sloop docked that I hadn't accounted for. The pirate hunters had six sloops, so why were there now seven?

"Get on your knees! Get on your knees!" Lucky's voice boomed as interim captain. "Restrain them now!"

I whirled around to the beginning of the pier to see that whatever intruders we had didn't get any farther into town. *Good.* I wanted security as tight as possible.

"Wait! I need to talk to the leviathan," a thick Skadian-accented voice insisted. "*Erm...* Ronin?"

"You'll be tossed in with the prisoners until he's available. We're cleaning up *your* mess," Lucky snarled.

I know that voice.

The same voice that accompanied the man who skewered my Mae on his sword.

I saw fucking red. I flexed my wings and sprinted forward, seeing both a white-haired Skadian and a lanky blond man next to him, both on their knees, wrists given over in surrender.

"Fucker," I growled as Lucky got out of my way. I would've knocked him over if he didn't. My hand snapped out and closed around a bruised violet throat. The Skadian heir's yellow eyes blew wide as I lifted him clear off the ground.

I was too angry to care about the scabs all over his previously pierced ears or the way his lilac skin was deeply purple around his wrists. I didn't care about the brand on his neck or the freshly healed blisters.

The heir choked out a few words, but I didn't hear them as he clawed at my hand. My heart pounded in my ears, and my entire face felt hot. This fucker burned my home to the ground. He killed my girl. He was *there* in my cabana when Mae and I gave each other a vulnerable night before our peace was stolen away.

"Wait!" the blond man shouted. "Please!" He got up, grabbing at my other arm, but I shoved him backward, prepared to snap the Skadian's neck and be done with him.

The heir's face turned a deeper purple as my people fanned out behind me, not doing anything to stop me. I doubted they'd be able to.

"Mae said to find you!" the blond man yelled from back on the planks.

At the sound of her name, my murderous rage was sliced right in two. *Only her friends ever call her Mae.* The heir wheezed, lips nearly blue. I glanced over at the lanky man. "Mae did?"

He nodded furiously, panic written all over his face.

I looked back at the heir and released him. He wheezed as he hit the planks, holding his even more bruised throat, croaking out, "I told her this would happen."

Through narrowed eyes, I hissed, "Talk. Now. I won't give you another chance."

He cleared his throat and got to his feet. "I am Prince Freynir Skadisyn. The first of my name. The eldest Skadisyn heir."

I lowered my head so we were at an equal eye level. "Why are you here, Skadisyn?"

"I'm repaying a favor."

A favor? My eyebrows came together in a seething expression of disbelief. I scoffed and threw Lucky a glance. "Throw him in the hold with the other prisoners."

"Wait—" The heir grabbed my arm.

In reaction, my fist flew back and snapped forward, splitting his lip and laying him out against the planks. "You're on *my* island, Skadisyn. The same island I took back from the raid *you* led. You are not permitted to touch me."

He swore, blue blood dribbling out the side of his mouth. He wiped it away with the back of his hand. "You're a prick."

I rolled my eyes. "Get him out the fuck out of here."

The blond man stared at the dark elf in disbelief. "What are you doing? Tell him, Frey."

"Clearly he doesn't give a fuck what I have to say," Freynir replied as two of my sailors pulled him to his feet. He didn't fight, didn't use magic, only hung his head in surrender. "I don't blame you. For what it's worth, I'm sorry. Mae told me to come here, and I wasn't going to refuse her."

Hearing her name on his lips caused another spike of rage to well up in my belly, spitting like water on a grease fire. "Let him go and step away," I snarled.

My sailors obeyed, stepping back to watch with the rest of my people.

"You stuck a sword in her chest. You don't get to speak her name if you've tasted her blood."

The narrowed pupils of his yellow eyes contracted even more as he leaned back to look up at me. I towered over the elf, using my physical size to intimidate him.

But he didn't back away. He only stared up at me, spine ramrod straight. "I never meant to hurt her. I was after you."

"Why?" Lucky asked from behind me.

The dark elf maintained eye contact with me and replied, "Varric Cross spun the tale that you were the one who had my wife assassinated."

It was then that I noticed what looked like an elven marital pendant around his neck. Luella wore one, too, but it wasn't for Andra. It was from her life before she was ship-wrecked here.

"And you believed him?"

Freynir lowered his head in what appeared to be shame. "I was a weapon, and Cross pointed me where he wanted me." He sighed heavily and held himself upright again. "Mae showed me that my faith was misplaced."

"Where is she?" I asked. My heart knocked against my ribs as I glanced at their sloop, hoping she'd be there. But deep inside, I knew it wouldn't be that easy.

"She saved our lives," Freynir said. "More than once, actually."

Emotion cracked my voice when I replied, "Of course she did. She always had too much heart."

With conviction, the blond man who'd accompanied Freynir said, "She's a good person. She doesn't deserve what they did to her."

I tensed. "*What did they do to her?*"

Freynir didn't falter under my dark tone, even if the blond man did. "I will tell you anything you want to know. Only in exchange for lunch."

"Lunch?"

"I've been stuck on that sloop for two weeks and chained in a cell on Pike's ship before that. I want lunch. And a mattress. I want some *good* sleep and half-decent food." Freynir crossed his arms, drawing my attention to yellowed bruises and barely healed blisters on his wrists. Injuries I knew well from the time I was in Pike's care.

"I'll pick something up from the galley," Lucky offered. "Would you like me to get your mother?"

"If she isn't needed elsewhere. Thank you—"

A shout of surprise interrupted me. "Caine? Oh Gods, Caine!" Robbie's voice came from behind me as the kid glee-fully sprinted up beside me, not remotely intimidated of me anymore. He'd taken his role as Lucky's first recruit seriously.

Robbie would never see combat if I had anything to say about it, but he was learning a lot under Lucky. I had faith that he'd be a great sailor one day.

The blond man slowly stood up, shock painted all over his face. "Robbie? Oh my Gods! I thought you were dead!"

I noticed that there were stark similarities between the two young men as they embraced each other, clapping the other hard on the back.

Robbie leaned back, beaming. "I'm a pirate now!"

I shrugged. "Honorary pirate."

"This is Captain Leviathan. I have so much to tell you," Robbie babbled excitedly before he finally read the fucking room. "Oh… did I interrupt something?"

"Take…." I trailed off for a moment. *Who the fuck is this man?*

"My brother," Robbie supplied. A true childlike smile of glee made him look his age.

"Ah. I've heard a lot about you." I gestured to Caine before looking at Robbie again. "Take your brother. Show him the ropes. Get him something to eat." As far as I was concerned, a naval officer who'd defied orders could join the other defectors. I'd speak to him later if necessary. "Get back to work!" I ordered, and the crowd scattered.

Hesitantly, Caine looked at Freynir, and the dark elf nodded his permission. Then the two brothers took off toward the town, leaving the dark elf and me relatively alone. I nodded toward my ship docked near the other vessels.

Freynir looked me up and down. "Did you always look like this?" He hummed and tapped his lower lip. "I think I would have remembered the wings, and the—ahem—*legs*."

I blinked. "Excuse me?"

The Skadian waved off my tone and replied, "Under different circumstances…."

Is he flirting with me? My forehead pinched together, and I felt an overwhelming urge to smack him again, but I refrained and decided to ignore whatever else came out of his mouth. "Move it. Hands above your head."

Freynir sighed, putting both hands above his head. He walked up the gangway and stopped when he got to the top. "Nice ship you got here."

"Up the stairs and behind the helm," I directed him. My helmsman opened my cabin door for us, and I closed it when we were both inside. "Take a seat at the table by the window."

"Can I put my hands down now?" Freynir asked.

"Keep them on top of the table," I replied. Judging by his state of dress and the wounds scattered across his bare skin, I doubted he had a weapon. I also doubted he'd bathed or cared for his injuries properly.

He obeyed, keeping both his hands palms down on the table. He put on this show of being unbothered, but I knew a man on edge when I saw one. His shoulders were stiff, fingertips twitching with the desire to hold on to something.

"Try to run, and I'll bind you to the ballast," I warned.

"Don't threaten me with a good time, Leviathan," he joked, fingers still twitching nervously. Then he took a deep breath and said with conviction, "I have every intention of keeping my promise to Mae. Take whatever precautions you think are necessary."

I hummed under my breath. From our interactions in the past, I knew he was dangerous. Freynir was a formidable warrior, but there was a resigned gleam in his eye. I didn't know him well enough to recall if it'd always been there, but I remembered the vigor in the swings of his broadsword.

I remembered his thirst for blood.

I remembered the smell of smoke like a burning hearth.

He was all rage then, but he didn't seem like that man anymore.

I turned into my side room to fill a bowl with water from the reserve. We weren't in motion, so the filter system wasn't working, but thankfully, fresh water was delivered every morning while we were in town.

On my way out of my washroom, I grabbed a jar of salve and a washcloth.

Freynir was still sitting there when I walked out, hands exactly where I told him to put them. He looked up at me with mild surprise when I placed the bowl and the jar of salve in front of him.

"Did Pike do that?" I asked, gesturing to the ripped cartilage on his extended ears and the blue blood caked around his hooked nose.

The dark elf hesitantly took the washcloth, watching me closely as he cleaned the wounds on his ears. "Pike is a bastard. He did a lot of things, but he didn't rip my piercings out. That was Adams."

Adams. His name sparked the memory of a man standing over me, a steel-toed boot colliding with my gut and the sensation of unwanted touches. "I know Adams."

He paused his ministrations. "I'm sorry." Then he gestured to his chest. "Do you mind?"

I shook my head, and he pulled his ill-fitting shirt over his head to reveal an angry wound on his chest where it looked like he used to have a nipple ring.

"My mother is a physician. She can take a look at that for you."

"It could've been worse," he replied. "I would've died if it weren't for Mae."

There was a brief knock on my cabin before the door opened. Lucky came in first with a plate of hearty bread and a bowl of soup while Mama tailed him close behind, a kit with her.

Lucky placed the food in front of Freynir, and he dove right in, completely ignoring the silverware to dunk the bread into the broth like he didn't know when the food would be taken from him.

Between bites, he said, "This is heavenly. Forgive my lack of manners. Pike only gave us scraps, like we were animals."

Mama stepped up beside him to observe his visible wounds. In her presence, he relaxed, letting her examine him. "Do you have any other injuries?"

With a mouth full of food, he said, "Maybe a broken rib or two." He picked up the bowl to slurp the soup down as quickly as possible.

She prodded the wounds on his chest. "These are warm to the touch. You have an infection."

"At the tail end of one," he corrected. "It would've taken me if Mae didn't get me off that ship." Then he chuckled. "She said she'd drag me back from the Hells if I died on her. Kicking and screaming."

Mama placed a small bottle of antiseptic on the table. "Keep it clean. Find me if it gets worse."

"Where is she?" I asked. "Why isn't she with you?"

A serious expression took over the dark elf's face. "Adams was taking her to a back room while the officers were distracted with disembarkment. She took the opportunity to set the ship on fire. I hope to the Gods that Adams burned with it."

That's my girl..., I thought, even if my heart ached.

"Seymour—*Caine*—was our guard. He's the one who snuck her the key. If I weren't so weak with the fucking infection, I could've dragged her to the boat with us, but...." Freynir looked away from me, clearly awfully ashamed. "She was shot getting me off that ship. She told me to come here.

She told me that after everything I'd done, I owed *you* my help."

Lucky looked over at me and said, "I could always use more help with the ships."

"I'm useless with a hammer," Freynir replied. "I'm more useful on the front lines."

Mama's blue eyes flashed over to me, and she shook her head. I understood that look well enough to know that she was saying, *"He's not fit for battle."*

"I know she's in the Ivory Keys. I know she's being held there because of the royal ship docked at the harbor. The one with the dragon skull and eel stamped on the flag."

"Cross is in the Ivory Keys," I repeated, looking between Mama and Lucky. "How long?" I asked.

"Long enough to have a full guard detail and a mountain of supplies," Freynir answered. "I assume you're going after her."

I didn't answer.

"If you're not, then I will. I owe that woman my life."

"*You're* not leaving the pier," I ordered. "We're going to need to plan a strike to take both Pike and Cross."

"He's telling the truth," Lucky pointed out before he sighed. "Skadians are many things. Rarely liars. And there's this—" He pulled the collar of his shirt down, revealing a nasty blister that matched the Skadian's.

The dark elf's eyes widened. "They used one of those collars on you too?"

Lucky readjusted his collar. "They called them magic inhibitors. Burned like a motherfucker." He shot me a glance. "Draconite."

"Mae shattered mine so we could escape. They had her restrained as far from me as possible so she couldn't reach it," Freynir recalled. Then he blew a breath out of his nose. "I should've known I was being used when she threw herself in front of you at that merrow colony." His upper lip pulled into a snarl, revealing pointed canines.

For a split second, I could smell that smoky hearth scent that I'd quickly associated with his rage. There was a long line of people Cross had misled, and Freynir wouldn't be the last.

"It's what Cross does," Mama said. "And he's so godsdamn good at lying that no one questions it. Not until we fight back."

I looked down at the dark elf from the bridge of my nose, and he met my gaze with an equally intense one. "We're out for blood, Skadisyn. I need to know where you stand."

"Cross played me for a fool. I *will* make him pay for it." He looked up at me with conviction glimmering in his stark yellow eyes. "I'm a weapon, Leviathan. *Point me.*"

30

RONIN MURDOCH

SIGNAL FLAGS

"What are you going to do with him?" Lucky asked, coming to sit next to me on the upper deck directly above my cabin.

I'd been talking to Freynir for so long that the stars had come out, and I stared up at them. They made me feel insignificant in the grand scheme of things. But I *needed* to feel small, like the entire world wasn't on my shoulders. Just for a moment.

I left Freynir in my cabin with Andra and my mother keeping guard. I didn't trust him, but this nagging sensation in the back of my head told me that he wasn't a danger to me. He answered every question—even the ones I didn't want answers to.

He told me how he arrived in Farlight Isles and how Cross led him to believe that I was responsible for his wife's death. Everything he'd done came into focus. Freynir was after vengeance, not after a political alliance.

Cross used him. *Always the opportunist.*

"He's an asset," I replied. "I hate to admit it, but if what he said was true, he has every right to vengeance, just as we do."

Freynir was a formidable fighter, but if he was here, then Skadi wasn't aligned with Cross as we originally thought. Both a relief and another layer of bureaucracy that I *really* didn't want to deal with.

"Last time you saw him, he killed Maeve," Lucky said, eyeing me carefully with his purple irises. "Are you prepared to let that go?"

"Fuck no," I retorted. "I'm going to hold that over his head every moment of this alliance. But I'm… I'm not as angry as I was."

"Good. Angry men act irrationally. We don't have time for that." Lucky leaned back, braids cascading down his spine as he looked up at the setting sun. Then he brought up one hand and counted on his fingers.

"What?" I asked.

"Seabird told me that it took Cross a few weeks to determine how to remove draconite from the host. Ivory Keys is about a twenty-day voyage." Lucky's eyebrows came together, concern deepening the wrinkles around his mouth. "With the slower sloop and judging by Freynir's injuries, they've probably been at sea closer to a month. Maybe longer."

A tic formed in my jaw. "That's how long he's been experimenting on Mae," I said, finishing his thought. That familiar warm anger simmered inside me.

"If Cross can get her magic… then we're fucked. We're *royally fucked*." Lucky got up, his boots tapping as he paced back and forth. "The boats aren't ready. We should've been on course weeks ago, but we didn't have enough men until recently."

"How long?" I asked.

"Well, I assume that Cross doesn't know the source of her magic, so that would buy us time—"

"I'm not going to dwell on factors I can't control," I said, which stopped Lucky in his tracks. "How long until the boats are ready?" I got to my feet and crossed my arms.

He adjusted his hat and replied, "Between finishing the frames, making it seaworthy, and stocking it for the crews, we're looking at three months. At least. Maybe seventy-five days if the new recruits cooperate."

"Are they causing you problems?"

He waved me off. "No more than any freshies. They want what we all want. Freedom." Then he paused and pulled something out of his trouser pocket. "Speaking of—Boats came to me a few days ago. She wanted me to draw up some plans for her."

Andra hadn't brought anything up to me, but we were drowning in work. And with new mouths to feed, sourcing materials, and the variable of where to put the defectors so I wouldn't be risking their lives or the townspeople, we were hardly ever in the same room together.

I perked up and took the outstretched paper. "She didn't mention anything," I said.

"Don't take it personally. All our plates are full. Yours more so," Lucky said. "Take a look at it."

I unfolded the paper, revealing a sketch of a three-wheel chair. There were notations of what materials to use, where to sew cushioning into the seat, even names of artisans who'd offered their help.

"It's for Howler," Lucky said. "Boats wants to get him out of that bed and back home."

My throat felt thick, and I handed the schematic back. "This is really thoughtful."

"He's well loved. If we can help him regain his freedom, at least a piece of it, then using the resources is worth it." Lucky's brow furrowed again as he retrieved something else from his jacket pocket. "I need a favor if you have time."

"Anything you need. I'll make it happen," I promised.

"Take these to Siggi. We'll need signal flags for the fleet." He sighed as if realizing how much more work had to be done. "And *then* we'll need to train everyone on my system. It's worked for my fleets, and I'm hoping to implement it here as well."

I'd never had more than one ship under my command. Lucky had more experience than I did, but these were still more personnel than he'd ever had at once. But between the two of us and all our allies, I had hope.

All ships utilized signal flags to an extent. It wasn't like we could shout out orders across the sea. So, we'd raise a Jolly Roger or a white flag, and some ships utilized a red flag of death. Lucky's system was more advanced. We needed a way to communicate directions, signal a stop or standby, issue warnings for sea beasties, and indicate when to charge the beaches.

"I trust you, Lucky," I replied. "I'll take care of the flags."

He tipped his head, and as he turned to descend the ladder back to the main deck, he said, "We'll get her back."

"I know we will."

WHEN I DUCKED BACK INTO MY CABIN, ANDRA WAS WATCHING Freynir as he fiddled with his ears, smearing salve over the raw flesh. I felt conflicted over whether or not to restrain him, but I didn't actually think it was necessary.

Not only was he missing his sword, but he wouldn't be able to outrun me if he tried.

Andra glanced at me and said, "Mama had to go back to the chapel to change some dressings." Then she shot Freynir an intense glare. "Or maybe she was tired of this one's questions."

"I'm new to Farlight. I've never been anywhere so tropical," Freynir explained.

"What was he asking?" I inquired.

"Go ahead. Ask him, since you're so intent on *blabbering*." She tipped her chin toward me, arms crossed.

Freynir crooked a pale brow and asked, "Is it always so fucking hot here?"

"Usually," I replied.

"What about—"

"*Ugh*. I can't listen to this anymore. He's your problem, Levi." She grabbed her hat from the coatrack and perched it on her head. Then she groaned and looked over at me. "Unless you still need me."

"You can go." Then I stopped her. "Oh, and thank you for taking care of our brother."

A smile pulled at her lips, but it didn't touch her eyes. "After all he's done for us, it doesn't feel like enough."

"No, it doesn't," I agreed.

"Good night, Levi," she said before shooting the Skadian a seething glare and leaving.

Once the door was closed again, Freynir said, "I don't think she likes me."

I pinned him with a hard glare. "You almost murdered her wife and succeeded in kidnapping a member of our family. Be thankful Wraith isn't here."

He blinked. "Wraith?"

"The moment she's alone with you, she's going to kill you," I stated. I wasn't sure if the news of the Skadian heir had reached Luella, but I knew she had every intention of taking her pound of flesh.

Hells, I had been too. But then I *saw* him. Pike had punished him enough. Luella wouldn't be as forgiving, however.

"Oh. The redhead. *Right*. I thought I only had to worry about you."

"Many people on this island want you dead, Skadisyn," I sighed, leaning back against the ballast as he continued cleaning and salving his numerous wounds.

"Not you, though?" he inquired.

"For now."

At my answer, the side of his mouth crooked up, revealing one of his extended canines.

"*Me-row*," Lieutenant Commander Lazlo announced as he wiggled up from the space between my bookcase and the floor. I raised my eyebrows as Lazlo marched over to the table, waggled his haunches, and pounced up right in front of the prince.

Freynir jumped but then hesitantly reached out to pet the purring feline on the ears.

Traitor.

"Aren't you a vicious predator?" Freynir grinned as he petted Lazlo. "Healthy and massive. You'd love all the rats on Pike's ship."

Lazlo blinked owlishly at me before bumping his nose against the prince's hand, demanding more attention. Then he flopped over onto his back and revealed a fluffy, inviting belly. Instantly, the Skadian fell into Lazlo's trap.

His hand came down to rub the massive cat's belly. I swore that cat smiled as his claws latched onto the dark elf's arm and he attacked. Freynir shouted, flailing as Lazlo scratched up his arm.

A laugh bubbled out of my chest before I could stop it.

Lazlo released the prince, looking awfully pleased with himself as he jumped off the table and wove between my legs, purring.

"Good boy," I chuckled when I rubbed his chin.

Then Lazlo disappeared, and I looked over at the prince.

His mouth was gaped open, scratches down his arm. Not very deep, but it still looked like it hurt.

"What the fuck?" Freynir demanded. "Ow. Shit." Then he muttered some swear in Skaditung before adding salve to his new injury.

"You're not around a lot of cats, are you?" I asked, still grinning because the fucker deserved it.

"We have wolves in the longhouse. The cats stay at the farms," he retorted. Then his eyes snapped back up to me. "You trained that beast on purpose."

I shrugged. "Maybe. Maybe not. Can you walk?"

"As long as I'm not required to use this arm," he huffed.

"Get up," I ordered, turning toward the cabin door and opening it wide.

He raised both eyebrows and stood up. "Where are we going?"

"I have responsibilities, and I'm not leaving you alone. Come on." I tilted my head toward the door, and he stepped out first.

I appraised Freynir as we walked. I could tell he was a little younger than me, but not by much. And even if the man knew how to swing a sword, he still moved with an entitlement only royals had. He seemed considerably more at ease than he was earlier. I was sure the lack of torture was a relief.

The sun was low on the horizon, but I knew the path to my cabana well enough to walk it with my eyes closed.

"Why are you taking me into the woods, Leviathan?" Freynir asked as we walked through the thicket to the beaten path that led to Anchorage Cove. "There're quite a few cliffs over here."

"Even though I *am* tempted to knock you off a cliff, I have business at my cabana." I walked behind him, feeling absolutely gargantuan with my staggering height. "Why don't you lead the way? Show me how you found it."

His shoulders stiffened. "I didn't think you or Mae would be there."

"How much did you hear?" *And answer the question carefully, or you'll be tasting the rock at the bottom of the hill.*

"Enough," he replied. "If it makes you feel better, a boot hit me in the face on the way out."

"Not two boots?" I asked.

He laughed dryly. "No. Just the one, I'm afraid."

We walked down the path in silence for a little while before I inquired, "What were you looking for?"

"Something incriminating," he admitted. "I didn't find anything. Nothing about a Dragon Lord who razed villages, seduced women, and ate children."

I sighed. "I don't know where the *eating people* thing came from."

"It's the oldest tactic in the book. If you want to instill fear, point the finger at any minority and say the children are in danger." Freynir shook his head. "I'm ashamed I didn't see it earlier. That's the same propaganda Edessa spread about Skadians. Most people know it's hogwash, but the damage has been done. Wars were fought over lies."

"Same story, different place."

His voice dropped an octave when he said, "And yet I believed the same lies."

It wasn't long before we reached my cabana. I waved at a few of the merrow who were swimming in the abysmal body of water down the hill. There were several things I kept in the inky depths and the cave system below, but I would've noticed if they lifted anything from my hoard. Not that I really would've cared.

My hoard used to mean a lot to me. Proof of my success as a pirate captain. But now, it seemed like such a small thing to care about.

A few merrows were outside on the porch and greeted me as I walked up.

"Come on," I murmured to Freynir as I walked past them to the far bedroom, where Siggi had been working on clothing patches.

The Skadian prince walked stiffly near me, not venturing too far. Which was wise because if he did, they'd assume he was an intruder, and I might not be able to protect him.

Hells, I don't know if I'll be able to protect him from Luella.

At least if Luella killed him, Mae could be mad at her and not me.

I knocked on Siggi's door, holding the designs Lucky needed in one hand.

"Yes?" Siggi asked loudly, and I could hear the hand crank on his sewing machine. Most of the time, he hand-sewed everything, but with so much work and so few hands, his machine got a good workout. He rarely ever used the machine for anything other than canvas or leather, and those materials were currently plentiful.

When I walked in, Siggi looked up at me with his magnifying spectacles and instantly stopped cranking. I recited a common greeting in Skaditung, which I knew would amuse the prince behind me.

Siggi repeated it before saying, "You'd better not have more work for me, Levi. I can barely keep up with patches."

"Unfortunately, I do," I answered.

He groaned and leaned forward, resting his head on the small desk that had fabric flowing over it like a cascading waterfall. "You need sails, don't you?"

"And signal flags," I added.

He threw his head back dramatically and made a motion of stabbing his chest with a sewing needle. "Kill me, then. I can't do this anymore."

I looked behind me at Freynir. "Can you sew?"

"What? Because I'm Skadian? You have a Skadian tailor and assume all of us can sew? That's awfully presumptuous," he said.

I stepped to the side so Siggi could see who I was talking to.

His eyes widened into saucers, and his mouth gaped open. "Is that—"

"Yes or no, Skadisyn?" I demanded.

His lips pursed, and he replied, "Yes. We're expected to mend our own clothing and—"

"Design our own wedding attire," Siggi finished. "When we have children, those same pieces are turned into baby clothes and blankets."

Freynir smiled genuinely. "It's nice to hear that even a continent away, my—our—traditions stay alive."

"There aren't many Skadians here," Siggi admitted. "But you're a Skadisyn? From the homeland?"

Freynir waved a hand toward Siggi, "No need for formalities. I haven't been acting like much of a prince lately." Then he looked up at me and sighed. "If I do this for you, will you take me with you to the Ivory Keys?"

"Yes." I lowered my head to look him in the eye. "If you want to eat. If you want a place to sleep. If you want to be considered worthy. You work."

He released a loud breath through his nose. "Fine. I also want a place at the table."

"*Fine.* At the end of the day, you come back to my cabin. I will have a cot for you," I stated. I wouldn't have him gallivanting unmonitored. Not until I was completely sure he could be trusted. At least Siggi would have dozens of merrow ready to defend him if the prince turned on us.

"And soap. And a fresh set of clothing."

I crooked a brow. "You're awfully demanding."

Freynir didn't back down from my stare and tilted his

head to the side. "You might be used to this *musk*, but I'm not. I need a bath."

With one more exasperated breath, I asked sarcastically, "Anything else you want, *milord*?"

"Keep that redhead away from me. I like my head attached to my body."

I lowered my own head, staring down at him from the bridge of my nose. "Fine."

"Splendid." Then Freynir grasped the designs from my hand and spun on his heel to say something I hadn't heard before in Skaditung.

In response, Siggi tilted his head back and laughed.

I narrowed my eyes, and Freynir threw a wink at me.

"I'll be with Udine in the other room. Try anything, and your life is forfeit."

"Order me around some more, *Captain*. I like it."

This is going to be a long few months.

MAEVE CROSS

A BREAKTHROUGH

I lost track of the days that passed.

My hours were full of experiments. Varric prattled on about my healing and how I seemed to heal faster and faster with each wound inflicted. The pain didn't last as long as my body made me whole.

Whole in appearance, but my spirit wavered, like I was a galleon being devoured by shipworms under the surface. It was only a matter of time before I sank. The only thing that kept me from falling apart was spite. The simmering rage that cauterized my splintered spirit. It felt as if my very soul had been enveloped with an armor born from the scars.

But in the middle of the night, I'd whisper to Penelope through the wall, soft enough that the guards couldn't hear us. Hope colored her tone as she told me about her dreams. About the first things she'd do when she saw her family again. About how she wouldn't be so afraid to tell Caine her feelings.

She didn't seem to be as afraid as she was before.

But her source of fear wasn't there.

Nathaniel spent weeks in the infirmary, and according to

Penelope, he was battling a nasty infection. After the nurses and physician sewed his face together, they were working day and night to monitor his infection so he didn't have to eat through a tube.

I would go to sleep hoping he would be dead when I woke up. I hoped that infection ate through him until nothing was left but a husk. I hoped he died *screaming*.

That news never came.

I dreaded the day Nathaniel came back, but the next time I had the opportunity, Nathaniel Pike was going to die by my hand, and it was going to *hurt*.

Penelope thirsted for freedom as badly as I did. I could hear it in the way she stumbled over her words in longing as if her mouth were parched.

In how she sang into the darkness as if that were enough to battle the abyss.

Some days, it was.

Other days, I'd hear her crying, and I'd press my palm against the wall and ache to comfort her. I wanted to take her into my arms and promise her that I'd find a way to free her. I'd unlock her cage so this songbird could finally *fly*.

There were times when I'd look out my balcony in Farlight and wish I were brave enough to leap from it. Just so I'd know the freedom of flying once before it was over.

I could imagine how beautiful her song would be once she was free.

Sometimes I'd fantasize about listening to her sing while Ronin played his violin. I imagined that it would be beautiful. A melody of liberation.

For her part, Penelope would tell me how she longed to feel the sea air in her locks and how wonderful a life of adventure sounded.

She reminded me of myself. Perhaps a softer version of

me who spoke quietly and did as she was told. But on the inside, she was as wild as I was.

"They can't take anything away from you."

Death had lied to me.

Physically, everything regenerated, but Varric still took my dignity. My free will. I kept thinking back to the dinner when I mutilated Nathaniel. To how smug Varric looked when I drew blood.

Did he plant that seed of spite in me on purpose?

Was he counting on Nathaniel's cruelty to get that reaction from me?

Gods, he's in my head. Like when I was a child.

I tried not to let him, but Varric was an earworm occupying my subconscious. I didn't know whether I was falling into his trap or not, and that doubt sat heavily inside me. It didn't matter if I was on the table or confined to my quarters, Varric was always there with me.

Whether I wanted him or not.

With each death, I got stronger, withstanding more brutality before I succumbed to the dark, the reprieves further and further away.

Now, as Varric split my chest open, I watched him poke around, unable to escape it.

It was a surreal sight.

I saw my own heartbeat, my lungs filling with each breath. I observed how my body struggled to keep me alive, but only for a moment until my skin came back together.

"I know it's here," Varric said, trying to clip my flesh back to itself to see how I ticked, but my body snapped them away and rapidly healed. "The body is a magnificent feat. So fragile, but so resilient."

My head tipped back as I fixed my gaze on the ceiling tiles. The neglected golden filigree. I counted the flowers sculpted there and the stars flecked with gold leaf. That ceiling was so ingrained in my mind that it was painted on the insides of my eyelids.

And every time I saw it, I wondered whose masterpiece it was that had been left to rot.

I ached to stare up and see the real stars. I wanted to remind myself of the times Ronin and I would stay up too late and talk with only the stars to witness us. When I was underneath that vast sky, everything else felt insignificant. All my problems felt so small.

The weight wasn't so heavy.

I missed the sky. I missed the sun. I missed the *sea*.

Now that I had a taste of freedom, nothing else could compare.

Varric's chair scraped the stone as he stood up suddenly. "Of course," he murmured.

I didn't say anything, glancing over at him as he wandered to his potions and elixirs and gathered the tube filled with a clear liquid that he would test my samples with. He came back and retrieved the scalpel again.

My head rocked against the table, and I screwed my eyes shut. *No more. Not again.*

"This won't bring her back," I hissed, desperate for anything to stop him. The information I held so closely stumbled out my mouth before I could catch it.

Varric's eyes snapped to mine, that cruel storm brewing in his gray irises. "*Her?*"

He poised his scalpel over my naked abdomen, which was still saturated with blood from hours of relentless experimentation. My hands twitched in their restraints, aching to snap the silver.

Then I'd take the chain and hang him with it.

But the keys were always on the other side of the room, next to his potions and his journal where he notated every awful thing he did to me. *And who knows what else?*

"Who was the woman in the mirror, Varric?" I snarled.

His upper lip curled into what looked like a sneer before it was gone, and he slid the blade down my chest. Blinding pain exploded in my brain. I writhed, crying out to get out of my own skin. Desperate to tear it all away to be free of the pain.

"And how do you know about that, Maeve?" he asked, but I couldn't focus on answering when he reached into the incision, uncaring of the pain it put me through. My ribs cracked as he pried them open with his bare hands. "I'm the only thing that stands between her and you. You think this is torture? This is *nothing.*"

I hissed through my teeth, black spots dancing in my eyes. The pain was so acute that I couldn't think as he took the vial of liquid and poured it into the cavity of my chest. It sizzled and burned, and I *screamed.*

A blue glow reflected off Varric's blood-splattered face. Then his eyes lit up, and he thrust his entire hand into my chest, taking my beating heart in his fist. My flesh closed around the intrusion as I thrashed, bucking my hips and kicking my legs as much as I could.

"Get off! Get off!" I bellowed.

An excited laugh sounded from Varric's mouth as he grasped my heart harder with a pressure that made my fingertips cold. "Your heart. Of course it was your beating heart."

The chill crawled up my arms as he obstructed my blood flow. I trembled violently.

My heart. The thing in my chest that feels too much and loves too strongly. The organ that breaks too easily.

Varric murmured a phrase in Antediluvian. The force of

the magic took my breath away as his eyes glowed, sapping the energy directly from my body. My shoulders shook as shock wreaked havoc on my body, the adrenaline running dry as he took everything for himself.

My eyelids fluttered, and I fought to stay conscious as Varric said something else, the beakers and equipment shuddering and levitating with the surge of magic. He laughed in exhilaration and withdrew his hand from my chest with an awful squelching noise.

Finally, I could take in a full breath as my healing mended all the damage. Tears thickened in my throat. It was different from the other experiments. This didn't feel clinical and restrained.

No.

Varric had his *hand* inside my chest. My ribs cracked apart. I could feel the pressure and the touch remain as a phantom. He grasped my heart like it belonged to him, but it was *mine*.

My heart was *mine*!

His bloodied hands cupped my cheeks, a wide, sinister smile on his face. "Now that was a breakthrough. Oh, isn't that lovely, Maeve?"

I swallowed down the emotions as they crested in my chest. I felt *violated*.

I'd heard all the stories of Varric's brutality from fellow sailors. How he did as he pleased completely unchecked by the Houses. I stared up at him and saw him as a madman, someone unmoved by empathy.

Varric raised me. He was, for all intents and purposes, my father.

He never cared about my pain before, but I didn't think he was beyond redemption. Not the way I viewed Nathaniel as irredeemable. But now, for the first time, I saw the *monster* that my people feared. He was so much worse than the Pikes.

It finally clicked. This man was *never* my father.

Varric was unbothered by my horror as he pulled away from me to jot notes into his journal. "You deserve a moment to relax," he stated. "I'll have the guards bring you to your room for the handmaidens to cleanse you. A new dress is a rightful reward, yes?"

"I don't want a fucking dress," I choked out, curling onto my side as far as the chains would allow me. I didn't care about my nakedness. I wanted to cross my arms over my chest and protect myself.

"Don't make a scene," he said, waving his hand and dismissing what he'd done to me. "I can't take it from you, but I'm sure I can find a way to share it."

He spoke like my heart was a commodity to divvy up, not like it was a vital piece of me.

"No," I hissed, a sob tearing through my throat.

"You gave up any autonomy when you betrayed me—"

I shook violently. "It's *mine!*"

He chuckled. "No, Maeve. It's always been mine. Ever since I found you."

Varric snapped his journal closed and left the room. Shortly after, the guards came in to retrieve me. And when they hoisted me off the table, their hands curled around my arms, I couldn't stand it anymore.

I cried.

"DON'T FUCKING TOUCH ME!" I WAILED AS THE HANDMAIDENS tried to wash me.

My hands were bound to the sides of the tub. I'd hoped they would leave me alone to bathe myself in peace, but I was too *dangerous.*

They scrubbed and probed, and I couldn't escape. Spite

and rage fizzled inside me, and I screamed, throwing my head forward and headbutting one of the handmaidens when they got close enough.

The other two jumped backward and went to her aid.

I panted like a trapped animal, desperate to hold on to one part of my autonomy. "Get. The. Fuck. Off. Me." I punctuated every word with a snarl. I felt wild inside, like any part of me could snap in two.

The tension was too much.

The horror I'd experienced was too much.

Everything was *too much*.

The handmaidens scurried out of the room, but I could hear them speak.

"I can't work under these conditions."

"King Varric will punish us if we can't follow his instructions. He specifically said he wanted her clean and fed before the next meeting."

"She broke my godsdamn nose!"

"We have to follow instructions!"

They went silent, and a few moments later, the door opened again.

"She's dangerous. Don't unlock her from the tub."

"O-Of course," a familiar voice said, stumbling over her words.

A cascade of red hair entered the room, and she closed the door. I could only see her narrow back as she turned around slowly. Her warm eyes widened slightly when she saw the state I was in.

I was sure my eyes were red, and I could still feel the blood drenched and crusted all over me. I knew I looked a bloody mess.

Penelope offered me a hesitant smile and quietly said, "H-Hello, Mae."

A sob retched from my chest, and I looked away, unable

to respond.

She came to my side quickly, and I tried to flinch away, but I couldn't, and another cry left my lips.

"I won't touch you, Mae. I promise."

I swallowed, feeling like a skittish animal when I slowly looked at her. Her blue eyes were so kind when she took the key and unlocked the chains from my wrists. I brought my hands up to inspect them, and the relief that ebbed through me made me bury my face in them.

"Thank you," I whispered.

"Can I-I keep you company?" Penelope asked.

I nodded, that suffocating feeling slipping away as I was granted the ability to clean myself. "You aren't worried that I'm too dangerous?"

She perched on the corner of my bed, fiddling with a loose stitch on her skirt. "I-I think you're too smart to try to run away. They'll bring y-you back." Her voice got even quieter. "I-I learned that the hard way."

I ran the sponge up my arms, making the water pinker with each movement. "What happened?"

She fidgeted with her hands. "I-I tried to run away, and he punished me on our wedding night." She tucked a tendril of red hair behind her ear. "Nathaniel said it was his reward for catching me. I-I was on my way to an apprenticeship with the opera school when Samuel Pike approached my father. With our tax debt, he had no choice."

"I'm going to get you out of here, Penelope," I said firmly.

"D-Don't make promises you can't keep. T-This is my life now," she said with a note of surrender.

"You can't accept that," I replied.

"I-I have, Mae. What's the alternative? The P-Pikes have all the power here." Penelope stood and moved around my room to flatten out my sheets and fiddle with the locked window covering.

I rinsed the blood from my hair. "You stand up."

Penelope looked at me from over her shoulder. "Not all of us can be brave like you, Maeve. I-I'm not strong. I've never been brave."

"You don't need strength to be brave."

She took something out from around her neck, a small pendant with a key. "You make me want to be brave, b-but I'm not like you." She paused. "I'm not supposed to do this."

I stood up from the bathtub and gathered the towel and robe that had been placed on the rim of the tub. "Not supposed to do what?"

"O-Open the windows." She unlocked the window covering. "They're barred, but I like to look out at the stars. Nathaniel gave this to me as a reward for behaving. H-He likes to pretend he gives me the world when he only gives me breadcrumbs. But he isn't here to take it away."

My heart squeezed at the small gesture. "You'd do that for me?"

She nodded, opening the window wide. Instantly, a sea breeze tickled my nose, and I inhaled deeply. It was the scent of home. The sound of crashing waves filled the room, and a joyful smile pulled at my mouth.

"Look up and kn-know that these are the same stars your family sees. No matter how far away, th-they're seeing the same stars."

Hesitantly, I reached out and squeezed Penelope's forearm in a show of appreciation. "Thank you, Pen."

She gulped and shyly looked down. "I-I thought you needed a smile."

"I needed to be reminded of home." I chuckled to myself, recalling a memory that I thought about fondly. "You know, when Ronin and I were… *courting*…," I said cautiously.

"Courting?" she inquired. "H-How do pirates court? D-Do they give you treasure?"

No. He gave me stars behind my eyes. I bit my tongue, remembering my company. Despite all the time that had passed, it wasn't the sex I missed the most. I missed everything else.

I shook my head. "Not quite. He did give me this wonderful turnover from a bakery. Gods, what I wouldn't do to taste that filling and feel the pastry flake in my hands." I hummed, remembering how he teased me by biting into a second one before giving it to me.

My heart ached in my chest again.

"I-I can find you a turnover," she offered, cheeks flushing. She looked so endearing when she fiddled with her skirt.

"You don't have to do that, Pen," I said.

"I like being called Pen…." Her gaze came up from her shoes to meet mine. "A-And I want to give you something for being my friend." Her cheeks were so pink when she said, "I want to make you smile again."

Tears welled in the corners of my eyes at the thoughtful gesture. "You deserve so much, Pen," I murmured softly as I reached forward to hold her hand. Her fingers felt clammy as they curled between mine.

She leaned into my gentle touch, and we stared out the barred windows at the stars and the crashing waves together.

32

RONIN MURDOCH

A TASTE OF FREEDOM

"Up we go," Andra said as she and I lifted Wesley from his infirmary bed into a seat that she'd crafted from spare parts that Lucky found while he was building ships. "Careful! Careful!"

"I'm not going to drop him!" I retorted, one hand on his back to keep him upright.

"Wouldn't be the first time you dropped me, Levi," Wesley teased while his arms shook on either of our shoulders.

I scoffed. "Your fault."

He was referring to the time he tried to climb on my back when I was in my full leviathan form, and I bucked him off into the big blue. He didn't land correctly and sprained his elbow, but that wasn't my fault.

I'm not a fucking pony.

Wesley grunted when we lowered him down. Luella watched anxiously, her good hand holding the chair still so it didn't roll away.

The back frame was comprised of iron welded together by our resident blacksmith, Ingrid.

Siggi sewed custom cushioning so it would support his back.

Butcher helped Andra design it, since he'd put together his own aids.

The whole town came together to make sure it was perfect, but ultimately it didn't matter what they thought, only if Wesley liked it.

"How does it feel?" Luella asked.

Wesley wriggled his shoulders, using his arms to get more comfortable. He looked up at us and grinned that radiant smile. "So much better than the bed."

The chair itself had three wheels: two in the back and one in the front so he could stretch out his legs. He grasped the handles on either side, and his hands shook violently. His throat worked down a swallow, and his smile no longer reached his eyes.

"I'll never be able to take the girls on a walk, will I?" The joy was no longer in his voice. "This is real nice, but it doesn't change the reality, does it?"

I parted my lips to tell him that I knew what it was like to be injured, but I stopped myself. I knew what it was like when *I* was injured. I didn't know jack shit about how this felt for him. I could still walk—Hells, I could fucking *fly* now.

"You don't know that, Howler," Andra said. "With enough practice, you might—"

"*Might*," he pointed out.

"Listen," Luella said, crossing her arms and kneading that sore spot where she was still nursing her stab wound. "You're right. It won't be the same. We don't know if you'll walk, Howler. That's the truth of it."

He folded his hands in his lap.

"*But* your girls are going to want you to let them take a ride in that chair all the time. Think of how big your arms are going to get. Isa is always squeezing your arms," Luella teased. "Gods, it makes me sick. If you didn't get snipped, you'd have twelve kids by now."

The gleam came back into his eyes again.

"It'll be different, mate," I said. "But that doesn't mean it's over. You don't heal by feeling sorry for yourself."

"You'd know all about that, wouldn't you?" Wesley teased, looking up at me and grinning even wider.

"You wound me." Warmth expanded in my chest. It felt nice to lift his spirits. While it would be a long road to recovery, he wouldn't travel it alone.

"Now, are we going to take this for a spin or not?" Andra asked, walking over to the door and opening it wide.

Wesley grasped the wheels on either side and said, "I've gotten rather pale in the infirmary. I look like a ghost. Like Wraith!"

"You wish you looked this radiant," Luella snorted.

He laughed and wheeled himself out of the room and down the hallway to the front of the chapel. Andra opened that door, too, and he quickly got himself outside. The warmth of the sun beat down on him, and he stopped completely, tilting his head up to bask in the breeze.

"I missed this," he murmured, eyes fluttering closed.

"Aye, mate, Boats and I have to work on stocking *The Ollipheist*," Luella said, clapping a hand on Wesley's shoulder. "But you can bet your sweet ass that we'll be there for dinner tonight before the big embarkment."

Wesley nodded. "Well, you better bring your drinking bellies for cards tonight!"

Andra and Luella gave him a smile and me a final wave before they took off.

At the pier, I watched sailors stock the freshly crafted ketches. Bliss worked with Pinky to assign roles to each of the vessels, and they were the best for the job.

The largest ships we had were *The Ollipheist*, which I

would captain, and two of Pike's galleons that had survived. Lucky would be my second considering he had experience commanding multiple vessels. He would report to me, but I would lead the charge.

Lucky and Bliss would captain the galleons at my flank with their assigned officers, but even the ketches needed a proper roster. A crew of seven for each ketch: at least one captain, gunner, bosun, quartermaster, helmsman, and two floating crew members. The defectors would be split among the crews to limit the chance of a mutiny.

This would be their chance to win any favor with me.

Over the past few weeks, there had been other pirate hunters who hung up their hats to join my cause. I supposed it helped to see how happy their peers were to be treated like people and not pawns.

At that moment, the whisper of autumn wind cut through the air.

"Ooh. That's nice," Wesley whispered, enjoying the fresh breeze.

The seasons were starting to change. According to Siggi, fall and winter felt the same in the tropics, but it was a nice reprieve from the scorching summer.

Gods, has it really been five months since I held Mae? Since I've seen her face?

The wind didn't soothe me. It was a bitter reminder of how I turned my back on her to save our people.

Would she understand anymore? After all Pike and Cross had put her through by now?

I didn't want to think about it, but at night, when the nightmares came back, I didn't see myself anymore. I saw each and every thing that they'd done to me happening to her. The humiliation. The violence. How it broke me. After a point, I succumbed to it. I let it consume me.

But Mae was stronger than I was.

"Levi?" Wesley asked.

I blew a hot breath from my nose, snapping out of my thoughts. "Sorry, mate." I wanted to be present for my friend, but whenever I had a moment of happiness, the dread came back.

"I won't hold it against you if you have work to—"

"No," I said. "I'm going to enjoy an afternoon with my best mate while I can."

"All right, then. When was the last time you ate something?" Wesley inquired, glancing up at me.

When was *the last time I ate something?*

When I didn't answer right away, he said, "Come now, mate. You're what… eight feet tall now? You gotta eat."

"I haven't had much of an appetite—"

"You're too worried making sure everyone else eats that you forget about yourself. You're like a big horned mama hen," Wesley said. "Let's go to the homestead, yeah? I want to give this chair a proper test."

He had a point. But I'd always been like that. It was my responsibility to make sure he and Andra ate while Mama was out captaining. Now instead of the twins, I had hundreds of people counting on me to keep them safe. But I was nothing if not stubborn.

So, I ignored the comment and asked, "Do you want me to push you?"

"No. If I get tired, I'll ask," Wesley determined. "But I need to do this myself."

"All right, mate. I'm sure the girls are excited to see you. Let's not keep them waiting."

I walked nearby in case he needed my help, but he wheeled himself willfully, determined to take control of his freedom. As we went, we tried to avoid shop talk, but conversation always rounded back to *The Ollipheist.*

The ship was such a big part of our lives together, but

given Wesley's injury and his family, he knew his sailing days were over. During those late nights that I'd visit him while everyone else slept, I knew he missed it.

Being my first mate was a job, and Wesley loved his job. However, he didn't belong to the sea like I did.

"A little help."

Wesley strained as we came up to a hill on the path that led to his homestead. I went up behind him and lightly pushed him so he could get over the steepest part. I barely did anything, but that was enough.

"Thanks."

When we got to the doormat, I knocked and was instantly greeted by Wesley's daughters. But I wasn't who they wanted to see.

"Daddy!" the littlest ones, Ellie and Dina, screamed as they rounded me to hug their father, tears in their little eyes. Maya and Lissy were also in tears the moment they saw him.

"Babies!" Wesley exclaimed, reaching to embrace as many of his children at once as he could.

There wasn't a dry eye as his daughters cried their hellos, trying to catch him up with everything. He beamed when he kissed their cheeks, so excited to be home.

"I was about to get him," Isa said from the doorway. "But thank you for saving me the trip, Levi."

I nodded at her, turning to see a large baby on her hip. Well, *baby* wasn't the right term for Brax anymore. He'd grown into a chunky child, almost one year old. I knew he'd be walking any day.

"My darling," Wesley said, grinning brightly at his wife. "Do you like my new ride?"

She leaned down at the waist to kiss him. "I do."

For a moment, it felt as if they'd forgotten everyone around them. Isa's delicate hand curled around Wesley's cheek, and he reached up to cup the back of her neck. Their kids were making obnoxious gagging noises when they leaned in to rest their foreheads together.

"I missed you," Isa murmured.

"I missed you more," he rebutted, capturing her lips one more time before releasing her. Then he took Braxton from Isa, and his son immediately made himself comfortable on Wesley's lap.

"Come inside. Let's get you both something to eat," Isa decided, ushering the kids back into the house. "All four of you get to help me make something special for your daddy."

"Me too?" Ellie, almost six, asked excitedly.

"You're old enough to help. Come," Isa replied, nodding inside so Wesley and I would follow.

I waited for Wesley to get over the lip in the entryway before closing the door behind him. Andra, Isa, and the kids had clearly worked hard to move all the furniture to make sure he had enough room to maneuver around.

"Sit down, mate," Wesley said, rolling up to an open spot next to the table. "It's hard to talk to you when you're so much higher up than usual."

"Fine." I sat across from him, folding my wings behind my back on the bench seat. "Do you want to play a round of bones?"

"I'd love to."

With two glasses of rum between us and a set of bones pieces, we played a leisurely game while his family chatted and prepared some food in the kitchen. Braxton watched eagerly, but I was sure it was because he wanted to stick a game piece into his mouth.

Occasionally, I caught sight of one of the other children who Isa had taken under her wing. They were working on various activities, whether it be catering to the chickens or marking up schoolwork my mother gave them to keep them on track.

"How does it feel knowing you'll be bringing Mae home soon? I miss that lassie," Wesley asked, rolling a bones piece to get a matching number, only to roll the wrong one. "Godsdamnit."

He passed the pieces off to me, and I rolled them. "It's been so long, Howler, and I don't know what the fuck Pike or Cross have been doing to her." Something tugged in my chest, and I didn't care that I rolled poorly. "But even so, I miss her like nothing else."

"She's strong, Levi. More than you and I combined."

I nodded even if I hated the idea that she'd have to conjure an armor of her own like I had. "She is." I paused, thinking about whether or not I wanted to tell Wesley what I'd been thinking.

If not him, then who?

"Do you remember when you got married?" I asked, passing him the bones.

He crooked an eyebrow. "Every year on our anniversary, Isa reminds me how I forgot my vows. Why?"

"I want to ask Mae to marry me."

Wesley's eyes shot up from his roll to me. "*You* want to get married?" Then he laughed. He fucking *laughed* at me. His son stared up at him, mimicking his father by giggling.

"I didn't realize that was fucking hilarious, Howler," I commented, frowning.

He waved his hand at me before clapping it over his mouth. When he finally got his fucking chortle under control, he said, "It's not that. It's *you*. When we were growing up, you were so godsdamn against marriage—"

"You've met our mother," I retorted. It was safe to say that she was an extremely poor role model when it came to romantic relationships. "And I'm not the same little shit I was back then."

Wesley waved at me again, trying to shut me up. "I was

going to say, before you fucking interrupted me, that I'm proud of you." He leaned onto his elbows and gave me that big beaming smile, but it didn't reach his eyes. "I'm sorry to be the bearer of bad news here, but if everything goes as planned with Cross, you're gonna be king."

I swallowed down my distaste for the title. That was what all this loss was for, wasn't it? I'd take on the mantle that had claimed so many lives. It didn't matter if I wanted it or not. "And?"

"Would Mae want that? To be queen?" Wesley asked. "That lassie is a free spirit. She ran from royal life."

I felt cold. I already knew the answer, but I didn't want to shatter the life I'd imagined for us. One on the seas, far away from castles and bureaucracy. The life where we'd finally get the peace we so desperately wanted.

But that was a fantasy.

In reality, once this was over, we'd never get a moment of peace. We'd be tugged in each and every direction. Someone would always be demanding something of me. Could I truly subject Mae to that life with me?

"I'll cross that bridge when we get to it," I answered. I could speculate all I wanted, but there was only one person who could tell me what Mae wanted, and she was trapped in a tower somewhere. "And I don't want you telling anyone about this. We don't even know if she'll say yes."

"Oh please, mate. You love her. She loves you. That makes your relationship the simplest thing in your life right now." He chuckled and added, "For what it's worth, even if the king thing doesn't work out, you know you have an island full of people who would love to attend the Great Captain Leviathan and Unkillable Mae's wedding."

"Unkillable Mae? That's what we're going with?" I asked.

"That's what those defectors call her when I eavesdrop on all their gossiping. I think it suits her," he replied.

I smiled and grabbed the set of bones. "I suppose it does."

Shortly after I rolled, Isa and the girls brought out a nice hot meal. Wesley didn't leave me alone until I took a bite.

"You better make a happy plate!" Ellie shouted. "That's what Daddy always says."

"Yeah, make a happy plate, Levi," Wesley tagged on.

I rolled my eyes. "You're lucky that you're my brother."

When I finished eating, more energized than I'd been in days, Andra and Luella joined us to drink the night away. But after the kids had been put to bed, Wesley was drunk and laughing his ass off with Luella. Andra's head was in her lap, Luella putting her to sleep by preening her braids.

It was nights like this that made me forget about all the bullshit. A perfect snippet in time when things weren't so complicated. But then I said my goodbyes and went to the front door, ready to head back to my cabin. Unfortunately, I was sharing it with Freynir, so I wouldn't get any alone time. Though as far as roommates went, he was clean and quiet when he wasn't fucking annoying.

"Levi?" Isa intercepted me from the kitchen, cocking her head to indicate that she wanted me to join her.

I glanced back at my mates one more time, committing the simple moment to memory. Then I ducked under the doorway to step into the kitchen. "Yeah?"

She tilted her head to the side. "I never said thank you. For getting Wesley back."

"No. Don't thank me. I was merely correcting a mistake I made."

"So serious," she mumbled. "You know, a proper response is *You're welcome, Isa*."

I pressed my tongue into my cheek to repress a smile and grumbled, "You're welcome, Isa."

"There you go. Not so hard, is it?" she asked before

looking past me at our family in the living room. "You'll make sure Andra and Luella get back safe, right? Mama too?"

A heaviness settled in my chest again, sinking into my stomach. I didn't know what would happen at the Ivory Keys, but I knew I'd try my best. "I'll do everything I can."

"Take care of yourself out there. No more missing meals. They're counting on you too much to neglect your health."

"Yes, ma'am," I answered.

She crooked a brow. "If I hear you've gotten yourself killed because you skipped breakfast, I'll bring you back from the grave to kill you again."

The corner of my lips twitched upward. "I will make sure I eat, Isa."

"Good. Now git." She shooed me before adding, "And bring that Mae back with you. It's hardly a family without her."

That heavy stone in my stomach dissipated, and I gave her a firm nod, then left to enjoy the quiet walk back to my cabin.

33

MAEVE CROSS

A FLEETING MOMENT OF WARMTH

The window was still open when the sun came up. Its warmth licked at my feet, slowly climbing up my body to bathe my face. I wanted to lie out under the sun like a cat with my belly up to bask in it.

Pen left the window open for me when she left, telling me that I had to close it when the guards came around. Even if she wasn't allowed to, she'd given me a tiny piece of freedom. I gained back a little bit of my autonomy with that window.

The sun had crested the horizon now, and I watched the colors wash over the bay. The waves crashed against the cliffsides. I closed my eyes and pretended I was at Wesley and Isa's homestead.

Like my mind's eye version of Ronin, the details were blurred like a watercolor painting, but the image gave me comfort. If I tried hard enough, I could imagine the laughing of their little girls, the splashing of the bin we used to wash the dishes, and the clucking of the chickens.

For a moment, the chill around my wrists wasn't chains. I was wearing thick golden bangles like the ones I'd seen in Ronin's wardrobe. Too big for my wrists, but he chuckled all the same when I put them on and accidentally slung one at him.

I curled my arms around myself and thought about how safe I felt when Ronin's arms were around me, his chin on top of my head, his smell surrounding me like a delightful fog.

I inhaled and smelled something warm and sweet like crispy sugar. Bubbling, tart fruit macerated in honey. Savory, salty bread. Flaky pastry soaked in butter.

Sure, Nathaniel's staff fed me, but I'd never had anything like what the baker in Shipwreck Bay made. That was a man who loved his craft, and I could taste it in every bite. Then there was Butcher, who made every meal taste like it was made with love even if the main ingredient was nearly spoiled potatoes.

With another inhale, I realized the smell of pastry wasn't in my head. I blinked, looking around my chambers to figure out where that delightful scent was coming from.

"You can't come in here," my guard said outside my door.

"Please, Gregor. I-It's only breakfast. He doesn't have to know," Pen answered, voice so quiet that I had to strain to hear it.

A heavy sigh. "I have my orders. Only the handmaidens are allowed inside."

"Th-The handmaidens aren't g-going to serve her after last night. Are y-you going to let the king's daughter miss breakfast?" she asked, stuttering heavily. I could imagine her shuffling from foot to foot, deeply uncomfortable.

"Fine," the guard decided. "But you don't get a key to her cuffs this time." There was a clattering sound. "And she doesn't get silverware."

Pen didn't answer as the door opened, and she walked in, a silver tray held in both hands. She wore a violet gown that covered most of her skin like always, but the bruise that was around her neck had finally yellowed.

When the door closed behind her, she looked up and offered me a nervous smile.

I lifted my nose and inhaled deeply. "You didn't."

Pen nodded excitedly. "I-I told you I would."

Emotion welled up in my throat as she placed the tray on my table. I nearly darted toward it, but then I was overcome with excitement as I dragged Pen into a hug. She froze up, both of her shoulders coming up around her ears.

Ronin used to freeze up like this too. I pulled away instantly, putting a few feet of space between us. "I'm sorry. I shouldn't have jumped on you like that."

Pinkness flushed her face as she clasped her hands in front of her chest. "I-I was surprised. I-It's all right." She took a deep breath and released her hands. "You can embrace me now. I'm ready."

I looked into her guarded eyes. "You don't owe me a hug, Pen."

She shook her head and outstretched her arms. "*I-I* need one."

I slowly approached her and curled an arm around her neck, bringing her into a tight embrace. She was a little taller than me, but she slouched, tucking her face into my neck. Her hands pressed against my waist.

I patted her back, letting her relax. She squeezed me like she was desperate for any affection that didn't have a price. I let her pull away first, and when she did, there were tears in her eyes that she quickly wiped away.

"I-I'm sorry," she apologized.

"Don't," I said, reaching up to cup the side of her face and wipe away another stray tear with my thumb. "Don't you ever feel sorry for that. Not with me. Not with anyone."

She gave me a watery smile and nodded, mouth opening

and closing as if the words had escaped her. Instead of speaking, she turned to the tray and lifted the lid, revealing savory breads and turnovers with burnt sugar around the edges.

"Oh Gods," I hummed, practically vibrating with excitement. "May I?"

Pen dipped her head up and down, gesturing to them before she sat on the edge of a chair, her skirts billowing around her ankles.

My eyes practically rolled back when I bit into the turnover. The filling wasn't warm, but it reminded me of home. I moaned to myself, savoring every bite so it could stay in my memory a little longer.

"I-Is it good?" she asked softly.

"Lovely," I replied. "Would you like one?"

She nodded, and I handed her a pastry. Crumbs coated her skirt as she bit into it, crumbling the flaky crust and getting jam on her mouth. Quickly, she wiped it away, fear mottling the joy on her face. Her body went rigid, and I wondered how often she'd endured a beating just for getting crumbs on her dress.

"Do you like it?" I asked, hoping my voice would snap her out of her spiral.

Her eyes darted up to mine and she smiled, nodding and taking another messy bite. I enjoyed her company as we shared the food, talking briefly about music or what it was like to be a pirate.

Then the door swung open, and Pen flew to her feet, panic etched all over her face.

"A little birdie told me you were misbehaving," Nathaniel said. "You forget yourself, darling."

I twisted around to see him standing there, bandages on his face and dark circles under his eyes, but he looked whole. *Not for long.* Rage boiled inside me as I stood up, stepping closer to Pen as if my presence would save her.

"Come a little closer, Nathaniel," I hissed. "Why are you so far away?"

He glanced at the chains, then at me. He didn't spare me another glance as his gaze swung to Pen. "Come here."

"I-I-I—"

Nathaniel threw his head back and laughed. "Oh, my pathetic wife. Can't get a word out? And yet you had the audacity to take pastries from the kitchen like a little pest."

I knew as well as anyone that Pen didn't do anything wrong. This was an excuse. "She is the lady of the house. She should be able to do what she wishes."

"Mae... p-please," Pen whispered, her throat bobbing as terror swallowed her. "I-I—"

I looked up at her as she struggled to speak, unable to say anything as Nathaniel grinned that cruel smile. "Come here, darling. Stop making a fool of yourself. I'll be lenient."

I reached for her, curling my fingers through hers. "Stay here. I'll protect you."

Her lips trembled when she looked down at me. Tears welled in the corners of her eyes, and I could see the battle taking place. She wanted to believe me, but she didn't believe there was a way out. She squeezed my hand like it was a lifeline, but that wouldn't stop the riptide from claiming her.

"She can't protect you, sweet thing." Nathaniel glared at our hands.

Pen didn't move. She held on tighter despite how fear had sunk its claws deeper into her.

Then Nathaniel turned toward the door. All niceties vanished when he snarled, "When I'm finished with your brothers, they'll only be able to idomitify them from their teeth. But at least you'll have a piece to remember them by." Then his mask was back, a coy look of false kindness. "Or you could come here and save them."

We stood there in silence, but it didn't take long for Pen's fingers to unwind from mine. I grabbed onto her harder, but she looked at me with tears in her eyes.

"I have to, Mae," she whispered.

My grip tightened momentarily. I was terrified to let her go, but I understood.

Gods, I understood.

I released her, and she took those long steps right into Nathaniel's embrace. He was a solid wall of muscle, a man who could easily overpower the average person, but instead of making her feel safe, he was Pen's prison.

Nathaniel's cold eyes met mine.

This was never about Pen.

He wants to hurt me.

He curled his hand into her hair and threw her onto the ground. She cried out as his boot thudded heavily on her chest. "What punishment fits stealing food?" he asked, but his eyes never left me.

I ran toward him as far as my chains would let me. "Let her go!" I screamed, thrashing as hard as I could in the hope that it would snap the chain.

It didn't.

"How about I take you into the high tower, Penelope?" Nathaniel asked. "Let's see how you fare *without* food. That would teach you to avoid feeding the vermin."

As he dragged Pen away, I tore my room apart, agony ripping through my bones. Then I took out the needle I kept embedded in my pillowcase and began to pick at my locks.

I will get out of this. I will get out of this.

I will.

34

RONIN MURDOCH

BACK ON THE BIG SALT

Most of my childhood was a blur.

I remembered bits and pieces—

Like how my brothers teased me relentlessly, but it never felt like teasing because at least I was being included. Even if I had forgotten what they looked like, I remembered how much fun we had together.

Or how the servants were always retrieving me from the roof or scolding me for hanging off the tapestries.

I vaguely recalled how I convinced the sentries to spend the whole afternoon hunting for frogs in the pond that turned swampy in the summer.

But my coat of arms had forever evaded my memory until I looked up at the flag that whipped back and forth from the mast on *The Ollipheist*. It looked nothing like the mockery Varric had procured for himself.

The design was a vibrant turquoise that boasted the whole body of a leviathan in all its glory, full of life with wings completely extended. Lightning erupted from its open maw. It proudly displayed the power of my lineage.

It represented resilience in the face of Varric Cross's relentless pursuit of power.

He awoke a beast when he ordered Shipwreck Bay to burn. When he tore Mae away from me and murdered my friends. When I came for him, he would feel the Isles shake beneath his feet and lightning split the air.

He wouldn't live long enough to regret it.

Pride expanded in my chest when I gazed down the pier at my fleet of ships, all proudly displaying my coat of arms. Twenty-five ships adorned with my flag. Surreal wasn't the right word. I'd never imagined that I would lead a battle against the men who scorned my family and stole the livelihoods of so many people.

If Mae hadn't entered my life, I'd either be dead with my draconite adorning a pointless piece of jewelry, or I'd still be fucking around while the Isles fell to shit around me. For the first time in my life, I looked in the mirror and I was *proud*.

I wasn't hiding. I wasn't pretending. I was finally where I was always supposed to be.

Let's get my girl back. And take the Ivory Keys, of course.

I flexed my wings and gave Shipwreck Bay's pier one final wave goodbye before I ordered, "Pull the anchor!"

Andra and the ship crew pulled up the gangway and cranked the anchor up and off the sea floor.

"Plankwalker, set course for the Ivory Keys. It's time to pay Nathaniel Pike a visit."

My helmsman dipped his head, smiling widely as he shifted the helm and replied, "Aye, aye, Cap."

Luella, my new first mate, shouted the next order. "I want to hear those canvases crack on!"

I directed Udine to lift the secondary signal flag under the other one to alert the fleet to follow and fan out behind us. She obeyed, watching the ship crew closely to learn the ropes. There were merrow stationed on every ketch to make sure things ran smoothly. They weren't familiar with these waters, but if anything happened, the merrow could transport sailors safely.

Bliss and Lucky captained the galleons behind me. We were trained on Lucky's signal flag system, but I would still be meeting with them in person for updates and orders.

The fleet was on the move, and I gave Luella a wave before ducking into my cabin. Near the ballast, Freynir was sitting on his cot. He'd done a significant amount of work during the shore leave, but he still retired in my cabin every night.

While I liked my privacy, Freynir was decent company. As much as he enjoyed fucking around and trying my patience, he still gave me my much-needed space.

But there was more than one reason he didn't claim his bunk in the officer's quarters.

"You can't avoid her forever," I commented, taking a seat at my desk.

"Red won't kill me if you're around," Freynir replied and made his bed. Even if he didn't want to admit it, he'd been hiding in my cabin all night.

"Only because she doesn't want to get blood on my floor." I tidied some of my papers and Gunny's blueprints.

My cabin door opened, and Luella came in.

Luella and I both took great pleasure in how skittish Freynir was around her. For someone who bragged about being a great warrior, he folded like a clam when she walked into the room. Her green eyes locked onto Freynir, and I knew it was only a matter of time before it came to a blistering head.

"You're still hiding him in here?" Luella asked.

I shrugged. "He's hiding. I just live here."

"Good day, Red," Freynir said, his back ramrod straight.

"Save it, cunt," she retorted and looked back at me. "I'm

here to report that the filtration system is working as intended."

"Good. I was worried that all that sitting around would clog the system." I leaned back. "How's morale? How are the defectors taking to the ranks?"

"Morale is high. The defectors seem to be getting on well with the crew, but I'll keep an ear to the ground," Luella replied.

"How are you?" I asked. She'd settled into the role of first mate well. Udine had stepped up to be acting quartermaster, but I had no doubts that Luella could do both roles if necessary.

She shot me a toothy smile. "Pleased as I could be to be back on the Big Salt. It feels good to sail again." She tilted her hat back to glance at Freynir. "It'd be even better if you let me throw him overboard."

I chuckled. "Sorry, Wraith. He stays."

She hummed and tilted her hat back down to shadow her eyes again. "Few places to hide here, Prince. Levi may have found you worthy, but you still shoved your sword through my best friend's chest. I'll be coming for you sooner or later."

Then she turned on her heel and left Freynir shaking in his boots in the corner.

"GOOD MORNING," I GREETED ANDRA FIRST THING THE NEXT day. Now that we were sailing again, I slept surprisingly well. It was only a matter of time until I had Mae back in my arms. We were no longer waiting.

Of course, the sea air and the breeze whipping through my hair also relieved a lot of the restlessness that lingered. Lieutenant Commander Lazlo seemed to sense the change in me as well, coming up from the lower decks to purr against my side while I slept.

Andra had the rigmates climbing the rigging to adjust the canvas to the wind. *The Ollipheist* cut through the water with both Lucky's and Bliss's galleons at our flank. We moved as a unit, close together.

Strength in numbers. If sirens or the kuru struck, we were more than able to fight them off. We'd also run several drills so the ketches at the back of the fleet knew how to respond before the song seized them. Each of the ships was outfitted with harpoons to defend against the kuru.

Cannons wouldn't do jack shit against tentacles, but harpoons would stun a kuru enough to scare them away. There were many stories about the kuru's massive cousins, the kraken, but I'd only ever seen the small, shy, tentacled beasts.

Kuru were hungry and quick, but they were nothing like the ship-destroyers sailors liked to tell stories about.

Andra waved me over and handed me a spare breakfast ration. "Mornin', Cap."

I gratefully accepted the food and enjoyed the final moments of sunrise. It wasn't much more than boiled eggs and crusty bread, but it still filled my belly. Plankwalker manned the helm and kept us on route, taking over for the night helmsman.

"Watch," Andra said, gesturing toward my cabin where Luella waited by the steps, out of sight from my door. "This is gonna be good."

Shortly after, my door opened, and Freynir stuck his head out, looking around before slowly exiting when he didn't see Luella. As soon as he closed my door, Luella grabbed him, eliciting a sound of shock from the Skadian prince.

Andra and I continued eating our breakfast.

"No one fucks with my family and gets away with it,"

Luella snarled and shoved Freynir down the steps and flat onto his back on the planks.

The dark elf's yellow eyes darted around the deck and landed on me, silently pleading for my help. I took another bite from my bread as sailors came up from the lower decks to see what the ruckus was about.

Freynir put his hands up. "We don't have to do this, Red."

Luella dragged him up to his feet and took a sparring stance in front of him. The prince was a formidable warrior, but she was also a force to be reckoned with. There was only one way Luella handled conflict, and it was through a good fight.

I should know. We fought constantly over who would be captain until we finally settled it through battle. I could still feel the bruises after nearly ten years of friendship.

"Show me you're worth your salt," she hissed.

Sailors gathered while Freynir rolled his shoulders and took a defensive stance.

"I don't want to hurt you," he said, nervously looking around at all the new faces.

Luella swung out and hit him hard upside the jaw. "Worry about yourself."

The scent of a winter hearth filled the air as Freynir retaliated, letting his hesitations go and fighting back. When he struck her, Luella grinned and attacked. To any untrained eye, it would look like she was trying to kill him, but I knew her better than that.

She dodged Freynir's strikes, but they were evenly matched. The wintery smell got stronger, but he wasn't trying to berserk and take advantage. He wasn't blinking into a plume of smoke. Blue blood spilled from his split brow and melded with a splash of crimson from Luella's bloodied lip.

"There! You drew blood! Are you happy?" Freynir shouted.

Luella moved like lightning with remarkable footwork. Meanwhile, Freynir kept up surprisingly well. Considering how injured he was when he arrived at Shipwreck Bay, I was pleasantly impressed.

"That's my wife, Levi," Andra sighed, enjoying the entertainment as much as I was.

The corner of my mouth turned up. "You're drooling."

"Yeah, I am," she replied.

Luella ducked around Freynir's strike, getting behind him to kick out his knees. He crumpled, and in the blink of an eye, she drew her dagger, holding it near his throat. Everything went quiet, and Freynir became still.

"Now we're even," Luella said and sheathed her dagger. "You came for my family. You do not pass me unscathed."

Freynir got up to his feet, and they stared each other down. Then he reached out a hand. "You fight well."

Luella took his hand in a solid shake. "You took your loss well."

"Are we good now?" he asked.

"We are," she decided before dragging him close and threatening him once more. "If you hurt my family again, my blade will kiss your throat."

They released each other from the handshake with newfound respect.

MAEVE CROSS

MUCK ON THEIR SHOES

I STARED AT THE WALL, AGONIZING OVER EVERY MOMENT THAT Pen's room was silent. The silver chains rubbed abrasively against my wrists so deeply that I swore I could feel them grind bone.

Days had passed, and the same questions pelted my mind.

Did Nathaniel kill her?

Is she all right?

How can I save her?

Without her, the castle felt *cold*. Void of any warmth or kindness. The handmaidens and guards felt it, too, and were equally on edge as I was.

Was he really starving her? Had he really locked her away in a tower as punishment for giving me a taste of home? My chest felt tight as I rounded back to the same conclusion every time.

It's my fault.

I promised to save her, but I was just as useless as everyone else.

My breathing was loud in my ears as my hatred grew and

grew. I fixated on every hypothetical opportunity to go after Nathaniel. My throat grew dry as I thirsted for violence.

The isolation hung on me so heavily that I couldn't sleep. My appetite evaded me. All I craved was Nathaniel's death. Then Samuel's for letting his son act on cruel desires.

I wasn't sure what was worse: Nathaniel's brutality or Samuel's apathy.

They will both pay for it.

They had given up their chance at mercy.

I suspected that they knew of my bloodlust because they never came to retrieve me themselves. They always sent the guards or servants. And even if those people worked for evil men, we were all born into a world that put those men in power.

To say no meant death.

As violently as the hatred ran through my veins, I'd never take my aggression out on the staff unprompted. They were as trapped in this prison as I was. They didn't know they had the power to leave.

My door swung open, revealing my guard detail. "Your Highness, we've come to collect you," the one up front announced.

I scoffed. He always referred to me as *Your Highness* or *Princess*. If they truly viewed me as worthy of the title, I wouldn't be chained to my bed. "Save the formalities."

"Come with us, my lady."

The two men slowly approached me as if I was a skittish animal. I couldn't run even if I wanted to, but I doubted they wanted to wrestle me out of the room.

My breaths were labored from the fucking corset I'd been strapped into as I stated, "I'll go easily if you answer a question."

"We don't know where Lady Penelope is. We aren't permitted to enter that wing," the guard answered before I asked. He swallowed thickly, averting his eyes for a moment before taking a deep breath. "Please, Princess Maeve, come with us."

"What does Varric have on the docket for me today? Hmm? More torture? Perhaps some humiliation?" I asked. "Will he give me more nightmares?"

His eyes crinkled around the edges, a frown deeply creasing his mouth. "Please. We can't delay."

Was it the fear in their eyes or the pity that made me relent? They patted down my dress for any weapons and checked my shoes but found nothing.

They hooked my chains to the hoop around my waist. To any onlookers, it appeared like ornate jewelry was draped around my arms, elegant silver looped around my neck like a dog collar. Additional measures after Pen was taken away.

I felt like a flaunted pet as the guards took me down the halls, but this time I wasn't taken to the room near the dungeons where my screams were muffled. They took a different turn toward the Great Hall.

Two of the Cross guards I recognized waited outside a large door. They didn't look at me as they opened it into a grand suite. Were they avoiding my eye from shame or disgrace?

Inside, there was a sitting room in which I recognized several nobles from the dinner weeks ago. Including Samuel Pike, who gave me this smug look like he knew more than I did.

The suite had several rooms and high ceilings painted with the same neglected flowers. As we passed one of the rooms, I caught a glimpse of a familiar mirror in its black frame with golden filigree. The mirror itself looked other-worldly, as if something floated between the glass and our reflections.

The calling mirror. I could get a message out to Frey's wife, Elinora.

If I could figure out how the blasted thing worked.

A small part of me imagined putting my hand through the mirror to watch the shards fall like shooting stars. I wanted to see that ghostly woman shatter. I wanted to hear Varric cry in agony as I *stole something from him.*

"Ah, I see she's finally made an appearance." Varric's voice snapped me away from the mirror, but I committed its location to memory. "Was she difficult?"

"I was reasonable," I replied.

"Well, you must be wondering why I've gathered our allies into one room," he began, gesturing to the House leaders.

It wouldn't be out of character for him to enact a violent coup, but he still needed their cooperation. I believed that as soon as he got what he wanted, he'd betray them in a moment. They thought they were special enough to be spared from Varric's coup almost twenty-six years ago, but they were part of a longer game.

"I cannot take Maeve's gift and give it to all of you. Unfortunately, it remains bound to her. But I can tether *one* life to hers," Varric said.

Over my dead body.

I thrashed in an attempt to get out of the larger guard's grasp, but he held on to my chain tightly. "Get the fuck off me!"

"Oh, don't be difficult. Can't you see? This is what you were meant for," Varric crooned, his stormy eyes brewing a swirling cocktail of malice and a mad glee.

I snarled. "You're a liar." I looked over the small crowd of nobles and shouted, "He will betray you! He will let you all die!"

"Poor thing," Varric sighed. "Your mind is still muddled.

I've been nothing but faithful to my word. I've granted you all power and prestige that the leviathans had hoarded for themselves. I will even test this magic on myself, to make sure it's safe."

Liar. But it didn't matter. The fools heard what they wanted to hear.

"Go along, then," Samuel said. "Show us your magic."

"Bind her to the table," Varric ordered.

I tried to break away, but the guards hoisted me up and slammed me flat on the table. I may have been immortal, but they still overpowered me. The chains clicked and locked my hands above my head.

"I should've asked the handmaidens to avoid dressing her," Varric mused, tapping his chin as he glanced at my gown. "No matter. Use these to cut away her clothes and expose her chest."

The closest guard hesitantly took the shears from Varric's outstretched hand. Slowly, he lowered them to the top of my bust and looked deeply uncomfortable as he snipped the fabric open. It fell away from me, and he averted his eyes, placing the shears on the table before backing away completely.

The eyes that flickered across my bare skin felt like unwanted fingerprints.

The nobles crowded around the table as Varric gathered his instruments. When he came to my side, he showed two stones to the audience. "I have carved two runes. One will be placed at the source of Maeve's power, and the other, I can wear to draw upon her life force whenever I need it."

No one said a word or raised a finger. Not when I shouted for liberation. Not when my blood saturated everything. I wasn't a person. I wasn't even a body. I was a resource to be depleted.

To my horror, they weren't only bystanders. They were

active, excited helpers. Two nobles joined to hold my chest cavity open as my body fought against the torment.

Varric spoke in Antediluvian and pressed the rune into my pounding heart. "Hold it open. We're not done."

It. Not her....

Even when he made a small incision in my heart, my body didn't expire. Each death had strengthened me, allowing me to take more and more damage.

Will I ever know Death's peaceful embrace again? Will I ever be free of this?

I already knew the answer.

My head tilted over to Varric, and I saw the crimson staining his hair and his face. The evil that radiated from him. The excitement in his eyes as he tinkered with me like I was nothing but a collection of gears and cogs.

I will never be free until I unseat the usurper.

He tucked the stone into the incision. "Release it."

Everyone removed their hands as my body closed around the rune, suspending it in my chest. The intrusion stole my breath away as I fought agonized tears. It was another violation.

A haunting that I could never be rid of.

"Step away," Varric ordered as my ribs cracked back into place and my skin stitched itself together, leaving behind nothing but phantom sensations and red smears. He grasped the other rune with a bloodied hand, slippery like oil. He spoke Antediluvian, and instead of his amulet glowing, the rune in his hand lit up.

I slammed my head into the table as the rune in my chest *burned*, searing me from the inside. A muffled cry spilled out of me as black dots danced in my vision, the pain so intense that I couldn't think straight.

Varric released a bout of manic laughter as he shouted

another spell, and the guard behind me flew into the air and... *imploded.*

I didn't know what I was looking at until the man who I'd been talking to this morning became a puddle of viscera on the floor. Horror enveloped me as the second guard screamed, but before he could leave, he, too, became nothing more than red mist.

I knew them. I just talked to them.

"Miraculous," Samuel whispered. "Will I be able to cull my ranks with a snap of my fingers?"

"Soon. But now, we can celebrate knowing that such power is possible."

The nobles cheered in response, but the noise sounded distorted as I gazed at what was left of the two men.

But they didn't care. They didn't share my horror. All they saw was muck on their shoes.

Varric clapped his hands together. "Now, would you get some servants to clean up this mess?"

My stomach tensed as revulsion spread through my body. Bile burned in the back of my throat. Tears glazed my eyes as I stared at Varric and the nobles in their celebration.

I needed to stop this, but I also feared that now it was too late.

RONIN MURDOCH

OLD SECRETS

Magic inhibitors.

That's what the defectors called the collars and chains they dressed the magic users in. Lucky had them strewn across his desk, and he tapped his chin as he examined them. His cabin on the galleon was considerably less personalized than mine was, but after I'd found some of his trinkets scattered in the ocean, he was able to give the built-in bookcases a little piece of his personality.

"You think you can reverse engineer them?" Freynir asked.

The Skadian prince insisted on joining me for war talks, but I told him he'd have to find his own way onto Lucky's ship. I wasn't going to fly him back and forth from *The Ollipheist*. That should've been the end of it. But it turned out that he wasn't bluffing.

Thank the Gods that I wasn't a betting man, because Freynir had proceeded to throw a rope to the other ship for a crew member to tie to their rigging before he literally climbed there.

Meanwhile, I extended my wings and landed on the deck

before he could get a quarter of the way across. Luella only laughed her ass off and told me to catch her up on any new information.

Lucky fiddled with the collars, clicking his fingernails against the draconite crystal. "With your permission, Ronin."

I crossed my arms and asked, "What did you have in mind?"

"We know Cross uses draconite to cast spells. And I have to assume he's found a way to take at least a portion of Mae's invulnerability," Lucky said slowly, his violet eyes gauging my reaction carefully.

I frowned. "It would be foolish not to."

Freynir didn't like that any more than I did. He tensed but didn't say anything.

"These chains are used to prevent casting, but I have a theory that I could flip the enchantment," Lucky explained, "and create a shield against Cross's spells."

A conflicted feeling unfolded in my chest at the idea of using draconite. Something so pivotal to my people had been twisted into a weapon, and now I was going to use it for my own gain. I sighed and reached forward, touching the black crystal that twinkled with blue.

"I wouldn't suggest this if I didn't think it was necessary. If Cross has gotten stronger, he could use his power to thin us out before we get close. I also wouldn't do this without your approval." Lucky fiddled with the chains that were used to bind wrists.

I was hesitant.

But wouldn't it be a bigger injustice to let Cross win?

As I stroked the crystal with a black-tipped claw, it didn't feel like I'd be contorting their memory into something ugly. Leviathans were meant to protect and guard.

"A shield?"

"Not a weapon," Lucky confirmed. "They've suffered enough."

"Who would carry it?" I asked, well aware that there wasn't enough material to supply the entire army.

He counted on his fingers. "I can break these into ten pieces. Then we can hand them out to those who will be the closest to Cross on the battlefield."

"When this is over, we return them to the trenches," I said.

Lucky dipped his chin. "I promise."

"All right," I agreed, turning to leave. "I'll catch up with you tonight."

Freynir followed me back to the main deck, where I greeted a few members of the ship crew. Even though it had been several days since we set sail, morale was still high, and everyone took to their duties easily.

I could tell who the defectors were because they seemed the happiest out of all the sailors. They smiled and joked with one another, enjoying the hard work and the rewards that came with it. With respect and security in their positions, they seemed to blossom.

Even the Seymour brothers, who were rather skittish when I first met them, relaxed under Lucky's captaining as if they had finally found a place they felt like they belonged.

That was really all it took to gain loyalty. Respect, honesty, and full bellies.

"You know, this would be a lot faster if you flew me back to the ship," Freynir commented cheekily. He brought it up frequently, always joking about how much fun it would be to ride a dragon.

I never knew if the double entendre was intended or not.

"Maybe then I'd forget about you and Andra letting Red beat the shit out of me over breakfast." He adjusted his collar, pulling his pendant out so it rested proudly against his clavicle.

"No," I replied, extending my wings to fly back over my ship.

When I landed on my upper deck, I could still hear him shouting things at me, but I didn't turn back to look at him.

How did Mae tolerate being cellmates with him?

THE STARS NEVER LOOKED SO BEAUTIFUL. I STARED UP AT them, my heart thrumming excitedly in my chest because I knew that tomorrow, I'd see Mae again.

Hang in there, sweetheart. Just a little while longer.

A big portion of me wished that when I got to the Ivory Keys, Mae wouldn't be there. My girl would've escaped in a flurry of fire and destruction. Mae would've taken the whole fortress with her.

Wishful thinking. I could hope all I wanted, but that wouldn't change the reality that she had been held prisoner for months. There was a chance that I wouldn't recognize her anymore. That too much had changed, and we wouldn't work anymore.

That didn't matter.

I was going to get her out of prison whether she still wanted me or not.

She would still hold that little piece of me. I'd never get it back. It would be hers forever. And I wished that the piece I held of her would still fit any misshapen socket it left behind.

I stared up at the stars from the top of my cabin, remembering the quiet, gentle nights when Mae would lean against me and we'd wonder if the Gods were watching us. Now, I knew they were.

Gods, I missed her.

"You up for company tonight, Cap?" Luella asked, drawing my attention to where she stood a few rungs from the top of the ladder. She had a bottle of rum with her.

I sat up and said, "Yeah." Then I noticed she was alone. "Where's Andra?"

"Sleeping," she answered. "She always falls asleep when I fix her hair."

"She's been working hard. I'm glad she's getting some rest." I scooted over, and Luella came up to sit next to me.

She took her hat off and combed her hair back behind her extended ears. "You're not. The night before the big battle, you should be sleeping."

She held out the wax-sealed bottle to me, and I used my claws to slice it open, popping the cork easily.

"No sleep for the wicked." I took a gulp and passed it over to her.

She chuckled and tipped the bottle back. "What does that say about us, Levi?"

"That we're as wicked as we need to be." We passed the drink back and forth, enjoying the quiet as the night crew worked beneath us on the main deck. "Besides, I'm always restless before a battle."

"You're restless, period."

"Eh." I shrugged. "What's keeping you up?"

She grunted under her breath and reached beneath her collar to pull out her old marital pendant. While Freynir wore his proudly, Luella hid hers like it was a source of shame she couldn't get rid of.

We sat in silence for a little while, passing the bottle between us.

"Did you know that I've been in Farlight Isles for thirteen years today?" Luella asked quietly, an unusual softness in her voice.

She always got distant on the anniversary, though I never

knew why. She kept her secrets, and I kept mine. We understood each other in a way that my other mates never did.

"I remember," I said.

"That Skadian prince is proof that I *can* go back to Algar." She twisted her pendant. "I just don't want to."

"You always have a place here, Luella," I offered.

She dipped her head and took another healthy swig. "My daughter turned thirteen a few days ago."

Daughter?

"I was expected to fancy men. I was expected to have a child. My wants didn't matter," Luella stated. "Once my daughter was born, I had fulfilled my requirement to my husband. He took the child, and I went back to work. I was still bleeding when I took to the water."

I remained quiet, letting her confide in me.

"I don't know why I still wear this," she murmured, twisting the marital pendant again. "I remember praying to Zerenyth that the ocean would take me so I wouldn't have to go back. I didn't expect my God to answer."

"Does Andra know?" I asked.

"She knows I was married," she replied. "I don't want her to look at me and see a mother who abandoned her child." Then she sighed. "He wasn't a bad man, Levi. I just didn't love him."

I glanced at the magic glittering off the pendant. Luella was guilty, but she didn't need me to tell her that.

"I would've never amounted to anything in Edessa. I would've been a working mother who resented her husband. Here… I'm free. Here, I matter." Luella looked up at the stars. "The fact of the matter is that the battle tomorrow is one step closer to a life I never wanted. Andra will find out eventually. I don't want her to hate me for it."

I tilted my head to the side and said, "I'm sorry you had to carry this alone for so long."

"It's lighter with company," she replied, taking another drink. "You're a good friend, Levi. I don't think I say that enough."

"I don't think you've said that ever," I teased, effectively getting Luella to smile.

"Back in Edessa, I don't think I had a friend." She paused and pinned me with an intense gaze. "I know she's your sister, but when the time comes, promise you won't shut me out."

"You're family. You stuck with me through all this bullshit. It would only be fair to return the favor."

Her smile didn't touch her eyes, but she still nodded. "You know, I expected you to devolve into a prick after Mae was taken, but you've surprised me, mate."

I snorted. "Thanks, Luella."

"For what it's worth, I miss her too." Her voice shook for a moment, revealing how vulnerable she felt. "But we'll get our girl back."

"We will," I concurred before taking another drink and passing the bottle back to Luella. Then we fell into a comfortable silence, staring up at the stars and enjoying the quiet before the next battle.

MAEVE CROSS

THE CALLING MIRROR

IN THE MIDDLE OF THE NIGHT, I WAS AWOKEN BY A HORRIBLE sensation of agony.

I grasped at my chest as the rune seared my heart, a wordless cry leaving my lips. Black spots danced in my vision. Then the blinding pain ebbed away, and my body fell slack.

Varric exercised his new magic constantly, no matter the time of day or night. It felt like he grasped my heart in his hand every time he used my magic. It wasn't enough to gut me or bleed me. He had taken any peace I had during the night. No sleep. No relaxation. Everything was swallowed by Varric playing with his new toy.

Reaching into my pillow, I felt for the needle.

I prodded it into the keyhole as I did every night. It was a miracle I hadn't broken the thin metal by now, but I wouldn't give up. After all, with enough practice, I could pick these fucking locks.

The pins tapped against the tip of the needle. *Carefully now.*

Nothing. I needed leverage, or I'd never get this thing

open. The pin was long enough to poke inside, but I needed something flexible to hold it. Another wave of powerful magic came over me again and I gripped at my chest, causing me to lose my focus on the lock.

Keep going. You'll never get out of here if you give up. You'll never save Pen.

You promised her that you'd get her out of here.

The pain ebbed away again, and I swallowed thickly. I didn't know where she was, but if I got out of here, I'd find her. She deserved a life outside this fortress. I'd also warn Frey's wife so she wouldn't lead her people into a trap.

I can't fail. I can't.

Sweat beaded along my hairline as I searched for something that would give me leverage. I got down to the floor, looking for loose nails or a—*there.*

A long strip of the hardwood had splintered on the floor. I curled my nails around the splinter and followed it, careful not to bend or break it. Then I put the needle between my teeth and attempted to bend it.

Please don't break.

Please don't break.

Gods, if you're there, please let this work!

A shock of nerve pain went through my molars as I bent the needle into a slight curve. I took a deep breath and focused on the lock that bound me to the bed. The chains around my wrists, I could deal with another time.

I stuck the thick wooden splinter into the hole as leverage before carefully inserting the needle to poke the pins into place. My mind reeled, desperation shaking my hands.

When the lock clicked open, I stared at it, dumbfounded that it actually worked. I'd been memorizing where the pins were and how to hook them into place, but a small part of me thought I'd be trapped in this prison forever.

I stood up, and the chains slipped from the anchor,

pooling on the floor. An exuberant feeling filled my chest, but I had to remind myself that I wasn't out of this yet. These chains would be my weapons.

I swung the silver around my wrists, curling them around my knuckles to pack a nasty punch. Then I tucked my makeshift lockpicks into my nightgown pocket in case I needed them.

It was the middle of the night, when I knew I had only one guard stationed outside—my new guards were much louder than my old ones and liked to shout their goodbyes, making it easy to keep track of how many there were. I tiptoed to the door and knocked on it, hiding behind where it would open.

"Uh, Princess?" The guard stepped in, sounding perplexed. Then I closed the door, and he paused, looking at me in surprise.

Before he could react, I swung, breaking his nose. When he hit the ground, I didn't hesitate to kick him in the face, rendering him unconscious.

I dropped down, hunting for my key to get the blasted chains off my wrists, but I didn't see it. Did the guards not have it anymore?

Why?

It didn't matter. I didn't have time to dwell. I took off down the hall. I didn't know where Pen was, but my first stop was the calling mirror. I knew where that was. Then I could find Pen. Time was precious.

As predicted, the guard rounds were thinner than the other times I'd been taken around the castle. They were easy enough to avoid. I walked quietly, using my small size to my advantage. Keeping to the shadows, I snuck all the way to Varric's quarters.

He's not there. I wasn't sure how I knew that, but I did. He had a piece of me, so in a way, I was with him. I *knew.*

As I closed in on Varric's quarters, I saw two guards stationed outside wearing the Cross coat of arms. I hid behind a pillar.

How in the Hells am I supposed to get past them?

Another guard came sprinting down the hallway. "She's gone!"

"Gone?"

"Yes! I must speak to King Varric," the Pike guard insisted.

The guards all looked at one another, and a Cross guard said, "He's not here, but let me take you to him!"

I glanced up at the ceiling, thanking my lucky stars for good timing. When their footsteps got far enough away, I crept across the hallway and opened the door.

The awful memory of what they did to me here lingered, but I couldn't let it distract me. I knew exactly where that damn calling mirror was. I ducked into the side room and came face-to-face with the grand black frame.

"Now, how do I get you to work?" I murmured, glancing around at the wardrobe and side tables.

No instructions. Fantastic.

I stepped forward and tapped on the glass with my finger. "Um… hello?"

Suddenly a woman appeared in front of me, tapping her foot incessantly. I gasped in surprise, taking several steps back.

She was draped in thin flowing fabric that was cinched around her waist. Her thick dark curls cascaded down her back. The dress left little to the imagination, revealing ample thighs and generous breasts. Her tawny, golden complexion made her appear unbelievably radiant.

"You're late," she said. "We agreed to meet again after speaking to King Bjorn of Skadi and now—" Finally, she noticed me. "Who are you?"

"Maeve," I answered. "Maeve Cross."

"Ah. The daughter." The woman waved her hand dismissively.

That was when I noticed a cuff on her forearm. It looked like it had been carved out of eternal ice, made of exactly the same element that Frey's pendant was.

"I heard about your imprisonment. My condolences. Now, if you don't mind getting—"

I blinked and looked up at her. "*Skelmis?*"

She froze. "How do you know that—"

"I don't have time. You're Elinora. Frey's wife?"

Her dark brown eyes narrowed into slivers. "Where is my husband?"

"He's safe," I promised. "He's with my people."

"Wait. Wait. Your father said the pirates kidnapped him when he went to rescue you," she said.

"No. Varric is lying to you. Frey and I were tortured relentlessly, not by the pirates but by *Pike*," I said, trying to tell her as much as possible before they found me here.

"Tortured?" she repeated, then parted her lips to say something else before I cut her off.

"I don't have time, Elinora! Varric and his army are planning an invasion of Algar. You cannot close the gap. Not yet." I swallowed thickly. "Freynir is all right. He thinks you were killed. He's... grieving."

"With all due respect, there is not a force in this world that can keep me away from my husband. I will scorch the seas and drown the land if that's what it takes," Elinora said. "Thank you for the warning. We will be ready."

I shook my head. "You don't understand. You won't be prepared—"

A wave of agony washed over me again. I shouted and grasped at my chest.

"Maeve?" Elinora asked.

"Maeve?" Varric asked from the doorway, both Samuel

and Nathaniel accompanying him. His gaze flickered up to Elinora, then back to me. "Ah. I see."

Panic swallowed me as he used another Antediluvian phrase to immobilize me.

No. Not again!

I fought against the pain and dragged myself to my feet. I glanced between the Pikes and Varric and turned on my heel, fleeing from the room.

"Get her," Varric ordered. "Make it hurt."

"My pleasure," Nathaniel said before taking off after me.

MAEVE CROSS

SING AND BE FREE

RUN, MAE, RUN.

Warning bells sounded all around the fortress as I sprinted down the long corridors. I could hear the heavy footfalls of Nathaniel close behind me. Guards ran toward me, but they weren't coming after me.

Instead, they ran toward the main gate, weapons in hand.

What's going on?

No. No distractions.

I glanced at the rising gate, knowing freedom existed beyond the iron, but I continued to race down the hallways.

I'm not leaving without Pen. I promised.

Taking hard turns down winding hallways, I tried to lose Nathaniel. I didn't know where she was, but I'd find her. It didn't matter if she was dead or alive. She wouldn't be left in this awful place.

While Nathaniel had brute strength, he wasn't as fast as I was. I ducked behind a pillar, obscured by shadows. Down the hallway, I could hear his labored breaths as he finally lost sight of me. The warning bells roared loudly, hiding any noise of my light steps.

My steps swayed and I stumbled every time pain erupted in my chest. Varric was actively trying to incapacitate me, but that seething spite inside me *wouldn't let him*.

Fuck him.

"Come on out, bunny," Nathaniel yelled as I fought another wave of anguish.

I clenched my fists tight, eyes watering, but then... it stopped. With a heavy breath through the nose, I steadied myself.

As I glanced around a pillar, I was tempted to go on the offensive, but I'd never win a fight against him. He'd snap my neck, and I'd be a prisoner again. If I attacked him, I'd never save Pen. My best chance was to hide.

My temper simmered as I thirsted to spill his blood. But I wouldn't if that meant Pen's freedom.

The guards stormed down the hallways in a panic.

"Where is Maeve?" Nathaniel shouted.

Both the Pike and Cross guards were flustered as they pointed down a different hallway, giving him completely wrong directions. Nathaniel took off. I released the breath that had been trapped in my lungs, battering inside my ribs like my rapid heartbeat.

Move. No time to delay.

My mind raced with the possibilities of where Pen would be. I didn't know the layout of the fortress, but I knew she had to be in one of the four far towers, where she'd be completely isolated. A heavy sensation collided with my chest as I thought about how afraid she must be.

I wondered how often she prayed for someone to save her. How often she cried for freedom. I wondered how many songs she'd sing before her spirit had waned to nothing.

Had she succumbed to it? The hopelessness?

No. I won't let her give up.

Following pure intuition, I climbed up a staircase, seeking

a locked room. At the top of the seemingly endless staircase, a heavy lock was clasped onto a cast iron door. *This must be it.* I retrieved the makeshift lockpicking set from my pockets and got to work.

Nathaniel wasn't the most intelligent man, but it would only be a matter of time before he found me. I wriggled the curved needle and the wooden leverage splinter to click the pins into place much faster than I'd been able to downstairs.

My mouth curled in disgust as I held the sprung lock, eyeing the greasy smudges and rust around the corners. Knowing the wailing of the warning bells would mask the noise, I tugged it free and hurled it down the spiral staircase. I heard it crash into a wall not far down.

Then I threw the door open, and—

"Oh Gods, Pen," I murmured.

Her frail wrists were bound to the wall. Her red hair obscured her face. She was barely more than a heap on the dusty floor. Her gown, the same one from the day she was locked away, was torn and hanging off her in a way it never had before.

I ran toward her, and she barely moved as I picked the locks that pinned her hands above her head. Lethargically, she looked up at me with glassy eyes. Her face was gaunt.

They were starving her.

"M-Mae? Is... is—" she tried, but she couldn't get the words out.

"No talking, Pen. I've got you," I said, unlocking the binds.

She cried out in pain as her hands collapsed onto the ground. She had no strength to hold them up.

"M... My arms," she whispered. "Hurts."

"I know, Pen. I know. Please, try to stand," I urged, crouching down to loop one of her arms around my shoulders.

She sobbed. After having her arms contorted for so long,

it gave her a great deal of pain to use them. She couldn't move. She was too weak.

A whimper left her lips. "Y-You came for me. I didn't think anyone would come."

Even though she'd lost a considerable amount of weight, I struggled to lift her. The muscles in her legs had atrophied from lack of movement, and even more so without any food. From what I could tell, she only had water from where it leaked in from the ceiling after it rained.

"Of course I came. I wouldn't leave you here," I said, grunting with exertion.

I tried to lift her. *I tried so hard.*

Pen cried as I leaned down to cup her face. Her chest shook, but she shed no tears. Her lips were chapped, cracking so badly, I could see blood smudged in the corner of her mouth.

"Please, Pen. Please get up," I begged.

"I can't." She swallowed hard, head weaving back and forth even with the support of my hands. Her jaw wasn't soft. Her cheeks weren't round. "You have to leave me."

"No," I ground out between clenched teeth. "I promised."

I hooked her arm around my shoulders once more and hissed as I used all the strength I had to lift her. But it *wasn't enough.*

Gods, I'm not enough.

Like the many times I'd suffered death, I could feel the cold breath of the Reaper. But Death wasn't here for me.

"You can't take her!" I shouted. "*I promised!*"

Tears tracked down my face as I uselessly tried to lift her again. My nose ran, and a choked sob tore through me.

"Do you remember what you told me?" Pen whispered, staring up at me with the kindness that softened all my calluses. Everything I'd suffered didn't feel so terrible when Pen was there. "About love?"

I blinked away tears. "It's the sweetest agony."

"I-I think I could've loved you, Mae." Her lips curved in the softest smile, and her fingers wove through mine. "Let me be brave. Just this once."

"You're already brave! You've been so brave for your family. For Caine. For me. Please, *please* hold on. Just a little longer, Pen. Please."

She blinked slowly, the sounds of her breath rasping and shallow. Uneven.

"*No*. No. Not here. Not here," I muttered, holding on to her hand like that would keep her with me.

"It... it was always going to end like this. But at least I'm not alone," Pen said.

I tried to give her a smile, some sort of reassurance. But I couldn't. "Your stutter is getting better."

"It's easier with you. I'm not afraid with you." Pen fell slack in my arms and said, "I wish I could've felt the sea breeze with you. Had one more taste of freedom."

The only time she ever felt free was when she sang.

"Will you sing for me, Pen? Sing and be free," I choked out.

With a wavering voice, she parted her lips and sang. Her voice croaked and broke, but I watched her eyes dance with a dying light. Joy unfolded on her face as she gave in to her passion. I listened to her voice get softer as she fell limp in my arms.

I held her, staying strong for as long as I could while her song became a final breath. I pulled her up, cradling her lifeless body. "Please be kind to her," I murmured as the ghost of the Reaper passed beside me.

I could feel their cold hand cover both Pen's and mine in a gentle gesture of compassion.

I could practically hear Death's voice and promise. *"She will know peace now, Maeve. There is no pain in my domain."*

Finally, I broke. I tossed my face up toward the ceiling and I wailed. My head throbbed with every agonizing cry. My throat closed up around a lump while my heart cracked in my chest. Every little bit of strength I had left drained out as emptiness swallowed me.

I didn't care about being caught. I didn't care who heard me. I didn't care about anything as I held Pen in my arms. She was my friend. She gave me kindness in a cruel place.

And in an instant, she was gone.

I clenched my eyes shut until the noise of a metal object clanged in front of me. I snapped them open as I glanced up to see Nathaniel standing there. His mouth was pulled into a cruel smile, and all that devastation within me changed into something else.

Bloodlust.

My chest heaved up and down, and all I could hear was the sound of my own breath.

"You know, if you hadn't found her, she'd still be here. I likely wouldn't have come until she started to smell." Nathaniel laughed and drew a dagger from his belt.

Slowly, I rose up, gently laying Pen on the ground. My muscles twitched, my nails cut into my palms, and a seething rage welled inside me.

"Finally, I have you all to myself. Let's have some fun together. When I'm finished, there won't be anything left of you that you didn't have to grow back. Except your heart. I can't touch that." He gestured to his face, to the massive slash and visible stitches. "It's a shame that I can't leave any marks on you. What I wouldn't give to mutilate you."

My ears felt clogged, his voice sounding like it was several miles away as my pulse roared.

"You're so precious when you're angry."

With every word, he stepped closer to me until he grabbed me by my hair, thrusting my neck back. I couldn't think. My mind spun like a whirlwind of leaves, each a new thought and new sensation.

"Let me watch the light leave your eyes," he said, staring deep into my eyes as his dagger thrust into my belly. He twisted the blade, but I couldn't feel it anymore.

It felt like... nothing. Nothing compared to the torment I'd endured, and certainly nothing compared to the loss of my friend.

The rage simmered like a volatile brew inside me. I watched confusion dance across his face as I whispered, "You think I'm trapped in here with you."

My hand shot up to the stitches on his face, and I hooked my fingers into them, tearing them open. He released the dagger, crying out in pain and surprise as he threw himself back from me. He cupped his face as crimson dripped down his alabaster skin. Fear contracted his pupils.

I reached down to the dagger suspended in my belly and ripped it out.

The same wound had killed me multiple times, but like any magic, mine had strengthened with practice. In an instant, my skin closed, leaving only the rip in my nightgown and blood pooled at my feet. A biting laugh spilled from my lips.

All the pain I'd suffered, all the friends I'd lost—it was time to *collect*.

His eyes were wide as he watched me heal while wielding a dagger that he so willingly gave me.

"Are you frightened, Nathaniel? Are you afraid of what you've created?"

Nathaniel stood up, his face a gaping wound. "I'm no more afraid of you than a python fears a bunny."

He came at me with every intention of disarming me, but I wasn't the same woman he'd fought in my bedroom all those months ago. I was *better*. I dodged his move, flinging my silver chains off one wrist to strike him across the chest.

With a grunt, he swung out to hit me, and I fell back with the force of the blow. I dropped the dagger, and it clattered against the wall. I tasted my blood in my mouth, but I recovered instantly.

Then I felt Varric use my power again, sapping it out of my chest.

I cried out, grasping at my chest to weather the pain. But I wouldn't crumple. Not now. Never again.

"You foolish little girl. You think you can take me in a fight?" Nathaniel barked.

I stood back up. "Hit me again. That tickled." I wiped the blood off my lip with the back of my hand.

He took the bait, swinging toward me while I dove for the dagger. I grasped the hilt and drove it upward into Nathaniel's belly. He gasped, all words escaping him as I jerked the knife out and stabbed him again.

"That's for Ronin," I growled.

I thrust the blade into his belly again. "That's for me."

Crimson coated my hands as I stabbed him again. "This is for every person you brutalized."

Blood streamed from his lips, and I plunged the knife in once more. "And this is for Penelope, you son of a bitch." I sliced the knife upward like a tailor's seam splitter, and he collapsed onto his knees, grasping for the threads of his life. "How does it feel to bow?"

The light left his eyes as he collapsed into a bloodied heap of his own viscera.

With one last look toward Pen's body, I promised I'd be back to lay her to rest under the stars. But first, I had to get to Varric. I had to bleed the Besieger once and for all.

I raced down the stairs, following the pull of the magic in my chest. Each time Varric used it hurt like the Hells, but it became easier to endure. Unfortunately, that meant his magic would also get stronger.

Blood coated my face, but it wasn't mine. I wore Nathaniel like war paint as I tore through the halls. The dagger was an extension of me as I wove through the guards, ready to fight to the bitter end. Swords clashed around me, but I moved between them. I didn't care who they were fighting.

But then I realized bullets were zipping beside me as well.

Strange. The guards never carry flintlock pistols.

Screams of terror cut through the air around me as rubble fell from the ceiling. The ground shook beneath my feet. But even the rumbling roar couldn't break my focus.

All of it hummed in my ears.

My vision was narrowed, my sights set solely on Varric. I turned down the corridor toward the room where I knew his calling mirror was. He wouldn't leave without it.

Pain rippled through me as Varric used my own life force to drive his magic. But nothing could stop me as my bare feet left bloodied footprints.

Another bolt of pain went through me as Varric used my body as a conduit, but I pushed it down, refusing to get distracted.

Then I caught sight of grayed curls and a white-gold crown. Varric stopped and glanced behind himself, clearly running toward me and away from something else, but I couldn't see what it was. Then those stormy eyes saw me, and his face broke into an awful grin before he waved his fingers.

He grasped his cracked amulet. The draconite shattered, releasing the soul trapped within as a portal opened up in front of him. Violet light spat from the portal as unstable magic shot in every direction.

"No!" I shouted, cocking my arm back and throwing the

dagger toward the portal. The blade disappeared along with Varric as the portal slammed shut, locking everyone else out.

I failed.

The chaos around me faded into the background as my vision tunneled around a dragon head that came crashing through one of the big hallway windows. His sheer size crumbled the stone like it was nothing but dry bread.

Two massive feet anchored into the wall and tore it away.

The guards around me cried out in horror. "There's a fucking dragon!" They fled, only to be cornered by other fighters bearing a leviathan coat of arms. The dragon roared, forcing his body into the fortress, though most of it still hung out the window.

The Cross and Pike guards tried to run, but me? I was mesmerized.

Is it really him? Has he come for me?

He bore a mouthful of razor teeth in his massive maw. Two ornate golden horns protruded from his head and curled around it like a crown. Those eyes...

Oh, those eyes.

I'd know them anywhere.

My hand came up to touch my lips, and all my rage fizzled away, leaving nothing but exhaustion. I moved toward him, no longer in control of myself.

Gods, he was beautiful.

But he's always been beautiful.

If I stripped away every power, every Gods-given gift, every mortal coil and tether, his soul would shine brighter than the stars above.

A horn wailed in the distance. But I didn't care about the victory.

His eyes focused on me, hot breath billowing out from his nose and blowing my hair back from my face.

"Is it you?" I whispered. "Has Death finally shown me something beautiful?"

That massive head lowered, and he pressed his nose against my outstretched hands. My shoulders trembled, and I bit back tears. I'd already cried so much, but I couldn't help it. I collapsed onto the ground, both my arms stretched as far as they could go around his maw.

His rumble shook my bones and soothed my soul. Like a massive cat preening in front of their favorite person.

Finally, *finally*, I was home.

39

RONIN MURDOCH

THE SIEGE OF THE IVORY KEYS

I'D DRAWN A LINE BETWEEN MY LEVIATHAN AND ME. HE WAS A beast, and I was a man. But as we closed in on the Ivory Keys, it became more and more apparent that my leviathan *and* myself were one and the same.

And now, as I stared at the moon cresting behind the Ivory Keys Fortress, a place I'd feared for a large portion of my adult life, it was time to seize what was mine.

In the name of lightning, the sea, and the rumble beneath my feet, I was ending it.

"Raise the Jolly Roger," I commanded.

At my order, the signal flags were changed from *Standby* to the cobalt blue flag embroidered with a roaring leviathan. We closed in on the Ivory Keys port. The fortress stood tall and dark in the distance.

I'm here, Mae.

The draconite Lucky crafted into a shield hung from Freynir's, Luella's, and Andra's necks as well as the necks of a few sailors who were charging the front lines. Not me. Draconite magic wouldn't work on me. I didn't need the protection, but there was something cathartic about draconite being used to protect when so often it was used to destroy. Luella clapped a hand on my shoulder, and I looked down at her, armed to the teeth and adorned with war paint.

"I'll see you on the other side, yeah?" I grasped her hand and dipped my head down. Andra stood next to her wife, hair tied up in braids. We all smiled, knowing this may be the last time we saw one another. "Keep each other safe."

"Likewise," Luella said, glancing over at Freynir. A broadsword was attached to a sheath on his back. "If he dies, so do you," she warned before sparing me one more glance. "Bring our girl home."

"I'll tail him in case he needs me," Freynir promised. "Though, he could agree to let me fly on his back—"

"No," I said for the fiftieth fucking time before I looked at each and every sailor watching me on deck. "Live or die, we bring freedom back to the Ivory Keys. Good luck."

Everyone had their orders. It was time to act before the warning bells rang. Gunny was already in the lower decks with the gunnery crew. No one leaves. Surrender or death.

"Good luck, Captain," a few voices called out.

I shed my vest, stepping up onto the half wall. With a final goodbye, I dropped into the big blue, extending my wings and willing a shift. It was a gamble to fully shift for an extended period of time out of the water, but Mae was worth it. And if I failed, Freynir was there as my backup.

I swam away from the ships, letting Cliohde breathe the full power of the sea into me. I could feel her nearby, watching but not interfering. My legs extended, shredding my trousers to grow into my leviathan form.

A tail dropped down behind me, swiping through the water. The sea embraced me, and I let my leviathan break through my skin. I tilted my massive head and breached the water. My powerful wings swept behind me, and I landed on solid wood, making the entire pier shake.

I am an earthquake that shakes down the walls of Cross's oligarchy.

I am the lightning that cracks through the stormy sky.

I am what the sea fears.

And you can't hide from me.

I spread my wings and flew into the night sky as my ground forces charged the pier and the beaches. From my vantage point, I could see Freynir berserk, using his magic to cut through the forces easily. He occasionally looked up at me, doing his best to tail me.

Gunny prepared to unload cannon fire onto Pike's docked ships, preventing anyone from fleeing. The Seymour brothers had taken a liking to the gunnery crew, so I knew Gunny wouldn't be fighting alone.

Luella screamed into the sky and charged ahead. She moved like the wind, fighting alongside Andra like a familiar dance. They were always perfectly in tune, and I knew they would keep each other safe.

Lucky and Mama led a flank attack, heading straight toward the fortress.

Bliss and Udine took a ketch around the island to catch any stragglers.

Freynir insisted that he didn't need to pair up, and I could understand why. His rage was a sight to behold with his broadsword and how he vanished into a column of smoke to move through the guard detail even faster. He delighted in each clash of the sword. He lived for the battle.

No one would be able to keep up with his berserk. And anyone who did would only get hurt if they got in the way.

Our intention was to take as many prisoners as possible. They weren't who we were after.

I landed on top of the fortress, using my claws to break through the roof like it was paper. The stone was no match for me as I tore apart the walls, slashing one of the towers open to stick my nose inside. I inhaled deeply, looking for—

Blood.

For a moment, I didn't know what I was looking at. Warning bells rang and screams bellowed through the hallways, but this tower was dead silent.

A body was hunched over in a kneeling position. I knew it was Nathaniel Pike. I knew his smell, especially in this form. Rot and iron. He was disemboweled, bloodied footprints leading away from him and down the stairs.

Another body lay against the wall, eyes closed in an expression of surrender. If it weren't for her gaunt cheeks and frail body, she could've been asleep. I inhaled again and caught the scent of cinnamon and berries.

Mae.

I broke through the walls and saw the chaos of guards sprinting through the halls. It reminded me of stepping on an anthill, but instead of coming to defend the colony, they were fleeing. Lucky and Mama had made it to the back of the fortress, their forces flooding the halls and taking prisoners.

The stone crumbled as I tore through the fortress. If Mae was here, then so was Cross. He wouldn't leave without her.

I flew around to the other side and crashed my head through the windows, letting the glass break as numerous guards shouted—

"Oh fuck, they have a dragon!"

My eyes darted down the hallway before I caught a glimpse of grayed curls and a white-gold crown. A red velvet cape hung from his shoulders, the train saturated in blood. He spun around, and I caught his gaze.

Instantly, he shed his cloak and took off.

Not this time, fucker.

Electricity crackled in my throat as he shouted something

in Antediluvian at me, but all it did was tickle my nose. *You can't use my own magic against me.*

I unleashed the storm from my throat and sent it rippling and bouncing off the walls and right into Cross. For a split second, he was stunned, but where my electricity should've left a scourge of burning flesh, he was whole, the draconite a glowing shield around him as he muttered the spell in Antediluvian.

A vile grin pulled at his lips as he examined a trinket on his wrist and the blue shield disappeared. He turned on his heel to flee down the hallway.

But suddenly Cross stopped in his tracks. He looked back at me and then at whoever was in front of him. He taunted them with a wave of his fingers.

Then he grasped his draconite amulet and spoke one final spell, splitting the veil between the Ivory Keys and Farlight Castle.

Fuck.

Violet energy spat from the portal as the draconite amulet shattered into nothing in his hand. The soul trapped inside didn't waste any time before flying to the trenches. I opened my massive maw to strike Cross with lightning, but as soon as I did, the portal vanished.

On the other side, all I saw were wide brown eyes and a white nightgown soaked in blood. But that didn't make her any less lovely.

It felt like my heart broke and mended at the same time. *Gods, has she always been this beautiful?* The second scourge of lightning died in my throat, and I suddenly felt exhausted. But I held on to my dragon form tightly. I wouldn't let it fall away until I got her to safety.

As the guards around her fled for their lives, she looked at me the same way she did when she first saw me like this—

with awe and wonder. Her wide eyes filled with helpless tears as she came toward me.

I needed her to touch me. I needed to know she was real.

A victory horn wailed in the distance, and an answering one came from inside the fortress. Without leadership, everything was destined to fall apart.

I focused on her face as she came closer, looking every bit like how I remembered. Her hair was shorter, but even though so much time had passed, everything about her magnetized me. Perhaps more than it already had.

My breath came out through my nose, blowing her hair back.

"Is it you?" she whispered, voice breaking. "Has Death finally shown me something beautiful?"

I'm here, sweetheart.

She stood there, hands trembling. Then Mae hesitantly reached out, but I couldn't bear resisting her touch anymore. I pressed my face into her hands, and she cried, stretching her arms around my maw and crumpling to the ground. I rumbled, rubbing my face deeper into her embrace.

I needed to get her out of here. I needed to bring her home.

Hesitantly, I leaned back until she let go. Then I dipped my head down to encourage her to climb onto the back of my neck. I'd given everyone so much shit about riding my back, but all I wanted to do was take my girl away from all this.

She sniffled and gave me a watery smile. "I thought you weren't a pony."

With another rumble, I let her climb up. Her hands tightened around my leathery skin, and I could feel her face press against it, giving herself over completely.

As she nuzzled me, I flew her back to *The Ollipheist*, and

that little piece of my heart she had taken away from me found its place back in my chest.

PART III

THE SENTRY AND HER KING

40

MAEVE CROSS

PAY YOUR PENANCE

THE SCENT OF CEDAR AND SEAWATER FILLED MY NOSE, offering a bit of comfort. Happiness swelled in my chest, but I was terrified that this would be taken from me next. Despite the happiness and hope, my rage still lingered beneath the surface.

Varric escaped. Shattered his trophy amulet to portal away. What a fucking coward. He got away before I could end it.

The rune in my chest warmed, but it didn't hurt anymore. My face felt wet, and devastation weighed heavily.

The fight wasn't over.

Get yourself together.

I could feel the power wane in Ronin's dragon form beneath me, and I wondered how long he had sustained it. Last time I'd seen him, he couldn't shift, but now…. Now he was *glorious.*

A memory of something flickered inside me. Even more so as I curled my hands around his golden horns as far as my fingers would go.

Which wasn't far.

He rumbled again, but this time, it sounded like a purr.

He really was just a big cat. It was no surprise that he and Lieutenant Commander Lazlo got on so well.

Above the clouds, I could smell the sea and feel the breeze in my hair. I lifted my head and closed my eyes, embracing the sensation. I was untethered from the ground beneath me. The chains around my wrists dangled, but they didn't restrain me.

I am free.

When my eyes fluttered open, the moon was in her full glory. Then I looked down toward the pier and saw *The Ollipheist* docked there, and if this was a dream, I never wanted to wake up. My home was *right there.*

I'd dreamed of that ship so many times. The sanded floors. The hand-worn helm. The familiar rigging that gave me so many calluses. The windows of the stern that glowed yellow from the lamps inside.

But I didn't remember the flag at the top of the mast. A Jolly Roger of a lightning-breathing dragon. The fleet of ships behind it toted the same flag. A smile overcame me again as I pressed my face behind the crown of his horns, wanting to hold him as closely as I could.

I was *so proud* of what Ronin had accomplished.

A massive crowd of people gathered on the pier near *The Ollipheist* with a handful of prisoners on their knees. I couldn't make out their faces from where I was, but the crowd all wore Ronin's colors.

Ronin landed nearby, making the entire island shudder in response as if he were more god than man.

He stretched his neck, allowing me to slide off, my bare feet touching the moonlit grass for the first time since I'd been taken prisoner. I wiggled my toes, delighting in how scratchy it felt beneath my feet. I had half a mind to drop into it and feel how it tickled my nose as I inhaled the green.

"Mae! Mae!" a familiar voice yelled as someone broke

away from the crowd. Numerous fast footsteps ran toward me. Before I could look up, my face collided with a soft chest. Luella's arms wound around me tightly.

"Hey, Lulu," I murmured, happy tears finding my eyes as I hugged her back.

Shortly after, Andra joined her, her braids brushing my neck as she embraced me from behind. "Oh, lassie, we missed you."

Joy flooded me, and I couldn't stop shaking with relief.

Cornsilk-blonde hair came into the corner of my vision as Enya embraced me, wrapping her arms around all three of us. They pulled away, and Enya cupped my face, examining me for any external injuries. "Oh, don't cry, love. You're back where you belong."

I nodded fiercely, helplessly smiling.

Ronin shifted behind me, falling to his knees as he finally released the leviathan. He was completely naked, but he didn't look as I remembered him. He was already tall, but he was so much taller than I remembered. He seemed to be in between his human and dragon forms. Horns curled around his temples, and wings extended from his back.

His tattoo had bloomed across his chest like a watercolor painting. But I didn't care about any of that when he offered me a soft, almost sheepish smile and those two dastardly dimples dented either side of his mouth.

The sight of him loosened that awful lump that had taken refuge in my throat. I reached out to grasp his shaking hands. As soon as I did, he pulled me into his chest, both his arms and wings curling around me. His scent filled my nose, and I felt *safe* again.

Words were never enough. Not to express the expansive feeling in my chest when he touched me again. I pressed my hand to his chest, and goose bumps pebbled across his skin. He bent down to rest his chin on top of my head.

Gods, I missed you.

Suddenly, I heard panting and footsteps. Smelled the scent of a winter hearth on the breeze.

Frey kept his promise.

Luella laughed. "I thought you said you could tail him."

"Shut it, Red. I did, didn't I? It's not my fault he's fucking fast." Frey panted harder as he came to a stop. "I brought your shit."

Ronin's hand shot out to catch the pack that Frey tossed at him. I didn't want him to pull away from me, but we still had work to do. He pressed a tender kiss on the top of my head before he pulled away completely.

"What happened with Cross?" Enya asked as Ronin tugged on a pair of trousers.

"Fled," I answered.

"Where?" Andra countered. "We covered all exits."

I gestured to my collar, my throat feeling so sore. I was tired of talking.

"His amulet," Ronin said for me. "Shattered it to make a portal."

Frey blinked. "So he abandoned all his allies?"

"Are you surprised?" I scoffed.

Luella snorted. "Fucking coward. What about Pike's shit son? All the others are accounted for."

"Dead," Ronin concurred. "I found him while I was looking for Mae."

A complicated feeling tightened my chest. I brought my bloodied hands up, and I could finally feel it also crusting on my face and neck. It stuck to my nightgown and was plastered to my abdomen. *Did he ever think my soft hands could be those of a murderer?* Shame reared its head, and I didn't understand why I felt that way ending Nathaniel's life.

Ronin reached out, his long-clawed fingers curling between mine. "It was nothing he didn't deserve."

His statement dampened the shame, but it was still there.

"Well, that's one bastard dead. What about the others?" Frey asked.

"They're awaiting your judgment, Ronin," Enya answered, looking at her son. "Lucky is holding your place."

Lucky is safe. That's good. I thought back to Shipwreck Bay's siege and wondered how many people were lost under the rubble. Was Wesley all right? Did Gunny survive? What about Spider?

So many questions, but not enough time to have them answered.

Then I realized Samuel Pike was on his knees with the other nobles. A handful of guards also awaited judgment, but I didn't disdain them as much as I did the pirate hunters.

"You're not done. Collect," Death's voice whispered.

All eyes flickered to me as I walked beside Ronin and his advisers. I noticed several of the guards standing among the sailors, likely having turned against them during the fight. I turned my attention back to the long row of prisoners, prepared for any sudden movements.

At the left, Samuel had that smug grin on his face. As if he knew something I didn't. It *pissed me off.* I thought about how many women he'd handed over to his son, knowing what their fate would be.

He thought we needed him. But all the riches and power in the world wouldn't save him. Not from me.

The woman I had been, the one killed so brutally all those years ago, came to the surface as Ronin addressed the nobles. I wasn't listening as he laid out terms for them to follow. It was an amicable attempt. Perhaps it would even work on a few of them. But Samuel believed he was above it. I knew the first chance he got, he'd finish the coup he started with Varric.

It was my sworn duty to protect Ronin, and Samuel didn't deserve my mercy.

The other nobles weren't innocent, but they were pawns. Samuel wasn't.

"King Varric abandoned us!" one of them shouted in disbelief.

I stepped away from Ronin, eyes set on Samuel. "I warned you that he was liar. But you already knew that, didn't you, Samuel?"

Those soulless blue eyes met mine, the same ones I stared into when he speared my belly and threw me from a window. The sentry I used to be tasted her own blood as she held on long enough to save her queen.

"I don't know what you're talking about," Samuel said, his hands bound behind his back, blood creasing in his hairline. Then he looked away from me as if I were nothing more than the muck beneath his shoes. "Your terms seem appropriate, *King Ronin*."

The rest of the nobles nodded in agreement, and even if it was a bad idea, Ronin would keep his word. Ronin was a good man. Underneath his reputation, he had honor. His word was his bond. His own oath. That was the reason he didn't kill Varric when he had the chance. He'd never kill an unarmed man.

I glanced back at the man I loved, and he furrowed his brow as if he were trying to see into my head.

Oh, you sweet man. I'll forfeit my honor so you can keep yours.

"Do you recognize me, Samuel?" I asked, turning my gaze back to him. "I'd hoped all the blood might jog your memory."

That cruel glimmer in his eyes flickered. "I see a pirate's bitch, if that's what you're asking."

My friends reacted behind me, but I raised my hand, stopping whatever they were going to do in my defense.

"Twenty-five years ago, there was a girl, barely nineteen at the time, who gave her life so Queen Enya could rescue her son. And you skewered her like a piece of meat," I recollected, watching the gears turn in his head.

Out of the corner of my eye, I saw Enya touch her lips, a million emotions in her soulful ocean-blue eyes.

"What if I told you that when that girl died, she didn't cross over. In fact, she waited. And waited. And waited. For her bond was to her queen, and she refused to abandon her for *years* before Death granted her a new life."

The crowd listened intently as I continued, shock unfolding on Samuel's face.

"You see, Samuel, you *created* me with your violence, but your son, he fine-tuned me. It's time to pay your penance. And I'm here to *collect*." With every word I stepped closer.

Samuel flung himself backward, and the crowd moved back as he shuffled away from me. "Wait. Wait. I can explain. It was—"

"If that isn't enough, tell me what's worse: someone who brutalizes and tortures their wives, or someone who finds those women and sells them like common cattle, knowing their fate is to die a horrible, slow death."

"Wait—"

"Is it worse to be a rapist or someone who *looks away*?" I was locked onto him. He scrambled back, but he'd never be able to get away from me. "Because from where I'm standing, there's no fucking difference."

As Samuel tried to get away, Seymour took a step up behind him so he bumped against his legs. A line of sailors and guards closed around him as he stared up at me, terror the only emotion in his eyes.

"I thought a python couldn't be afraid of a bunny," I stated as one of the sailors held a blade out to me. I accepted it gratefully, and my chains rattled as I struck Samuel through the chest. "How does it feel to choke on your blood?" I sneered in his face. "To feel your life drain away as agony rips into you? I've felt this *over and over again*. You're fortunate you'll only feel it once before you burn in the Hells."

Blood sputtered from his lips as I twisted the knife before Death's cold embrace blew over me, taking him away with them.

I straightened up and gave the knife back to the sailor. "Feed him to the sharks. I want nothing left to bury."

I gazed down at Samuel Pike's body, and I didn't feel a damn thing. Numbness tingled in my hands, and I felt empty.

Ronin and Enya were both staring at me, their gazes nearly indecipherable. The nobles, human and elf alike, looked at me in horror, but Ronin took the advantage.

"You lot are on borrowed time," Ronin said to them. "If you're lucky, you can still repent. If not, we'll give you a coward's death." Then he looked over at Luella and said, "Take them to the dungeons. I want the fortress scouted for supplies."

"Aye, aye," she replied, giving me a look of kindred understanding. Before she could leave, I grasped her jacket.

"There's a woman in the tower." I didn't think I could bear seeing her again so soon. "Lay her to rest under the stars. She was my friend."

Compassion filled Luella's eyes as she squeezed my forearm. She nodded and gestured for a few sailors, including Frey and Andra, to transport the prisoners to the ruined fortress.

Ronin looked to Lucky, who returned a slight nod, announcing, "Tonight is a victory! Let us celebrate after the supply scout. Let's save the rest of the work for tomorrow."

The crowd cheered and dissipated, but I remained. Ronin's eyes never left me as he gestured toward *The Ollipheist* with his head. I nodded, my body feeling overwhelmingly heavy as I came toward Ronin and his mother again.

"That was you?" Enya asked. "You helped me get away?"

I fiddled with my fingers. "Yes and no. Maybe she was me, but that's not who I am anymore. But she wanted you to know that her greatest shame was that she never got to help you save your other sons."

Enya gently touched my shoulder with her three-fingered hand. "She did what she could. And with Samuel's death, you've avenged my boys. Now there's only Varric left."

I nodded, not feeling like it was enough. Especially since I knew I'd given him an advantage. My power was his. Frey's wife, Elinora, was going to close the gap, and I had to be there to stop whatever Varric had planned.

"I'll join Lucky for the celebrations and keep an eye on our new defectors. You two have a lot to catch up on," Enya said, giving me one more squeeze before leaving Ronin and me alone.

Ronin approached me and held my wrists, still clad in draping silver chains. He grabbed the cuffs with both hands in turn and physically bent the metal away from me, freeing my raw wrists once and for all. The blisters closed instantly, leaving only the memory.

My voice felt thick. "Thank you."

"I'll understand if you want to be alone," he rumbled. "I'm sure this is all very overwhelming."

I swallowed. "It is, but I've spent enough time away from you." I gazed up at him, losing myself in his eyes again.

He took my wrists to kiss them and sufficiently washed away the memory of the shackles.

I couldn't feel the phantom of them biting into my wrists. All I could feel was Ronin's lips erasing all the pain. I took him in, bathing in the love in his eyes. Even saturated in blood with a dead man not far behind me, he still looked at me like I was the same woman who stole his heart away.

Perhaps we hadn't changed as much as I feared. Maybe we'd changed in the same way. We both grew armor, but his was on the outside and mine was inside.

We curled our fingers together and walked toward *The Ollipheist*.

41

RONIN MURDOCH

A SOUL-DEEP BOND

Sparing Samuel Pike wasn't an option.

Sooner or later he would try to finish what he started. But I was a man of my word, and I wouldn't have struck unless necessary. My people needed to see that I was honest, even with someone as vile as Samuel Pike.

But even after seeing Nathaniel's body in the tower, I didn't expect Mae to take Samuel's life into her own hands. In that moment, she solidified herself as someone who would do whatever was necessary.

It was more than that. My sweet girl had been pushed to her limits.

I didn't need to know the details. My temper rose at everything she'd endured and the bastards who hurt her, but I pushed it down. Mae handled it, and she needed comfort, not an angry man she'd have to soothe. But now, we had our answers.

Mae was my sentry. And I was her king.

Our fates were woven together. I would always find my way to her, and she would always find me again. I already loved her, but this bond was soul-deep, embedded in my very being.

Mae's fingers, woven through mine, were shaking violently. Even my touch couldn't quell them. I guided her back to my cabin, a special place that was ours. Despite everything we'd suffered together or apart, this was the one place that felt like mine.

The memories of what Pike and his men did to me slipped further away, because all that came to mind were the late-night talks and all the times I'd held Mae while we slept. I thought about her smell and the way she made me feel safe.

The few sailors on deck got to their feet and waved excitedly at Mae. She returned their greetings with a smile that didn't reach her eyes. I knew how it felt to steel yourself to keep up appearances. It didn't matter if I was broken inside. We still had work to do.

She felt different. Mae had always been on the slight side, but she was incredibly thin now. The pronounced muscles on her arms had atrophied. Her sun-kissed complexion had paled, and her freckles weren't as dark. Even her warm brown eyes weren't as sweet as honey anymore. She had a… haunted quality about her that I didn't like one bit.

But she hid it. Her other fingertips danced along the half wall, tracing the woodgrain. She seemed lost in her head when she dragged her feet over the planks to remind herself what the deck felt like. I let her take her time as we walked up the steps, her hand passing over the helm.

I slipped my hand away from hers to get the door to my cabin. She jolted in surprise and reached for me again immediately. Then Mae caught herself, wringing her hands together when she shyly looked up at me.

I held the door open for her, and she ducked under my arm into the cabin. I closed the door behind us, watching as she took note of everything. The books in the bookcase. The papers strewn across my desk. The cot in the corner. The table by the stern windows where we'd have dinner. Our bed where her pillow had an imprint of my horns from how often I'd bury my face in it to feel like she was with me again.

Her shoulders slouched when she exhaled deeply, visibly relaxing.

"Are you all right, sweetheart?" I asked.

She jumped slightly, and I hated that I'd startled her. "I need a minute. Can I...?" She trailed off, rubbing the back of her neck, cringing at the sensation of thick, dried blood all over her.

I knew most of it was Pike's, but judging by the tear in her nightgown and the scent of her own blood, she'd sustained a wound. My temper flared again, but what the fuck was I going to do?

The Pikes were dead. Cross was gone. I had Mae back, but I didn't think either of the Pike men had suffered enough. If I had my way, I would've strung them up the same way Nathaniel had me displayed in my cabin, at the mercy of any lowlife who was bored.

They'd be made into that same spectacle so many fellow pirates suffered, hanging from their toes in the gallows before being bled like a pig. But I wouldn't be deranged enough to stuff them as a trophy. In fact, I wanted nothing left. I wanted their corpses to be picked clean and lost forever.

What would be a better fate for a Pike than to be forgotten?

"You get into the shower, love. Do you want something to wear?" I asked, deliberately not moving any closer. I didn't want to startle her again.

She nodded, walking toward my wet room. "Something that smells like you."

My heart fluttered like it did when she kissed me the first

time. Gods, my mouth felt parched—I was aching to taste her lips again. Hold her against me like we were the only people in the world. I wanted to forget about the outside world and our failings.

I wanted a beautiful distraction.

But we'd been through this once before. I wouldn't make the same mistake again. We wouldn't fall into a cycle of sex and distraction like we used to. This bond between us was far more important than that.

"Anything you need, sweetheart," I promised. "I'll be in here."

Her head dipped down, and she entered the wet room. A few moments later, I heard the water. I busied myself with finding something she would like to wear. Her request was more difficult than she meant it to be.

Nothing fit me anymore, but I'd be damned if I couldn't fulfill the one thing she wanted. Freynir had taken a large sum of my clothing. The mates and I liked to joke that he'd fit Luella's clothes better than mine, but he wouldn't hear of it.

I dug through a trunk and found one of my shirts. I brought it to my nose and sniffed. *I wonder what I smell like.* The shirt smelled strongly like my cedar trunk and a little like the ocean. I hoped it would suffice.

Then, over the noise of the pounding water, I heard a soft sob. Hard intakes of breath and stifled cries.

Oh fuck, she's crying.

My heart fucking shattered into a million godsdamn pieces. I hated it when she cried.

Before I could even think about it, I was already in my wet room. Her bloodied nightgown had been left on the floor, and a few red smears led to the shallow shower basin. She had curled into the corner, her knees pressed up to her chest.

The water, a deep dark red, circled the drain.

"Baby," I murmured, getting to my knees in front of the basin.

Drops of salty water clung to her eyelashes, indistinguishable from her tears. "Why won't it go away?" Her shoulders curved inward as her body shook. "It's too much." She held her hands out, still stained by the lives she'd taken. "It won't go away."

She looked so small there, so tormented. Memories riddled my mind of when I'd gotten back from Farlight Prison and was too exhausted to clean myself but too prideful to ask for help. That was the moment when I wanted to be comforted more than anything else in the world, but to ask for it meant I was admitting weakness.

I'd cut everyone off, but in return, I was emotionally unavailable. Mae suffered, and I let her because I was too caught up in my own shit.

But I wasn't that man anymore.

I reached through the water to gently cup the side of her face, meeting her wide eyes. They swam with darkness. With grief. Shame. With every ugly emotion that had claimed me numerous times before. "I got you," I murmured. "Come here."

I climbed into the too-small shower still dressed in my trousers and took her into my arms. The basin was a tight fit, but I made it work so Mae could feel safe. She curled against me and pressed her face into my chest. Carefully, I reached for my soap to lather her trembling back.

Her cries grew quieter as I cleansed her of the night. I took her hands and meticulously washed them, cleaning under her nails. I did everything she was too worn out to do herself. I wove my fingers through her hair, and she slouched deeper into my chest while my wings curled around her.

She'd been so strong, but she didn't have to be strong

with me. It was time for me to hold that weight for a little while. I'd carry it as long as she needed me to.

Finally, she looked up at me, fully bare both physically and emotionally. I could see the doubt in her eyes, the disbelief that I was actually here. With my thumbs, I wiped her cheeks clean. "There you are," I murmured. "I knew you were there under all the muck."

The sides of her mouth pulled up in a watery smile. "You're still here too. Under the teeth and horns, you're still mine."

I pressed her hand against my chest where she could feel how hard my heart pounded. "I've always been yours, Mae."

"So much has changed, Ronin," she whispered. "How can you still be mine if I'm not the same person I was?"

"If so much has changed, my love, then why does it feel like no time has passed at all?" I replied and ducked down to give her a kiss on the tip of her nose.

"I've killed people since we saw each other last," she said, holding my gaze as though if she so much as looked away, we'd both vanish back to our own circle of the Hells.

"So have I. More than two," I said. "And I don't count the Pikes as *people*." I reached over to the lever and shut the water off. My trousers were saturated, but I didn't feel cold with Mae in my arms. I groped blindly for a towel, knocking over numerous things before wrapping it around her shoulders.

She tilted her head to the side, watching me closely as she walked her fingers along my jaw to my horns. Sensation exploded across them as I tipped my head back, a low rumble billowing from my chest. Amusement lit up her eyes as her fingers moved to my wings and my skin pebbled, basking in her caress.

It felt like the taste of sugar after a long voyage at sea.

I wanted more.

My throat bobbed as I tilted my head farther back so she could trail her touch down my neck. She then leaned in and stuffed her face into the juncture between my neck and shoulder, taking a deep breath.

"I killed Adams too," she murmured.

At the sound of his name, I scowled, but that instant feeling of dread ebbed away just as quickly as I imagined my girl putting a knife to his throat. "Who else?"

"There was a group of men on Pike's ship who liked to talk about what they did to you," she said. "I made them choke on their words. Then I set the ship on fire."

I hummed, absolutely delighted. My skin tingled, warmth flooding all over my body at the realization that my girl took the lives of the men who'd tormented me. "Did they die screaming?" I asked, nuzzling my nose in her wet hair.

Cinnamon and berries. My springtime.

And like spring, she sent the darkness away. She warmed the cold and grew stronger after. Because in reality, spring was just as brutal as winter.

In the cold, you fight to survive.

But in the spring, you fight to bloom.

"Yes." She pressed a kiss to the side of my neck, and my entire body fucking *sang*.

I pinched her chin, tilting her face up to look at me again. So godsdamn lovely. "Can I kiss you, sweetheart?"

Her eyes darted between my eyes and my mouth. "I was wondering when you'd ask. I only had to bring up eliminating a long list of your enemies."

A smile pulled at my lips, and Mae had made her choice to focus on my mouth. I didn't answer, instead dipping my head to capture her petal-pink lips. She sighed into the kiss, arching her neck toward me.

Her lips parted, and her taste flooded my mouth. The tether that bound us to each other tightened, bringing us closer together. My eyes fluttered closed, and I surrendered to sensation.

Her hands explored my body, and I felt a caress across my chest before she grabbed my shoulders hard enough to dimple the skin. She searched my mouth with her tongue, devouring me with a sense of urgency. I let her do whatever she wanted, careful not to prick her lips with my fangs.

I released her chin and moved my hand to the nape of her neck, trying not to get too carried away. I wanted to grab her and hoist her onto my lap, but I was acutely aware of how sharp my nails were. I didn't get her out of that prison to make her bleed during a kiss.

Her hands trailed from my shoulders to the soft skin of my wings. Then she pulled away, laughing a little under her breath.

"Hmm?" I hummed, slowly blinking as I tried to focus on her.

"Your wings," she said with a smile, gently stroking the moleskin.

I practically vibrated. "That feels nice," I admitted. The sensation was completely new to me, but all it made me want to do was spread out on my belly to feel her stroke my wings. Heat pooled in my groin, excitement flushing my entire body. I rumbled again in contentment.

"I can tell," she teased. "They're trembling. And you're billowing like those salties from the swamp at Violetta's Haven."

She's right. "Oh."

"Don't stop. I like it." She cupped my face and pressed one more kiss to my lips.

Even if I wanted more, I let her stand up and dry off. Her body mesmerized me, and my own reacted. It wasn't the right time, but I couldn't help it. My desire had been completely dormant during her absence, and now that I had her in front of me again, everything turned back on.

Helplessly, my eyes climbed her freckled thighs to the thatch of dark hair between her legs, then the soft belly and dimples in her hips, those small, teardrop-shaped breasts that I ached to devour.

But my heart ached worse.

I wanted to bathe her in as much affection as we could tolerate. I needed to refill that well and kiss every lingering sensation away. Every awful memory would be replaced until all she could remember was how much I loved her.

Then I noticed it right before she tucked the towel around her.

A glow in her sternum. Barely there and flickering.

What the fuck is that?

Discomfort pinched her expression as she turned away from me completely. She pressed her hand into her chest as if to offset some internal pressure.

"Mae?" I asked, rising up to my full height and following her out of the wet room. My shirt was draped on the bed for her, and she didn't waste any time dropping the towel to pull it on and fasten the top buttons. "Mae?"

The narrow line of her shoulders pulled in, and she sighed. "I wanted to forget it was there."

"What's there?" I asked, crossing my arms. *What the fuck did they do to you?*

She shook her head. "Varric put something inside my chest. It lets him use my accelerated healing as a magical amplifier."

Oh, fuck. That's why my lightning didn't kill him. He used Mae to throw up a shield.

With a roll of her shoulders, she turned around to look at me. "His magic…. Even without his allies, it'll be difficult to keep him from razing the entire continent."

Shit.

"Is there a way to…?" I trailed off, not finishing the thought because I already knew the answer.

"You want to cut me open, too, Ronin?" she snapped, the utter agony in her voice breaking me. "Be my fucking guest. I don't know if you can even get it out."

Too?

I held up my hands, wanting so fucking badly to take it away. Take it all away. "No. No, Mae."

Her face flushed as anger flooded her expression. "I'd like one—*one* blasted night—" She shook all over again, and in a moment, I was by her side, both my hands on her quaking arms.

"No," I growled, my voice dropping an octave. "No. I would *never* do that to you."

Her lips trembled. "I… I know. *I know.*" She broke away from me and ran a hand through her hair before she hissed in barely contained anger, "They took my hair. They took my dignity. They took everything. Varric stuck his hand in my chest like my heart was his *property.*"

I'm so sorry. I'm sorry I couldn't protect you.

I had to get past it. "Sweetheart, sit down. Please. Come here."

"I don't want to *sit down.* I want to stop feeling like this." She pressed her hand into her chest again. "I'm out of the tower, but Varric still has his claws in me."

"Come here. I won't repeat myself again," I demanded, taking a seat on my bed, cold, damp trousers be damned. I leaned over to my trunk and gathered some supplies: a hairbrush, hair oil, a few things here and there.

Mae looked at me skeptically as I patted my thigh. "What are you going to do?"

"Let me give you a little piece of yourself back."

Her eyes were so warm as she sat beside me, laying her

head in my lap. I brushed the tangles out. Then I reached for the hair oil, warming it between my hands. It smelled herbal, like rosemary and mint. I took my time massaging it in, carefully scratching her scalp with the slightest amount of pressure so I didn't cut her by accident.

Her eyes fluttered closed, and she gave herself over to me.

"I want to take care of you, baby."

Her eyes opened again, eyebrows pinched together. "You have so many people to take care of, Ronin. You don't have to do this for me."

"I don't consider taking care of you to be a chore. I've been aching for you the past six months. I have crews and people to keep fed, paid, and alive, but you…. You're the only person I've ever *wanted* to take care of."

Mae released a lovely sigh and tilted her head back, accepting my affection. "You're too sweet to me."

"I disagree."

Her lips pulled into the smallest smile, and I played with her hair, braiding a small section of it like Andra braided Luella's. I enjoyed preening her hair. The fine strands slipped through my fingers like silk.

She mumbled her appreciation, and her eyes fluttered closed once again. I felt her abandon her stresses as she rolled onto her side. I rubbed the back of her neck, kneading her tense shoulders. Her muscles fell slack, and she made a noise of delight.

Over the next several minutes, her breaths slowed.

Warmth spread through my limbs at the realization that she felt safe enough to sleep.

I kissed her forehead, murmuring, "I love you, sweetheart. With everything I have."

She stirred, but the concerned pinch in her brows went away with a deep wheeze. I tucked her into our bed, changed into some dry, loose-fitting trousers, and took her into my arms. I had to maneuver myself to accommodate my hulking form, but my comfort was secondary to Mae's.

I fell asleep to the smell of her hair and the sound of her breathing.

She's here with me.

I'm safe again.

42

MAEVE CROSS

MALICE

PANIC CAUSED ME TO JOLT UP IN BED. BLEARILY, I LOOKED AT my surroundings, my breath coming out fast and hard. *Where am I?*

A big arm had slipped from my chest down to my hips, and Ronin stirred. His dark hair was in complete disarray, strewn over his face. By now his undercut had completely grown out but was still noticeably shorter than the hair on the crown of his head. He grumbled loudly and tossed himself onto his other side. Our cabin came into view, and my heart finally began to slow.

I knew his back well. It had enticed me on numerous occasions… but where were his wings? Instead of the new wingspan, their outline was now etched into his back, slightly raised. I reached forward to touch the new tattoo, and he grumbled again.

His skin was warm to the touch, and I plastered myself against his back, hooking a leg around his hips to eliminate as much space between us as possible. I wrapped my arm around him and pressed my hand to his chest. He wasn't as large as he was last night, but I didn't care how variable his appearance was.

It felt like a dream to touch him again. But this time I wouldn't fall through him like he was a specter. He was here. And he was mine.

"Sweetheart?" he murmured, his fingers weaving through mine. Then he guided my hand to curl around him tighter. Those talons he seemed so afraid to scratch me with weren't there. Just those big, familiar hands.

Ronin froze and released me, bringing his hand in front of his face. His entire body grew taut with alarm when he untangled himself from me, sitting up on his bed.

"What the fuck?" He reached for where his horns had been. He touched his teeth. Then he threw the furs off his feet to see that they weren't elongated like they were before. *"What the fuck?"*

I watched him get up and have to pull his trousers tighter around his waist.

"What's wrong?" I asked.

"My feet," he answered, staring down at his normal toes.

"I… don't see the problem," I replied, my voice going up a bit at the end. The tattoo on his chest was still that lovely blue watercolor painting, and now he had an additional one on his back.

He shook his head. "No. Cliohde gave me this form to protect myself. Where did it go?"

My initial reaction was alarm. "*Cliohde?*" Then I sighed. "Well, I've been having chats with Death, so that shouldn't surprise me."

His eyes locked with mine. "*Chats* as in plural?"

We still had a lot to catch up on. I pointed at myself. "I spent a lot of time dying the last six months. Death might as well have laid out biscuits and tea." Then I shook my head. "But let's focus on your lack of wings for a minute."

"For the past six months, Cliohde blessed me with that form. I was only ever able to change into my full leviathan. I couldn't transform back into this." He ran a hand through his hair. "Gods are really fucking abstract when they talk to you—"

I snorted. "Tell me about it. And then they get really annoyed when you don't know what in the Hells they're talking about."

The corner of his mouth twitched in amusement before he shook it off. "Did I do something to offend her somehow?"

I pursed my lips. "Give me a little spin."

"What?"

"Spin for me," I insisted, wiggling my brows.

"What are you getting at, Mae?" He crossed his arms and drew my attention to his forearms.

Dragon or not, he still takes my breath away.

My lips pulled into a cheeky grin. "Stop being stubborn and spin. I want to see something."

He tossed his head back and sighed before slowly turning in a stiff circle.

In the space between us, I could see magic thrumming through the outline of his tattoo, flickering from dark blue to oil-slicked black, just like his scales in his full form. "I take it that you don't know about the tattoo on your back."

"The what?" he huffed, reaching back to touch the raised ink. "Wait a fucking second."

I watched the outline glow as he willed it to come forward, his hands elongating into claws. He rolled his shoulders, and the outline rose into two wings exploding from his back. But the rest of him didn't grow to that staggering height.

"That's new."

"You couldn't do that before?" I asked.

"No," he answered, flexing his shoulders again. The wings disappeared into the ink under his skin. "Do you know how many garments Siggi tailored for me? How many pieces of clothing Freynir stole?"

He sighed and turned around to face me, and I didn't miss the pink that flushed his face. Ronin looked awfully sheepish as he pulled at his trousers, then stepped over to his trunk to gather some fresh clothes.

My face heated as warmth expanded in my chest. I'd thought he'd grown a sort of armor in my absence, but I didn't realize how literal that had been.

"Do I make you feel safe, Ronin?" I asked. "Is that why you put your thick skin away?"

I watched with delight as his face flushed completely red. He looked away from me. "Or it could be because Pike's dead," he deflected.

"If it makes you feel any better, last night was the first time I've felt safe since Shipwreck Bay," I admitted.

His eyes softened, and he came toward me. He leaned forward over his bed to stroke my chin with the backs of his knuckles. "Me too," he murmured, leaning down to kiss me.

I reveled in the feel of his lips against mine, our breath mingling. "I love you," I murmured against his mouth.

He traced my bottom lip with his thumb. "I love you too. Gods, I missed you more than I want to admit." Ronin sighed, pressing his forehead against mine briefly before taking a step back. "You can stay here if you want while I speak to the new recruits. Lucky and I have much to do."

"I need to talk to Frey. His wife is alive," I said. "There was too much going on last night for me to tell him, and frankly, I don't know how he's going to take the news."

Frey led a siege on a town full of innocent people because he was so blinded by grief. To find out that all of that meant nothing? I truly didn't know if he'd be overjoyed or even more horrified at his actions.

Both those thick dark brows went up to his hairline. "Seems like we'll both be busy today," he commented. "Though I'd rather not let you out of my sight."

"The feeling is mutual," I said, pressing my face deeper into his grasp, losing myself in his eyes for as long as possible. "But I'll see you tonight."

"Tonight," he agreed, kissing me one more time before letting me go. Then he jumped up from his spot and rushed over to his trunk.

His sudden movement startled me, but then he pulled out a few of my favorite garments to wear when we were at sea: a fitted linen shirt and my navy wool trousers.

Did... did he bring me some fresh clothes? My heart soared, and a smile pulled at the corners of my mouth.

Ronin presented the items to me "I wanted you to have something that was yours. Something clean. I didn't know when I'd see you again, so—"

I cupped his prickly jaw before he could finish speaking, kissing him with all the appreciation I could muster. He hummed, eyes fluttering closed as he fell into it. I stroked the side of his face before I pulled away, delighted in how his eyes sleepily opened again.

"Thank you."

He tucked a stray piece of hair back behind my ear and murmured, "You're welcome, sweetheart."

When I got dressed, all I could think about was how I was finally wearing something that belonged to me again and that it smelled so distinctly like cedar and seawater.

I found Frey in the camp outside the fortress. Several sailors were sitting there, stuffing their faces with breakfast. Butcher and Conway had prepared a giant cauldron of porridge over a roaring flame. It smelled like butter and oats, reminding me of the very first meal I had on *The Ollipheist*.

The one where Gunny called me spoiled and I swallowed my pride.

So many familiar faces lit up around the camp when they saw me. One of these days, while we recovered from the battle, I could join them and reminisce on our lost time.

Frey looked up from his bowl, pinning me with his stark yellow eyes. "*Ylgr!*" He stood up, tossing his bowl into a tub of soapy water. He sped toward me, the broadsword clapping against his back. I noticed that his shirt was too big, as were his trousers that he'd tightened to his narrow waist with a belt.

Those were definitely Ronin's clothes.

"You look good," I said, gesturing to his extended ears. The wounds where his piercings had been healed nicely, leaving purple marks that would fade over time.

"Your kin have treated me well," he replied, looking awfully content. Then he tilted his head to observe me, his marital braid slapping his shoulder. "You, however, still look haunted."

"We need to talk. Walk with me?"

He crooked a silver-blond brow and nodded. "Sure."

I headed toward the fortress. I wanted to show Frey the mirror and find a way to get through to Elinora again. He walked in step with me, slowing down his usual pace to accommodate my much shorter legs.

"It feels strange to walk beside you without having to deal with bullets or chains," Frey mused. "I'd forgotten that for such a ferocious woman, you're also very short."

To emphasize his point, he rocked onto the balls of his

feet, looking directly over me before he literally patted me on the head like a well-behaved puppy.

I glared up at him. "It's not my fault that Death put me in this body." Though, I did find myself wondering why I wasn't given a body with more physical strength.

He ruffled my hair, a few of my new braids wiggling around. "Stature aside, I did miss your company."

It was nice to walk under the sun and feel the breeze without the threat of battle or injury. Some of Ronin's sailors watched the front gate, while others were inside scouting for supplies. The fortress had always felt like a stormy cloud was cast over it, but without the Pikes, it felt like an entirely new building.

"I enjoy a good battle as much as the next warrior, but watching you ride that dragon to victory surpassed it. I kept telling him that I should take him for a ride—"

Gods, he hasn't changed one bit since the brig.

"Do you *hear* what comes out of your mouth?" I interrupted, a helpless smile curling the side of my own.

Frey grinned, showing off his extended canines. "Enough to know that I'm hilarious."

A small laugh slipped past my lips. "I'm glad you weren't trapped here with me, but I missed your sense of humor."

He shrugged and followed me down the hallway. "Sometimes all you need is a laugh to know you're not totally fucked."

I hummed in agreement, taking in the massive damage Ronin did to the fortress. The ceiling was cracked open in many places, and there were significant holes from his talons. Warmth flooded my belly at the thought of his strength.

But he was always so careful with me.

My lips tingled as I subconsciously pressed my fingers to them, remembering how good it felt to kiss him again. It had been so long that I'd forgotten how it felt to be consumed by his presence. It could fill the whole room.

And when he stood in front of hundreds of sailors, he *commanded* the entire island with nothing more than a look.

Sometime soon, I'd like to remind myself how he knew how to command my body.

"Stop that," Frey retorted.

"What?" I asked, breaking out of my thoughts.

"In all the time we were stuck together, I smelled fear and rage off you, but never *that*." He shot me a knowing look. "Do you remember the time I told you about my ability to smell pheromones? It was one of the few times I was absolutely serious."

Heat flushed my face, but instead of sputtering in embarrassment, I said, "Have you *seen* the man?"

He snorted. "I have. I get it. But please, *that* is very distracting. I can only imagine how you two *stink* when you're together. Remind me to avoid his cabin completely."

"Why would you be in his cabin?" I asked.

"Well, because your friend Red was trying to kill me—"

"Reasonable."

"Shut the fuck up," he retorted with a roll of his eyes. "And Ronin was nice enough to set up a cot in his cabin so she didn't slit my throat in my sleep."

"Is she still trying to kill you? I could talk to her," I offered. As irritating as Frey could be, I'd grown fond of him. Like a ship hull grows fond of their favorite barnacle.

He waved his hand. "She got it out of her system. But she still stares at me like she's imagining what I'd look like without a head."

"That's how she looks at everyone. Except Andra."

I found my way to Varric's old room. The calling mirror had to still be there.

Frey followed me inside and glanced along all the various

things Varric had left behind. Clothing. Surgical instruments. Various alchemy concoctions. "What did you need me to see, Mae? I'm sure Red or Andra would've joined you for a little errand. Even the dragon if you asked nicely."

I opened the door to the side room, and lo and behold, the large black-framed mirror was still there, the glass glimmering as if something floated between the reflection and our world.

"I wanted you to come with me because your wife is alive, Frey."

He stopped walking completely, and I caught a whiff of a wintery hearth. "That's not fucking funny."

"I wouldn't joke about that," I replied, looking over my shoulder at him.

His yellow eyes blazed. "I saw her body. She was lifeless with that fucking Face-Stealer over her. Then I tackled them through the portal, and all this shit fell from their pockets."

"Do you know what this is?" I asked, gesturing to the mirror.

"A calling mirror," Frey replied, deeply suspicious. "We have a few in Skadi. Any reflective surface will do for communication with the right spell. I prefer the water because mirrors can play tricks on you."

"She was in the mirror," I explained. "She's alive, Frey."

He crossed his arms, and that wintery smell only got stronger. "What did you do to see her?"

Nothing. "She just appeared—"

Suddenly, a chuckle echoed around the room. The hairs stood up on the back of my neck as the noise chattered and chittered like a flurry of insects. Frey's eyes widened, shooting to the mirror behind me.

"That's not Elinora," he stated firmly.

"No. No, I'm not," a gleeful feminine voice giggled. "You look an awful lot like your granddad, Son of Skadi. Shame we couldn't bleed your *skelmis* like your grandmother." A barked laugh. "What a fitting end."

Slowly, I turned around, catching glowing amethyst eyes. I felt a blaze of Frey's rage and heard the *shiing* of his broadsword leaving its sheath.

"*Draugr*," he growled, tensing his entire body.

"You think so little of me," she crooned, floating between the realms, flesh bloated and gray. Her hair hung off her scalp in clumps. She grinned a bloody smile. "This is *my* calling mirror, Prince. It does nothing without me."

"You called Elinora for me, didn't you?" I realized.

Her neck snapped to the side when she looked at me. "I did."

"Then bring her here!" Frey demanded, voice nearly breaking with hidden desperation. "Prove to me she's alive."

The woman's tongue flicked at her teeth, her movement undeniably serpentine. "Why would I do that when your despair is so *delicious?*"

Death's voice echoed in my ears. "*Shatter the mirror. Collect the soul.*"

"No," I hissed between my teeth. "*I didn't kill Pike for you.*"

I took the Pikes for all the horrors they committed.

I took Adams and his band of murderers.

I would take Varric Cross for his crimes.

I was Death's champion, but I would never be Death's executioner.

"Ah," the woman in the mirror said. "I know you, Sentry. Same soul, different body. Similar to my King of Ashes. Shame he hasn't found a vessel sturdy enough for me. At least one he's willing to part with."

What?

Then she chuckled. "Death is here for me again, aren't they?" Her eyes pinned mine with an intensity that only the

Gods were capable of. "Shatter the glass, and you'll never know Death's lies."

A cold hand gripped the back of my neck as if Death were pleading for me not to listen.

"What are you talking about?" Frey demanded.

"Gods can't interfere in the mortal world. But they can make mortals do their bidding. *Champions*. They shouldn't be surprised that I'm only living up to my name," she continued, twisting around herself like a thorny vine.

"And who are you?" I asked, not sure if I wanted the answer.

"I used to go by many names. Some called me Cacia, the Skadians called me Fenrir, but I prefer *Malice*. And you two could *feed* me for eons."

Frey drew his sword to break the mirror, but she tsked.

"Son of Skadi. You shattering my door won't kill me. It'll release me," the woman teased.

"Then why don't you want us to release you?" I asked.

Her fingers walked along the glass. "Because it'll be so much *work* to use you, Sentry. And I prefer to watch. My pieces are already in motion."

Death's grip tightened. "What are you talking about?"

"Few mortals can withstand the essence of a god. I've only met one worthy vessel. Without one, I'm impossible to kill. With one, Death can finally claim me. But, my darling sentry, I'll enjoy myself first."

The ice-cold grip evaporated, and Death vanished.

"You're lying," I whispered.

"Maybe. Do you want to risk it?" she taunted. "You know, mortals are too sentimental. My King of Ashes told me your spirit was stronger than mine, opting to borrow your power instead. I think he's fond of you. Even now." Her eyes bounced between Frey and me.

Frey's hand closed over my shoulder as I grew tense. He sheathed his sword. "I'm not going to risk it."

My lips curled into a snarl. "I'm just something to use."

"You have always lived and died for someone else." She sighed. "Now, next time you come here, bring that dragon. When I have your body, Sentry, I'd like to see who would do *anything* for you. Maybe I could trick him long enough to hear what he sounds like in the throes of passion."

Rage spat up in my belly.

"It's been so long, and Ronin is as good a name to call out as any. I hear he likes it better with your voice."

I thrust my hand forward, slapping it open-palmed against the glass. It rattled, and her eyes danced with excitement. "Keep his name out of your fucking mouth."

"Malice tastes like heaven on you. Decadent as the wars. Death may have stripped my godhood, but they won't be rid of my influence that easily. The hate only makes me stronger. Even Death won't be able to stop my ascension." She looked at Frey and wiggled her fingers. "Ta-ta for now."

I slouched against the mirror, radiating with anger. I glanced over at Frey. "She mentioned your grandparents."

A tic jumped in his jaw. "It doesn't make any sense. During the war when Farlight Isles was banished, the Queen of Nyland murdered my grandmother. Was that... the queen?"

Same soul. Different body.

"What about the King of Nyland?"

The gears were turning in Frey's head. "That's not what they called him in the history books. They taught us about the tyrant—"

"Frey," I snapped. "What did they call him?"

"In Skaditung, it was *Alfri Askhon*...." His head fell back. "In Common, it's translated to *the King of Ashes*."

Fuck.

43

RONIN MURDOCH

FUCKING MINE

Mae stood in front of a table of our advisers, all of whom were as lost as I was. "Varric Cross—reincarnated. Me—reincarnated. Lady in the mirror—Goddess of Malice." She squeezed the bridge of her nose and said, "I don't think I can explain this any simpler, Ronin."

Along the massive table in the Great Hall, my mother and Lucky sat on either side of me, then Luella, Andra, Udine, and Freynir. Everyone was accounted for.

Bliss was the interim commander with Pinky while we discussed our next steps. Something Bliss complained about greatly, but at least it was a promotion from cabin boy. I warned them that if they fucked it up, they'd be back to swabbing decks and Pinky would captain their boat.

They still had work to do before I forgave them for that fucking mutiny attempt.

It felt nice to be back in my human form again, and my mates and advisers also seemed pleasantly surprised to see me like this. My appearance was now more variable than it had ever been, but I also felt more like *me* than I had before.

"I didn't believe it either," Freynir said. "You have to see her to really understand what we're dealing with."

Mae's eyes snapped over to Freynir, and she snarled, "Over my dead body. No one is going into that room."

What had this Malice said to Mae?

"But if Malice knows Varric's plans," Lucky said, scratching his graying beard, "then we could get the leg up on him."

"*No*," Mae hissed.

Lucky sighed. "Lass, we can't go after him blind."

Luella cleared her throat. "I'm with Mae on this. The Gods are tricky. I've never heard of a Goddess of Malice, but whatever she is, she's trapped in a mirror. Let's keep it that way."

Mae's eyes softened, and she offered Luella a look of appreciation. "Varric is still our greatest threat. I can feel it when he uses magic, and it's getting stronger. He threw up a shield to withstand Ronin's lightning."

Guilt rattled around in my chest. "We know he went to Farlight Castle. We know the gap between Farlight Isles and Algar is going to close. This is more than we'd ever had before. And when I find Pike's calling mirror, we can finally contact Elinora."

"We didn't call him the King of Ashes for no reason," Freynir said, crossing his arms. "His cult scourged the—"

"Cult?" Udine questioned.

"Do they teach you nothing in the Isles?" Freynir asked.

"Not all of us have a royal's education, Freynir. Not to mention, history books were burned and blacked out when Varric came into power," Andra pointed out. "Many sailors and common people still don't know how to read because education is considered a luxury."

The Skadian prince's mouth twisted in discomfort, but he dismissed it and said, "Well, it seems we'll have to fix that when Cross is unseated, yes?" He tapped his chin. "The long and short of it is that the King and Queen of Nyland led a cult that scourged the entire continent. It caused so much unrest that people turned against their own kingdoms. It wasn't until they were banished that it came to an end."

"Why banish and not kill them?" Luella asked.

Freynir shrugged. "That's a good question. Ultimately, the Guild of Sorceresses was merciful. The king's and queen's memories were tampered with, and they were given the chance to repent. As soon as they did, they'd be welcomed back to Algar again."

Udine stood up. "So the torment my people have suffered at the hands of the Besieger was because the Guild of Sorceresses were too good to get blood on their hands?"

"I wish I had a better answer for you," Freynir replied. "A lot changed in Algar after that ruling. Laws and treaties were put into place to keep it from happening again."

I wished his words felt like a comfort, but they didn't.

FOR DINNER, CONWAY AND BUTCHER HAD LAID OUT A SPREAD of sandwiches. Cured meats and cheeses weren't available at sea, but the Ivory Keys Fortress was laden with fancy fixings. My sailors were thrilled to dive into the salty meats and the chewy, crusty breads.

We found several staff members hiding in the kitchens and in storage closets. They'd expected the worst, some of them crying for mercy before we could get a word out. They were unarmed, so we let them go to spread word about the Pikes' demise.

Despite it being a hostile takeover, I wanted to make it clear that we weren't there to harm the townspeople. I even sent a few locals out to gather recruits.

Some of the servants stayed if they had nowhere to go. But most of them left. Word traveled fast, and I expected civilians to trickle in to join our ranks or size us up. We were after Varric Cross next, but I also had to appoint a leader to handle whatever unrest happened after we left.

I had a lot of good people behind me. We'd be all right.

With two sandwiches in my hands, I walked back to my cabin, where I'd left Mae to get ready for bed. She'd been acting strangely since she left with Freynir earlier, and I knew it was because of Malice.

I was even tempted to see this mirror for myself, but Mae *did not* want me anywhere near it. Curiosity buzzed in my head, but I respected Mae. We'd go to the mirror together.

There were very few people on deck. Most of them were gathered around the various bonfires, enjoying the night. I opened my cabin door. Mae stood in front of one of my bookcases, wearing nothing but one of my shirts. The white linen had slipped down one of her shoulders, and I wanted nothing else but to trail my lips along the freckles.

She looked over her shoulder at me, but her eyes were distant. The way she held herself was different now, even in the privacy of our cabin. Her back was ramrod straight as she turned back around to glide her fingers over the spines of what was left of my book collection.

"What did she say to you, love?" I asked.

Mae's shoulders rose and fell with a heavy sigh. "A lot of things that I didn't like."

I sat down at my table near the windows. "Come and eat. Tell me about it."

"All right," she murmured, sitting across from me to unwrap her sandwich. She couldn't make eye contact with me as she took a big bite.

Then she slowly told me everything that happened in that

room. That Death had lied to her. That Malice wanted the mirror to be broken to possess Mae's body.

"She gets into your head. I could feel it," Mae said between bites. "Gods, being around her made me so gods-damn *angry*. You know as well as I do how fast that anger can turn into malice. There is one thing that's certain: She's dangerous."

"Do you think she's telling the truth?" I asked, reaching out to wind my fingers through hers.

Her shoulders hunched forward, and she brought my hand up to her lips for a tender kiss. I could feel the crumbs on the corners of her mouth leaving little scratches.

"Your guess is as good as mine." Her dark eyes met mine, and I watched those layers of armor peel away to reveal that soft, warm gaze that I loved so much. "I think she wanted to watch me squirm."

"I won't let her take you, Mae," I said.

Her eyes drifted down to where my shirt was unbuttoned, and she murmured, "It's not me I'm worried about."

Amusement curled the side of my mouth upward. "Yeah?"

She finished her sandwich and stood up, bracing herself on her palms. She pinned me with her wide eyes, leaning forward in a way that made the shirt droop down. My mouth watered, and suddenly I wasn't capable of thinking of anything else but how her tits felt in my mouth. In my hands. Pressed up against—

"I'm going to make something clear to you, Ronin," Mae said, then snapped her fingers, drawing my gaze up to hers. "My eyes are up here."

"What's clear?" I asked, throat bobbing as my tongue darted out to wet my lips.

She leaned in again, and I found myself mesmerized by her. A cluster of braids was tucked behind her ear, and her petal-pink lips beckoned to me. A lovely flush brightened her cheeks, and heat cascaded down my spine like hot water.

The way she looked at me made me fucking hard.

"I'm in love with you. Do you know what that means?" she asked.

I watched her round the table, and I leaned back in the chair, parting my legs so she could stand between them. All I wanted her to do was sit her pretty ass on the table so I could bury my face between her legs for dessert.

The chairs were nailed down, so I couldn't scoot backward, but I rather liked her being close enough that I could seat my hands on the dip above her hips.

"Sit on the fucking table and tell me," I ordered.

Mae's eyes got all heavy lidded as she propped herself on the table in front of me. My gaze dropped to her thighs as she parted them. My chest rose and fell with every breath as I stared at the wet mess between her legs.

What I wouldn't do to lick it up and taste exactly what I did to her.

My cock thickened in my pants, and the sight of her cunt threw me to the edge of finishing in my trousers. I tilted my head back and groaned. Mae was going to fucking kill me one of these days.

Suddenly, her foot shot out and pressed against my chest. "You seem distracted."

"Obviously," I retorted. "I'm thinking about how good you taste when you—"

"Look at me, Ronin," she demanded, a slender hand coming to my jaw to direct my gaze up to hers. "I'm in love with you," she repeated, pupils blown to the Hells but ferocity blazing in the inky depths. "Which means that if anyone touches you, they're dead."

"I would say the same, sweetheart, but I much prefer

watching you take your own pound of flesh," I replied. "Then I'd wash the blood from your hands."

For my entire life, I was the one who'd fought for the people I loved. Right or wrong, I would get my hands dirty to protect my family. I was the captain. I was the big brother. I was heir to the throne.

But I didn't have to be any of those things with Mae. She was right when she said I could put my thick skin away when she was safe in my arms.

I would take care of Mae, but I'd never had anyone willing to take care of me the way she would.

I took her hands into mine. Her fingers curled between mine like they were meant to fit there perfectly.

So small. So dangerous. So *fucking lovely*.

She was vicious, bold, and brave. But she was soft for me. I watched her grow from a spoiled princess into a force to be reckoned with. Truth be told, I'd loved every step of it.

She was my match in every way.

I rose up from my seat to pinch her chin between my thumb and pointer finger. She leaned into my touch, staring up at me like she didn't believe I existed. Like I was a dream she was destined to wake up from.

My heart pounded hard in my chest, blood buzzing in my ears with excitement.

"Telling you I love you isn't enough, sweetheart," I murmured, hypnotized by the way her lips parted. "Because this is deeper. I'm devoted to you. I never wanted to be a better man until I met you."

Her throat arched up toward the ceiling, and my hand slipped to the nape of her neck. "You're everything to me, Ronin." Tears welled in the corners of her eyes as she added, "I'm so afraid that you'll be taken from me."

A single tear fell down her flushed cheek, and I leaned

down to kiss it away. "There wasn't a single day that I didn't think about you."

"All I wanted was you. When it got bad and worse, all I wanted was you."

"You have me. You have all of me," I promised.

She took my hand and brought it to her chest, where her heart pounded rapidly in time with mine. "I know."

I captured her lips, groaning deep in my chest when she opened up for me. Her taste filled my mouth, and the smell of cinnamon and berries surrounded me. Her heartbeat kicked faster when I kissed her.

The feel of her lips wasn't enough. I needed to kiss every freckle, hear every sigh of surrender, and taste her when she came apart.

Slowly, I slid my hand from her chest down to her soft stomach and then to the wetness between her thighs.

It was the fact that she was always fucking soaking for me that made a whimper of desperation crawl up my throat.

Mae reacted to the noise I made with a whimper of her own. "Please?" she asked as her thighs parted and trembled. I trailed kisses down the curve of her throat, nipping where her pulse pounded.

My name spilled from her lips when I stroked her clit, which was already swelling in anticipation. Licking up her neck, I took her earlobe between my teeth, and she squealed when I sank a finger into her cunt.

Instantly, she got wetter, squeezing my finger with quick flutters. Her hips lifted, demanding more.

How fast can I get her to come?

My hand that wasn't busy between her thighs dove under the shirt to grasp her breast, pinching her pebbled nipple. She folded against me, quivering when I added another finger to join the first. I rubbed gentle circles on the swollen bud with my thumb.

I hooked my fingers upward to the firm spot behind her clit, and it didn't take long before she was shaking, clenching around my fingers faster and faster with an impending orgasm.

"Ronin," she moaned, repeating my name over and over again like it was the only thing she knew how to say.

I was tempted to make her come right then and there, but we'd been apart too long. Her first orgasm would be against my face.

Withdrawing my fingers, I gripped her jaw and kissed her hard before taking a seat in front of her. Her head was reeling back and forth, her eyes unfocused as I gripped her thighs and dragged her to the edge.

Mae screamed when I lowered my head between her legs, licking up everything I could. Fuck, I was nothing more than a man worshipping at the altar of Mae's cunt. She tasted heady and hot and *mine*.

She was *fucking mine*.

My cock thickened in my pants even more, and my eyes rolled back. I didn't think I'd ever finished untouched to the taste of a woman on my tongue.

Fuck, I was going to.

I ignored my need to breathe as I devoured her, my nose nudging her clit as she thrashed above me. I glanced up to see her neck thrust toward the ceiling, both of her hands tangled in her hair. Two glorious tits peaked with tight pink nipples obscured her face. Her hips rocked against my face, lost as she was in the throes of passion.

So godsdamn beautiful.

Heat bunched at the base of my spine, swelling in my cock. I tried to repress it, but I was too far gone, Mae tasted too fucking good, and I hadn't so much as fucked my own fist since she was taken from me.

I latched onto her clit, fucking her with my fingers, and

she came apart right as I did. She clamped down on my fingers, and I imagined how good she'd feel around my cock. My groan was muffled against her, her spend gushing all over me and the table.

Fucking Hells….

Another wave of my orgasm hit me, my hips bucking up, and I spilled into my trousers. My vision narrowed, and I broke away from her to toss my head against the back of the chair. The force of it made me dizzy, both my legs shaking uncontrollably.

Out of the corner of my eye, I saw Mae fall backward so her spine was flat against the table, panting heavily.

The next words spilled from my lips before I could stop them. The tether that bound us, whether by fate or love, grew tighter. Intimacy flared between us, and I couldn't waste it.

"Marry me, Mae."

44

MAEVE CROSS

BEAUTIFUL

Ronin demanded something of me, but I didn't hear him. My head was reeling, the stars still dancing behind my eyelids. My legs were quivering fiercely, and even if that orgasm was enough to cast every dark thought away, I desired more.

He hadn't said anything else, and I propped myself up on my elbows, finally coming back into my body again. Ronin's face was flushed, his pupils devoured his irises, and he was panting and shaking as if he'd already….

My eyes widened, and I asked, "Did you…?"

"Yes," he answered.

"From…?"

"Yes, Mae. Turns out your cunt tastes better than I remember." His eyes finally locked on mine, completely consuming me.

My insides clenched around nothing, and my eyes darted to the mess I'd made on the table, then to the wet spot on the front of his trousers. I wanted to make him do it again. And again.

Until the only reason he knew his name was because I kept screaming it.

"You didn't hear me, did you?" he asked, tilting his head to the side as a wicked smile curled his lips. Those two blasted dimples dented either side of his mouth, and my mind went blank.

I was lost in his gaze. In the way our very essence wound together tighter than a knot. His smell filled my nose, and I couldn't focus on anything but the color of his lips. My hands itched to pull him closer and tear his shirt open. Then his smile fell, and I wanted it back. Immediately.

He sighed and grumbled, "It was a bad time to ask. Forget I said anything."

When he stood up, he looked absolutely dejected. I sat up straight, shooting my hand out to grab him, holding him by his linen shirt. "No. No. What did you say?"

It wasn't the orgasm that made his face flush even deeper, his expression almost sheepish. "I said, '*Marry me, Mae.*'" Ronin paused, watching my face closely. "Obviously not now, but it'd be something to look forward to when it's all over.

"You want to marry me?" I asked, a ball of emotion welling in my throat. My entire body soared with delight. A smile spread helplessly across my mouth, but it was all too much for me at once. I slapped my hands over my face as my cheeks heated.

"What are you doing, Mae?" His hands came up to pry my hands away.

"Hiding," I replied, smiling so wide that my cheeks hurt. "I can't remember the last time I smiled like this."

"Well, let me see your smile, pretty girl," he replied, successfully separating my hands from my face. "There you are."

I brought my lower lip between my teeth, trying to repress it. "And you asked me right after—"

"I'd been thinking about it since you were taken from me, but now that I've tasted you again, *I need you*," he declared with conviction.

My eyelashes fluttered as I scooted closer. "I need you, too, Ronin. Sometimes it scares me."

"I know the feeling," he said, stroking my chin tenderly with his thumb. "Is that a yes, love?"

"I don't remember you asking a question. It sounded like a demand," I teased.

"Oh, it was. But demand or not, you can still say no." I could feel his breath against my face, and it made my lips part, utterly parched with the desire to drink in his kiss. "Do you want to marry me, sweetheart?"

I wiggled on the table, parting my legs to get closer to him. "More than anything."

"Yes?"

"Yes, you irritating man!"

He grinned and said, "You pronounced *scoundrel* wrong."

I laughed. "Scoundrel."

"That's right."

He captured my lips, and I hummed in contentment. I encircled his neck with my arms, dragging him against me so my chest was flush against his. Our mouths molded together in a searing kiss.

My eyes closed as I parted my lips so our tongues could dance together. I could taste myself on his tongue, and it made a rush of heat dampen between my legs again. He groaned deep in his throat, his hands dropping down to my waist to eliminate any space.

It didn't take long for his cock to stir again, growing hard as he pressed against me. My body cried out for him, demanding to feel him everywhere. I hooked a leg around him, trapping him between me and the chair behind him.

"You're wearing too many clothes," I murmured against his lips.

I trailed my hands down to his shirt and tore it open, letting the buttons make music as they bounced off every hard surface around us. His chest rumbled and he pulled away, hand shooting up to my throat to pin me flat against the table.

Lust flared through my system, and a desperate noise spilled from my lips. My eyes snapped open, and I licked my lips as I raked my gaze up and down his chest, ogling the dark chest hair and the tattoo that bloomed and blended into his skin. I caught sight of one vein that went from his collarbone and down his torso to disappear into the waistband of his breeches.

Gods, he's beautiful.

Time slowed down, and desire flooded every nerve ending. Wetness gathered between my legs. I loved how he looked on top of me and how his hand felt fastened around my throat. The calluses on his fingers were rough on the soft skin on my neck, and I wished he could leave marks on me.

I'd wear the bruises of our passion proudly. I craved him so deeply, it was painful.

He never squeezed, only demanded my attention.

Ronin was remarkably attentive and gentle when I was spread out beneath him, careful not to drive me past my limits. After everything I'd endured, I found security in how he knew my body.

And I needed to lie beneath the man I loved and let him cherish me. I'd never grow tired of how my heart soared or how he looked down at me like I was everything he'd ever wanted.

Like I was powerful and precious all at once.

"You're going to help me repair that shirt tonight, sweetheart," he said.

I arched my throat upward, a silent offering. "Can it wait? I've only finished once. And I want to see if you can come again like that."

He crooked an eyebrow and chuckled. "I'm afraid that won't happen. You've taken the edge off. To think that I was trying so desperately not to finish in my trousers. I wanted to save that for when I was buried to the hilt inside you."

"Why? It was incredibly flattering." I wriggled underneath his grip. "I take it there wasn't much relief with a certain Skadian prince taking refuge in your cabin?"

He laughed again. "I don't think his wife would approve."

"No. She seemed rather possessive when I talked to her. Something we have in common, I suppose," I added cheekily.

With a hum, he tightened his hand around my throat. He drank up my reaction as I curled my fingers around his hand, encouraging him to squeeze.

"I've never been a possessive man, Mae. Not until you. Even so, I want you to have a life outside of me. I'm not greedy enough to demand you all hours under the sun."

Excitement buzzed under my skin.

"But when you're like this, underneath me in the dark, I feel greedy."

I felt the same way. Our lives would be busy, but at the end of the day, Ronin would be with me. He could hang up his captain's hat and curl into my arms. I could kiss the weariness away, and I knew he'd do the same.

We would fight the battle and nurse each other's wounds afterward.

And then, when we were tangled up together, I found comfort in knowing he was just as possessive about the vulnerability as I was. We'd suffered too much and wore our trauma like a matching set.

When we were together, we were *whole*.

Ronin's gaze skated down my body to where my nipples

tightened into peaks. A desperate noise burst from him, cheeks flushing deeper. He released my throat, and I missed his hand instantly. He sat down in the chair again, staring at my body like he didn't know which piece of me he wanted first.

"You're so fucking pretty when you come." He leaned down and gave me another firm lick before leaning back to gaze at me.

I squealed, anticipation welling inside me again.

He gripped my thighs, his fingers leaving little white imprints. "Your breathing gets deeper, and your eyelashes flutter. Fuck, the shape your mouth makes. I need to see it all the time. I'd be a happy man, tasting you all night."

His chest was heaving, his nipples pebbled beneath a thick sprinkling of dark hair. I loved the way his face was flushed and how he chewed on his plump lower lip, aching for another taste.

I needed to feel him inside me, thick and demanding. My legs trembled from thinking about how good he felt when he finished, filling me with his spend. "That won't be enough for me, and you know it."

A knowing smirk curled one side of his mouth. "What can I say? I like it when you're needy."

My insides clenched around nothing, and I slid off the table directly onto his lap. Ronin groaned when I swiveled my hips against his, feeling his cock jump against me through his trousers. I curled my arms around his neck and kissed him thoroughly.

His hands fell to my hips, guiding me over his lap so my clit rubbed against him. The stimulation felt dulled in comparison to his mouth, so I pressed down harder, rocking like I was riding him. He made all sorts of gruff noises against my lips, moaning and whimpering. My clit swelled, and my breasts became more sensitive as I rubbed my chest into his.

Heat bunched at the base of my spine, and I wondered if I was going to come again.

My mouth fell open as he latched onto my neck, sucking hard.

I tossed my head back and cried out softly when another climax came toward me as his cock nudged my clit over and over again. Molten honey cascaded through me as I fell lax in his arms, sweaty and flushed but not satiated.

"Did you just come again?" he groaned. "Get in my bed. Fuck."

I blinked away dark spots in my vision and shook my head. "I'm too impatient for that."

He was about to demand something else when I slipped my hand down to his lap, quickly undoing the laces on his trousers. His eyes rolled back, and he said, "If you ride me too hard, we'll knock the fucking chair over."

"What is it you told me when you tore my shirt open the first time? When buttons went flying, and it wasn't even my shirt? Right before you made me see stars?" I asked, rising onto my knees to pull his cock out. It pulsed in my hand, hard and hot.

Most of his first climax had dried, and I needed something to slick him up for what I had planned. I held my hand out to him and demanded, "Spit."

Ronin swallowed another swear, his eyes going unfocused when he obeyed, wetting my skin so I could reach down and play with him. I stroked him up and down, knocking his length against my clit to tease myself.

It felt so good. But he always felt good.

"I remember you saying that you didn't care. If I fuck you so hard that I break the blasted chair, I really don't give a shit." I slid him back and forth against my slit, and it felt so decadent that I had half a mind to give myself another orgasm before I took him.

"If you don't fuck me right now, I'm going to bend you over my desk until you can't walk," Ronin threatened, but it teetered on a whimper.

Hearing my man whimper made me positively *feral*. "Is that a promise, baby?"

Before he could reply, I guided him right where I needed him. I sank down slowly, perfectly slick from all the preparation. He held my hips tight in his grip and moaned, a tantalizing noise that sounded far better than I remembered.

"Fuck, Mae. *Fuck.*"

His cock filled me to the brim without even a pinch of discomfort. My eyelashes fluttered and I murmured his name like a plea, sinking down until he was completely seated within me. His thighs trembled beneath me, that tendon in his neck straining.

I didn't deny myself the opportunity to sink my teeth into that taut muscle, Ronin jumping and groaning loudly at the sensation. I could feel him get thicker, and my body reacted in kind, squeezing and demanding satisfaction. At this rate, we'd be tumbling over that edge far too quickly.

Then we'll just do it again.

I kissed and sucked on his neck as I rocked my hips, bouncing on his cock. Ronin thrust upward, matching my speed. Pleasure erupted throughout our bodies. Goose bumps pebbled all over his skin, and I shoved what remained of his shirt off his shoulders.

"Fuck, slow down," he groaned, head tossed back against the chair. His cock thickened inside me even more, and I bounced harder, faster. "*Mae*. Fuck. Please."

"Why?" I asked, rocking back and forth, relishing the feel of him.

His hands tightened on my hips, eyes rolling back. "I need you to fucking get there before I do. I… I *can't*. I—"

I continued to rock back and forth, hypnotized by the way his jaw clenched. I barely even heard the crack beneath us. The chair tipped backward, breaking right off the nails that kept it from sliding around the boat. Ronin landed flat on his back with me on top of him, interrupting how hard I was fucking him.

The brief reprieve was enough to throw us backward from the edge.

He laughed, his hands kneading my hips. "I told you."

I placed my hands on his chest, leaning forward so my breasts swung in his face. He captured a nipple in his mouth, cutting off whatever bratty reply was on the tip of my tongue. A curse got stuck in my throat when he nipped it, pinpricks of delight rising all over my body.

My mind went hazy as he flipped us over off the chair and onto the planks. I squeaked in surprise, making him smile again when his forearms caged my head. As much as I enjoyed topping, my rebellion faded away into submission when he pinned both of my hands over my head with one of his.

He didn't move, holding himself inside me while I warmed his cock. I wriggled my hips, painfully unsatisfied.

He kissed my throat, trailing his lips down to some freckles scattered across my collarbones. He cradled me gently, showering me in affection. I cried out something, and there was probably an *"I love you"* somewhere in the nonsense that spilled from my mouth.

He slid out of me momentarily to kick his trousers the rest of the way off, but before I had a chance to whine, he thrust into me again.

My body fell slack, completely at his mercy. He rocked slowly, taking his time to pull out and press forward again. I could feel every ridge rubbing against all the right parts inside.

I arched my back, murmuring another declaration of love as I fell into a blurry haze where nothing mattered but us.

His dark eyes watched me like he was mystified, wholly lost in me the way I drowned in him. The hand that pinned mine came down to cup my face. "You're so beautiful."

For once he wasn't telling me how good I felt squeezing his cock.

He wasn't telling me all the filthy things he loved about me.

He wasn't detailing how many ways he would make me come.

I didn't think he was telling me how beautiful my body was. He was staring deeply into my eyes and telling me that *I* was beautiful down to my spirit. The part of me that was cracked and worn but never broken. No matter how hard they tried.

A warm glow radiated inside me, making me whole again.

Ronin leaned back onto his knees, lifting my leg to hoist it over his shoulder, then burying himself that much deeper. A soundless gasp left me as he pulled me forward, hooking my other leg around his hips.

He turned his head to kiss the quivering calf on his shoulder, fucking me until I was shaking on the crest of a glorious moment of bliss. Mindlessly, I reached for him, gliding my hands up and down his chest.

"Come for me, baby. Make a mess of me like you made a mess of the table," he said, his voice lowering.

I quivered, my walls pulsing around him. "I'm so close," I whimpered, needing more and less at the same time.

"I know," he replied, stealing my hand to bring two of my fingers into his mouth. It was so unbearably erotic that I nearly came right then. "Touch yourself for me. Let me watch."

I couldn't do anything but obey. My clit was hard and swollen as I stroked it between those two fingers, switching to my own arousal when I'd used up his saliva. I watched the place we were joined, where his length glistened from me.

Sweat beaded on his neck, cascading down his chest. Perspiration also soaked my brow, but I didn't care how filthy we got.

"Such a good fucking girl." He thickened inside me, on the brink of finishing.

My eyes rolled back, and I begged, "I need you with me. Please."

"You'll take me with you," he promised.

We worked each other to the precipice of pleasure, and when it hit me, I screamed his name. I clamped down on him hard, squeezing and demanding him to fill me with his spend. I needed it like I needed air. I wanted to satisfy him the way he satisfied me.

Another rush of fluid similar to earlier coated his cock, gushing all over me and him and the floor. White light burst behind my eyes as a potent sense of relief flooded my body, relaxing every muscle as my leg slid off his shoulder.

He groaned loudly, his hand slamming down next to my head when he swelled inside me. I reached for him, pulling him flat on top of me when he came, jolting and lost in his own powerful release. When he softened enough to pull out of me, my head was light.

A silly grin spread across my face as he leaned back to stare at me with blissed-out eyes. He returned my smile and kissed me deeply. I preened under the affection, humming happily under my breath.

"I missed you," he said when he pulled away, caressing my jaw with his thumb.

"Not just the sex, I hope." I stuck my tongue out at him.

He rolled his eyes, a smile playing on his lips. "The sex is fantastic, but no, that's not the only reason I missed you, you brat."

"You like it," I said, canting my head to land a kiss on his neck.

"Unfortunately," he replied, tilting his head to give me better access to that tendon that demanded a nibble. I obliged, and he hummed in delight. "As comfortable as the floor is, I'd rather hold you in bed."

He got up, leaving me cold. He glanced over at the damage: the broken chair, the ripped shirt, his soaked trousers, and the slickness still all over the table and the floor. Then Ronin looked down at me, probably noticing my frown, and leaned down to scoop me up into his capable arms.

I giggled, kicking my legs playfully as I nuzzled my face into his chest. "Don't tell me you're going to make me clean up the mess now."

He carried me into the wet room and turned the lever so the faucet sprayed out seawater. "You, darling, have worn me out. Let me take care of you, fix the braids I ruined, and clean up the mess we left. The buttons and the chair can wait."

We smiled at each other, incredibly satiated and happy as we stepped into the water and cleaned the night off.

45

MAEVE CROSS

A RICH MAN'S DIRTY SECRET

I woke up too early the next morning, restless. Ronin slept next to me, his broad form nearly squishing mine. A smile played on my lips when I thought about last night. His proposal. The wonderful night we spent tangled in each other's arms.

Despite how happy I was, guilt lingered under the surface. How dare I be happy when I'd lost friends? How dare I be happy when I couldn't uphold my promise and save Pen?

Sitting up in bed, I stared at the man I loved. Apprehension gripped my heart hard—even harder than the magic Varric used to seize my life force for himself. I was a cocktail of complicated emotions and trauma I didn't think I'd ever unpack.

I stroked the muscles on his back, and he unconsciously pressed into my touch.

Most of all, I was terrified.

Terrified that he'd be stolen from me.

Terrified that the woman in the mirror would manipulate him.

Terrified that Varric would use my powers to strike Ronin down.

I didn't want to fail him the way I failed Pen.

That would be the end for me. What was a sentry without her leviathan?

I stroked his spine, trying to rouse him so he wouldn't be alarmed if he woke up without me.

He grumbled and tossed so he was facing me, half asleep. "Mae?"

"I'm going to get up."

"Why?" he murmured, trying to blink the sleep away, but it had a firm grip on him. "Let me come with you."

I shook my head and kissed his wrinkled brow. "Sleep, love. You need it."

I didn't want company, and he seemed to understand that. "All right. Join me and the mates for lunch later?"

"I'll be there." I pressed a kiss against his lips. "I love you."

Before I could pull away, he grasped the back of my neck, pulling me into a deeper kiss. I sighed, relaxing in his hold before he released me. "I love you too. Take my sash for your gear."

"Your lucky red sash?" I prodded.

He nodded and yawned. "Rings will rip your fingers off. I meant to give it to you last night, but we were distracted. Besides, it'll look better on you." Then he pressed a kiss on the tip of my nose and collapsed back into bed again.

That blooming sensation of happiness once again warmed my chest. I gazed at him a little longer, falling deeper in love with him. As tempting as it was to curl into bed again, I crawled over him to find the stash of clothes he had for me: a linen shirt, trousers, and my favorite worn boots.

Then I reached into his chest and gathered his lucky red sash. It excited me to tie it around myself, using it to house a cutlass on my hip. It was so recognizably Ronin's that I felt even more special.

Plus, when he was in his half-leviathan form, he used a vest to hold his gear. His sash was ornamental. I'd get more use out of it.

When I was dressed, I slipped out of his cabin, closing the door behind me.

It had been only a few days since I asked Luella to take Pen's body from the tower. Even if I couldn't bear to see her, I also couldn't leave her alone in that dark, cold place, contorted around herself like a rose that had been pruned incorrectly.

Nathaniel's body could be picked clean by the rats and the birds, but I wouldn't let Pen be forgotten like that. It wouldn't be long until her body was taken back home to be buried by her family. That meant I didn't have much time to say goodbye.

Beneath the early-morning sky, oranges and pinks painting the horizon, Gunny gathered materials outside the Pike Garden. Tears pricked my eyes when I took him in. He wore an eyepatch over one eye, faded injuries along his face. He was clipping a few flowers and gathering dried pieces of wood.

"Gunny?" I called out.

He straightened up immediately and turned on his heel, pure joy radiating on his face. "Birdie!" He discarded his spoils and darted toward me.

I ran toward him, too, not wasting a moment in spreading my arms into a welcoming hug. "Gunny," I said again, tucking my face into the crook between his neck and shoulder.

Gunny wound his arms beneath mine as he squeezed my waist. He pulled away, smiling so wide that his twisted canine was visible. "I heard the news, but I knew you probably needed time before I bombarded you."

"You could never bombard me," I promised before dragging him into another hug. "Gods, it's good to see you."

He nodded against my head, enjoying the friendly embrace before we pulled away completely. "Is it true? You're a reincarnated sentry?"

"It is. How are you? How's Spider?"

As soon as I said Spider's name, Gunny's face fell. "He's dead, Mae."

It felt like I'd been punched in the chest. Spider was as good a friend to me as Gunny, always welcoming and kind. But he and Gunny were thick as thieves. A bond that was far stronger than friendship. "I'm so sorry."

"It's why I'm here, actually. Those flowers don't grow in Shipwreck Bay. I thought it'd be nice to dry them so they won't wilt by his grave." Gunny rubbed the back of his neck. "I thought I'd whittle something for him too." His grief was palpable.

"Do you want to talk about it?"

He shook his head fiercely. "No, birdie. I just need time. I'm not ready to say goodbye yet." His throat worked down a swallow. "I should go. I have rounds soon."

"All right. Would you want to get a drink sometime soon? Before we leave dock?"

A subtle gleam came back into his eyes. "I'd like that. Maybe you can find something good in that fortress, yes?"

I nodded and brought him in for one more hug. "If you need me, Gun, I'm here. You're family, all right?"

"I know," he replied, offering me a timid smile. "Cap's sash looks good on you."

We said another goodbye as he went back toward the flowers he'd snipped, and I stepped through the garden gates. Birds sang and perched in the trees. It had been overgrown and uncared for, but it felt far livelier than the stench of death that filled the fortress.

Penelope's body lay restfully in the grass, wrapped in linen. To my surprise, she wasn't alone. Seymour was crouched down next to her on his knees, his back to me. His hands were shaking as he lifted the fabric off her face to pull it back. It was just for a moment, and I saw the crimson of her hair spill out around the linen before he tucked it all back in. His eyebrows crushed together, hands curling into fists.

I watched his shoulders heave in silent sobs. He reached out to brush her cloth-covered cheek and murmured, "My Pen."

Brush crunched under my feet, and Seymour's eyes shot up to me. His eyes were red, jaw clenched. His throat bobbed several times as we looked at each other.

Seymour knew Pen? His Pen? What does that—

Then it hit me all at once.

"You're Caine?" I asked.

He swallowed. "I thought...." His eyes glistened with unshed tears. "I thought she was at that singing academy. She was so godsdamn *excited*."

"I'm so sorry," I whispered.

Caine's teeth ground together. "I didn't know she was here. Not until the guards mentioned her by name last night."

My throat grew thick as tears spilled down my cheeks. "I'm sorry I couldn't save her. I tried. I—"

Caine waved his hand. "You saved me, Mae. I know you tried."

"She didn't die alone," I said, hoping it would offer some comfort.

"To die beside a friend is what we all hope for in this war," Caine said quietly. "We wasted so much time, but I didn't realize we would run out of it so soon."

I knelt down in the grass beside him. We sat in silence,

but it felt so heavy. I thought of all the things Pen had told me and all the things she said she regretted. "She talked about you," I offered.

"What did she say?"

I didn't know if her words would help or hurt, but I said them anyway. "She loved you. She told me that she was so afraid to tell you how she felt, and she regretted it."

"I know how she felt. I was the one too afraid to ask her to marry me." His chest shook as he released a strangled sound. "I didn't want her to give up her dreams for me. I was just a farmer's son destined to die a worthless death in battle. She deserved more than I could give."

Hesitantly, I reached over to squeeze his shoulder in commiseration. "I'm sorry, Caine."

"Me too," he said, shrugging off my comfort to stand up and leave without another word.

My heart hung heavily in my chest, but I'd spilled enough tears in this place. I turned my attention to the body of my friend.

I didn't move the covering off her face like Caine had because I knew the decomposition had already started to set in, and I didn't want to remember her as a corpse. The brief flash I saw when he pulled it back was enough. I wanted to remember her as that kind girl who was a light in a dark place.

"I'm so sorry, Pen," I murmured. "Thank you for being my friend. I'll never forget you. I hope you finally find peace among the stars."

Slowly, I rose to my feet.

I wouldn't return to bed with Ronin. It was still early, and he needed rest more than I needed his company. I walked toward the door of the fortress that was ajar to the garden.

Something called to me like whispers and secrets. Without the Pikes or Varric, the fortress shouldn't scare me anymore, but I loathed the way the memories hurt me. A ghost of a scalpel kissed my sternum, and the rune inside my chest warmed.

I'd never rid myself of the remnants of pain Varric left with me.

But I wouldn't be afraid of a big empty building.

The energy that called to me wasn't Malice's dark manipulation.

It wasn't Death trying to lead me down a path they claimed was my destiny.

It wasn't Cliohde's touch when I freed a leviathan from their draconite.

It was bright. And it was mine.

Two sides warred inside me: the part that was terrified of everything that had happened to me in there and the part of me that desperately wanted to fight her own demons.

With hesitant steps, I entered the fortress.

It was too early for sailors to scour the halls for supplies. The silence was unnerving because even when I was locked away, I always heard guards or servants pattering up and down the halls. That didn't stop me from following my gut.

Or more accurately, my heart.

The pull guided me up a staircase on the far side of the fortress. A wing I'd never been to. A stale scent of decay lingered. A few of the rooms had been opened and tossed, stripped of anything useful.

But there was one with two massive doors that had remained untouched.

Why?

The cold metal tickled my palm as I opened the door wide and was greeted with...

The stuffed heads of pirates. The rumors were true.

Horror caused my hand to clamp over my lips. Outside in the hallway, I noticed vomit sprayed against the detailed golden trim. The scent of decay was heavy, and I knew this was Nathaniel's chamber. I wanted to turn and run. I wanted to retch.

But I didn't because whatever was inside called to me.

Pushing down my nausea, I rushed into Nathaniel's chambers and closed the door behind me. Mounted to the wall were several trophies, and now I knew why Pen never talked about what she saw in his bedroom.

Joined to the room was another bedroom, void of any personality but grander than Nathaniel's. I wondered if this was where his father stayed when he wasn't out on business. There were few books on the shelves that were mainly filled with morbid contortions of teeth and bone.

Disgusting.

A coating of dust lined the gold-painted ceiling. It was beautiful and detailed, likely from before the Pikes claimed this fortress during the coup. The ceiling depicted a scene of a fully dressed woman dancing in a field. She looked ecstatic and trapped in an eternal moment of joy.

I wondered how often Pen stared up at the mural and imagined that it was her.

The pull in my chest tugged again, drawing my gaze to the back of the chamber where panels of the wall were locked with a heavy bolt. *There.* If it weren't for the lock, it would look like decorative trim.

As if it had been a secret hideaway once upon a time.

With deliberate steps, I walked over to it and yanked on the lock a few times. It was heavy and bound the secret passage tight. Urgency rose within me, and I knew I *needed* to get inside.

I took note of the calling mirror perched on top of Nathaniel's desk before I tore the drawers open, scattering everything in search of a key. When one of the wooden drawers went flying, I heard the unmistakable *ting* of a key falling from a secret place under it. I snatched up the key and tried the lock.

It got stuck in the cast-iron lock, but when I twisted it harder, the lock popped off the door and clattered on the floor. When I reached for the panel and pulled it open, it was heavier than I expected.

The sound of metal on metal was surprising as it slid open like a cell door, clicking into place when I opened it completely. A plume of dust whirled around me like autumn leaves, the scent dank like a cellar.

Grabbing an oil lamp from Nathaniel's desk, I lit it and twisted the dial to light my way.

The passage went on forever, dark and winding. No source of light. I wondered if it was an escape route for the original family. The dust was unbroken as it clung to the walls, cobwebs hanging from every corner.

Something familiar hummed through my ears, though I knew I'd never been here before. The walls were lined with wooden crates and shelves filled with heavy tomes.

What is this?

I set the oil lamp down on the floor where it could lightly illuminate the shelf. Then I pulled out a thick leather-bound book and wiped dust and grime off the surface. I opened it, and my breath rattled from my chest when I read the text written in fine cursive.

The Murdoch Family Tree.

I thought Varric had burned all the history. I thought everything was lost when the libraries were torched.

Without thinking, I grasped another book, equally as ornate, and flipped it open to the first page. *Cliohde's Blessing: The First Leviathan.*

Another piece of history I thought was destroyed.

I tugged another book down and greedily read the title: *The King of Ashes and the Birth of Farlight Isles.*

Staring down the long tunnels, I saw there were innumerable shelves full of books. It was all here. Hidden away from the public eye like a rich man's dirty secret.

"Knowledge is everything to the powerful, Maeve. You best not forget that."

If the shelves were full of forbidden history, then what was inside the crates?

I turned to the closest one, my fingernails splitting when I tried to pull it open at the seal. No good. The nails had stood the test of time.

But then I prodded the wood and found it soft like dry rot.

I dug my fingers into it, the fibers falling apart at the press of my nails. The panel disintegrated into nothing, covering the contents with powder. Then I reached in and pulled. It was heavy and cold like a breastplate.

The plates of steel whistled, lightly scraping against one another. The light danced off the smooth metal as I turned it, wiping the dust away to reveal a Murdoch coat of arms. My heart hammered, excitement clouding everything else.

I traced every blemish in the armor, stopping at the gaping hole where a rapier had pierced through the mesh and tore through my gambeson.

This was mine.

Something caught my eye behind the crates—something flat and smooth. I grabbed it and knew it immediately as my shield. Then my insides twisted in disgust.

How long did Samuel Pike have this on display before he threw it in here with everything else he deemed better left forgotten?

I grasped the leather strap behind the shield and brought it up toward myself, remembering how it felt to fight and defend. It felt *right*. My foot flew through the crate underneath the one that held my armor, and several more sentry armor pieces spilled out.

The ones from my sisters in arms.

I inhaled hard, stilling all the feelings that threatened to breech the surface. Whatever came next, I would survive. Varric would pay for what he'd done. The battle was won, but the war would only get darker.

But I knew I would protect my people, and I would avenge those we lost along the way.

I hooked my shield to my back with the familiar leather strap and reclaimed what was mine.

To be continued in Book Four...

ACKNOWLEDGMENTS

The Indomitable Sentry was not an easy book to write. It's heavy. It's angry. When that rage crests over the surface, it's cathartic. With so much evil in the world, this book was my way of coping with it. Even when it feels hopeless, if you're willing to be brave and stand together, anything is possible.

Hope is the most powerful weapon when wielded correctly.

I couldn't have written this alone. I want to say a special thank-you to the best beta readers: my good friends Deana and Kendra. This series has been a crazy ride for me, but you two have been there every step of the way, bumps included, and I absolutely adore you.

Thank you to my mom, Libby, whose support has been unshakable since I started my writing journey at the age of twelve years old. And to my sibling, Kay, who is always there to flesh out my ideas and for their never-ending knowledge of pirate history when my brain won't cooperate.

To my husband, I couldn't ask for a better partner. I started going to events this year, and you've been there to help me set up, break down, and share my joy when I make a sale or meet a new reader. You've cheered me on when I complete a draft or power through a bout of writer's block. I love you.

A big thank-you to my editors, McKinley and Kristin. I never dread getting a round back, and I trust the both of you more than anyone else with my story. No one else understands the ins and outs of this series like you do, and I can't wait to finish strong with Book Four.

And of course, the acknowledgements wouldn't be complete without saying thank you to all my wonderful readers. You inspire me every day, and I want you to know that I write with the hopes that you'll see yourselves in my characters, feel empowered by my worlds, and have this story resonate long after it's done.

Like you inspire me, I hope to inspire you to stand up and be heard.

Be brave.

Be vulnerable.

Be indomitable.

And make a fucking scene.

See you in Book Four.

ABOUT THE AUTHOR

Anacostia Miller is a novelist and screenwriter with a background in filmmaking and prop creation. After ten years of writing and two years of ghostwriting, she found her niche in romantasy. She loves exploring different themes like found family and showcasing inclusivity.

World-building and developing intricate histories in her novels are some of her favorite things to do. She also grew up on classics like *The Lord of the Rings* and *Buffy the Vampire Slayer*, which have inspired her writing. Developing complicated lore and having moments of happiness are vital to the stories. Also, humor plays a big part. As dark as things will get, readers can always hold out for that moment of happiness to make it worth it.

During her days, you can find her trying out a new recipe to figure out how to describe it in her writing, daydreaming, or annoying her husband by telling him exactly how the lighting conveys emotion in every movie they watch together.

instagram.com/anacostiamillerauthor
tiktok.com/@anacostiamillerauthor

ABOUT THE PUBLISHER

Hot Tree Publishing loves love. Publishing adult romantic fiction, HTPubs are all about diverse reads featuring heroes and heroines to swoon over. Since opening in 2015, HTPubs have published more than 300 titles across the wide and diverse range of romantic genres. If you're chasing a happily ever after in your favourite subgenre, HTPubs have you covered.

Interested in discovering more amazing reads brought to you by Hot Tree Publishing? Head over to the website for information:

WWW.HOTTREEPUBLISHING.COM

facebook.com/hottreepublishing

instagram.com/hottreepublishing

tiktok.com/@hottreepublishing